HIGH SCHOOL
HERO HEIST

By
James Mascia

I'd like to thank all my friends and family
for their support as I continue to create
this magnificent series.

This book is for those who take the word impossible
as a challenge and not a roadblock.

Previous Books in the Series
High School Heroes
High School Heroes II: Camp Hero

PROLOGUE
JULY
SUMMER BEFORE JUNIOR YEAR

Savanah could really hit hard. I'd been hit by her before, but now I realized she'd really been pulling her punches. I'm just lucky I can shield myself from physical damage like that, because otherwise my head would probably be splattered all over the wall of that airplane hangar. As it was, I probably had a dislocated jaw.

As I soared through the air, mostly from the momentum the strike had caused, I couldn't help but think about how I probably deserved this.

I never believed in Karma before, but I guess it was a real thing. I'd cheated, I'd stolen, and I'd put my lot in with an unsavory element. True, I'd done it for the right reasons, but apparently Fate didn't care about that one way or the other. All it cared about was retribution for crimes committed.

And I had committed a lot of crimes. At minimum, I had to have racked up at least three felonies and more than a dozen misdemeanors. *So much for being a hero, right?*

It's not your fault, the voice said. *You only did it so you could save lives.*

But it still made me a criminal, I argued.

Not only that, but I'd betrayed Ethan, my boyfriend, without even meaning to. So yeah, after everything I'd done, I deserved getting hit in the jaw and sent flying through the air by the most powerful girl in the world.

The sky is so pretty up here.

I'd reached the top of the arc and was now descending back toward Earth. Still I did nothing to correct my course. I could still fly, but at the moment, I didn't want to. I had to figure out a way to correct this. I needed to fix everything between my friends and with Karma. If I couldn't figure something out before plummeting into the ground, then so be it.

Think, Christine, think.

It wasn't easy to do so while racing through the sky. Believe it or not, wind can be very distracting. But I had to think of something, and fast, before I ended up being nothing but a bloodstain on the Italian countryside.

No. You can't let that happen. You aren't going to let it end this way.

Then it came to me. It was the perfect solution. One that could redeem all the terrible things I'd done and rebalance my Karma. Not only that, but I'd be able to keep myself and my friends safe.

I slowed my rapid descent until I was floating freely under my own power, more than a mile above the Earth's surface. I was going to head back. No matter what, someone would be losing their powers today.

CHAPTER 1
ENDING A LONG YEAR
JUNE—SOPHOMORE YEAR
1 MONTH EARLIER

The final bell rang and a collective sigh of relief washed through the gym class. Thoughts of, *One more day,* and, *Twenty-four hours 'til we're free,* mingled in the air. I absolutely agreed. It would be nice not to have to meander the halls of Thomas Jefferson High School for nearly three months.

This past year had been... interesting, to say the least. Not only had I discovered I could read people's minds, control their thoughts and fly, but I uncovered a story that went all the way back to my grandfather's service in World War II. I'd also been captured by an Agent of the Meta-Human Detection Agency (M.H.D.A.), only to end up training with her in an attempt to foil some master plan of a shady science teacher who'd disappeared for the last two months.

Jeez... when did my life become a comic book?

Anyway, I was as eager as anyone for this school year to be over. All I had to do was get through the next twenty-four hours – which would be harder than you might think.

First, I had to run home and pick up my two-and-a-half-month old brother, Conner, so my mom could go to work. Then I'd dash back up to the school to watch my boyfriend win his track meet—and I do mean win. After all, Ethan is the fastest boy alive, and couldn't possibly lose any of his races.

After that was my training session with Abby, followed by going home, making dinner, putting Conner to bed, and working on my final project for history I'd been putting off for two weeks.

I was out of breath just thinking about it.

Heading out the main entrance, with the rest of the overly excited students, I raced to my car—the only symbol of my "normal" life.

"Hey, Chris," one of the twins, Lance or Kyle, shouted—I could never tell them apart. "Wanna help set up the senior prank?"

Heaving a sigh and rolling my eyes, I watched them pull a couple boxes from the trunks of their cars. I don't know why, but I felt the need to comment, "You guys aren't even seniors."

"We know," Lance or Kyle responded.

"But the seniors dropped the ball. So, we're gonna pick up the slack," the other finished.

"Well, you have fun, I gotta run home." I slipped into the driver's seat of my Mustang as the two of them walked back into the school, carrying the boxes with them.

Whatever the two of them were planning, I wanted no part of it. I didn't want to be grounded all summer. I'd just gotten off house arrest, and I had a bad feeling whatever they had planned would place me right back on it.

Driving off, I left those worries behind me, and focused solely on the last day of school.

My mother waited impatiently in the driveway when I got home. Even without reading her mind, I could tell she was afraid of being late.

"Come on, Christine!" she shouted as I stepped out of the car. "My shift begins at three. You're supposed to come straight home."

I neglected to mention I *had* come straight home, and the fact that it wasn't even two-thirty yet. When my mom was in a mood like this, it didn't do much good reasoning with her anyway. Instead, I simply said, "Okay."

She handed Conner, already in his carseat, to me and bounded into the car. Smoke practically shot from the tires as she sped off.

"That's mom for you," I told Conner.

He giggled as if he knew exactly what I said – he didn't. I did almost daily checks on his brain to gauge any cognitive abilities. After all, he shared the same genes I had, so he stood a good chance of developing some kind of mental ability. But so far: nothing.

"Okay, Conner," I said, loading him into the tiny backseat of my car and strapping him in. "Let's head back to school."

****

By now, Conner had gotten used to our trips to the school. For nearly the last month, I'd been bringing him up there, unbeknownst to my parents, to sit in on my training sessions with Abby Davidson. Today, however, was the first time I'd brought him into a crowd. I was a little wary as I approached the half-full stadium, not knowing how he'd react.

As I walked through the gate, a loud crack filled the air. I jumped just a little, always on the lookout for any danger—which seemed to follow me around. Quickly I realized it was just the starting gun being fired, beginning one of the races. I prayed it wasn't one of Ethan's races. He was the only one I really wanted to see.

Hefting my brother's carseat, I bounded up the steps. To my relief, I noticed the runners jogging, almost casually, around the track. It was one of the longer races. Ethan only competed in the sprints.

I took a seat on the bleachers, near the front row. I did my best to stay away from the majority of the people. I might have been able to control my mind reading ability, but I still felt apprehensive in crowds.

I lifted Conner from his carseat and sat him in my lap. I hoped he wouldn't get hungry soon – I forgot his bottle in the car, and didn't want to go back in case I missed anything.

As it turned out, I could have gone back and forth to my car about a dozen times. The first race was sooooooo slow. They ran a mile and the last runner – thankfully from the other team – came in at just over eight minutes.

The next race was even longer, with the runners going two miles before finishing. Last place came in at nearly twenty minutes. However, I stayed, glued to my seat because I had no idea how long any of the races would be until they ended.

Luckily, as they were getting ready for the next race, Ethan stepped onto the track, his gold "42" glistening on the crimson uniform. I let out a loud cheer of, "Go Ethan!" But no one else followed my outburst. My cheeks reddened and I stayed silent.

He lined up in the third lane, and placed his toe on the line as the starter shouted, "On your mark!"

The starter then raised an arm and pointed the gun into the air. "Get set!"

Ethan and the other runners all crouched slightly, ready to spring.

Those three seconds between "Get set" and the bang of the gun were excruciating. Just waiting in anticipation for the loud crack was enough to drive a person insane. When would he pull the trigger? I found myself holding my breath as I waited for the race to begin. And I was in the stands, I could only imagine how Ethan felt.

Oh, he's used to it, the voice in my head chimed in. *He's probably as calm as can be.*

BANG!

Within seconds Ethan was ahead of the pack. They were all moving pretty fast, but no matter how quick they were, they wouldn't get ahead of my boyfriend. The sad part was, as fast as he was going, he was barely even trying. This quick sprint for a normal person was little more than a casual walk for a boy like Ethan.

They only ran one lap, and Ethan beat them all by at least five seconds. This time, when Ethan crossed the finish line, everyone in the stands cheered, so I joined in. I will admit I was, by far, the loudest. Some of my fellow students gave me odd looks. I was never one to burst out cheering like that—but he was my boyfriend, after all.

I sat through Ethan's next two races—which he won, by the way. Then my watch beeped.

I groaned. "Four o'clock already?" Actually it was four-oh-five, according to my special watch. She was late today. Usually she'd beep me if I was only one minute late, forget about five.

Hoisting Conner back into his carseat, I blew out a long sigh. Sometimes Abby could be so annoying—and about as impatient as my mother. She knew what I was doing, and she still couldn't give me a little bit of leeway.

I stopped at my car to pick up Conner's diaper bag. He was going to need some food soon – and a diaper change by the smell of things. Then I went back into the school, and made my way to the wrestling room. This time of year it was vacant, since wrestling season ended in February. Plus, it was enclosed, so no one could look in, and it had mats on the floor and all the walls, making it a perfect place for the intensive training we did.

The door creaked open, and a musty smell assaulted my nostrils. I didn't think I'd ever get used to that smell. It was amazing that after nearly four months, they couldn't get that stale sweat odor from this room.

Abby stood in the center of the room, my friends with her, apparently watching the door as if she expected me to step in that very moment.

"It's about time," the woman said.

"Oooh, a whole eight minutes late." I laid the sarcasm on thick.

"Where's Ethan?" Savanah asked. If possible, she sounded even more agitated than Abby.

"Still at his track meet," I explained.

Tiffany rushed up and took Conner from me. The baby giggled as soon as he saw her familiar face. "Have fun with Aunt Tiff while I go and play." I sounded like an idiot. "He needs a change," I told my friend as I handed over the diaper bag.

You'd think news like that would be enough to deter someone, but not Tiffany. If anything, she was even more excited.

She's sick, I thought. There was really no other explanation. I've heard of girls being "boy crazy," but my friend was "baby crazy."

I joined Savanah and Peter in the center of the room, both anticipating and dreading what Abby had in store for us today. This was one major reason I never joined a sport—practice. Now, I found myself attending practices even more grueling than if I'd joined track with Ethan. If only my super-power was having an actual athletic ability.

As I came up to my friends, without explanation Abby walked off.

"How did Ethan do?" Peter asked. His voice said he wanted Ethan to have done well, his mind said he wished Ethan had fallen flat on his face. When was that boy going to get over the fact he had no chance with me? There was only one boy for me and that boy was Ethan Everett.

"He won all the races I got to see," I said, putting special emphasis on the last words, and turning my head so Abby would hear me.

She was already on her way back to us, carrying three white garments. "Here," she said, tossing one to each of us, "put these on."

Untangling the fabric, I noticed it felt stiff against my skin. Once I managed to totally unravel it, I recognized it for what it was.

"Why do we have to wear these?" I asked.

Savanah looked at me quizzically, then back at her own, identical garment. "Why? What's the matter with it? Aside from being a fashion disaster, that is."

"It's the same jumpsuit Tiff and Samantha found at Camp Hero. It's for people who have no powers." I turned on Abby. "But we have powers."

Abby barely missed a beat, again it was as if she'd expected the argument. "It's not just for unpowered people. It's a form of protection." She pointed to me, and at the same time, gestured toward the suit. "Put it on."

This time, I didn't say anything, but pulled the garment over my clothes. I could feel the difference in the way my body moved as soon as it was on. I suddenly felt like I could do anything, like jump and touch the ceiling without using my powers at all. It was kind of invigorating.

However, that all changed as soon as I saw the flash of movement in Abby's direction. Her hand quickly swung around, grabbing something behind her back. It slung back so quickly toward me, I didn't have the chance to react as an ear shattering BANG, not unlike the starting gun at Ethan's race, killed the silence. The next thing I knew I felt a brief pressure against my chest, where the bullet apparently struck me.

As quickly as she'd drawn it, she reholstered the gun behind her back. I, on the other hand, was still too shocked to move. My chest felt like someone had hit me with a tennis ball at about a hundred miles an hour. It stung, but not much more than that.

"The bio-suit increases agility and stamina," Abby continued the lecture as if she hadn't just shot me. But she had. My trainer and mentor had just pulled a gun out and shot me! Now she acted like that was a natural thing. "It can take a beating, leaving its wearer relatively unharmed. And face it, Christine, you take your fair share of beatings."

I couldn't argue with that—besides the fact my mind was still reeling and couldn't make my mouth form words. In the last year, I'd been hospitalized, suffered at least two concussions, sprained my knee and broken my wrist. Maybe a suit like this could be useful. The color was all wrong though. I'd have to dye it when I got home.

"Now, try them out. Get a feel for them. You're going to be wearing these a lot."

I did as she said, taking a few steps and a few practice jumps. Normally, doing anything beyond walking took great effort on my part. With the suit on though, I felt more balanced, and I could sense it taking the strain off my muscles. I had to admit, besides the ache in my chest, the suit felt great.

"Okay," Abby said once the three of us had a couple minutes to get acclimated to the suits, "let's start training."

CHAPTER 2
UNEXPECTED VISITOR

Dragging my feet through the darkened doorway of my empty house, I placed the sleeping Conner, still in his carseat, onto the couch. I wanted so badly to go to sleep myself, but I had way too much to do.

The first thing was make dinner. I was famished, having not eaten since lunch, and having an intense two hour workout, involving several crashes into the padded walls of the wrestling room, was making my stomach growl like a hungry lion. My father would also be home from work shortly and he'd want some dinner too.

Now, I don't pretend to be a chef, but I can boil water. So, I end up making pasta a lot. Tonight was no exception. While the water boiled, I opened up the finest jar of marinara sauce the supermarket had.

As I waited for my fabulous dinner, I checked the paper Mr. Murray had given us explaining our history project. Seriously, what teacher assigned a project and made it due on the last day of school?

I had to make a poster for the Civil Rights Movement—something someone might carry at a protest. I wouldn't have bothered with it, but I'd worked really hard this last quarter to bring all my grades up. I wasn't about to sacrifice my "A" because I didn't do my final history project.

Checking on Conner one last time, making sure he was still asleep, I returned to the kitchen to finish dinner. My stomach gave a little roar as if it knew it would be fed soon.

And it was. I think it only took about three minutes between the time I strained the pasta to when the meal rested peacefully in my stomach. After cleaning up, and leaving a plate for my dad, I moved quickly to get Conner in his crib so I could work.

Despite all I had to do for him, sometimes I did enjoy taking care of the brat. Tonight was not one of those times. Even though I tried my best not to jostle him too much, as soon as I pulled him from his seat, he woke and started wailing. It was like he knew I had things to do and didn't want me to accomplish them, because when I tell you this infant fought me every step of the way, I mean it.

It began with trying to feed him. First, he wouldn't take the bottle, then when he finally did drink a little, he spit up all over me. After that, as I was changing him – or attempting to, at least – he decided it was a good time to go to the bathroom all over me and the changing table. He struggled as I put on his pajamas, and wouldn't stop crying even as I rocked him, played with him and tried in vain to feed him again.

I have caught bank robbers, fought delusional psychotics, even stood toe-to-toe with a dragon, but Conner was the one who made me throw in the towel. Eventually, I had no other choice but to plant the suggestion in his still-forming brain that it was time to sleep. He finally quieted down and drifted off into dreamland. I hated using my powers like that, especially on my own family, but the little bugger gave me no choice.

Breathing a sigh of relief, I finally set him down in his crib. Quietly, I tiptoed out of the room, fearing I'd accidentally wake him up again.

Finally, I can get this project done.

A loud series of bangs filled the quiet air as someone knocked on the front door. Quickly, I shut Conner's bedroom door to muffle the sound.

"Think again, Christine." I sighed and trudged back downstairs to answer the door. I was never going to get the poster finished.

My annoyance at the unexpected visitor, whom I whole-heartedly planned on sending away as rudely as humanly possible, was quickly replaced by utter shock and confusion as I cracked the door open.

"What the hell are you doing here?"

He'd shaved his goatee, making himself look even younger than usual. But even without the facial hair, I recognized him immediately.

"Hello, Ms. Carpenter," came the deep, even voice of my former mentor and science teacher. "May I come in?"

"No," I said, beginning to close the door on him. "You have nothing to say I could possibly want to hear."

Quinn wasn't going to take no for an answer. He stuck his foot in the doorway and pressed his hand against the door itself, making it impossible to close. For a moment, I thought I was going to have to fight him off and quickly started erecting invisible barriers around my mind so he couldn't manipulate me.

"Christine, I just want to speak to you for a moment," he said. His tone never changed, making it difficult to gauge his actual emotional state. "Let me explain myself."

"Really? Explain yourself?" I shouted. I couldn't help myself. Of all the people who'd stabbed me in the back, his betrayal hurt the worst. "I trusted you, Quinn—or Quintus—or whatever the hell your name is. You lied. I saw the past—saw the actual day the photo was taken. You weren't there. You lied. And then, before I could question you, you just disappeared. No note. No explanation. And you left that imposter to take your place."

"Christine, I'm sorry." His unchanging tone made me wonder how sincere the apology really was. "I really can explain everything, if you'd let me in."

Quinn supposedly couldn't manipulate my thoughts like he could everyone else's, but still, I felt myself wavering and my shock and anger abating. The worst part was, I couldn't tell if it was because I wanted to or if he really was making me. And believe me, you don't know how terrifying it can be when you can't trust your own thoughts.

My tension release slightly, but I still didn't invite him in. "We'll talk at school tomorrow." An excellent solution, I thought. Especially if the talk turned into a brawl, at least there'd be witnesses, and I'd have my friends to back me up.

Unfortunately, I wasn't going to have my way. My father picked that exact moment to pull into the driveway. *Worst timing ever.*

Quinn's head turned, either from hearing the car or seeing the defeated look on my face, and he smiled.

My unwitting father slammed his car door and walked up the path to our front door. He whistled as he came toward us – much happier than he usually was. Normally he dragged his feet after an exhausting day. Whether happy or not, he still didn't take notice of my little standoff until he reached the bottom step of the porch. Only then did he stop whistling.

"Hello," my father said, extending a hand to Quinn. "Can I help you?"

"Hi there, sir." Quinn's voice picked up, becoming much more warm and jovial than it had been a few seconds ago. "My

name is Mr. Quinn. I'm one of your daughter's t
Thomas Jefferson High School."

My father groaned, giving me the evil eye and clea ,
the wrong conclusion. "What has she done now?"

"Oh, nothing." Quinn's smile got, if possible, even wider.
"She is a model student, and from what I hear, she shouldn't have
less than a 'B' on her report card."

"Well, it's about time." He was still glaring at me like I was a
criminal or something. "If she's not in trouble, then—"

"Why am I here?" He looked over his shoulder at me. "You
mean Christine hasn't mentioned it?"

"No," my father said, looking between Quinn and I in
confusion. "She hasn't said a thing."

"Oh, well than this will be a pleasant surprise then." He
smacked his hands together like an overly excited seal waiting for
someone to throw him a fish.

"Well, what is it?" my father asked. Even though he looked
on in interest, he still nervously loosened his tie, as if this news
wasn't going to be pleasant at all.

For some reason, I was pretty sure he was right.

"No," Quinn said, drawing the vowel out for a second before
continuing, "I think we should wait for Mrs. Carpenter to come
home. It was be best to hear this news together."

My dad was already getting impatient with Quinn. I didn't
blame him. After all, to him, Quinn was some stranger, coming to
give him some information on his daughter, yet refused to let that
information out. If I were in my father's position, I'd probably
have strangled the man by now.

I might have done it anyway, except I really wanted to
discover what Quinn was up to.

Walking past the science teacher, my dad sighed. Then,
without asking any further questions said, "Why don't you come
in and wait? My wife should be home soon."

My father then walked into the house, leaving me standing in
the dorrway, staring at Quinn.

Did you influence him?
Barely any effort. But, yes.

Quinn clapped his hands together again. "Now that he's out
of the way, can we talk?"

CHAPTER 3
STUDYING ABROAD

Reluctantly, I allowed my former mentor to pass through the threshold. I gave serious thought to manipulating my father into making him leave, or call the cops, but Quinn could easily use his power to reverse it anyway. That was a war I wasn't ready to fight – yet.

So, I brought him into my living room, plopping on the sofa, doing nothing to hide my frustration and annoyance with him.

I pressed the small button on my watch. This would send a signal to Abby and let her know I was in trouble. With any luck, she'd show up with an entire team and arrest Quinn on the spot. Maybe she'd stick him into a stasis chamber like she had with so many others she considered "too dangerous."

I was pretty sure I'd done it covertly, but Quinn gave me a knowing glance before he said, "I know you're angry with me. And I know I need to earn your trust again."

"Really? You're kidding!"

"Your usual wit is not at all helpful at this time."

"I know what you are, and I don't know what you're trying to do, but I'm going to find out, and I'm going to stop you."

"Stop being so dramatic." He waved a hand at me. Without his facial hair, he really did look younger, really no older than Abby, and she was only in her early twenties – so she claimed anyway.

"Christine, you don't know the whole story about me. But if you would allow me to explain, I will tell you what Ms. Davidson and your grandfather can't."

I was going to tell him Grandpa Carpenter hadn't told me anything. As a matter of fact the only time I mentioned Quinn's name, he turned pale and left the room. That was when I knew the man before me was no good.

I nodded for him to go on. Better to let him keep talking until Abby got there.

"Yes, my name is really Quintus. I don't have a last name, because I was never truly born."

How was it possible? The look of utter bafflement on my face must have told Quinn he needed to explain further.

"I am a product of good, old fashioned, German ii
was engineered, created in a tube, bred for the sole p
destroying the Allied forces in World War II."

It was beginning to dawn on me, but even as my mind was
still trying to comprehend what he was saying, he continued.

"I'm a clone. One of five. Actually, the last of five—hence
the name."

"Really? So your name is 'Five'?"

"Technically, I suppose. Primus, Secundus, Tertius, and
Quartus were all created before me."

"What happened to them?" I couldn't believe he was sucking
me in, and so fast. At least it would keep him talking.

"Killed during the war," he said matter-of-factly. "I'm the last
of my brothers, mostly because of... your grandather's platoon."

No wonder I had trouble mentioning his name to my grandfather. I
knew he'd been the cause. Now I knew why. If my grandfather
knew about Quinn, he might decide to come after him.

"Why do you think I never told you?"

"It doesn't matter," I shot back in response. "You're still a
Nazi, and you still have some hidden agenda. Plus disappearing
and having Jayson Johnson morph into you to take your place.
Everything is just... wrong."

"I'm sure it all looks very wrong to your untrained, teenage
mind. But I assure you, there is a logical explanation for the whole
thing."

"So, let's hear it."

He grinned at my apparent rudeness. "Impetuous as ever, I
see. You think all that matters in life is yourself. I assure you this is
not the case. Patience, Christine, and you will get the answers you
so desperately desire."

"I'm not playing your stupid games, Quinn. Either answer my
questions, or I'm gonna blow the whistle on this whole thing."

"Christine," he said as calm as ever, "Please don't make
threats you aren't prepared to follow through on."

He stared at me a moment, and I back at him. Both of us
daring the other to blink first, as if that would settle things. It
wouldn't. What I didn't realize was Quinn was using the moment
to assess me—deciding whether or not to call my bluff.

The coffee table and television shook as I mentally grabbed
hold of them. In response, the lamp from the end table rose in the

air. Quinn simply looked at me with a smile which said, "Don't try it."

We both blinked when my dad's footsteps came down the stairs. He'd changed out of his suit and into a Steelers T-Shirt and sweat pants. We'd replaced the furniture when we'd heard him and he didn't have a clue there was any tension between us, or how dangerously close he'd come to having a gaping crater where his living room used to be.

"Can I offer you something to drink, Mr..."

"Quinn," the villain finished, turning his head only slightly to keep an eye on me. As if I was going to attack with my father standing two feet away. "And, no thank you. I'm on a very special diet."

My dad's eyebrow arched, and he gave me a look, all the while thinking, *This guy's crazy. Special diet.* He rolled his eyes and walked into the kitchen.

If only he knew Quinn could hear everything.

"Now, where were we?" Quinn asked, looking amused. "Oh, right. You were accusing me of being a Nazi, and then some idle threat of telling on me. That about right?"

I nodded.

"As I've already explained, yes, I was in the German army during the war. But, it was also I who ended the war, and allowed the Allies to invade Berlin." He quickly held up a hand, silencing my protest before I even got it started. "An anonymous message was sent to Eisenhower, Chruchill and Stalin on April 28th, telling them when and where to attack. That message came from me. Just before ground troops invaded, as planes flew overhead, dropping bombs left and right, turning Berlin into rubble, I located and entered Hitler's secret bunker and killed him."

He raised his hand again, but this time he couldn't silence me. "Hitler killed himself, when he knew he was going to lose."

"Hitler was a sociopath and a megalomaniac with delusions of grandeur. The man nearly took control of as much territory as the Roman Empire in a fraction of the time. He nearly succeeded in exterminating an entire race of people. Do you really believe a man deluded enough to do all that could ever take his own life?"

I didn't answer. I couldn't answer. He made a good point, but it was so hard believing something when you were taught something completely different for years. History had Hitler putting a bullet in his own head, yet Quinn's argument sounded perfectly logical. I didn't know what to believe.

"I didn't think so," he said when it was clear I wasn't going to respond. "The bullet came from Hitler's gun and it was fired by Hitler's hand. But there was someone pulling his strings." He pointed to himself, as if I couldn't figure out who he was talking about.

"I timed his apparent suicide with the invasion to throw German Command into turmoil. Not to sound too full of myself, but it was quite a brilliant plan."

That was all well and good, if it was at all true, except for one thing. "But why would you suddenly—" I couldn't find the right words to use. My mind drew a complete blank.

"Betray my country?" he finished. Then he sighed rubbing the bridge of his nose like he did when I asked something completely inane. "If you had paid attention, you'd understand it was never really my country. They used me as a weapon. But sometimes a weapon backfires and harms the wielder."

"Nice metaphor," I said.

"I thought so. To add to why I turned on my creators, let's just say I didn't agree with their whole idea of the 'Master Race'."

"Riiiiight." If he could have been any less convincing with his response, I might have laughed in his face. However, he was just convincing enough to warrant a scowl and an angst riddled sigh.

"What would you do if you were told you needed to exterminate… let's start with five-hundred people? Could you do it?"

I shook my head.

"What if they told you your country would be destroyed if you didn't? Could you then?"

Again, my head shook.

"Really? You'd be able to trade five-hundred lives for hundreds of thousands, even millions?"

When he put it that way, my refusal sounded a lot worse. But it didn't matter, no matter what he said, no matter how high that number went, my answer would always be the same.

"I don't kill people."

"Not even one? Not even to save a life?"

"No. Not even then."

"Very noble of you." He scratched his hairless chin. "I wonder what happened to Thomas Fulton then."

I wanted so badly to make his head explode. And although the coffee table between us vibrated again, threatening to throw itself upon Quinn, I restrained myself.

"How dare you use that against me," I growled, barely containing my rage. "You know what I went through after that night, and you know it's because of what I did to Tommy I won't ever kill anyone again."

"I'm sorry," said Quinn. He didn't look at all apologetic. "I won't bring it up again." He looked away from me then, as if he were seeing a distant memory he wished he could forget. "My number was 20,000. They wanted me to murder 20,000 innocent people before I was able to say 'no'."

There was no response to that last statement. I could honestly not believe it. He could have been telling the truth, but he could just as easily be lying. It was impossible to tell. I wished I could read his mind.

"Where have you been?" I asked instead. I figured changing the subject would be better than continuing with the current line of conversation. "For the last couple of months, I mean."

Any revelation he may have been having was instantly washed away by my question. He snapped his head back toward me and a slight smile returned to his lips, though the pain he was feeling was still apparent in his eyes. "I dropped off the radar for a while and got back to doing some research. In the two months I've been gone, I did some travelling and managed to find something very special."

He was trying to draw me in again. I couldn't let him suck me in. He was a villain—the worst of the worst. If I let him play me, I would lose.

I sighed. I'd probably lost the second Quinn stepped through my door. "What did you find?" It would be my own morbid curiosity that would be my downfall.

"First, answer this for me," he responded. "Did you find something in Camp Hero when you were there? Something maybe a bit insignificant, yet special at the same time."

My thoughts immediately went to the spearhead I'd found in that old abandoned laboratory. Alone, the object was nothing special. However, something about it made me hold onto it. When

I'd shown it to Grandpa Carpenter, he said he thought it might have been the Spear of Destiny, the spear that had spilled Christ's blood while he hung on the cross. It was something they were after during the war, but never found.

I wasn't at all compelled to tell Quinn any of this, of course. After all, he was about as trustworthy as a crack addict who claimed they were clean.

"No," I lied. "We just found the M.H.D.A. facility and freed all the prisoners."

"I see," he said, leaning back in the chair steepling his hands in front of his face. He eyed me quizzically, and I knew he was checking my head to make sure I was telling the truth. I hoped my mental barriers were strong enough to hold him back.

Fortunately, I was saved by the doorbell. His concentration broke as we both jerked our heads toward the door. The fact I could sense no one on the other side told me I had been rescued. Abby was here, thought inhibitor and all.

In my head, I did a little victory dance. I did my best not to show any emotion. I'm pretty sure I failed since Quinn's gaze shifted between me and the door as he smiled. "I guess the cavalry's arrived. Just in time, I imagine."

I didn't move. The doorbell rang again.

"Christine, can you get that?" my dad called from the kitchen.

Only at my father's prompt did I find the courage to rise and go to the door. As predicted, when I opened it, Abby stood on the other side.

"Miss Carpenter," she said in an overly formal tone, even for the counselor she was pretending to be.

"Oh, Miss Davidson," I said, acting surprised – Quinn didn't buy it. "Won't you come in?"

"Christine, who is it?" my father yelled from the other room again.

I rubbed the bridge of my nose. He wasn't going to be happy someone else from my school was here. "Ms. Davidson, my counselor."

Why do I feel like I'm about to be ambushed? he thought.

"Can you come in here for a moment?"

Great. Now I'm gonna get yelled at for no reason. I trudged to the kitchen, glancing back at Abby and Quinn and praying they could be left alone for a minute without destroying my house.

As I'd imagined, my father sat at the table with a scowl on his face. "Do you want to explain why two of your teachers are sitting in my living room?" He didn't give me a chance to answer before adding, "What's going on? And I want the truth."

How I wished I could grant his request, but the truth wasn't an option. "I don't know," I answered.

"If I find out you're lying to me–" He let his voice trail off – the threat implied. He'd ground me again.

"Dad, I seriously have no idea what Mr. Quinn and Ms. Davidson are doing here. But I promise, I didn't do anything wrong. And my report card will be the best one all year."

Despite the fact that what I said was 90% true, he still didn't believe me. I didn't need my mind reading power to figure that out.

For a few minutes I stood, deadlocked with my father, trying my best not to lose my temper, while he tried his best to prove I was being dishonest. Thankfully, the front door opened again and we both knew my mother had finally returned home.

"Hello," she said, confusion wafting with her voice. She was still looking over her shoulder at the strange people as she came into the kitchen.

"Who–" she began.

Dad didn't even let her finish the question. "A couple of teachers from the high school."

"What are they doing here?"

"I don't know," he said, giving me the evil-eye. "Our daughter's lips are sealed."

"I told you," I said, at last raising my voice in the hope my point would get across, "I have no clue why they're here. Why don't you believe me?" It was infuriating. Just because a teacher comes to our house, I was being treated like a criminal.

"Christine, we aren't saying we don't believe you," my mom said, trying to be diplomatic. She didn't believe me either, but I didn't think it was the best time to argue the point.

"Why don't we go in there and find out what they want?" she asked, motioning me to take the lead.

I walked back into the living room, feeling like an inmate walking the last mile. My parents acted like the guards escorting me to the gas chamber. Both of them were very interested in what these two invaders had to say.

Quinn and Abby sat as if they'd been having the most pleasant conversation. Only I knew how much the pair wanted to tear each other apart.

Abby stood as my parents approached and reached out to shake hands. "Abby Davidson, I've gotten to know Christine very well over the last few months."

Of course she had. She'd only interrogated me about a hundred times before finally offering me a job. A job, I might add, I hadn't been paid for yet.

Quinn was next. He introduced himself, shaking hands with both parents. After all the formalities were done, we all sat down. There was hardly a pause before Quinn started speaking.

"I know you're wondering why we're here," he mentioned. "Well, a few months ago, Thomas Jefferson High School was given the opportunity to send our students on a historical immersion trip to Italy this summer—all expenses paid."

I had to stop myself from standing and shouting that Quinn was a liar and there was no such trip. But, my parents couldn't know what was really happening and if I called Quinn out, they would know everything.

"Only being allowed to send two of our students, the school decided to hold a contest. Every student was given the opportunity to write an essay stating why they should be selected for this sensational opportunity. Your daughter, Christine, wrote a wonderful essay about visiting Europe and seeing the places her grandfather set foot during World War II. It really captured our interest because it was so personal, not like the generic papers many of the other students turned in."

Wow! Quinn really could spin a lie and make it sound true. He'd totally taken my parents in and had them hanging on his every word – though to be fair, he could have been using his powers to cause that. My only real concern was discovering what Quinn was up to, and stopping him.

"As I said, two students were selected for this excursion, a freshman named Jayson Johnson, and your daughter."

Both my parents looked at me. The way their brows slanted you would think Quinn had told them I'd been caught shoplifting. Leave it to my parents to be upset about something positive—even if it was a sham.

"Why didn't you tell us about this?" my father practically snarled.

"I don't know," I said quickly, moving to the defensive. "I forgot, I guess."

"Forgot?" my mother added to the attack. "How do you forget something like this?"

"Mom, I didn't even know I won," I said, thinking fast to keep up with Quinn's game. "I wrote the stupid thing back in February. How am I supposed to remember stuff like that?"

"We only made our final decisions this afternoon, and with only one day left for the school year," Quinn added, "we thought it prudent to notify the families as soon as possible. Hence why we are here tonight, and why we waited to have you both here."

I half expected my parents to immediately say I couldn't go and send Quinn on his way, but when I glanced over at them, they were giving each other a look saying they should discuss it. I had to kill that discussion before it started. I wanted no part of Quinn's scheme.

"I can't go," I pretended to talk to Quinn, though I looked at my parents as I spoke. "My little brother needs to be watched while my parents work."

"She's right," my mother agreed, glancing in my direction again. "We'd have no one to watch Conner, and I was planning on taking extra shifts when school ended to make some extra money."

Internally, I breathed a sigh of relief. There was no way Quinn could convince my parents now.

My relief was cut off at the head, however, when Abby, who'd been surprisingly silent during the conversation, finally spoke up. "I think this is something you should take more time to think about Mrs. Carpenter. This is a great opportunity for Christine to expand her horizons, and learn who she really is. Being Christine's counselor, I can tell you she would greatly benefit from an experience like this."

Stunned into silence, I could only gawk at the woman. She was supposed to oppose Quinn, not agree with him – save me from the maniac, not send me into danger. I began to regret calling her in.

My father's skin turned a darker shade of pink as blood furiously pumped into his cheeks. "Neither of you have actually said what this experience is. How long will she be gone? What will she be doing? How will we stay in contact? You can't honestly expect us to agree to anything until we have all the information."

Abby smiled, and in that counselor-like demeanor she used when trying to diffuse a situation, she turned to Quinn. "I think I'm going to have to defer to my colleague for those details."

Yeah, she had to "defer" because she had about as much information on the trip as I did – which was none at all.

If Quinn was bothered at all by Abby's sudden compliance, he didn't show it. As a matter of fact, he acted as if the whole thing were planned.

Quinn cleared his throat, I think more to get my attention than anything else. "This will be a four week trip through Italy. We would leave July 1st and return on the 28th. While we're there, Christine will be helping conduct research at various sites around the country, learning about the history of Rome from all the way back before the time of Christ.

"We will also be touring many historical sites, like the Roman Coliseum and the city of Pompeii. Christine will be immersed first-hand into another culture. I promise, this is a once-in-a-lifetime educational opportunity for your daughter."

"July 1st? my father asked. "That's less than two weeks away."

"I know this is a major decision, and these usually take some time," Quinn said. "But I'm afraid we'll need an answer tonight."

My mother looked at my father. An almost saddened expression covered her face. "I don't know if we can," she said. "I need to work."

"Well," my father responded, his cheeks turning red, the feeling of pleasant embarrassment shot from him, "I was going to tell you when you got home, but our guests distracted me." The grin he'd been wearing when he'd arrived home returned. "I got the Johnson and Wales account today. It's literally a million dollar account. I can pay my brother back the money he loaned me, and you don't need to work anymore."

My mom looked as if she were torn between jumping up and hugging my dad and wanting to cry. After my dad's words sunk in, she regained her senses enough to say, "I'm not sure I should just up and quit my job, dear. We can still use the extra money."

I would have expected my father to be taken aback by the statement—I certainly was. My mother didn't want to work, but felt obligated to so my father could start his new business. For her to suggest she keep working when she had a way out was a strange occurrence. However, my dad acted like he suspected my mother would act this way.

"We could always get my parents to stay with us and watch Conner while Christine's gone."

For a half-second I wondered why my dad was advocating for me to go on this trip. He should have been the first in the line of opposition. All it took was once glance in Quinn's direction to know what was going on.

I had to do something before Quinn manipulated my parents into thinking my going to Europe was a good idea.

"Would you guys stop talking about me like I'm not sitting right here?" I asked indignantly. "None of you have even asked my opinion. But I'll tell you, I don't want to go."

It didn't work.

"Christine, don't you have a project to finish for Mr. Murray's class?" Quinn asked.

I was going to shout at him and say I'd finished it, but for some reason, I was compelled to tell the truth. "Yes," I answered in a rather meek voice.

"Don't you think you should go do it?" asked my father.

I wanted to scream. I wanted to throw things. I wanted to decapitate Quinn and use his severed head as a soccer ball. However, losing my temper would get my nowhere, so I stood, stamped my foot and turned in a huff.

I can't believe they just got rid of you like that, the voice said in a mostly mocking tone.

As I was going out of earshot, I heard Abby interject, "This is what Christine always does. She never wants to try anything new. We need to do something to get Christine out of her shell."

I stopped midway up the stairs, fuming. My cheeks were on fire and I gave serious consideration to charging back down the stairs and giving all four adults a piece of my mind. Either fortunately or unfortunately my self-control once again kicked in and I simply stood for a moment longer as Abby continued.

"The barrier Christine has created needs to be broken, and an extended trip away from her family, away from her friends, would be perfect for doing so. She will have the opportunity to do something important while interacting with other students from around the world."

There was a pause in the conversation, and I could still feel some apprehension from my mother. My father had been completely taken in though and was ready to sign on the dotted line.

"In my opinion, if we don't do something with Christine soon, this reclusive behavior will continue well into adulthood."

The really sad part of all this was, I wasn't at all an introvert like Abby was convincing my parents of. I mean, yeah, I wasn't a member of any sports team, and I had no interest in joining any clubs, and I only had a few close-knit friends but… Okay, I guess I was a bit of an introvert. But that didn't mean it was a problem in need of fixing.

It didn't take too much more talking before my dad said, "I suppose there's a consent form you need us to sign."

And with those words, I knew my fate was sealed. I sighed. I was going to Europe and be part of whatever sinister plan Quinn had in mind for me.

CHAPTER 4
CONFRONTATIONS

The effort I put forth on my poster was a little lackluster. I designed a sign for the bus boycotts, but I could have only spent twenty minutes on it and it was reflected in the quality. I was so disappointed in myself.

I couldn't keep my mind off of Quinn, Abby and this insane trip to Italy I was apparently being forced to go on "for my own good." Don't get me wrong, I really wanted to go to Italy, but the circumstances bothered me.

I couldn't help but wonder if the spear had something to do with all of this. He'd asked me about it right before Abby came in, and I was sure he'd have revealed everything to me if she'd waited two more minutes to arrive.

For most of the night, I twirled the rusted piece of metal in my hands, hoping the strange artifact might share some long-forgotten secret with me. It was stupid to think the spear knew what Quinn wanted, but the irrational part of my brain continued to press the matter anyway.

I barely slept, but thankfully it was the last day of school, so I didn't have to be completely alert.

Leaving my house before my mother even woke to feed Conner, I made my way to school as the sun was coming up. I was going to have it out with the science teacher and the counselor. Both of them had some explaining to do. Even if it killed me, I would make them spill their secrets.

I walked through the front door of the school, lame poster in hand, and realized how foolish I was. My footsteps echoed down the empty corridors. I was alone in the building. Now, I'd have to wait. But I was so antsy to get the confrontations over with I couldn't sit still. For a half hour, I walked back and forth between Quinn's classroom and Abby's office, pacing the long, vacant halls expecting one of them to arrive.

Unfortunately, neither of them showed in the thirty minutes, and I was already fatigued. My anger apparently walked off, and other students arriving, I decided to go to Mrs. Blank's classroom. She at least had arrived.

She was surprised to see me, to say the least. Shocked was more like it. School still didn't start for another twenty minutes and there I was, intruding on her quiet time. "You're here early," she muttered, turning away from her email. She thought I was there to discuss my grade.

"Sorry, Mrs. Blank. Just eager to get the last day over I guess." I gave her a half-smile and set my things down at my desk. "I'll leave you alone."

Surprised as she was for me to enter, she was even more so when I left. *Strange girl,* she thought as I exited back into the hallway.

I decided to give it one more try to see if my two nemeses had arrived yet. The worst that could happen would be they weren't there and I'd spend some extra time with my math teacher. Quinn's room was still locked and his light was out. Cursing, I walked to the guidance office. I hated to think I'd wasted my whole morning and wouldn't get the chance to at least verbally assault one of them.

The door was unlocked. At least that meant someone was in the office. I creaked the door open and peaked my head inside. On first inspection the room looked empty, but the sound of papers rustling came from one of the cubicles. The emptiness of the thoughts in the room told me all I needed to know.

My resolve returning, I stepped into the room and marched straight to the cubicle.

It was Abby.

"What the hell was that all about last night? I thought you were on my side!"

She tore her gaze from the papers she'd been perusing. "And how did I know I'd be seeing you this morning?" Her thoughts were less than amused, despite the mischievous smile she sent in my direction.

I wasn't amused either. "Answer the question."

The smile wavered. For a split-second she looked as tired as I felt. But Abby, never one to show how she really felt about anything, quickly brought the grin back. "Sit down, Christine."

I didn't move.

"Fine. Stand for all I care." She waved an agitated hand in the air. "Don't bother thinking that maybe I have more knowledge of the situation than you. You might have telepathy, but you still know very little about how people think."

"Then why don't you explain it to me." I hissed the words at her.

She shook her head. "Adjust the attitude, girl. It's unbecoming of an Agent to let her emotions out so freely."

"You're the one who hired me, remember?" I spat. "Speaking of which, when am I getting paid?"

This time she smiled, amused. The tension had been broken, but only for a moment. "Christine, please sit."

"No. Explain."

"If you were any normal Agent, I'd have booted you out on your ass about ten times by now. This level of insubordination to a superior officer is—"

I cut her off. "Why are you avoiding my question? I might not know much about how people think, but I can tell when they're trying to change the subject."

"As your superior, I don't have to explain—"

"Yes, you do. This is my life we're talking about, and I can either be cooperative or not. I have no intention of helping Quinn out on this mission of his. However, the question still remains— what the hell happened last night? Are you working with him?"

She took in a long, deep breath and slumped back in her chair. She truly appeared to be beyond exhaustion. "Christine, please—" She stopped, noticing the frown on my face telling her I was never going to sit in that chair. She sat up and leaned her elbows on the desk. "Fine. Christine, have you ever watched a spy movie? You know, James Bond or something like that?"

One of my eyebrows crooked at the question. Why would she ask me something like that? "No," I responded.

She rolled her eyes. "Of course not. I'm going to order Ethan to sit you down and watch a couple of them then." She thought for a second before continuing. "Sometimes when James Bond is trying to infiltrate the enemy and learn more about them, he has to pretend to cooperate. Only when he's inside can he gain any valuable information."

At least that made sense. I had to admit that much at least. It didn't change the fact she was using me as a pawn in this little info gathering game of hers. "Why me, though? I don't think I'm qualified enough to—"

"You are the only one who can. For some reason, you're important to Quintus. He didn't ask for any other member of your team. Just you."

Why? The voice in my head asked. *Why only me?*

I wasn't any more special than the others. Quinn wanted me for something specific, but what? My breathing grew heavy. "I don't understand."

"Neither do we," admitted Abby. "As far as we know, you share all of his powers, so he can't need you to fill in any of his gaps."

"And Ethan, Savanah, Peter?" I asked, knowing Abby would understand the full question.

"Calm down, Christine." Her voice was soothing. "You're not going in alone. I'm already taking measures so your team will be there if you need them."

"That's a relief."

"You can't tell them yet. If Quinn reads their minds, he'll know what we're up to. Make sure you don't let anything slip."

I nodded. It was unfortunate, but I'd become really good over this last school year at keeping secrets from my friends. First about my powers, and then about the horrific things I'd found out about Quinn since going to Camp Hero. It was too dangerous letting them know anything when Quinn could pluck information right out of their heads.

"That still doesn't answer, why he picked me… and Jayson." I thought about Jayson's power. He could turn himself into anyone he wished. Between us, we had mind control, and morphing. What could Quinn have planned that would require those two skills?

"We believe there are other members of this team Quinn is putting together. But as of yet, we haven't been able to figure out who. We do, however, know he's been recruiting for the last couple of months."

"Yeah, he told me last night he'd travelled virtually around the world. But he made it sound like he was searching for some-*thing*, not some-*one*."

"He was doing that as well. He spent a great deal of time in Northern Italy. But we still don't know for what purpose."

"You've been following him the whole time? And you didn't let me know?" If that weren't bad enough, she'd had him followed for months and she couldn't figure out anything about him.

"Every time we got close, he managed to give us the slip," she explained. "It's hard to perform surveillance on someone who can hear the thoughts of the stakeout team."

"Then have them wear those thought inhibitor things." I motioned behind my ear so she'd know what I was talking about.

"Those aren't foolproof either. Think about Christine, how do you know when I'm around?"

I thought for a second. I could sense when Abby was coming even when she was wearing the inhibitor. My mouth spewed the words before I'd even thought of them. "Because I can't sense anything. It creates a void, and that's what I feel."

"Now add nearly 70 years experience on top of that," she added.

Wow. It had to be nearly impossible to follow Quinn around. Was that why Abby thought I was so valuable? Because I was the only one who stood a chance of being in his midst without him being able to sense any duplicity? Was I the only person capable of discovering and passing along data on the man?

An expression of comprehension must have crossed my face, because the next thing I knew, Abby was speaking. "Now do you understand why it is so important you cooperate with him?"

I nodded, my jaw slack and unable to form words.

"Sit down, please."

I sat.

"Thank you." The politeness of her words was cancelled out by the way she rolled her eyes. "Now, we have two weeks to prepare you. The first thing we need to do is figure out where he plans on taking you, and what he plans on doing."

"I might have an idea." I spoke before I could stop myself. I'd been pondering it all night, but couldn't come up with any answer. Even though I'd never said anything to Abby about the spear, now seemed the best time to do so. After all, it couldn't hurt to have a second brain mulling over the thoughts and coming up with another hypothesis. "Remember how Quinn gave me that clue about Montauk Point, to lead me to Camp Hero?"

"Yes," she said. Even with the inhibitor on I could feel her frustration. That clue had almost made her give up gathering information on Quinn. He'd been crafty, giving me a note he knew only I would be able to read.

"Well, when we were at Camp Hero, I found an object. An old spearhead. When I showed it to my grandfather, he said he thought it might be the Spear of Destiny. And when I'm near it, the spear... I don't know... it's like it talks to me." I paused, trying to gauge some reaction from Abby. As usual, her expression was unreadable. "I think Quinn sent me there specifically so I could retrieve the spear. He even hinted at it last night, but you came in before he said anything specific."

"And you think he might be looking for something similar in Italy?"

"Yeah." The whole thing sounded so stupid. Why would Quinn be after some old rusted piece of metal, or some other artifact that was thousands of years old? It didn't make sense. "I guess." The words came out weakly.

She leaned back in her chair and stared at the files in front of her for what seemed like an hour. She must have been thinking about what I'd told her, trying to see if there was any plausibility in the words. The fact she didn't seem surprised about the spear meant she knew something about it.

The warning bell rang, telling me I only had five minutes to get back to math class before I was late. It also snapped Abby out of her daze.

"I'm going to look into it. In the meantime, see what you can dig up with Quinn. Report back anything you can find out from him."

And like that, the conversation was over. I rose and walked out of the counselor's office. When I stepped into the hallway once again, it was filled with students, none of which were at all eager to get to class. Thoughts of, *Last day,* and, *Thank God summer's here,* filled the corridor. I on the other hand, felt no such enjoyment anymore. Like last summer, it appeared this one would be spent working. Albeit I wouldn't be employed at a retail store for just above minimum wage, but I'd still be working.

I thought seriously about going immediately to confront Quinn, knowing the science teacher had to be in his room by then. But instead decided not to ruin my perfect attendance streak of the last couple months and meandered my way toward Mrs. Blank's room.

Fate was not to be kind to me today, however. I was stopped in the hallway by Lance and Kyle, who motioned me over to them. We were about forty feet down the hall from Mr. Philmore's office, and the principal was walking by. The twins' eyes followed him as he came by and the two of them snickered.

"What did you do?" I groaned, already backing away from the pair.

"Just wait," one said.

"You're not going to want to miss this," added the other.

Suddenly glued to the spot, I allowed my gaze to follow the principal, knowing he was the target of whatever prank Lance and Kyle had set up. He went to his office and fumbled with his keys at the door. Both twins interest piqued as their anticipation went to levels I didn't think possible. As soon as Mr. Philmore creaked the door open, the pair pressed themselves up against the wall as much as possible. I did the same, not wanting to be the only one caught in the middle of hall when the fireworks blew.

I counted the seconds, with each one my feeling of fear grew more and more intense. When I reached two, my heart was racing. By the time I made five I thought I might burst from the sheer terror I felt—and I hadn't even done anything wrong. By six, all hell broke loose.

First, Mr. Philmore stumbled backwards out of his office, papers flying all around him. He landed clear on his rear in the center of the hall. Next, several squirrels scurried into the hall, causing the few teachers and students left to scream and fling their belongings into the air. I was frozen, watching in both horror and amazement while trying to hold back the roaring laughter trying to break free of my throat.

How the two of them pulled this one off was beyond me. What it must have taken them to first capture the squirrels and then break into the principal's office was much more than I would ever be willing to do to pull off any prank. The twins were definitely dedicated to their craft.

Even more astounding were the pair of raccoons that followed the frightened squirrels into the corridor. One of them scampered across Mr. Philmore's chest in its hasty escape. His scream was so high pitched, I feared he'd break some glass.

"Time to go," Lance or Kyle said.

"Yep. Let's get to class," said the other.

I made my escape as well, dodging running squirrels and raccoons as I navigated the hall. I stepped carefully over Mr. Philmore and glanced into his office as I past. It looked like a warzone. There were papers, torn and chewed, littering the entire office. The desk was in tatters as well, since it appeared the squirrels had used the wooden legs and edges to sharpen their teeth.

Kyle and Lance really needed to be congratulated on this one—if they didn't get caught, that was.

I made it to first period right after the bell rang. Luckily it didn't look like Mrs. Blank was interested in marking tardies today. We didn't do much, but she gave us all candy and showed us our grades. I got an A in math for the first time in, like, forever!

After first period, I bolted from the room and navigated the crowded halls to chemistry. Mr. Jenkins looked incredibly happy because the year was coming to a close.

Two and a half months without these little— I refrain from adding the final word because it is totally inappropriate. I laughed as I walked by him, which caused him to stare intently at me for a second. It was such a comment which this man made when I'd first discovered my powers.

As I was walking in the door, I gazed down the hall to Quinn's room. The door was open and the lights were on. Reaching out mentally, I sensed his presence. I breathed a deep sigh, knowing the decision was already made.

Putting my books down, I stepped back out of the class. "Mr. Jenkins, I'm going to talk to Mr. Quinn for a minute."

He shook his head and his smile wavered for a moment. Then he waved his hand down the hall telling me to get out of his face.

I ignored him and strode toward my second confrontation of the day.

Quinn's room was impeccably clean. For the first time all year, it wasn't set up for some experiment. The man stood behind his desk, watching the door as if waiting for me. He probably was.

"You will tell me what's going on and you're will tell me now!" To emphasize the fact I wasn't playing around, I mentally grabbed hold of his door and slammed it shut.

He turned toward the window, but said nothing.

Fine, you want to play games. Let's play.

Looking at his desk, I saw his cup, the one he always drank coffee from. It was no ordinary coffee mug, it looked more like one of those old wine goblets you see in movies. Only this one definitely wasn't made of gold. It appeared more like it was made of wood.

I mentally took hold of the cup and drew it toward my hand. The object flew across the room and into my hand. I readied myself to hurl the old and worn item at Quinn, but as soon as it touched my skin, I felt the strangest thing.

It spoke to me—just like the spear.

I couldn't throw it. Instead, I lowered my arm and examined the rough surface of the cup. I was barely able to glance at it before it was whisked out of my hands and shot like a bullet across the room to the outstretched arm of Quinn.

If he could shoot lasers from his eyes to kill me, I'm positive he would have done so at that very moment. "Never touch this cup."

I wasn't even worried about his wraith. I was more concerned about the object in his hands. "What is that thing?"

The way he held it, checking it to make sure I hadn't damaged it, told me more than I needed to know. That cup was worth more to Quinn than his life.

"This is very old and very fragile," he said. "It shouldn't be flung around in this manner."

"It spoke to me," I said, stopping myself before letting out it was in fact like the spear I'd found.

"And why does that surprise you, Ms. Carpenter? You've come across an object like this before."

Even though I knew he was already wise to the situation, I still feigned ignorance. "I don't know what you're talking about."

"Don't play dumb." His eyes practically glowed red with rage. "I know you have the spearhead. I felt it in your home last night when I came in. Why you'd think you could hide something like that from me is beyond my comprehension."

"Well, you haven't been honest with me, so why should I be with you?" No matter how angry he got, there was no way he'd intimidate me into backing down.

He placed the cup back on his desk before stepping toward me. For a split second, I thought the man was going to attack. I backed away until I hit the wall. No attack came.

"No, I haven't. And I think you know why." His voice had an edge of anger in it, but still held onto the calmness it usually did. "I can't have you passing information along to the Agent in our guidance department."

"Even if I was passing information along to her, it shouldn't matter. You could kill her with a thought." It was a weak argument and we both knew it. So, I decided to try another tact. "Besides, since I'm apparently going on a trip with you, I think I deserve to know where we're going and what we're doing."

He moved away again. Again, he said nothing.

"I know it has something to do with the spear and that cup of yours. Are we going after another artifact?" I gave him a couple of seconds to answer the question. When it appeared I still wasn't going to get a response, I added, "You were going to tell me last night. Why can't you now?"

"Because I don't know where your loyalties lie. You called that woman in when you thought I was trouble. I don't know I can trust you."

"Then leave me here. I don't want to go on this stupid mission of yours anyway."

"That's not possible. You're key to my plans."

And there was the opening I needed to ask the question I really wanted to ask. "Why? Why me? What makes me so special?" Even after my conversation with Abby, and thinking about it for the last hour, I still couldn't figure it out. "You and I have the same powers. Why do you need me?"

"I cannot say," he said simply. "Not yet anyway."

"How convenient for you."

So, there we were, a stalemate. Quinn unwilling to give up any information, and me refusing to concede until he did.

"Where are we going?"

"Italy."

"For what?"

"I cannot say."

I eyed the cup on his desk once again. Thinking maybe I could get him to talk if I did something to his precious cup, I took a mental hold of it again.

But, though I was intent, the bell rang beginning class. Not wanting to really ruin everything on the last day of school, I simply exclaimed, "This isn't over!" Then I turned and marched out of the room, slamming the door behind me again.

CHAPTER 5
LAST DAY BLUES

I sat through science, and waited to hear my final grade from Mr. Jenkins. I received a B, which I think was most unfair, considering I hadn't gotten lower than an A on anything the entire quarter. But rather than argue with the man, I simply nodded my head and went back to my seat. Though I did laugh the loudest when at the end of class his chair mysteriously moved out from under him as he was sitting down. When he fell flat on his back with a loud crash, I couldn't help but feel a small amount of satisfaction.

History was no better, though I did get up to present my poster. It wasn't the best one, but Mr. Murray said I got a B on it. Good enough for me.

As I was exiting the room, I had a thought. Earlier in the year, we had gone over a unit about World War II. In that unit, Mr. Murray had spoken about the Spear of Destiny, and when I asked him about it, he'd had a lot of great information. I wondered if he could help me now, and knowing I probably wouldn't get another chance to ask him, I hung back as the class exited.

"Mr. Murray." My voice was meek, almost embarrassed.

"Yes, Christine. I don't think you're going to have to worry about your grade. You've shown great improvement this quarter. I wish you would've shown this kind of initiative earlier in the year."

"It hasn't been a good year for me," I commented. "But I wasn't going to ask about my grade."

The teacher sat behind his desk as he stared up at me. He felt concerned. Even if I couldn't read his mind, I'd have been able to see that much in his eyes. "What's the matter?"

"Nothing," I said a little too quickly. "I was remembering some things from earlier in the year, and I was wondering if you could explain them."

"You do know the year's over. There isn't going to be another test."

"I know. I was just…" I began, then stumbled over my own words as I thought up the best one to use, "curio… no, interested."

"Okay." He felt relieved I wasn't in trouble, but also contemplative as to why I would seek out such information. "What do you want to know?"

I explained how we'd had the conversation about the spear and how I wanted to know more and why Hitler was seeking it out.

A crooked smile stretched across his face, and I could feel his delight someone would ask him about this. It was apparently a subject he was very fond of. "Well, Hitler was after many artifacts he believed would help him win the war. And who knows, if he possessed any of them, he may very well have. The four main items were, the Spear of Destiny, which we already spoke about, the Holy Grail, the Shroud of Turin and the True Cross. Each of these items is associated with the death of Christ. The spear stabbed him, the grail held his blood, he was wrapped in the shroud and nailed to the cross. The four items are said to have unimaginable power."

"Yeah, like the Holy Grail can make you..." My voice trailed off even as the last two words escaped my lips. "Live forever." *Of course.* That's why Quinn was so protective of the cup. It really was the grail and if he lost it, he gave up immortality. *Why didn't I see it before?*

"That's the rumor," Mr. Murray responded.

Immortality. I couldn't believe it. So, Quinn's only true power was the mind abilities. He never did get another injection which made him age slower like he'd told us. He was still so young because he drank from that stupid cup.

"What about the other artifacts? What could they do?"

"The spear is said to bring victory in battle to the person who possesses it. People claim the shroud has healing powers, and can even raise the dead. But, I can't say what the cross can do. I will tell you people have fought for these artifacts for nearly two-thousand years now. King Arthur was the most famous hunter of the Holy Grail. Charlemagne supposedly possessed the Spear of Destiny until he lost it and then was killed. King Richard the Lionheart fought a whole crusade to take possession of the True Cross."

"Where are they? Does anyone know?"

"Why are you so interested?" He crooked his head and raised an eyebrow.

"I find things like this fascinating." It was a lie, and a weak one at that, but it was the best I could do on short notice.

"No one has ever found the Holy Grail—as far as we know, anyway. Also, there is no evidence anyone has ever uncovered the True Cross. However, the Spear of Destiny was said to reside in a church in Vienna, Austria until World War II, but then it disappeared. And the Shroud of Turin—well the whereabouts of the shroud should be obvious."

It was my turn to arch an eyebrow. How was I supposed to know where the artifact was? I was about to say as much, but Mr. Murray spoke again before I had the chance.

"The shroud is named after the city it is held in—Turin, or as the Italians call it, Torino."

I nodded, trying to hide the excitement filling my body. "Thanks. I should get to English." I walked to the door and turned just in time to say, "Have a good summer." Then I ran off to English as the bell rang and the halls emptied.

We had an end of the year party in English, but I mainly sat in my desk and talked to Sam. Then, it was off to lunch.

I was looking forward to lunch today. The last day I would get to sit together with all of my friends for a while. It was going to be hard though, because I promised Abby I wouldn't say anything to the others about my trip with Quinn. At least, after school I'd be able to say anything I wanted. None of them should have any contact with Quinn after the final bell today.

I gave a polite nod to Samantha as she came to our table to say hello to Sam. She gave one in return, but we exchanged no words. That didn't bother me. It was better off for everyone we didn't speak to each other. The girl might have saved my life back in May, but that still didn't mean we had to like each other. Being cordial toward one another was enough.

It wasn't long before I was joined by the rest of my friends. Peter came first, sitting quietly at the end of the table as usual. Ethan and Sam flanked me on either side with Tiffany and Savanah bringing up the rear, both sitting across from me.

"So, Mrs. Sampson gave a test today," Savanah announced. "I swear, I hate that woman."

"Eh, Mr. Clark did the same thing," Ethan said. "Fifty questions."

"Nothing for me," I said. "Stupid last day nonsense. But boy do I have something to tell you guys later."

"Tell us now," Tiffany insisted.

I shook my head. "I promised I wouldn't say anything yet."

Tiffany's bottom lip poked out as she did her best to look like a grumpy four-year-old. It didn't faze me.

"Really. I can't. Trust me. You'll understand when I get to tell you."

"Well, then I just won't tell you about Ryan Herbert asking me out."

She had my interest piqued. "Another summer romance, huh?"

"No. I think he could be the one this time." Tiffany's cheeks flushed red, and her smile got even wider.

"I don't know," I said. "You seemed to think the same thing last summer with you and David, and look how that turned out."

"You're right," she admitted. "But I'm going to make this one work."

I didn't say anything. Ryan Herbert wasn't the classiest guy in school, but I figured he would at least treat her right. I just didn't want to see her get crushed again like she had when she found out David was cheating on her.

"Well, I officially made the state team for track. The meet is in two weeks at Penn State," Ethan announced.

We all offered our congratulations, but he only received a kiss on the cheek from me. I was really excited for him, even though we all knew he'd make it. I mean, how could he not? The boy chase down a car on the highway—how could any normal human beat him in a race?

But then my excitement was replaced with another emotion—guilt. It filled my body like a bad flu, and I wanted so bad to sneeze it out. Ethan wouldn't get to go to the state tournament because in two weeks, he, like me, would be going on a forced Italian vacation.

All the joy I'd had from discovering one possible motive for Quinn dragging me to Italy, now felt like horrible and intense pain for the hurt I would be causing my boyfriend. The worst part was, I knew and I couldn't even tell him. It felt like the secret I held from Peter. Every day I promised I would tell him I'd once hurt him and how Quinn had erased it from his mind, but every day I couldn't bring myself to do it.

"What's the matter?" Ethan asked, always the first to sense a change in my mood.

Again, I was forced to shake my head. "I'll tell you later." Then I shoved the chicken sandwich I'd bought on the lunch line into my mouth. For the first time, Peter wasn't the quietest person at our table.

****

The day only went downhill from there. The morning's discoveries were a thing of the distant past, and weighing heavily upon me was the intense pain I'd have to cause my boyfriend when he found out he wouldn't get that state championship he wanted. I had a test in Art—yes, ART. I had to identify the painters for certain portraits and landscapes, like I was supposed to remember all that. I know I lost my A in that class because of one stupid test.

Then, when I stopped into the guidance office again, Abby was nowhere to be found. I must have looked like a crazy person, because all the real counselors insisted on speaking to me before I left the room.

Then, because gym wouldn't be complete without an injury or two, I spent the last period of the day in the nurse's office with an icepack over my eye after getting hit with a football. I told Coach Green I'd had worse, but he insisted.

All in all, it was a crappy afternoon.

When the last bell rang, I think every fiber in every muscle in my body relaxed.

The halls of the school had never cleared out as quickly as they did that day. You would think they were giving away free iPads in the parking lot. Papers flew in the air as the students raced each other to the doors. Thankfully, I wasn't among the stampede, because I probably would've lost my cool.

I didn't have the patience to hang around the school any longer. I'd been lurking about for eight hours and I needed to go home.

My car had never looked as pleasant to me than it did when I stepped through the school doors and out into total and absolute freedom. My bones were so weary, I wouldn't have even considered flying myself home. I took a few deep breaths of free air, reveling in the warm sunshine, then drove home at a nice, leisurely pace.

I was totally relaxed by the time I reached my house, but it was all for nothing since my mother was waiting to charge my car like a bull as I pulled up.

"I'm late!" she shouted. She handed me Conner before I even got out of the car, then jumped in her own car and drove off, almost leaving skid marks in our driveway.

I looked at my brother, fidgeting in my arms. "She's your mother."

Like yesterday, he laughed, making me think for a moment he understood me. But he didn't. I couldn't wait until he could. He'd be much more fun then.

My mother's car turned the corner and I grabbed my bookbag—empty thank God—and took Conner inside.

As soon as I opened the front door, I knew something was wrong. There was someone in the house, and they were waiting for me. Most people would think it was paranoia driving that feeling, but I could sense at least three people waiting only steps within.

They must have slipped in when my mother went outside to meet me. She never realized her house was being invaded by… invaders. Feeling their thoughts, I tried to sense their intentions. They were definitely waiting for me, but beyond that, I couldn't tell if they were hostile or not.

I thought about busting in, with mental guns blazing to take all of them out. With Conner in my arms though, that wasn't a possibility. I wouldn't risk him getting hurt. And I couldn't leave him on the porch while I went inside. Not only would Child Protective Services come knocking on the door, but who knew if someone would come by and kidnap him while I was occupied.

I could have turned around and left, but thought what would happen when my parents came home and found a bunch of strangers, possibly armed, in our house. It wouldn't be pretty—especially for me.

"Agent Carpenter," an impatient voice spoke before I could make a decision. "Step inside, please."

Feeling the need for continued caution, I slowly crept through the door into my living room. Standing by my couch were three Agents, none of whom I recognized. One was an older, dark skinned man, with white hair, keeping his hand on the gun resting in its holster on his right side. The other two, a man and a woman, were younger, maybe a couple of years older than Abby. All three wore those black business suits.

"Agent Carpenter," said the older gentleman, "I'm here to brief you."

"That's great," I said. "And who exactly are you?"

He relaxed his stance, moving his hand from his sidearm. His expression however, turned sour. "My name is Agent Smith."

"Really?" I closed my eyes and shook my head. "You couldn't come up with a better codename?"

It was barely above a whisper, but I still heard his response. "I hate teenagers."

Conner began squirming again, and starting making little groaning noises. I scanned his mind and saw an image of his bottle. Knowing what that meant, I moved toward the kitchen.

"Let's continue inside," I said. "The baby needs to be fed." I didn't hide my annoyance with the man, nor did I wait for a response, and disappeared through the kitchen entrance.

Agitation filled the room as Agent Smith followed me. "Agent Davidson said you were a handful."

My head was already in the refrigerator as I grabbed one of Conner's bottles. "Yeah, well so is she. You have any idea how whiny she is? I shoved the bottle in the microwave and set the time for sixty seconds. Then I turned on the old man and frowned. "You said you wanted to brief me. Let's hear it."

"Are you always so brash?"

"Only when someone breaks into my home."

He shook his head and sighed. His exasperation level was beginning to reach its limit. This man clearly had no patience. He definitely wasn't going to last dealing with me.

"In les than two weeks, you are going on an important assignment with a very dangerous man."

"Tell me something I don't know."

"Shut up!" he yelled. "A proper Agent listens quietly as her superior explains things."

"I guess I missed that lesson at the academy."

The microwave beeped, cutting off whatever response was mustering in the flustered mind of Smith. I grabbed the bottle and without bothering to test to make sure it was warm enough, put the nipple in Conner's mouth. He instantly began sucking the formula out.

"Look, I don't want to go on this assignment of yours," I told the man. "I promised to spy on Quinn, but I think asking me, a sixteen year old, to go into a dangerous situation is frankly ridiculous."

His face turned an even darker shade than it already was, and Smith looked like he was fighting the urge to let loose a string of curses. When he calmed a little, he let out some very tense words. "You are an M.H.D.A. Agent. You will do as ordered and you will not question it."

"Wait a sec. Don't your Agents usually get paid? After my first paycheck you can lecture me about proper Agent etiquette."

"I am not going to sit here and argue. If you continue, I will instruct my Agents to bind you and tape your mouth shut."

He waited for me to begin arguing, but I saw in his mind how serious he was, and though I was sure I could take on the three Agents, I was still not willing to risk hurting Conner in the struggle.

"As I was saying—two weeks—dangerous man. You are going to pretend to cooperate with this man Quinn, no matter what he asks you to do. The only intel we have thus far, is what you learned last night. For the next two weeks, we need you to get as much information out of him as possible."

"Actually, I'm not sure how much info I'll be able to get. I'm not sure he trusts me, since I'm working with you. But I can tell you this—"

"Hold on." He held up a hand then called over his shoulder. "Franklin, get in here!"

A second later, the male Agent stepped into the kitchen. The man practically saluted Agent Smith and said, "Yes, sir." He was way too eager to please.

"I need a record of everything Agent Carpenter tells me. Please set up a recorder."

The Agent pulled a small recording device, something like a news reporter used when getting the big interview in a movie, and set it on the table. "Ready."

"Is Agent Thompson putting the devices in place?"

"Yes, sir."

"Devices?" I asked.

"We need to monitor you from now on," Smith explained.

"Why?"

"Tell me what you were going to say a minute ago."

Conner had finished his bottle, but was still sucking on the rubber nipple like there was no tomorrow. I pulled it out, propped him on my shoulder and patted his back.

"Well, like I said, Quinn told me he doesn't trust me because he knows I'm working with you. But he also said he needs me."

"Can you remember the exact words he said?" prompted Smith.

"Why does that matter?" I continued patting Conner's back and rocked him back and forth.

He sighed and frowned so hard, at least seven wrinkled ridges appeared on his forehead. "Because sometimes the way someone says something, or the exact words they use can tell more than the simple information. Quinn could very well have been giving you a clue as to what he needs you for without actually saying it."

I rolled my eyes. All this covert nonsense was just that—nonsense. "Okay. I think his exact words were, 'you're essential to my plan'."

"That's it?" he asked. Disappointment radiated from him.

"Well, that's what he told me. But I did some digging of my own and I think I know what he's after."

"Elaborate." He motioned toward the recorder.

Conner finally burped, but I continued rubbing his back in hopes he would soon drift off to sleep. "Quinn drinks from this cup. It's a very old cup. I believe it's actually the Holy Grail, and that's why he's stayed so young all these years." I paused to make sure he understood what I was saying. He did. "So, anyway, I asked my history teacher about it and he said it was one of four artifacts."

"You asked your history teacher?" Smith interrupted.

"Well, I didn't say why I was asking."

Conner let out a deep breath that told me he was getting ready to drift off.

Tiptoeing toward the recorder, I continued in a quieter tone. "I think he's trying to collect these four artifacts. And one of them is definitely in Italy—in the city of Turin. The Shroud of Turin."

"The death shroud of Jesus Christ?" Smith asked. "You really think he'd want an old piece of cloth?"

"If you've got a better idea, I'd love to hear it," I whispered. "Now, please be quiet." I jerked my head toward Conner.

Smith motioned Franklin to turn off the recorder. The young man did as instructed.

"What else do you need?" I asked. "This hasn't been much of a briefing. I've told you more than you told me."

"If Quinn is smart," Smith continued in a low voice, "which we already know he is. He will know we are tracking you, so he's going to get you to remove pretty much everything that might be a tracking device, including the watch we gave you. So, we need to implant something inside you he can neither detect nor have you remove."

I suddenly had a bad feeling this was going to involve a needle of some kind. The last thing I wanted was some homing beacon implanted in my arm, or leg, or worse.

I didn't argue though. This was something that would help keep me safe, which was the most important thing. Instead, I said, "Okay. Let me go put Conner upstairs, and then you can do what you need to."

Smith nodded. Finally I'd gotten his approval on something—not that I was seeking it, of course.

I snuck up the stairs with Conner as quickly and noiselessly as possible, being careful not to jostle him into wakefulness. I lay him in his crib, grabbed his baby monitor, and went back downstairs.

Smith and Franklin were waiting for me in the living room, along with Agent Thompson, who I swear wasn't there when I'd gone up with Conner. She had probably been planting some surveillance system somewhere in the house.

"Okay, so this tracking device," I said as I walked toward them. "What do we have to do?"

Agent Thompson held up an item that had the shape of a futuristic pistol. Then she motioned for me to sit on the couch, precisely where I'd been sitting last night when I'd been talking to Quinn.

The device in her hand really was starting to freak me out. If she used it on me, it looked like it was going to be very painful. She must have noticed my wary glance at the device, because she said, "Don't worry, you'll barely feel it." Then she pointed at four points on my body—on each shoulder and then at each knee. "We're going to insert the trackers in four specific places, where they will likely not be found. They are no bigger than a pin head, but send out a powerful signal we can pick up by satellite."

Her words were pretty much doing nothing to ease my nerves. "That's all very interesting, but can you put them in?"

Her smile was apologetic. "Roll up your sleeves."

I did as instructed, and cringed as the cold metal touched my upper arm. I did my deep breathing to keep myself calm, but when I heard a whir followed by a click and then felt a sharp pinch on my shoulder I jumped.

"Ow!" I rubbed my arm where she'd injected the device in me. *So much for not hurting.*

Unfortunately, I had to sit there through three more—one on my other shoulder then lifting up my legs so she could place the other two behind each of my knees. Those areas were going to be sore for a week. I glanced at my left shoulder to see what looked like a hicky forming on the spot she'd shot me.

When she backed away, I was finally able to relax.

"You are to report any contact you have with Quintus before your trip," Smith said to me. "For the next two weeks your point of contact will be Agent Davidson. Do you understand?"

I nodded. Still mentally recovering from the assault on my limbs. Before I knew it, the three Agents had left my house. So, their very weak instructions to collect information was pretty much a moot point, since Quinn wasn't going to reveal anything anyway.

I picked up my cell, wincing from the pain in my shoulder as I lifted it to my ear. It was time to let my friends know everything.

"Hello, Ethan?" I said when he picked up. "I need you to come over."

CHAPTER 6
INTRUDER

Ethan took it better than I would have.

"Yeah, I figured something would happen," he said. "There's always next year. Besides, how many tenth graders win the state tournament anyway?"

The five of us were sitting around my living room. Ethan was to my right on the couch, with Savanah and Tiffany next to each other on the loveseat.

Peter sat alone on the armchair arcing lightning between his hands. "Why didn't Abby come to tell you this?"

It was something I hadn't thought anything of. I figured he was Abby's superior and wanted to handle things himself. But she hadn't been present at all. "I don't know," I responded. I honestly hadn't thought about it, leave it to Pete to make a single thoughtful comment. "She could have been busy."

"She is," mentioned Savanah. "I saw her running out of the school after lunch today. The way she was rushing, I wouldn't be surprised if something big happened."

"No. Nothing happened. If it did, we'd know about it," I said, sounding more sure of myself than I felt.

"And Quinn?" Tiffany asked. "You're actually going to help him get Christ's shroud?"

"That's what I've been ordered to do." I twirled a finger in my short hair, not looking at any of my friends. "If I can double-cross him, believe me, I will. He can't be allowed to have it if we can prevent it."

Savanah rose and tromped over to our television. It wasn't turned on, but she stared at her reflection in it for ten seconds before turning back to us. Her lips were curved down in a frown. Her jaw tightened. She looked directly at me. "It was only a couple months ago you were so sure we couldn't trust the M.H.D.A., but when you volunteered us to join we all followed. Now you're telling us we can't trust Quinn. So, which one is it? Who can we trust?"

I was about to respond when a wave of dread rippled through my body. Ethan called it my "Spidey-Sense". I knew it was a premonition. Danger was coming—but from where? I froze, trying to pinpoint where and when the trouble would come, but I couldn't. It would probably come to me in a dream like it had before I set off to find Eddie.

Shaking my head to clear feeling from my brain, I finally responded to Savanah. "I don't think we can trust either of them. But Quinn was a Nazi. If I had to choose between the two, he would be the least trustworthy. So, for now, we stick with the M.H.D.A.."

"And if it turns out Quinn is right?" She plopped back on the couch next to Tiffany, causing the girl to jump about four feet in the air before landing on the soft cushions herself. "I mean, he could be telling you the truth. He could be one of the good guys."

"I know," I responded. "But look at his actions. When he first met Ethan and me, he told us he was the reason we all go to Thomas Jefferson High School. He somehow manipulated our parents to moving here. Then he begins training us, but disappears, leaving a replacement—a replacement, I might add, he never told any of us about. Then he just shows back up with this wild mission he also refuses to tell any of us about."

"She's right, Savanah," my boyfriend added, "the evidence is against him."

The feeling came back. It felt like someone had dumped a bucket of ice-water over me. Whatever the danger was, it was close—and getting closer. I started to say something, but was interrupted.

"I'm not ready to give up on Quinn yet. I think he's going to surprise us," Savanah almost shouted.

"I can't believe you don't trust Christine," Tiffany said. There was venom in her voice. She never spoke that way to Savanah.

The girl was completely taken aback by Tiffany's remark. She wanted to respond, but her brain wouldn't allow her. She stammered a few times before finally getting out, "Don't you have a date to get ready for?"

"No one said she doesn't trust, Chris," Ethan said. "I'm sure she needs to see for herself."

Savanah turned and glared at Ethan. The gaze said only one thing to Ethan: "Stay out of this."

When Savanah did speak, her words were said very slowly and deliberately. "I'm more concerned my summer vacation is going to be ruined for absolutely no reason. This whole thing sounds stupid, and idiotic, and I honestly want no part of it."

"How do you think I feel? I'm being forced to go with Quinn."

"And from what you're telling me, we're being forced to follow you around for a month. Does that sound like a vacation to you?"

"No," I admitted.

"No one ever said it was a vacation!" Ethan yelled.

My sense of danger was completely overwhelming me now. I needed to tell them. Something was about to go down, and we didn't have time to keep arguing amongst ourselves. "Guys."

"I've got my own crap to deal with. I don't need to go running off whenever Abby tells us to!" Savanah shouted at Ethan.

"Guys." I wanted to calmly bring the argument to a close, but with each passing second, that seemed more impossible.

"You knew this would happen when you signed up!" he continued arguing. It was as if I weren't even there.

Tiffany and Peter were both intently watching the shout-fest in front of them, rather than help me out to calm them down. But the danger was coming and I really needed to alert them to it.

"I didn't sign up for any of this!" Savanah screamed. "I wanted to just have a normal life!"

"But you're not normal! None of us are. We have a responsibility to help those in need!"

"Hey, I'm normal!" Tiff interjected.

"Guys." I tried in vain to get their attention one final time.

Savanah stood again, as if challenging Ethan. He stood too, rising to the bait. If I didn't stop this soon, I was going to have a fight in my living room, and the two of them had the potential to destroy my entire house.

"Yeah! Well, who helped me when I needed them? Who came to my rescue when Bruce did… did those things to me!" A single tear rolled down her face. Usually this was the breaking point, when anger turned into grief and everyone apologized. Savanah's rage didn't subside. "Who helped my grandparents when they were murdered? Who helped my dad when he was in his accident? There are hundreds of us out there! Why don't any of the others help?"

I had to end this. I pushed both of them back down with a mental push as I shouted once more, "Guys!"

The both of them finally paid attention to me.

"We have something more important to worry about. There's something coming."

Before any of them could respond, the baby monitor blared with the sound of Conner crying. It wasn't his normal cry, he was screaming. There was the possibility he could feel the danger too and it frightened him, but I didn't think that was it. No, whatever the foreboding feeling was, was coming from the nursery.

"C'mon," I said, sprinting for the stairs. "It's in Conner's room."

I was the first up the stairs and I felt a split second of panic as whatever was in the room heard us coming. I heard a crash as the intruder dropped something to the floor. I ran for the door and flung it open with my mind before I reached it. Then, not hesitating for an instant, I jumped into the room, ready to face whatever was in there.

The room was empty, except for the crying baby. The light blue drapes over the windows wafted in the slight breeze coming through them. I hadn't left the window open. The changing table had been flipped over as the intruder made his hasty escape.

Ethan entered right behind me, not able to pass me on the narrow stairway.

"Check the window," I ordered. While he did that, I picked up Conner to console him.

With his head stuck out the window, searching the neighborhood for any sign of disturbance Ethan said, "Nothing out here."

I heard Peter call up from the driveway outside. "I'll check the other side of the house!"

"Be right down!" Ethan shouted to him. "Wait a second!"

Ethan then turned to me, his eyes were wide open and looking at me like a puppy might when it knows something's wrong. "You alright?"

Conner continued to cry very loudly in my ear. I rubbed his back and rocked him. My heart was beating about a thousand miles a minute and my breath was coming in very short gasps. I couldn't bear thinking what might have happened to him if I hadn't sensed something was wrong. "I'm fine," I managed to say. "Go and see if you can find anything."

A brief gust of wind, and my boyfriend was gone. Over Conner's crying I could hear him giving orders to Peter on where would be the best places to search. I started moving over to the window to watch, but felt a hand on my shoulder.

With my body in full on panic-mode, and with my heightened levels of adrenaline coursing through my veins, the girl was lucky I didn't tear her arm off when I spun around. Once I saw who it was, I relaxed, but only enough so I didn't kill her on the spot. "Tiffany," I breathed out, "don't ever do that again."

She held out her arms. "Give me Conner. Go and help the other's search."

I shook my head and clutched Conner tighter to my chest. There wasn't a chance in hell I was letting him go now. Besides, with me outside helping Ethan and Peter searching, there'd be no one left to protect Conner. "Where's Savanah?"

"Followed Pete outside."

Nodding, I sat in the rocking chair my mother had bought so she could rock Conner to sleep at night. Only when I started rocking in it did Conner's screams begin to calm.

"There," I cooed. I kept my voice soft and light despite my still rapidly beating heart. "Where all right now. All right now." I looked up at Tiffany and pointed briefly at Conner's crib. "His pacifier should be in there. Can you grab it?"

"Sure." She searched the crib, moving his tiny blanket to locate the pacifier. Suddenly I felt her tense and a tsunami of fear hit me. She froze, looking down at the sheets.

"What's the matter?" My stress levels were beginning to rise as well. Whatever she was seeing couldn't have been positive.

She looked over her shoulder. Her eyes were so dilated they looked perfectly black. She wasn't focusing on me at all, but looking directly at Conner. They began filling with tears as she pointed at the baby. "Chris... is he... is he bleeding?"

My heart skipped a beat as I pulled Conner away from my chest to inspect him. He didn't look like he was bleeding. I ran my hands up and down his arms and legs, then turned him around to check his backside. There was nothing on his clothes, nor any cuts on his arms or legs that indicated he was injured in any way.

All the jostling disturbed him, and he began crying again. So, I pulled him back to me and began rocking him again. Looking at Tiffany, I shook my head.

"Are you sure?" She turned back to the crib and looked back down. "Because there's a stain on his sheets."

I stood and walked to the crib. "Could it be something else?"

She shook her head. "It's definitely blood."

Peering down in the crib, I saw the stain Tiffany was looking at. It was a reddish brown color and from the shine on it, I could tell it was still wet, which meant it was fresh. Someone had bled in the crib only a few minutes ago. If it hadn't been Conner, then who?

"Let me see him," Tiffany insisted. She held out her arms to take Conner from me again.

I shook my head and pulled back from her.

"Chris," she said. "I'm not going to steal him. I want to make sure he's okay."

She was my best friend and I knew I should trust her, but at the moment, I didn't trust anyone with my baby brother. I was, pretty much the only protection he had. And if anything happened to him, it would be all my fault. However, I also knew Tiffany was trying to help, so, hesitating and with a bit of reluctance, I handed him over. But I still stood close enough so I'd be able to snatch him back at any moment.

She felt his body, ignoring the fact that Conner struggled and continued screaming in her arms. She moved his clothes out of the way, exposing more skin for her to scan. Tiffany was determined to find the source of the blood and the more she looked, the more I was sure she would find it.

Under his shoulder, she found something. "Chris, look." She indicated a mark on his skin which was sort of yellowish in color with a bluish ring around it. The blemish couldn't have been bigger than a dime, and was so faint I'm surprised she even saw it.

"What is it?" I asked. I'd never seen anything like it before.

"It's the beginning of a bruise." She rubbed her finger over the spot. It must have been sensitive, because Conner shook when she touched it.

"How would a bruise make him bleed?"

"He didn't bleed. But I think it is his blood."

I raised my eyebrows at her. She wasn't making any sense. If he didn't bleed, then how was a splash of his blood on his sheet?

"It's the same kind of bruise I get when I go to the doctor," said Tiffany. She eyed me with such intensity then and I could tell the next words were going to hit like a sledgehammer. "It's the kind of bruise I get when they draw blood."

My head spun as it tried to fathom what had happened. Nothing made sense.

I took Conner back from Tiffany and resumed rocking him in the rocking chair. I needed to figure this out. There had to be some kind of logic somewhere. I started speaking aloud, thinking if the words were said, I could begin to understand. "So, someone broke into the house—I'm assuming through the window—and drew some blood from my brother. I started sensing danger, but couldn't pinpoint it. When I finally realized, the intruder bolted back out the window, knocking over the changing table and, since I see no blood on Conner, spilled some of his collected sample. The question is: why?"

"Do you think this has anything to do with Quinn and this trip to Italy?"

I nodded. There was no doubt in my mind everything was connected. "What we need to figure out is how these puzzle pieces fit together."

Conner finally seemed to calm down from the trauma inflicted upon him. He'd gotten shots and had blood taken before, but my mother had always been standing over him, consoling him. He still cried, but at least he could feel safe in my mother's arms. Having some stranger wake him from a fitful sleep by stabbing him with a needle had to frighten him more than anything. I wouldn't be surprised if the boy was scarred for life with an irrational fear of needles.

Ethan came back into the room a second later. "We didn't find anything. Whoever was here is long gone."

Savanah entered behind Ethan. "They left no trace either. Nothing I can find anyway."

Peter came into the tiny room now, making me feel a little crowded. Involuntarily, I clutched Conner a little tighter to my chest and started my deep breathing. "Whoever it was couldn't have jumped out of the window and run off."

"If they jumped," Savanah mentioned. "He or she could have flown out, which could also be why we can't find anything."

There were only two other people I could think of sharing the power of flight with me, and one of them could be ruled out immediately. Which only left—

"And one more thing," Savanah said, interrupting my thoughts. "I'm sorry for what happened downstairs. I don't know what came over me. It's, like, the words weren't really coming from me. It's the strangest thing. It was like someone was playing with my emotions—guiding me to say those things. I mean, I think those things all the time, but I'd never say them out loud like that. Do you understand?"

I understood only too well. The person who was in this room had used Savanah as a distraction. With her yelling and arguing with the rest of us, none of us—especially me—would notice what was happening upstairs. By the time I had come to my senses and stopped the arguing, it was too late. Again, there were only two people in the world who had that ability other than me.

"It was Quinn," I said. "He's the only one who could have done this."

Then Peter said the one word on all of our minds. "Why?"

CHAPTER 7
PREPARATIONS

"No way! The psycho broke into my house and attacked my brother! I'm not going with him!"

Abby and Smith sat in my kitchen now. Smith looked as upset as he had earlier that afternoon, but Abby was, as usual, unreadable.

"We put surveillance devices all over this house, including your brother's bedroom," Smith said, glaring at me with those angry eyes of his. "We have no indication of anyone entering this house other than your *friends*." The way he said friends made it sound like a curse.

Does this guy hate everyone?

"Well, I don't care what your equipment says! Someone was in this house, and they took blood from my brother's arm. He has the bruise to prove it, not to mention the stains on his sheets. I'm not going, and that's final."

"Christine," Abby said, sounding more counselor than Agent, "I think you need to calm down. There's more going on here than you realize."

"Then fill me in. Isn't that what you *superior officers* do?"

Smith's face turned a darker shade, and he looked like he was going to flip his top. But Abby held up a hand. "It's okay Agent Smith. I know how to handle her." Then she spoke to me as if he weren't there. "I believe you. Despite evidence to the contrary."

"Really?" It wasn't the statement I'd been expecting from her. "How come?"

"Because I lost track of him right around the time of the break in."

So that's why she hadn't been here earlier. She'd been tailing Quinn to see what he was up to. But the man was obviously as crafty as they said. Somehow, the science teacher had not only been able to lose Abby, but also managed to enter my house without any security detecting him. If it hadn't been for my abilities, we probably wouldn't have known he was here either.

Smith eyed Abby with such intensity he must have been hoping for her head to explode. "Do the words 'need to know' mean anything to you?"

"I don't know," said Abby, turning in his direction, "do the words 'police work' mean anything to you?"

"I'm putting you on report, Agent Davidson."

She sighed. "What else is new?"

It was the first time I'd ever seen Abby act like—well, me. She rolled her eyes and made a face like I made whenever she gave me an order I didn't agree with. Even her tone matched mine.

"The point is," Agent Smith's voice sounded cold, like he was going to spit up ice cubes at any moment, "Agent Carpenter really has no choice in the matter. She *is* going on this mission and she *is* going to help us capture Quintus."

"Don't you care about sending me off with a dangerous maniac?"

He didn't answer, but I could see it in his eyes. I couldn't read his thoughts because he was wearing an inhibitor, but a word formed in my head as he looked at me. *Expendable.*

"You know what?" I rose from the kitchen table and began backing out of the room. I thought seriously about flipping the furniture over onto him, but controlled the urge. I couldn't believe I'd been so stupid. My grandfather had been right about these people all along. They were going to use me and then get rid of me when I wasn't useful anymore. "Get out of my house! I had enough reasons before not to do this, but this lack of sympathy takes the cake. Get out!"

Of course, Smith and Abby didn't move. My little temper tantrum had no effect on him.

"If that's your decision." Smith's voice was too calm and even for him. He wasn't going to let this go. He turned his head toward Abby and said, "Agent Davidson, arrest her."

"What?" I asked. This was also not a remark I'd been expecting. "What did I do?"

He rose, opening his jacket and putting his hand on his gun. "You are a highly dangerous meta-human who has not only broken into a top secret government facility but is now impeding a federal investigation. You will be incarcerated to the fullest extent of the law."

A breeze blew by me and suddenly Smith was unarmed. Ethan stood beside me as if he'd been there the whole time, holding Smith's gun by the barrel.

The footsteps of both Peter and Savanah filled the air behind me as the pair took up ranks in the entryway. We had Smith and Abby outnumbered. Neither of them would be arresting any of us today.

"What law?" Ethan asked. "Chris saw what you did to those kids that were too dangerous. None of them were ever given a chance." Ethan was referring to the underground bunker we'd all been held in. The metas they considered "too dangerous" were frozen and put into stasis—no trial, no rights, just captured, sedated and locked away.

"No one's being arrested today." Abby rose to stand beside Smith. She never took her eyes off me though, even though Ethan was technically the one with a weapon—not that he'd actually use it. "Everyone, calm down."

"Tiff's with the baby?" I asked Ethan in a low voice.

Ethan nodded.

There was going to be a fight and everyone in the room knew it. Everyone also knew it would be us four teenagers who would be claiming victory. The only problem was, even if we won against Abby and Smith, there's be about a hundred Agents descending on my house within minutes. And then we would lose.

"Everyone relax!" This sounded like an order being given to soldiers in basic training. It was said with such force and gusto we had no choice but to listen. Abby stepped forward, coming in between Smith and the four of us. "You're all acting like children. Yes, even you, Agent Smith."

Smith looked like he was going to protest, but a sneer from me made him think otherwise.

"We're all on the same side here. We all want the same thing. To see Quintus ended. We may not know what he's doing, but we do know if he succeeds it's going to be bad." She paused and looked at all five of us in turn, making sure she had our attention. "For all of us."

I eased up my shoulders, relaxing my posture from attack to neutral. As much as I hated to admit it, it was the second time she'd been right today.

"Christine, as I told you before. You are going on this mission, and your team will be there to back you up. We've implanted you with four tracking devices. We'll never be more than a minute or two from your position. Yes, it's dangerous, but you will be in the safest danger possible."

"Safe danger?" I asked, arching an eyebrow. "You just make that one up?"

She ignored the comment, but I could see her tense up, which told me the remark had agitated her. "We leave in under two weeks. We have plenty to do. Christine, you must act as if you have no idea it was Quinn who was in your house this afternoon. Confide in him you think it was one of us, and make him believe you're returning to his control."

"But—"

"No. Agent Smith is right about one thing. You need to follow orders without argument. If you want to continue being an Agent, then that's what you need to do. Do you understand?"

I shook my head, but reluctantly answered, "Yes."

"Agent Smith, you may be my superior, but you will never talk to me that way in front of any members of my team again. Understand?"

"Yes." He answered, but in such a tone that told me he actually didn't understand.

"And you need to have more patience with them. They are only teenagers. I wasn't so different when I was first recruited, was I?"

He didn't answer, but he didn't need to. From the way he huffed, it was clear he thought she hadn't changed much since her first day on the job. Could it be she really did have the same attitude as me when she first started? Might I turn out to be a good soldier like her one day? I cringed at the thought. Once I used the M.H.D.A. for my own means, I intended to be rid of them forever.

"I think we should leave," Smith said. He stepped around the table and walked past us into the living room.

"Agent Smith," Ethan called after he'd made it a couple of steps.

The Agent turned, looking impatient. "Yes?"

"You forgot this." Ethan tossed Smith his gun.

Smith caught it, then nodded and put the gun back in its holster. He then turned and walked out.

"How did you get mixed up with this guy anyway?" Ethan asked as soon as he heard the front door close.

"He trained me." Her voice was far away as if remembering times long past.

"Nice guy," Savanah commented. She turned and walked into the living room.

Peter followed.

"He's probably one of the best Agents we have," Abby said quietly to me and Ethan. "He's been so obsessed lately with finding Quintus that... well, you see how he is."

"Yeah, like Savanah said, he seems like a really nice guy."

"Well, you better get used to him. Especially you Christine. Because he's going to be your contact in Italy."

"What about you?" She couldn't abandon me now. Not when I needed her the most.

She began walking past me, but stopped just as she stood between me and Ethan. "I'm too recognizable. Quintus doesn't know Smith. He's the better choice." Everything from her posture to her tone of voice said she didn't actually believe what she was telling me. But as quickly as I noticed it, she returned to her normal self. "There'll be around the clock guard of this house until you depart, just to be safe. So, don't do anything stupid."

Then she walked out of the house after Smith.

****

The whole next week was a blur. With school out, and this impending mission, Abby felt it necessary to have training sessions twice a day rather than only once in the evenings. Luckily, with my mother taking extra shifts at the store, I didn't have to make any lame excuses for why I was sneaking out with Conner in the morning.

I met with Quinn twice, and did as Abby told me to do. But when I explained how I thought it was the M.H.D.A. who'd broken in and hurt Conner, Quinn didn't look like he believed a word of it. I made no mention of finding out about the shroud and what I thought we were doing. But even with my fabulous acting ability, he didn't trust me. Needless to say, I didn't get any new information out of him.

It was hard making preparations for a mission when all you had to go on were a few hunches.

It was three days before we were set to leave. Quinn met me in the morning at Starbucks to finally give me my airline ticket. We were departing at 7:20am on July 1st from Pittsburgh International Airport and flying first class into Torino with only two brief layovers in Philadelphia and Rome. If I needed anything else to confirm my suspicions about what we were after, this was it.

I headed over to my training session. Abby had found a nice secluded place near Lobb's Park, since we couldn't use the wrestling room for the summer. It was a nice clearing in the middle of the woods where no one would see us. After I showed her the ticket, Abby made the preparations for the rest of them to take the following flight out. I would be completely alone with Quinn in Torino with no support for exactly five hours. It didn't sit well with me, because anything could happen in those five hours, but I supposed it was better than nothing.

Tiffany wasn't too pleased, especially after Abby told her she wouldn't be joining us on this mission. She wasn't officially an Agent, and Abby wasn't going to take responsibility for her.

"If you want to pay for your own ticket, however, we'll be glad to have you shack up with us," Abby told the girl. "Besides, what would Ryan think?"

I'm kind of surprised Tiffany didn't slap her, especially after the jibe about her new boyfriend.

"Line up," Abby ordered. We obeyed. "Today, you are going to do something a little different. But it is something that's going to hone all of your abilities. Quintus is a very dangerous individual, as I'm sure you know. He can take control of your mind in an instant. While you all will be wearing thought inhibitors to prevent this, you still need to learn how to fight back."

She paced the ground in front of us like a drill instructor, making me feel like we were in the military. "Christine, you will be Quintus today. You are going to repel the others in any way possible. Ethan, Peter and Savanah, you three will try and grab hold of Christine. Once someone has a firm grip on her, the round will end."

"How does this help me keep Quinn out of my head?" I asked.

"You already can repel Quintus' influencing thoughts. You are going to work on taking control of the others, because when the crap hits the fan—and believe me, it will—you are going to be the first target. And if you think Quintus isn't going to have allies, you are dead wrong. You are going to have to take control of those attacking you and turn them on the man. That's what you're going to practice today."

"Everyone okay with this?" I asked my friends. I made a promise to them I wouldn't even control their thoughts again, after almost losing them all for just that reason.

They all nodded.

"Yeah, Chris. We trust you," Peter said. That hurt. Of all my friends, he had the least reason to have faith in me.

"How touching." Abby motioned for me to take a place at the edge of the clearing and then for the others to take the opposite side. "When I say go, you may begin. Remember, the round stops once someone has a firm grip on Christine."

She waited for us to get into position and then yelled, "Go!"

I didn't even have a chance to latch onto any of their minds before I was whisked off my feet and Ethan had me in a bear hug.

"Stop!" Abby shouted. "Christine, you need to be faster. I assure you, Quintus will have control of them long before anything serious happens."

I nodded, knowing exactly what she meant. While Ethan and the others got back into position, I readied myself for the second round. This time I latched onto their minds before the battle began, ensuring Ethan couldn't pull the same trick again.

This time, when the command to start came, I made Ethan think he was running in the wrong direction. The boy completely turned around and ran off into the woods the wrong way. Savanah and Peter then advanced cautiously. I reached out to them and grabbed their thoughts. Savanah was going to try and distract me while Pete came around to flank me.

Seeing an opportunity, I allowed Savanah to think they were continuing and made Peter back off to the side. I backed up, looking frightened as Savanah approached, but as she was going to lunge and attack me, I had Peter send a bolt of lightning, shocking her. She fell to the ground momentarily before picking herself up and coming at me again.

Before she took another step, a set of arms once again wrapped around my middle and lifted me off the ground.

"Stop!" Abby shouted.

As soon as I my feet touched the ground I spun on my attacker. Ethan had come up from behind and grabbed me again. He was too quick for me to react.

"Christine, you need to attack multiple targets at once," Abby criticized. "You need to work harder." She stopped Ethan as he was walking back to his starting position. "It was too easy for her to get into your head. You need to learn to block her out."

Ethan's agitation could be felt across the clearing, but when he responded, he was nothing but polite. "How can I do that?"

"Focus on your objective. Think of nothing but getting the job done. Even when thoughts keeping you from your objective push into your head, push back. The key is focus." She looked him right in the eye and repeated the word. "Focus."

"Got it," Ethan said, though he definitely didn't feel all that confident.

We tried again, and without much effort, I was able to get into Ethan's head and deter him from coming for me. This time, I made him think Savanah was me. The girl fought him and quickly broke free of his grip, but Ethan was so quick he had her in another hold almost immediately.

Unfortunately, with my concentration set on the two of them, I didn't notice Peter sneaking up on my right. By the time I saw him, it was too late. He shocked me with a lightning bolt, sending me tumbling to the ground.

When the tingling sensation of the electrical current coursing through my body stopped, I dusted myself off and rose. But the round was over, so I gave no more fight as Peter came and grabbed my wrist.

"Stop!" She came running over to me this time instead of shouting her ridicule out in front of everyone. "Multiple targets! You have to be aware of multiple targets at once. Do you think Quintus isn't going to use every person around against you?"

"No."

"Then make sure you keep your mind locked on all of your opponents at once!"

I looked away from her, but nodded anyway.

She stepped even closer to me and lowered her voice. "Christine, if there is a confrontation, Quintus is going to use your friends against you. You can't be afraid to hurt them. If they aren't disabled, they will hurt you."

"I won't hurt my friends."

Sighing as she stomped off to berate Ethan again, Abby gave us a rare glimpse into her frustration. What did she expect? We'd run through the exercise three times. Did she want perfection already?

We ran through the scenario another five times. Each time I lasted a little longer, but someone always managed to grab hold of me. Abby yelled each time we finished a round. Her screams were mostly directed at me, since I was apparently the most important piece in this puzzle.

I'll admit, there were a couple of times I could have stopped Ethan or Peter from "capturing" me, but it would have meant throwing them into a tree or hitting them with a rock. I wasn't willing to risk injuring them.

No matter what my friends did, they couldn't totally block me out. If they couldn't keep me out, there wasn't a chance they'd be able to keep out Quinn. I hoped the thought inhibitors Abby would give them would help.

While we were walking down the path back to the cars, Abby walked beside me, once again speaking in a voice only I'd be able to hear.

"You have to fight harder. Quintus will use them against you. I know they're your friends, but under his control, they won't hesitate to kill you. The only way to defend yourself is to disable them, and that might mean using potentially lethal force."

"You can't ask me to kill my friends."

"I'm not asking. I'm ordering. If it comes to it, finishing Quintus is more important than any of them—any of us."

"You can order me all you want." I stopped, turning on her. My eyes bored into hers to show how serious I was. "I'm not going to hurt my friends."

"Then we've already lost." Abby continued down the path without another word, disappearing around a bend.

CHAPTER 8
KINGS AND PAWNS

The evening after our less than successful training session in the woods, my grandparents showed up. Since the two of them were going to take over my babysitting responsibilities they wanted to be brought up to speed.

The truth was Grandpa Carpenter really came early to talk to me. He'd heard everything my parents knew and wanted to hear the whole story. I was the only one who could provide it to him. He took it much better than when I'd told him I was chasing one of my dreams to New York City.

"You can't do this."

Driving in the car, on the pretense of going to get some milk, I almost crashed into the car in front of us when my grandfather proclaimed this.

"Why not?"

"It's too dangerous," he said. "They are asking too much of you. You're only fifteen."

"Sixteen," I corrected.

Despite being the only person in my family who not only knew about, but shared my powers as well, my grandfather was also the most overprotective of me. The problem was, with what I told him, he knew how much was at stake. He also knew I wasn't being given a choice.

When I'd told him two months ago I'd joined with the M.H.D.A., he'd told me he thought I'd made a terrible mistake. Listening to this first official mission they were putting me on, only helped to confirm that fear. And yes, as hard as he tried to hide it from me, I could feel how afraid he was.

"It'll be fine," I assured him. "Ethan and the others will be there backing me up. They're not going to let anything happen to me."

He patiently explained how Quintus was a dangerous man.

I rolled my eyes. *Like I didn't know that.*

"Grandpa, what did you do in Italy during the war?" This was the first question I'd asked that sounded more like a normal teenager talking to her grandfather.

The problem was, while he was willing to talk to me about our shared powers, and was perfectly open about his training, he didn't like talking about the war. "Why do you want to know about that?"

He'd told me very little about his involvement in World War II, and the information I had gotten out of him, I had to squeeze out of him myself. This was no exception. "I'm wondering. You told me you were in Italy for a little while. I want to know what you did."

"I was only in Italy for about a month, hun," he said. "What I did wasn't very exciting."

Yeah, the "wasn't very exciting" line was what he used on me a lot. I wasn't giving up so easily, though. "C'mon, tell me. I'm a big girl now, I can handle it."

He didn't respond, but gazed through the windshield as I pulled the car into the supermarket parking lot.

Once I parked the car, I pressed for answers again. "Does it have anything to do with Quinn?"

He shook his head. His eyes were far off, staring nearly seventy years into the past. "No, it didn't. We were hunting one of his brothers, Secondus."

"Really?"

"He was protecting Benito Mussolini. It wasn't long after the Allies had invaded Normandy, and we'd been asked to handle the growing problem in Italy. Mussolini had already been taken out of power, but Hitler was protecting him in a hotel high in the Abruzzi Mountains called Campo Imperatore. We were asked to take out Secondus and capture Mussolini."

"So, what happened?" I asked. I had to wheedle as much information I could out of him. "What could Secondus do?"

He considered the question for a second, turning toward me finally. "He could literally shake the Earth. He nearly caused an avalanche that buried us all when we went in. We were able to stop him before he did too much damage. We managed to kill him, but unfortunately, Mussolini escaped. Russian forces caught up with him about a year later, and he was executed.

"Christine, understand, Secondus wasn't half as dangerous as Quintus. You don't have the ability to take him on. We were trained soldiers and we were barely able to survive against Quintus when we faced him. I don't want to lose you."

"You're not," I told him. "I'm more capable than you think."

That ended the conversation, both of us too tired of trying to convince the other to see their point of view. We both knew I was going no matter what, so it made any further argument on the subject useless.

We went into the store and bought the milk we didn't need and then drove home. I wanted to hear more about his battle with Secondus. Maybe I would be able to use some of the information when I eventually had to battle Quinn. But I didn't want to push my luck getting any more out of him. The fact he'd divulged anything was a victory in itself.

We ended up picking up some Chinese food for dinner. Then we made our way back only speaking about the end of the school year and how I'd been able to pick up my grades.

I pulled up into the driveway, and we got out of the car.

"Christine, hun," Grandpa started, then wiped a hand across his forehead. "You know I'm only trying to protect you, right?

"Yeah." The response came out more like a question, mostly because I knew the question was only a setup for what else my grandfather was going to say. Nervousness shook my very core as I waited for him to continue.

A shadow covered his face for a moment, giving him an evil look. Then, like that, it was gone, and the loving face of my grandfather returned. "You know how to play chess?"

The question took me off guard. I froze while my brain tried to formulate a response to the simple question. I must have looked pretty foolish standing in my driveway, staring blankly at my grandfather.

Finally my mind understood and I responded. "Yes. I mean, a little I guess."

He responded warmly, throwing an arm around me and starting toward the house. "Why don't we dig up your dad's old set and play a game?"

"Okay," I said, a little confused at the sudden change of tone and topic this conversation had suddenly taken. "I'll go get it."

****

It took me nearly a half hour to find the chess set, hidden among the rubble of junk in our basement. The sheen of dust covering the box told of the years it had spent laying forgotten on the shelf.

Blowing the dust off the cover, I climbed the stairs back into the kitchen where I found my grandfather waiting patiently for me. He smiled and motioned to the seat opposite him at the kitchen table.

He took the box from me and opened it. The smell of old cardboard hit my nostrils as the long pent up air inside escaped. "Where did you learn to play?" he asked.

"Ummm, dad, I guess. He showed me how to play when I was like eight. I haven't played in years though."

He nodded, but didn't say anything more as he set the pieces on their individual squares. As he was doing that, my grandmother walked in, cradling Conner in her arms.

"You two decided to play a game," she remarked. "How nice."

"Yeah," I agreed. It was nice, or at least it would have been if I had any idea why Grandpa Carpenter had suddenly decided to play. But, I've learned in the last year or so everything he does is for a reason, so I generally try to go with the flow when it comes to his sudden whims.

My grandmother grabbed a bottle from the fridge and gently placed it in the microwave as if it were made of porcelain. It was like she was afraid to spill a drop of the formula and upset my baby brother. "Maybe we can play some rummy later, Christine."

That would have been great, if I had a clue what rummy was. I'm sure my grandmother would show me, and besides, I could always leech the rules from her head. Ethan was supposed to come over to hang out—God, it felt like we hadn't done that in so long—and he wouldn't mind learning a new game, especially if he could beat me at it.

"Sounds good," I said.

The microwave beeped and she pulled the bottle back out. She squirted a few drops on her arm to check the temperature— something I never did—and put the rubber nipple in Conner's mouth. "Well, I'll leave you two alone then. This little fella and I've got a date of our own, don't we? Don't we?"

When my grandmother started doing what I lovingly referred to as her cartoon character voice, I promptly went into ignore mode. It was sad how childish a grown adult could be to entertain an infant.

"Chess is more of an art than a game," my grandfather said, recapturing my attention after my grandmother left. "You need to be creative with your strategy, or your opponent will read you and claim victory."

"Creative," I said, "got it."

The board was completely set up. The white pieces were sitting in front of me, waiting for the "war" with my grandfather to begin. He simply waved a hand over the board and said, "Your move."

I reached out to grab one of the pieces, but as my hand grazed one of the pawns, Grandpa Carpenter stopped me.

"No hands."

I cocked my head to the side, scrutinizing him. He had never been an advocate for using my powers needlessly. *So, why is he now?*

Again, knowing there must have been some purpose to all of this, I went with it. I grabbed hold of the same pawn I was going to move before, this time with my mind, and slid it forward two spaces.

My grandfather did the same, mentally taking one of his pawns and sliding it forward two spaces so it was diagonal to mine. I cocked an eyebrow at him, it was like he was inviting me to take the piece. He must have realized what a bad move he'd just made.

I picked up my pawn and moved it into the space his pawn was occupying, then I removed the black piece from the board and put it on my side of the board.

"Chess is not for the timid," he said. The statement was almost an under the breath remark, but it was loud enough so he was sure I would hear it. "You have to be willing to sacrifice for victory."

He moved his knight, and I moved a pawn ahead one space. He moved a pawn, and I moved my rook. He moved his knight again, placing it directly in front of my rook. I moved the rook forward and took the knight.

The game went on with my grandfather moving his pieces in a haphazard way, allowing me to take piece after piece. *Is he letting me win?*

As the thought escaped my head, he glanced at me and grinned. But he didn't comment this time. He moved another of his pawns to a black square where it was sure to be taken by one of my knights on my next move.

What's the point of playing if you're going to let me take you down?

Again, no comment.

I shrugged, but moved my knight to take his pawn and on my next move, the same knight took one of his bishops.

"Logic and knowledge," was all my grandfather said as he slid his queen diagonal across the board until it took one of my rooks.

I looked at the board then, I still had many of my pieces, and had any number of moves I could perform. His king was ready to be taken and I was sure I would have it in three moves. I moved my bishop to the right side of the board, so on the next turn it would be able to take the king.

"Check." My voice sounded so proud as the word came through my lips.

My grandfather studied the board and nodded, smirking at the game as if he finally noticed the trouble he was in. He moved the king forward one space, as I hoped he would. I moved my knight so his king would be taken if he moved one space to the right. He couldn't move his king forward, because if he did, one of my remaining pawns would take it. He couldn't move it back, because my bishop would take it. My queen was in position to take the king if he moved to the left. Which pretty much only left him the option of moving diagonal to the right. Once he did that, I would move my last rook into position and it would be checkmate, because he'd have nowhere else to go.

But he didn't move his king at all. Instead, he moved his queen again, so it was two spaces in front of my king. "Checkmate," he said with grim satisfaction.

"What?" I practically jumped from my seat, to hover over the board. There was no way he could have beaten me. He only had five pieces left. He had to be looking at it wrong.

But he wasn't. It didn't matter what I did on my next move, if I left my piece there, his queen would kill the king, if I moved it to the left diagonal, his knight would take it, to the right, his rook was waiting. No matter what move I made, I lost the game. So, I gave a push to the top of my king, toppling him over. I couldn't believe it.

Crossing my arms, I huffed and looked away from the board. I shouldn't have lost that game.

"Look at all the pieces you have," my grandfather said.

I sighed and turned my head back toward the game. I had almost all of his pieces, while he only had four of mine. My mind still insisted there was no way I should have lost.

"I moved you into position with every move I made— sacrificing my own pieces to give you a false sense of security. You thought you had me, you were ready to call out checkmate and claim victory. But at the last moment, I struck and delivered the deathblow. A blow, I might add, you never saw coming. Am I right?"

Heaving another sigh, I had no choice but to agree with him. "Yeah, I guess."

"This is the way Quinn plays. I've done this with him. He is the coldest, most logical thinker I have ever come across." Again, his eyes glazed over as some memory from his past danced through his vision. "Heck, we thought we'd beaten him before. I thought we had for seventy years. But now, he's back."

I sat, not speaking and not moving, taking the words in.

"You can't trust where you stand with him. He is constantly evaluating the situation and moving you into the position he wants you in. It may look like you're winning, but you never are. You are playing his game, by his rules. Do you understand?"

"Yes."

"That's why I don't want you to go. Now, I know I can't stop you." He said, seeing the protest rising into my conscious thoughts. "And I'm not going to try. But I can show you some techniques that will let you survive this trip."

"Okay," I was ready to listen to whatever mental technique he had for me. All the things he said, had been what was nagging me at the innermost portions of my being for weeks. I knew all these things, which was why I didn't want to go on this cursed trip. Whatever he wanted to show me, I was sure it would be something Quinn didn't know about, or at least it would be something he wouldn't expect when I unleashed it upon him. "What do I do?"

"First," said Grandpa Carpenter, chuckling at my eagerness, "reset the chess board. I'm going to get us a couple of sodas."

CHAPTER 9
OLD ENEMIES

Garry Kasparov once said, "Chess is mental torture." At least, Grandpa Carpenter told me he said that. I don't think he ever played four games straight, only using mental abilities to not only try and read his opponent, but to simply move the pieces as well. Once we were done, and me not winning a single game, my brain was pretty much wiped out.

My grandfather attempted to teach me how to think creatively. I'm not sure how successful he was, but in order to try and beat him, I had come up with some new tactics, thinking "outside the box" as he said.

Needless to say, by the time we were done, and Ethan had come over, my brain could barely function. It felt like I'd done and learned more in the last twenty-four hours than I had all year in school.

We played rummy with my grandmother and my dad for about an hour. I picked up the game quickly, but still didn't win. My mind was so muddled, I couldn't concentrate enough on the cards in my hand.

Finally, I was able to retire from the game, and Ethan and I sat in front of the TV, and I fell asleep in his arms.

I woke the next morning, still laying on the couch, but with a pillow under my head and a blanket covering my body. The smell of coffee filled my nose and there was a loud banging on the front door. I looked at the clock on our cable-box—10:30.

Jeez, did I really need to sleep, I thought as the pounding continued.

"I'll get it," my grandfather called from the kitchen. I felt him begin to come into the living room, and something in my gut told me that would be a horrible idea.

I sprang from the couch and bolted to the door. "I've got it, grandpa!" I shouted as I reached the door. He seemed to accept this and stayed put in the kitchen.

I checked over my shoulder, to make doubly sure he wasn't coming in, then creaked the door open. Standing on my porch, like he'd been nearly two weeks ago, was Quinn, dressed in the most expensive suit I think I'd ever seen him in.

"Good morning, Ms. Carpenter," he said. "May I come in?"

Looking over my shoulder once again, feeling the mental tendrils of my grandfather reaching out toward me, I said, "I think that would be a poor idea." Then I forced my thoughts to remain calm so Grandpa Carpenter wouldn't think anything was amiss out here and want to come to investigate.

Instead of inviting him in, I stepped outside, shutting the door behind me. I kept a mental lock on my grandfather, just in case he wandered toward the front door.

"My grandfather's inside," I barely whispered. "Are you crazy coming over here like that? Do you want to start World War III in my front yard?"

Quinn stood on his tiptoes, looking over my shoulder as if he could see through the walls into my house. His expression did nothing to hide the excitement and intrigue he clearly felt. "So, good-old Frank is inside, huh? I'd really like to see him. You know, to catch up. For old time's sake."

If I didn't know he was joking, I might have had a heart attack right then and there. Who knew what would happen if Quinn actually set foot inside my house and said hello to my grandfather. Stroke or aneurism came to mind. And even if those worst-case-scenarios didn't happen, I knew the encounter wouldn't end well.

"You have to go," I said, pushing Quinn lightly to get him off the porch. I kept looking over my shoulder, fearing my grandfather would open the door at any moment and stare into the eyes of his long lost enemy.

Then, looking down the street, I saw the black SUV. The Agents assigned to watch my house were getting antsy, they saw the target in plain sight and wanted nothing more than to take him down now. Obviously, they were under orders not to unless trouble erupted, but I did notice the driver's side window roll down briefly so the Agent could peek out and see what was happening.

"We aren't in any danger, Christine," he said, crossing his arms and planting himself on the topmost step. "Relax."

I eyed the car, this time so Quinn would be sure to see where I was looking. "They've been watching me all week. You've really got them worried." Hopefully if he thought the Agents were staking me out he would trust me a little more and reveal a little bit about his plan. I was, after all, still under orders to get as much information out of him as I could.

No such luck.

"I'm sure I do," he said, not even bothering to glance at the SUV. He casually leaned against the post and looked me up and down. "What else can you tell me about what the M.H.D.A. is doing?"

"Is that all you're here for, information?"

"What else?" he said. "If you really want me to trust you, you'll tell me what they've been preparing you for."

"To take you down," I said. "They've been about as giving with their information as you've been. They don't trust me either." It wasn't entirely true. Hell, it was an outright lie. I hoped, however, I said it with enough conviction it at least sounded like the truth.

Then I thought about some of the things my grandfather told me during the chess game: giving your enemy a false sense of security and letting them think they're beating you. Why not actually tell him the truth, or at least, part of it. Maybe if I did give him something, it would pave the road to trust I needed.

"I think they're onto you too. They know you're trying to steal the shroud."

If this was news to him, he didn't show it. As always, I couldn't get a read on him at all. "What do you think?" he asked.

"I think it's true. The shroud is supposed to be in Torino and that's where we're going. You already have the Holy Grail and the shroud must have some kind of power too. Am I right?"

"Yes, the shroud has power, much like the spear you're hiding in your bedroom. Surely you've discovered what it can do."

"It's supposed to make the holder unbeatable in battle, but even when I did have it, I almost got myself killed." I was referring to my brief assault at Camp Hero on the giant dragon Eddie Eagan had dreamt up. If it hadn't been for some quick thinking, I'd have literally been scorched beyond recognition.

"And the Grail?"

"Everlasting life," I said almost immediately. Why did I feel like he was quizzing me all of a sudden? I needed to get back on even footing and ask some questions of my own. "So, I guess that's why you haven't aged in seventy years?"

"Oh, I've aged. I've gotten older—wiser. Just because I look the same doesn't mean I'm not old in spirit."

I jumped at a sound of a car door closing. My heart beat rapidly in my chest again. I'd stopped paying attention. That could have easily been my grandfather coming to check on me, or the Agents deciding to bum-rush Quinn. I was getting distracted with all those questions. I needed to stay focused.

"Are we after the shroud?" I asked.

He didn't answer right away. When I was convinced he wasn't going to answer at all he said a simple, yet firm, "Yes."

"Why?"

"That's something you are going to have to figure out for yourself." With that, he turned and stepped down off the porch.

He was right out in the open, standing in the middle of my driveway. Why the M.H.D.A. didn't have a sniper take a shot and end this, I still don't know. It would have made everyone's life a whole lot easier.

"Why did you come?" I called after him. The whole visit seemed rather pointless.

He didn't even look over his shoulder as he continued to walk, back straight and shoulder's back, as if daring someone to challenge him. "To find out what you knew, of course," he said.

I stood on the porch until he was out of sight. He didn't have a car, and seemed content to stride down the street. My heartbeat returned to normal, so did my breathing. I needed to calm my thoughts as well before I went back into the house, otherwise my grandfather would know something was wrong. And I had no desire to explain why my brain was in such turmoil.

The Agents never moved, but no doubt they were calling the Quinn sighting in to Abby or Smith. *Could they have heard the whole conversation?* I wouldn't have put it past them to bug the porch as well as the house. But even if they had, there was always the possibility Quinn had disabled the devices when he'd come close, like he had the other day in Conner's bedroom.

Resisting the temptation to flip the Agents the bird—you know, as a thank you for helping me out with Quinn—I opened the door and went back into the house.

"Who was it?" my grandmother called from upstairs as I came back in.

"Just the paperboy, trying to collect his payment," I lied.

"You were out there for a while, is everything okay?"

"Yes, grandma," I said. "He's got a major crush on me." Being that our "paperboy" was a fifty-year-old man, the statement was really, **really** creepy, but it was the only thing I could think of on the spot. I shuddered at the thought, then walked into the kitchen.

"Morning," I said, opening the fridge to get some juice.

"Hey, sleepyhead," my grandfather said from behind the paper. "Why're you up so late?"

"I'm a teenager," I explained.

"How's Mr. Quinn?" he asked.

I dropped the orange juice container and the liquid started spilling out, creating an orange pool on the floor.

"What do you mean?" I asked. Then, trying to cover up my shock, I quickly grabbed some paper towels to clean the mess up.

"Hun, I'm an old man, not a fool. I can sense him from a mile away." He laughed, but it was a sad sort of laugh.

"Then why didn't you—?"

"What? Run outside and have some epic battle the like humanity has never seen? I'm not crazy." He got up from the table and stepped over to me, grabbing my hand and pulling me away from the spilled juice. "I'm not a soldier anymore, Christine. I can't fight him."

His eyes drooped, making him look like a sad puppy. It was like he'd lost something in himself, and he knew he would never get it back, no matter how hard he tried. He looked into my eyes, and for a second, I could feel all of his pain as if floodgates had opened.

His want to be young again and his need to feel useful hit me like a hammer. His concern for my safety and my family in dark times burst forth like cannonballs. His desire to go back and fix past wrongs, including his mistake in not defeating Quinn, plunged through me like a sharp sword. Memories upon memories attacked my senses, all of them horrible experiences he wished he had never been a part of.

A tear rolled down my cheek, and I almost broke down and cried, but my grandfather broke the connection as quickly as it'd formed. Then, embarrassed at letting me see what I had, he stumbled off.

I wanted to call after him, but I simply couldn't speak. How come he'd never shared that with me before? Why had he kept all that inside him? Grief like he felt, being penned up inside a person, had to have been torture.

The emotions of the briefly shared experience were beginning to fade. All of his memories too were erasing themselves from my mind as if I'd never seen them. I'd finally understood why my grandfather was so against me going out and playing hero. I always knew he was afraid for my life, but he was trying to protect me from so much more. So many horrors waited out there for someone like me.

I bent down, and finished cleaning the orange juice.

****

Friday, July 1ˢᵗ—the day I would first set foot outside my home country. We left before sunrise, that morning, trying to beat rush hour traffic. My dad said traffic on I-376 was usually at a standstill if you tried to leave after 6am anyway, so we were better off since my flight was leaving so early.

My parents and my grandfather came to drop me off. My grandmother stayed home with Conner. I couldn't believe it was going to be a whole month until I was going to see all of them. The longest I'd ever even been away from my parents was five days, and that was only a few months ago on my trip to New York.

Will I get homesick? I'd never had the feeling before, and I wondered if I would even know if I had the feeling or not.

I kept sending soothing, calming thoughts to myself to prevent my blood pressure from reaching critical levels. My parents, especially my mother, could tell I was nervous, but their reasoning behind my panic was totally off base. Sure, I'd never been on a long plane trip before, and sure I'd never left the country, and of course this was only my second trip anywhere without my parents, but all those reasons were trumped by the fact I would be spending the next day or so sitting only a few feet from arguably the most dangerous man in the world.

When we pulled into the temporary parking lot, I gave serious consideration to throwing open the door and flying off. However, my sense of duty (which I must have inherited from my

grandfather) won out, and I slowly got out of the car and grabbed
my suitcase.

Right, another first, I had a suitcase instead of a duffle bag.
My parents had loaned me their rolling luggage, making me swear
I wouldn't destroy it on my trip.

"I want you to have this," said my dad, slipping a few bills
into my hand so my mother wouldn't see.

I looked at it for a moment then tried to hand it back to him,
but he wouldn't take it. I didn't need or want the money. I would
have tried to explain, but he had already changed the subject.

"You are to call once a day, no matter what. I think you are
seven hours ahead of us, so even if it's early in the morning there
you can call."

"Uh huh." I nodded.

My mother came around the car then, followed by Grandpa
Carpenter. She looked like she was going to start weeping at any
moment. My grandfather looked worried.

Even though the memories he'd shared with me had long
since disappeared, the feeling of them remained. It wasn't a feeling
I think I'd ever be able to forget.

"Are we ready?" my mom asked.

"You know you can't come to the gate with me." I hoped I'd
be able to get them to say their goodbyes here instead of near the
busy line of the security checkpoint.

They didn't take the bait.

"I'm going to at least make sure you hook up with Mr. Quinn
before we leave you."

Not wanting to argue, I shrugged and started walking toward
the terminal. Each step I took was harder than the one before it. It
was like a giant magnet was pulling at me from behind. The closer
we got, the more I wanted to turn around and head for home.

But, as hard as I was being pulled, and as much as I prayed
some meteor would descend from the sky and obliterate the
airport at that very moment, we safely made it to the terminal.

I checked my bag, and then it was time to seek out Quinn. He
wouldn't be hard to find. All I had to do was reach out and ping
him with my mind, much like a submarine uses sonar to locate
enemy battleships.

He was waiting at the security checkpoint. So, pretending like
I was looking for him, I guided my family over to that location.

The terminal was crowded, but not so much I thought I would lose my cool. There were so many people though, with so many chaotic thoughts, I couldn't even block them all out.

The checkpoint wasn't too far, and soon enough we were all able to see Quinn standing with Jayson, both waiting for our arrival.

I looked over at my grandfather, who appeared as calm as could be. This was the part I was dreading. The encounter I'd tried so hard to prevent the other morning was about to happen. Two fierce enemies of the distant past were about to come face to face again and...

"Hello, Mr. Quinn," my father said, reaching out to shake the fake science teacher's hand.

I tried not to draw attention to myself as I positioned my body in between my grandfather and Quinn. It wasn't like I'd be able to stop them if they decided to go at it, but I hoped at least if they saw me there they'd think twice about throwing a punch.

My movement hadn't gone unnoticed, Quinn's eyes shot toward me, even as he continued smiling at my father. "A pleasure as always, Mr. Carpenter. How was the trip over this morning?"

My father bragged about how he'd made good time, and he and Quinn continued their small talk. In the meantime, making sure I kept myself in between the two old soldiers, I stared at Jayson. I still didn't know what to make of the boy. At the beginning of the school year he was Tommy Fulton's punching bag. I'd even rescued the little twerp a few times from the bully. Then, all of a sudden, he appeared in Quinn's office, pretending to be Quinn. Other than that, I knew next to nothing about the boy.

The first thing I needed to discover about him was if could I trust him when things went south with Quinn. It would be nice to have another ally on my side, but I wasn't counting on it. For some reason, I was sure Quinn had his claws firmly rooted in the boy's consciousness.

Jayson nodded at me and said, "What's up?"

I could only shake my head and then turn back to the conversation between my dad and Quinn—a conversation that had taken a turn for the worst.

"This is my father, by the way—Christine's grandfather." My father motioned to Grandpa Carpenter.

Quinn looked up at him, as if he'd just noticed the man was there. He wasn't at all surprised though, as no waves of shock rolled from his body. Again, as he stuck out his hand to shake my grandfather's I feared someone was going to die right then and there. But Quinn merely smiled as my grandfather accepted the handshake. "A pleasure to meet you."

They both wore smiles, like absolutely nothing was wrong, not unlike how Quinn and Abby had been able to sit next to each other in my living room a few weeks ago. Under the surface though, I could feel the rage boiling in both of them.

If you hurt my granddaughter, came my grandfather's voice in my head, *I will find you, and I will kill you.*

Empty threats are unbecoming of a soldier, Frank, Quinn projected back.

Just try me, Grandpa insisted.

Quinn broke the handshake and said, "All right, I think it's time we get going." He peered down at me and Jayson, acting like a teacher talking to a couple of his students. "Are you two as excited about this trip as I am?"

"Yeah!" Jayson said enthusiastically.

"Uh huh." I rolled my eyes. He was overdoing it a little.

He handed a paper to my mother. She nearly snatched it out of his hand and looked at it. Her nerves of letting me go off with him were getting to her.

"This is our itinerary," he explained. "If you need to get in contact with us at any time, these are the places we'll be."

"Can I get one of those?" I asked. I would very much like to have seen what it said on there. Maybe I'd even be able to pass some of that information along to Abby and my friends.

"Why don't we let it be a surprise for now?" Quinn said. He slung a backpack over his shoulder and then guided Jayson into the security line.

"Goodbye, hun," my father said, giving me a hug.

My mother kissed me on the cheek and simply told me, "Have fun. I'll miss you."

Then came my grandfather. He scooped me into a big bear hug, and as my feet were lifted off the ground he whispered in my ear. "You be careful."

"Listen, when I come back, after this is all done, I promise, no more hero stuff." It was the only real promise I could make.

After all, "careful" was probably the one thing I couldn't be on this excursion.

If possible, my grandfather hugged me even tighter. "I love you."

"I love you too."

He let me go. My feet hit the ground and I turned to walk away. Before I got into line behind Quinn and Jayson, a thought came to me.

Walking back over, I whispered into my grandfather's ear. "The spear is under my bed in a duffel bag. Keep it safe."

He knew exactly what I meant. He gave me an almost imperceptible nod, but he pushed a wave of reassurance toward me.

This time I got into line, looking back only once as my family departed. Then I was all alone with at least one—probably two—potential enemies. I kept my guard up as we were ushered through security, keeping myself open to find any weaknesses in my opponents.

CHAPTER 10
MEETING THE KAISER

After transferring in Philadelphia and spending only an hour on the second plane, I was already ready to get off. It didn't matter I was sitting in the cushy, comfortable seats of first class, I would rather have flown myself beside the plane the few thousand miles.

It didn't help that I was seated by a boy who couldn't seem to sit still and kept kicking me every time I'd come close to nodding off. I was pretty sure he was doing it on purpose, because whenever I looked at him afterward, he would pretend like he didn't know what was happening. The boy was lucky smashing him through the window would decompress the plane and suck the entire first class cabin out with him.

He was only a year or two older than me, and had blonde hair cut short and gelled up so it stuck in place. He had only some blonde stubble coming in on his chin and around his mouth that I doubted I would have even noticed if I hadn't been sitting a foot away from him. What stood out the most on him though were his clothes. Black leather jacket, with a black t-shirt underneath, black jeans and large black combat boots—in other words, dressed in my ideal style.

I'd already given him a few mental jabs to make him leave me alone, but it seemed my manipulations of his brain weren't taking hold. After the fourth time of trying to take a nap only to be suddenly shocked to wakefulness, I decided to give up and play on my phone.

I pulled up a game I'd only downloaded yesterday. Since I couldn't play against my grandfather, I figured I would try my luck against the computer. I knew it wasn't the same as playing against a human opponent, but maybe there was still something I could learn by playing.

I started off with the computer set to amateur, but I beat it too easily. Deciding I might as well go for the hardest setting, being it was the closest I would get to playing an actual person, I made the computer a grand master.

I lost the first game in only ten turns. The second game lasted a little longer, ending in fifteen.

"What are you playing?" a voice came from beside me.

I almost bumped heads with the annoying blonde boy. He'd been leaning over my shoulder watching me play. For just a second, I stared into his eyes, looking into the pools of deep blue. I had to look away, embarrassed by the proximity we'd been in. I'd never looked closely into a boy's eyes other than Ethan's.

"So, you do more than kick."

"Yah. Ist dat a problem?"

His accent was a little difficult to understand, but I could tell it was German. At least, he sounded like all the German villains in those bad action movies Ethan made me watch.

"No, I guess not," I said. I started a new game and moved my left-most pawn forward two spaces. "Do you have a name? Or should I call you Kicking-Guy?"

"My name ist Klaus," he answered. "Klaus Kaiser. Und you?"

I was only half paying attention to the boy. I was still angry with him for bothering me. Plus, with my new strategy, I was sure I'd be able to beat the computer this time. "Christine Carpenter," I said.

"Vhat are you playing, Christina?"

"Christine," I corrected. I moved a pawn and took one of the computer's pawns. "And I'm playing chess."

"You vill lose," was all he said.

A shiver of rage shook my spine, and again I gave serious consideration to ejecting the boy from the plane. Not only was the boy annoying, but was rude as well. I was about to tell him off, but the screen suddenly read, "Checkmate".

I'd lost.

I shut the phone and shoved it back into my pocket. I'd done it so hard it actually hurt my leg.

Glaring daggers at the boy, I snarled. "Any other helpful advice?"

"Yah. Relax."

"Thanks." Why was this boy so annoying? And why did I have to sit next to him for—I checked my watch—another seven hours? Oh God, I might actually kill him!

I pictured slamming his head into the wall until he passed out. While it did make me feel better, it wasn't nearly as satisfying as it would have been if I'd actually done it. Instead, I turned away, intent on ignoring the boy the rest of the trip.

"Vhy you have—how do you say—stick up the butt?" Then, he kicked me again.

My hand came around so fast he didn't even have time to react before a red handprint darkened his pale cheek. The slap was hardly satisfying. He didn't even look phased by my strike. As a matter of fact, he actually seemed to enjoy it. He smiled as he ran his thumb over the mark, then nodded his head.

"I alvays heard American vomen had nasty tempers." He winked at me, making my stomach tie into a knot. "I guess it's true."

"And are all German guys such dip-wads?" I asked, staring long and hard into his eyes.

"Nein." He shook his head and smiled. "Not all."

I can't take this anymore. Pushing into his mind, I'd meant to plant the suggestion he was really tired and needed to take a nap. At least that way I would get some peace from this mental moron. But something hit me in the forehead, right between the eyes, breaking my concentration.

"What the—!"

Klaus opened his mouth and caught the peanut he'd ricocheted off me. He chewed it happily, making a satisfied groan deep in his throat. "Vould you like a peanut?" He held out the small bag the attendant had given him after takeoff. I seriously considered grabbing the bag and cramming it down his gullet.

Why was this creep bothering me anyway? Didn't he have anything better to do? It seemed that no matter what I tried—no matter what I did—he was intent on making this plane trip miserable.

Someone came up the aisle and stopped right beside my chair. I breathed a long sigh of relief. At least for a moment, I wouldn't have to deal with the aggravating boy.

Looking up, I gazed at Quinn standing above me. It had been the first time I was happy to see him in months. Maybe he could rescue me from the pain that was Klaus.

"How are you doing?" he asked.

"Terrible." The pleading look in my eyes didn't seem to give the man the hint. So, I synced my brainwaves to his and added, *Please switch seats with me.* I nodded my head in the boy's direction.

"Actually, it's why I came over."

The words sent a rush of gratitude flowing through my body—another positive emotion toward my sworn enemy. I would have stopped the thankfulness where it started, but Quinn was saving me from this idiot.

"Don't get too excited," Quinn added, obviously having felt my intense emotion. "What I meant was, I came over because I could feel you. If you're not careful, you're going to have everyone on the plane trying to murder one another."

"So, switch with me. You can deal with this social defective."

He shook his head and pursed his lips. "Can't do that."

"Why not?"

"Because the two of you are going to have to learn to get along. You're going to be partners on this mission, after all."

I was definitely going to be sick. How could he expect me to work with someone who was so—insert many derogatory words here.

Turning back toward Klaus, my body filled with red hot rage. He was sitting there, popping peanuts into his mouth and grinning like the village idiot.

"You can't be serious," I said. Then turned back to face Quinn again, only to find he'd already returned to his seat.

I hesitated, knowing when I turned around, I was going to find the boy still staring at me. I needed to calm myself down before I knocked out every single one of his teeth. I took several deep breaths, cleansing the rage from my body. I didn't want to hurt the boy, really, I simply wanted him to stop annoying me. Eventually, I had no choice. I turned to face him.

"You sure you don't vant a peanut?"

Ignoring the question, I instead went for the more tactful track. "How do you know Quinn?"

He leaned back in his seat, but didn't take his eyes off me. He felt around the inside of his bag of peanuts, searching for one he missed. Then, finding none, he crumpled the bag up and tossed it aside. "He came to me a few months ago. He vanted me to show him my—how you say—abilities—yah abilities. So, I show him, und he ask if I vant to help him get zomething. He promised to pay me lots of money."

"Vat... I mean, what can you do?"

The words were barely out of my mouth before he answered, "Vatch."

He pulled another bag of peanuts out of his pocket and then pulled a peanut out of the bag. He held the single nut between his forefinger and thumb. With a lopsided grin, he curled his index finger under the nut and then nodded his head to indicate a direction.

I followed the motion, and looked across the first class cabin at an older man in a business suit laying back, sleeping with his mouth opened.

The next thing I knew, I heard the peanut whiz past my ear as it flew clear across the aisle, speeding right into the man's mouth. The man convulsed as he woke up. The impact at the back of his throat must have stung, because he reached a hand up to massage his neck. He scraped his tongue on the front of his teeth as if trying to get a bad taste out of his mouth. Then he fell back to sleep.

I had to admit, I was a little less than impressed. "What kind of power is that?" I asked. "There are plenty of people that can do that. I mean, they teach people how to hit targets like that in the military."

"But your American marines cannot shoot vings off fly at fifty yards avay."

The pride he felt was painfully apparent. He didn't think I could possibly come up with a comeback for his boast. He simply stared at me, making me want to hit him even more. Luckily, I didn't do either—no comeback, no punch. Maybe if he thought he'd won, he'd leave me alone.

Wrong again.

"So, vhat do you do?"

"I read minds." I said it so uncaringly, as if my powers weren't a big deal at all. I didn't want this idiot to think I was challenging him in any way—it would only make the flight that much longer if he thought he had to one up me the whole time.

Instead of taking it as a challenge, he saw it as a game. "That's very interesting. You know vhat I am thinking right now?"

I didn't even need to push to get into his mind. "You're thinking you want more peanuts."

He nodded. "Do you have any?"

I gave him my bag. I wasn't going to eat them anyway. Peanuts weren't my favorite.

"Tell me about more about your abilities." He poured the whole bag of peanuts into his mouth like he was drinking them. Then he chewed them, making loud crunching noises I was sure Quinn could hear from his seat. "Dhey zound very interesting."

"There's nothing to tell," I tried explaining, but I was speaking to deaf, or just plain stupid, ears. "I read minds and I can make people hear my thoughts." I didn't think I needed to reveal my other abilities. Especially if I had to use them against this boy later, it would be best if they be a surprise.

"So modest," he said. "Be proud of your abilities, like I am."

"I am proud of them. When they aren't making my life a living hell, that is." Then not wanting him to delve any further, I decided to change the subject. "Why don't you tell me how much Quinn promised to pay you?"

"Enough to take care of my parents back home. Dhey do not have much money. Live day by day. I vant dhem to be proud of me too. I vant dhem to live very comfortably for rest of lives."

Maybe I was wrong about him. Even if he was in it for the money, it sounded like his intentions were noble. There was the possibility he and I could get to be friends, as long as he didn't make me kill him.

I saw an opportunity in what he said to plant a doubt in his head. Annoying as he was, when the time came that I needed to face Quinn, having him—no matter how lame his ability was—on my side, would be helpful. "How do you know you can trust him?"

"He is good man," Klaus responded. "I know."

So much for that, I thought. Maybe another opportunity would arise. But for now—

"Listen. I'd really like to get some sleep. So, if you could leave me alone for a little bit—"

"Of course. Of course." He motioned for me to lay back down. Then he turned his head to look out the window.

Maybe all I had to do in the first place was ask nicely. Maybe the boy wasn't so bad after all.

I lay back and closed my eyes, willing my brain to relax and my muscles to untighten themselves. It took a few minutes, but eventually I felt myself drifting off to sleep. My breathing became deep and even, and I knew I was ready to saunter into dreamland.

Hopefully, if all went well, I'd be able to sleep until we were ready to land.

As I was about to fade into unconsciousness, he kicked my leg again.

CHAPTER 11
THE SAFE HOUSE

Ah. Italy.

Of course, I wasn't as excited to be there than to be off the plane. Don't get me wrong, the emotions filling me of actually setting foot in this foreign territory was covering my arms in goosebumps. But the fact I was no longer sitting next to Klaus trumped that about ten times.

No matter what thrilled me more, I had to admit, even the view through the airport windows was breathtaking. The snowcapped mountains far in the distance, looming over little towns and cities dotting the landscape made me wonder why I'd fought so hard against coming. Even the dangers involved were worth what I was seeing.

I pulled out my camera and snapped a photo. At least I'd have something to show my parents that resembled a normal vacation.

As I made to shove the camera into my pocket, someone crashed into me from behind, nearly sending the camera tumbling to the floor. Luckily, I grabbed it mentally an inch before it shattered into a thousand pieces and floated it back up to my hand.

As I looked at my assailant my blissful moment with the landscape faded.

"Apologies." This time I was pretty sure Klaus meant it. However, all the bruises I was sure to have on my left calf from the constant abuse on the plane, made me a little less than forgiving at that moment.

Stepping out of striking distance, I stood next to Jayson. I figured it would be safer that way. The boy was also staring out the giant glass window like I had been.

"Amazing, isn't it?" I asked.

"I'll say." Even his voice sounded transfixed on the Italian countryside before us.

I looked out again and couldn't help but be taken in by it all. I couldn't help but think: if it looked this wonderful here at a crowded airport, how great would it be to see it up close?

I couldn't dwell on it though. I hadn't gotten to say more than two words to Jayson since leaving Pittsburgh, and I needed to know where the boy stood.

"What has Quinn told you about this whole mission?"

He shook his head and shrugged his shoulders. "Not much. We're going to steal some old object."

"And you're okay with that?"

He shifted from foot to foot, and purposely averted his gaze from mine. "Not really. But if it means my mom doesn't have to work three jobs anymore, then I don't care."

Quinn had a firm grip on him, but at least he could be saved. I still wasn't sure about Klaus—not that I'd want him on my side anyway. If I could at least pry Jayson free of Quinn's clutches, I could at least consider it a small victory.

"I'm not sure I'll be able to do it." It was the absolute truth. I hadn't ever so much as stolen a piece of candy. How was I going to react when the time finally came to steal something important?

"We'll do fine," Jayson said with such conviction, he almost made me believe it. He looked up and smiled. The smile seemed confident, but there was a hint of fear in his eyes. This boy was as unsure of what we were doing here as I was.

I gave him a warm and caring grin in return—one that told him he wasn't alone.

"Our transportation has arrived," came Quinn's deep voice.

I nearly jumped out of my skin. *How long had he been standing behind us?*

Spinning on the man, I made sure my stony expression returned. I didn't need him knowing what had transpired between me and Jayson.

"Let's go. The two other members of our team are waiting at the safe house."

"Safe house?" I asked aloud without meaning to.

"Yes, a place where no one should be able to find us."

"Great," I muttered.

I'm not sure if Quinn heard me or not, but no matter what, if we were going to a place where I couldn't be tracked, that was definitely a bad thing for me.

Jayson, Klaus and I were led by Quinn through Torino Airport, following the signs to the pick up area. As we made our trek through the crowds, I was surprised at how many people were speaking English. I always knew many people around the world spoke English, but I still figured I'd hear more people speaking Italian.

My eyes went wide with surprise as we walked through the doors and gazed upon a young man in a black suit holding a sign reading "Quinn". It wasn't the man though that caused my eyes to bulge from my head. It was the limousine he was standing in front of.

I'd only rode in a limo once, when I was five and a flower girl in Uncle Murray's wedding. I felt like a princess, getting to ride in such a big and fancy car, wearing a beautiful white dress (yeah, me in white—I know). The limo sitting in front of me was twice as big and twice as nice. But I must have grown up quite a bit in the last eleven years, because this car didn't make me feel special in any way.

"Let me get those for you." The young man said as he grabbed my luggage. He opened the trunk and then put my bag in, followed by everyone else's. Quinn slipped him some money and then ushered us into the back.

The back of the limo could probably have fit a dozen people, so there was plenty of room for the four of us. I sat first, and Klaus insisted on sitting next to me. I made a noise that sounded much like a lion's growl and then moved.

"Hotel Chelsea," Quinn told our driver, and the car rolled away from the airport.

We rode away from the airport down a two lane highway. It was very wooded and I thought for a moment the driver was taking us in the wrong direction. As I was about to say something about this to Quinn though, the entire landscape opened up and before us was a city sprawling out in all directions. There weren't very many tall buildings to be seen—at least, I couldn't see any skyscrapers like we had in Pittsburgh. The city looked old, much older than anything I'd ever seen. From a distance, I could tell there were just as many—if not more—old brick buildings as there were cement ones.

"Mr. Quinn?" Jayson asked. "How are we supposed to understand what's going on if we can't tell what anyone's saying?"

"What do you mean?" I interrupted before Quinn could respond. "Everyone's been speaking English. We shouldn't have any problems."

The way Jayson looked at me then, his head crooked and his eyes half opened, made me feel like I was crazy. "What are you talking about? No one's said a word in English since we got here?"

It was my turn to gaze upon Jayson quizzically. One of us was insane, and I was sure it wasn't me.

We'd been staring at each other for what seemed like a few minutes, when we were broken apart by Quinn's slight chuckle. When I turned to look at him, I was greeted with a very amused look.

"Jayson, I wouldn't worry about understanding what anyone is saying. Christine is right. Most people understand English here, and if you speak to them in English, they will do their best to help you."

I was about the give Jayson an "I told you so" look, but Quinn continued.

"And Christine, he is absolutely correct. No one has been speaking English."

I shook my head, hoping maybe it would unscramble the words Quinn spoke into something coherent. "What? It sounded like you said no one has been speaking English."

"Yes," he responded. "I did."

"But, I've been understanding everyone."

"That's because of your ability. You can hear people's thoughts, and thoughts, are universally understood. So, when someone speaks, you are hearing what they are thinking and not their words. Do you understand?"

"Not really," I admitted. It sounded like English. I would think I knew what my own language sounded like.

Shaking his head, but still wearing that same amused visage, he said, "Your brain translates for you. No matter what people say, you hear it in English. Just as when you speak, everyone will hear you in their own native language."

"Does that mean Kaiser-Boy over here has been speaking in German this whole time."

"No," Klaus responded. "I speak very good Ameri-caan English."

"Well, your accent could use some work then." I rolled my eyes and turned away.

We rode through the city then, winding down some very narrow streets in our car. I took out my camera and took some pictures of some interesting looking buildings. Some of the old architecture was like something I'd only seen in old movies. It was almost like stepping into the past.

I wasn't the only one staring out the windows though. Jayson too was as amazed as I was. Klaus, however, didn't seem too impressed, and that was probably because he'd grown up with stuff like this his whole life—after all, he was from Europe.

Eventually, we stopped in front of a small five floor building, with a gray and green canopy over the door which read, "Hotel Chelsea."

"I suppose my mind is translating the sign too?" I asked.

The driver had come around to open the door, and before Quinn stepped out, he looked over at the sign and said, "No, it really says 'Hotel Chelsea'."

We all climbed out of the car, the driver helping each of us step out. And I stood in front of a tiny little storefront that appeared to sell picture frames and other little knick knacks. Next to the window, on the corner of the building was a small sign. I assumed it was the street sign and it read: Via XX Settembre.

20 September Street?

"You three grab our bags," Quinn said. "I'm going to check us in." With that, Quinn walked off.

I looked at my watch. It was nearly 2 o'clock local time. The others would arrive in about five hours. I needed to tell them where we were staying so they'd be able to procure a room nearby. This might be my only chance to do so, because I doubted Quinn would let us leave his sight this afternoon.

Pulling out my cell phone, I found both Ethan's and Abby's numbers and sent one simple text message: Hotel Chelsea – Via XX Settembre. I was sure they'd be able to find the place. Now, I would just have to figure a way to get away from these people.

The driver handed me my mother's rolling luggage and then got in the car and drove off. We three teenagers stood in front of the old hotel, staring at it and holding our bags like lost little kids.

Klaus was the first to move, walking across the narrow street. Jayson and I turned to each other, both wondering what we were getting into, and then did the same. The inside looked as old as the outside. The walls were painted in a faded yellow color, but looked like it had been painted recently. Though the age of the place was apparent, it had been very well maintained. An old man sat behind a small brown desk and he was busily talking to Quinn.

"You and your children will love the sites. Be sure to take them to see Porta Palatina and the statue of Julius Caesar."

"We will be taking in all the sites," Quinn assured the man as he slipped the room key from his hands. "Thank you for the advice."

"No problem. Remember, if you need anything, just call down and ask for Gianni."

"Will do." Quinn turned to us and motioned toward the stairs. "We're on the fourth floor."

"Have a good holiday," Gianni said as he eyed all three of us and then sat back behind his desk and turned to his computer.

There was no elevator, which hardly surprised me, so we had to carry our bags up the stairs. Thankfully I packed light, otherwise the steep, narrow stairway would have been hell to traverse.

There were only three or four rooms on each floor, and as we walked up the stairs, I didn't see anyone else. However, as we approached our floor, I began to get an uneasy feeling. One of those feelings I usually got when something I didn't like was going to happen.

I looked over at Quinn. If I felt it, he must have too. But, as usual, the man gave no indication he had any emotion whatsoever.

We got to out room—402. Quinn unlocked the door and we stepped inside.

When I entered the room, I instinctively threw my bag to the ground and lunged at the two people I saw in there. I had taken them by surprise and the three of us fell to the floor. I had barely gotten to throw a punch before a pair of hands yanked me away. I struggled to break free. Whoever was holding me back didn't understand how dangerous these two were.

"Get the hell out of here! We have nothing for you to steal!" I spat at them.

I continued to fight desperately to get free of the grip. During my struggles I noticed it was Quinn who'd grabbed me and who was trying to drag me from the room. "Let go!" I shouted.

"You never said this psycho was part of your team." The young man in the trenchcoat said this. His face was unshaven and left him looking scruffy. I'd met him three months ago when he and his sister robbed me on the train to New York.

"At least I'm not a lowlife thief!"

The boy looked like he was going to hit me. If he did, not even Quinn would be able to hold me back from beating the boy to a pulp.

As he stepped forward, the girl grabbed his arm and stopped him. "Johnny. No." She was the more sensible of the two.

"Gina! Control your brother!" Quinn yelled at her.

At that moment, I felt myself lifted off my feet as Quinn used both physical strength and a mental push to toss me back through the door. Now Jayson, Klaus and Quinn stood between me and the two thieves.

I tried to shove myself back through, but I was rooted to the spot. Quinn had mentally locked my feet to the floor. Fighting against his mental prowess, I did my best to move.

"Everyone calm down." Quinn said. "Johnny, Gina, sit over there." He pointed to the bed furthest from the door.

Then he looked at me, still fighting against his hold. I pushed hard against him, fought hard until, my right foot lifted from the floor and stepped forward. As if there was a magnet under the floor, my foot was pulled back down.

A wave of shock smacked me as Quinn watched me take another step with my left foot. Like the first time, my foot only moved a little bit before it was pulled back to the floor. Even if it took me an hour, I was determined to make it to Johnny and Gina and get rid of them.

"How do you know each other?" Quinn asked. I would have thought it was an act, but the look of mingled anger and confusion on his face said he seriously had no idea how we could possibly know each other.

"They robbed me. Then left us all to die at Camp Hero!" I took another step toward them. Each step I took seemed to get easier, either because Quinn's grip was weakening, or because I was fighting harder against it—I couldn't tell.

"Will you stop fighting me!" yelled Quinn. "They're here because I asked them to be here. Now stop acting like a child!"

"Fine!" I stomped on the floor with my final step, then made no more movement. "But as long as they're here, I'm not. You said you needed me. So make your choice. What's it going to be?"

Quinn's face became hard as steel at that second. I swear I saw his eyes glow with a raging fire. "Your attempt to bluff me is nothing short of pathetic. You've come all this way, and you're not going to stop now. You have as much to gain from this as I do."

My heart beat against my ribcage. A thousand thoughts ran through my head as I went over his last sentence. The foremost one that came to mind was, *Does he know I'm planning on betraying him?* If he did, then my rebellion was killed before it began.

"You are going to have to learn to get along. We are all on the same team." Quinn looked between Johnny, Gina and myself.

Gina looked at my and then flicked her head back, sending the purple streak in her hair whipping out of her face. She appeared about as pleased with this arrangement as I was. At least I did have one advantage over her—she was afraid of me. The same couldn't be said for her brother.

"Okay," I said as calmly as my vocal chords would allow.

"I can live with it," Johnny said.

"Good," Quinn said. He finally moved out from between us and broke his mental hold on my feet.

I lifted my legs easily, to make sure I could move if I had to. Apparently he'd had a similar grip on Johnny, because he too flexed himself to make sure he could defend himself if I decided to attack again.

"You have an hour to settle yourselves in," Quinn informed all five of us. "Then we're moving out."

"You still haven't told us vhat ve're doing here," Klaus said, mirroring all of our thoughts.

Quinn stopped then and looked at each of us in turn. Every one of us, including Johnny and Gina, all looked at him in anticipation. I may have been the only one who had any idea what was going on, and only because I had done some digging.

He'd promised each of *them* money in return for their commitment to this mission—me, a web of lies and deceit. The way I glared at him now told him he better not try and dodge the question. The others' emotions echoed those feelings.

The man decided he couldn't hold out any longer otherwise he'd have a mutiny on his hands. "In the 1930s, as Adolph Hitler rose to power, he began a search for, shall we say, powerful artifacts. The first item he found was a spear. Not just any spear, but the spear that stabbed Christ in the side when he hung from the cross—The Spear of Destiny.

"He had some of his top and most trusted scientists study the artifact to determine what gave it its power. They found blood permeating through every pore of the metal. Yes, the blood was old, crusted, dried, but genetic material was still found inside. They developed a serum from that material which, when injected into a human being, gave incredible powers.

"As the war began, he sent his agents to the far corners of the Earth in search of the other artifacts. The only other object that was found was the Cup of Christ, otherwise known as the Holy Grail."

He didn't brandish the cup, and he sent me a mental shove that told me I better not say a word about it. He didn't want them to know about it, probably because knowing he had the cup that held the key to eternal life would make him a target. I didn't blame him for this particular secret.

"Yo, man!" Johnny spoke up. "I don't care about the history lesson. The only reason my sis an' I are still sitting here is because you promised us a payday. So, let's get on with it."

"And as I've told you before, I will not tolerate this insolent behavior."

Suddenly, Johnny was screaming, like his body was filled with intense pain. Gina jumped away from him and wailed too, but hers was more out of fear than pain. Nothing seemed to be happening to either of them. However, knowing my own powers, I had a pretty good idea what Quinn was doing to them.

Concentrating on Johnny, I saw flames licking his clothes, charring his flesh. Quinn was mentally torturing the boy for a simple comment. If he was trying to teach the boy a lesson, it had already been learned. He didn't need to continue, yet he was still pushing into the twins' minds, making them both believe he was burning.

Acting quickly, I pushed out with all the mental force I could, slamming Quinn into the wall. In my haste, I think the unfocused blast caught Klaus a bit, because he tumbled into the bed. No big loss. The important thing was, Johnny and Gina had both stopped screaming.

Quinn quickly straightened and composed himself. He didn't look happy, but he also didn't appear angry either. He shook his head at me and I prepared myself for the inevitable attack.

But it didn't come.

Instead, Quinn turned to Johnny. "I'm assured you have seen the error of your ways." It was apparent to everyone he was containing some barely restrained rage. He had to be losing his touch, because he used to be able to stay so calm, no matter what the situation.

Quinn opened the door and stepped back into the hall. Our eyes all followed him, but none of us moved. Johnny and Gina were still recovering from their bit of torture, and Jayson and Klaus were a little shocked at what they'd seen. None of the four had ever seen Quinn use his powers like that before. Hell, I'd never seen him use them either. I'd been on the giving end of that particular power.

Do I look like that when using my powers? Is that how Peter had seen me when...?

"Are you coming?" Quinn's tone was friendlier, making him seem almost bipolar. "You wanted to find out what we're here for. Follow me."

CHAPTER 12
THE SHROUD OF TURIN

We marched out of the Hotel Chelsea and made a left down the narrow street. Only one block away, the street opened into a wide courtyard, and in front of us was a white building, seemingly standing away from the buildings surrounding it. The building could have been brand new, or it could have been hundreds of years old, I honestly couldn't tell. Near it was a tower made of a dark brick far older than the building itself.

The cross on the tallest steeple of the white building was all I needed to see to understand what the building was—a church.

I would have said we looked conspicuous, standing on a street corner, staring at the church, but there were many others gawking at the building. People entered and exited the large wooden doors at the front of the building, while others stood at various points in the square taking pictures.

"This is what we're here for," Quinn informed us.

"What is this building?" Jayson asked.

"Turin Cathedral," Quinn announced.

I took in a deep breath. Even though I had known all along this was what we'd been after, standing here, in front of the building made it more real.

"We're going to steal the building?" Jayson was a little more than confused.

"No," I explained. "We're after what's inside."

"And what's that?" Johnny's voice was once again short and gruff, as he tried to regain his tough-guy façade after us seeing him scream like a girl earlier.

I wasn't about to let him think he could intimidate me though. I stepped to him and leaned in so my face was right on top of his. "Maybe you should have paid more attention in history." Even though he stood a few inches taller than me, I felt like I towered over him at that moment. "We're in the city of Turin and there is only one artifact associated with this city. The Shroud of Turin."

He sneered at me and pushed me away. "Get away from me!"

I barely stumbled and gave the boy a smirk. But then I turned to Quinn, to ask one of the many unanswered questions I had. "But can you explain what you want the shroud for? I mean, it has the same genetic material on it as the spear and the cup. What difference does the shroud make?"

"All the difference in the world." He shook his head as if the answer to my question was obvious. "We literally have the blood of God pumping through our veins. There are many, including your own M.H.D.A., who would kill to get their hands on any one of these artifacts. If they did, they could create an army of super powered soldiers who have the potential to make the Holocaust look like a game of capture the flag. By gathering these objects, I make it impossible for anyone to get their hands on them."

"Except you," I said.

"Better in my hands then theirs."

"If dhey are so dangerous, vhy not destroy dhem?" Klaus interjected.

"Could you honestly say you could destroy an artifact that ancient and important? No, these artifacts mark our history. They mustn't simply be burned, or melted, or harmed in any way."

"So, essentially, you're trying to protect the world?" Jayson asked.

Quinn considered the question with pursed lips for a moment, then nodded. "Absolutely."

I didn't know how much of what he'd said to believe. Could others be after these artifacts? It seemed strange anyone else would even know what they could do. Could Quinn really be trying to protect the objects? Was the M.H.D.A. really after the shroud like Quinn?

No. It wasn't possible. They were supposed to be the good guys.

But, weren't they trying to do what Quinn said he was trying to prevent? The room I'd found the spear in had been set up as some kind of lab. They could have been creating soldiers in that very room. Plus, until I found it, they had possession of the Spear of Destiny. They were probably extracting genetic material from it all this time to create the super-human formula.

Was the M.H.D.A. the true bad guy?

"So, let's go get it," Johnny said, striding toward the cathedral.

Gina grabbed his arm, stopping him before he made it three steps. "Johnny, be patient. If we don't follow orders, we won't get paid."

He rolled his neck around as if trying to remove some kink. Then he glared at her. The longer the two gazes were locked, the more Johnny's face softened. Finally, he let out a sigh. "All right, whatever you say, sis." He turned back and rejoined our little group.

"Now that our little outburst is over, we're going back to the hotel and you all are going to get some rest. We begin first thing tomorrow morning."

"And what do we begin?" I asked.

"You might know all about history," Johnny shot at me, making me want to give him another dose of mental torture, "but you know crap about heists. The first thing you need to do is stake the place out and come up with a plan."

"This coming from Mr. Smash and Grab." I shook my head.

"You think you're so high and mighty."

"And you're an idiot."

I turned away from him then, satisfied I managed to get the last word in. I walked the block back to the hotel, with the others not too far behind me. I could hear them murmuring. I heard Quinn several times tell Johnny he needed to calm down and needed to work with me. I was pretty sure I'd be hearing similar words later.

I didn't care. I wasn't going to be cordial to Johnny under any circumstances. No matter what Quinn's true motive was, whether he was telling the truth and really wanted to protect the world, or if he had darker motives, he didn't know Johnny and Gina like I did. Even though there wasn't much trust to be had in our little group, the two of them were probably the most untrustworthy.

I made it to the corner of the hotel, stopping underneath the big neon sign glowing overhead. Leaning against the wall, I saw someone across the street, seemingly hiding in the shadows. I wouldn't have thought anything of it, but the person standing there had no thoughts whatsoever. Obviously he was an Agent.

Quinn and the others were only about thirty feet away, and if I could sense the man in the shadows, I was sure Quinn would too. Not wanting to be seen by Quinn, I turned slightly so he couldn't see my right arm and while pretending to study one of the potted bushes, lining the sidewalk, I motioned with my hand to make the Agent go away. I then held up my five fingers for him to see. Hopefully he got the message I'd be back in five minutes and would be able to talk to him then.

He didn't move for a moment, but it looked like he was talking. *Probably getting orders from someone,* I surmised. Then he slinked further in the shadows as Quinn and the others strolled up.

"Vhat are you looking at?" Klaus asked me.

I was still staring down the street, into the shadows where the Agent had been. Klaus was trying to follow my gaze to see what held my attention.

"Nothing really," I lied, turning toward him. "I was wondering if this bush was real or not. It looked like it might be fake."

"Silly American," he said. "Vhy vould anyone plant a fake bush? You can be so foolish zometimes."

I wanted to tell him I wasn't a fool. I wanted to come up with a hundred reasons someone might plant a fake bush. Instead, I forced myself to smile and giggle a little like he'd said something amusing.

He took it the wrong way. He laughed a little bit too, then punched me lightly on my shoulder. "I break your icy exterior. You no longer hate me? Yah? Vee be friends?"

Instead of answering, I punched him back. "If you stop hitting me, maybe I'll consider it."

"It is, how you say, a deal."

"Klaus, Christine," Quinn called from the doorway. He sounded like a teacher leading his class through the city streets and was trying to corral the stragglers. "Come on, we have to get some rest. Big day tomorrow."

"Be right there," I shouted back.

Quinn looked at us through half-closed eyes. Then he smiled and gave a wink before he went inside. I wondered why he had that reaction. It didn't take too long to figure out he'd sifted through Klaus' head. Unfortunately for me, his thoughts weren't what one might call appropriate.

"So, vee are alone," he said with a wink of his own.

He leaned in on me and closed his eyes, expecting to get a kiss. How could the boy be so stupid? I pushed him, both physically and mentally to get him to back off. He stumbled back and opened his eyes up in shock.

"I thought vee be friends. Vee have a deal."

"Yes, friends, not lovers."

He looked uncomprehendingly at me, as if in his mind there was no difference between the two.

Grunting, I walked away, using the disagreement as a reason to leave. I had to meet the Agent and find out what he wanted. Besides, my need to get away from the boy was all too real. If I stayed , I probably would have killed him.

"Christine, vait for me!" The boy was persistent. I had to give him that.

I stopped in the middle of the street, which probably wasn't the best idea. But since the only car I'd seen so far was our own limo, I was pretty sure I wasn't about to be hit by anything. In a second, he was standing in front of me again.

"I apologize."

"It's okay. I think we should get away from each other for a little bit." It wasn't a lie. I couldn't meet with the Agent if he was hovering over my shoulder. I had no idea where Klaus' allegiances were. He could potentially run right back to Quinn and reveal everything.

He didn't look like he was going to bite though. He stayed put, as if I might change my mind in a second. Persistent as he may be, the boy didn't take a hint.

I started to retreat, backing away from him slowly, but Klaus matched my every movement. I had no choice but to send him a much harsher message. I grabbed hold of his thoughts, and altered those thought patterns so his infatuation became disgust.

His entire demeanor changed in less than a second. Where lust and attraction had filled his eyes a moment before, now only confusion and a look of distaste remained. He stopped his advance and allowed me to back away from him. By the time I made it to the opposite sidewalk, he'd already turned and was trudging back to the hotel.

The feeling would pass in a few minutes, and I was sure he would figure out what I'd done, but a few minutes was all I needed to find a meeting place with the Agent.

As soon as he was out of sight, I ran down the darkened street where I saw the Agent escape. I reached out, trying to sense the emptiness I was all too familiar with. It didn't take long to find him, less than a block away, hiding in a small courtyard filled with trees. He had his back on one of the trees, waiting casually for me to walk up.

Once I was close enough, I was able to tell who it was. I honestly hadn't expected him to come out to the field. I pictured him as one who delegates tasks such as this to his subordinates.

"Smith, what are you doing here?"

"Agent Smith, if you would Agent Carpenter." He groaned in frustration at my informality. "Nice work slipping away."

Wow. A compliment from Agent Smith, the world might come to an end.

"We only have a few minutes before you're missed, so let's get to the point. What intel have you gathered thus far?" I had to hand it to him, the man really did put himself entirely in his job. He didn't even have time for a "hello, how you doing?" He went right to the conversation.

Not that it was much of a conversation. I explained how we'd been right about the target, and I told Smith about what Quinn had told us about saving the world. I explained about the three added members of the team and how Quinn had promised each of them a big payment on completion of the mission. Smith didn't betray anything. If someone were watching us, they'd probably think I was telling him about my day seeing the sites of Torino.

Which begged the question, if Smith didn't react to Quinn's motive, did he already know about it? Maybe Smith was hiding something. On the other hand, he could be as good at hiding emotions as Quinn and Abby were. Either way, I still had no real answers.

"Do we have a timetable?" Smith asked when I was finished.

I shook my head. "He hasn't said anything, but we are doing surveillance tomorrow. If I'm right, we'll be hitting the cathedral by the end of the week."

He made a barely perceptible nod. "Keep me informed. Your team should be arriving at their location in just under two hours. We will be watching."

He pulled a matchbook and a cigarette out of his pocket. I would never have pegged him as a smoker. But he pulled a match from the book and lit the cigarette, inhaling a small puff of smoke and causing the tip to light bright orange. He blew smoke out of his mouth and then tossed the burnt match and the matchbook on the ground.

"Text me at this number if you need to meet. I will be here ten minutes after I receive the message." I expected him to hand me a paper or a card with a phone number on it, but instead, he walked away, tossing the barely smoked cigarette into the grass as he did.

He was gone by the time I thought to call to him and ask, "What number?" Why did Smith always have to be so cryptic? If it were Abby, she would have given me the number to dial with specific instructions. Smith seemed like he wanted me to pluck the number from the air through some clairvoyant power I didn't possess—okay, I sort of possessed it.

Smith hadn't even given me any information either. My team was going to be here soon, but where? What were they planning on doing to Quinn? How were they going to stop him? Where would they be watching from? I wanted so badly to howl and curse, but all I did was kick the trunk of the tree he'd been leaning against.

In kicking the tree, my foot moved the matchbook Smith had thrown in the grass. It flipped over and revealed words on the cover. It read: Smith's Auto-Service – 011 555 2626.

"Oh, he's good." I picked it up. If Quinn saw this, he wouldn't think anything of it. A simple matchbook for some auto mechanic wouldn't raise any eyebrows. My frustrations with the Agent simply vanished as I walked back up the street to the Hotel Chelsea.

However, the good natured feelings too vanished, when I saw Klaus, standing in the doorway of the hotel, waiting for me.

CHAPTER 13
EARLY MORNING RUN

I haven't shared a bed with someone in a long time. It really sucked I was all but forced to do so with Gina, though thinking of my three other choices of bedmates, she was definitely the least of the evils.

I admit, the bed was comfy, and after the long, restless plane ride the previous day, I slept better than I had since hearing about this trip. My biggest problem: the room didn't have a private bathroom. The hotel had a common bathroom shared by all the guests. According to Klaus, that was pretty standard in Europe, so I didn't put up too much of a fuss. I was still less than thrilled at sharing a bathroom and shower with twenty other people.

I looked at my watch—6a.m. So early, and the sun was already pouring through the window, covering my tired body with warmth. I slipped out of bed, being careful not to disturb Gina. I don't think my efforts mattered. The way she was snoring, I doubted a jet crashing on the roof would wake her.

I stepped over Jayson, who was sprawled, tangled in his blankets on my way to the window. The other two boys, being bigger, had agreed they would share the bed and forced the little guy to sleep on the floor. I opened the curtains to peer outside.

It was a beautiful morning. The sky was that perfect shade of blue—the color it always is in those travel brochures for exotic destinations. Little fluffy clouds dotted the sky casting small shadows on the city.

From our room, I could see the cathedral, it looked so peaceful without hundreds of people bustling around the outside. The whole city, it seemed, had yet to awaken, as everywhere my eyes fell, I saw almost no signs of life. I took out my camera and snapped a picture.

Then, deciding this would be the perfect time to take a shower, I rummaged through my bags for something suitable to wear—black tanktop and shorts. Then I tiptoed down the hall and washed.

It was about 6:30 when I returned to the room and found Klaus sitting up in the bed, hunched over like he'd woken up. He wasn't wearing anything but a pair of boxer shorts, and for the first time I got a clear look at his body. Underneath his clothes, who would have thought the boy looked that good? To say he had a six pack would have been an understatement. He was completely toned from head to toe, devoid of even an ounce of fat. The boy had to work out all the time to keep up that physique. My cheeks flushed from gazing upon his perfect form.

He yawned and then turned his head in my direction. "Good morning."

I looked away, my cheeks bursting with color. I hadn't even seen Ethan with this little on before. "Uh… yeah. Morning."

"Vhy are you up dhis early?" he asked.

"I could ask you the same thing."

From the corner of my eye, I saw him pull a t-shirt over his head and slip on a pair of sweatpants. Only then could I bring myself to look at him again.

"I go for run," he said. "Want to join?"

"Stifling a laugh, I said, "I don't think that's a good idea." And it really wasn't, despite my powers, I was probably one of the least athletic people I knew.

He walked up to me, clapping me on the shoulder. "I vill go slow. You need exercise. Get the blood pumping."

"I'll pass." I stepped away from him and shoved my sleeping clothes and towel into my suitcase. Then, from the side pocket, I pulled my cell phone and checked to see if I had any messages. There was one from Ethan. It had apparently come somewhere around 2a.m.

Need to meet… text back when you're free, it read.

I heard the creak of the door as Klaus headed out.

"Wait!" I called, not believing my own words. "Give me a second to get my sneakers on."

Klaus' face lit up like he'd just won the lottery. But he shut the door and waited as I returned Ethan's text instructing him to meet in front of the cathedral in ten minutes.

"Vhat made you change your mind?" Klaus asked while I slipped socks and sneakers on my feet.

"I guess I figured you were right. I could use a little exercise. I'm a little out of shape."

"You look fine," he said, not making any effort to hide the fact he was now checking me out.

A groan came from the boys' bed, as Johnny rolled over. "Who cares how she looks? Just shut up and let me get some sleep."

Again, I stifled a giggle and Klaus did the same. It was the first moment we'd shared where we were both of the same opinion.

Not wanting to disturb Johnny any further, Klaus waved a hand toward the door and slowly opened it to step outside. I followed him out. However, I was definitely not as nice as my temporary roommate, and I slammed the door behind me.

The loud crash of Johnny falling out of bed was all I needed to confirm my action had the desired effect. I felt Jayson stir out of his dream-state as well while I strode proudly down the hall behind Klaus. Gina was still in a deep sleep.

It might seriously take a plane crash to wake that girl up.

I waved to the man at the desk as we went out the front door. He didn't say anything, but gave the two of us a cordial wave in return.

"Vhere vee go?" Klaus stretched out his legs and twisted his upper body as he prepared to get started.

I on the other hand, who had never gone on a run unless it was to get a passing grade in gym class, looked around, trying to pick the best direction to go where I could easily lose him.

I pointed down the street in the opposite direction of the cathedral. "Let's go that way."

"Good." Klaus jogged in the direction I'd indicated and I was forced to go with him.

The only reason I'd wanted to go on this stupid run was to have an alibi if anyone wondered why I was missing so early in the morning, but after only a quarter mile, I was already trying to think up another alibi. My breaths came in and out in deep spurts, and my legs, especially around my ankles, were on fire. The cramp I was planning on faking to get away from Klaus might not need faking after all.

We'd run a block, and Klaus was being very patient with me. He badly wanted to go at his usual speed, which was probably much faster than the pace we were running at, but he kept checking to make sure I was able to keep up with him. The worst part was he didn't mind. He was happier having me run with him than if he'd let me stay behind in the hotel.

I felt bad having to deceive him, but I had no choice. As nice as he was being, I still couldn't trust he wouldn't betray me the first chance he got.

We hadn't gone very far before I knew I couldn't go much further. Ahead I saw a small café called Mordillo. It was an odd place, claiming to sell pizza and hamburgers (the sign was in English, as I noticed many of the signs were). The thing that made it strange though was the sign outside the place claiming that the burgers inside were McDonald's hamburgers. The golden arches were unmistakable. I figured this would be as good a place as any to stop. It would be a good landmark to meet Klaus at after I met with Ethan.

I wheezed loudly, only putting a little bit of acting into it. Then I bent over and made like I was going to vomit. "I can't… go any more."

Klaus stopped his jog and walked back over to me. He put a hand on my shoulder and pushed me upright. "It's not good to do that. Straighten up and get more air." He was being infinitely patient with me, and another pang of guilt hit me for having to lie to him. He was annoying, and I hated he couldn't stop touching me, but he really did seem like a decent guy.

"Why don't you go on?" I gasped again, this time only for effect. "No reason for me to hold you up."

"You be all right?" he asked.

Damn. There was real concern in those eyes.

I leaned on the wall, turning my head back the way we'd come. We'd barely run two blocks from the hotel—not even a half mile. And though I was only half faking, I still wanted to kick myself for being so out of shape. I should've been able to run three times as far without getting tired. He was going to think I was such a wimp.

Who cares? the voice in my head said. *Are you trying to impress him?*

No, I answered quickly. The response came so quickly, I hardly believed it.

I nodded. "Yeah. I'm fine. I got a cramp and…" I wheezed again. "Having a little trouble catching my breath." I waved him off. "Go on. I'll wait for you here."

"Okay. You vait. I be back in ten minutes. Dhen vee run back." He really was too nice.

I watched him run off, and at first, I couldn't help but admire his backside. Even in sweats, it looked good and I couldn't help but wonder why I hadn't noticed it before. He looked back once and caught me gawking at him. He laughed and then continued on, seeming to pick up his pace.

Great, I thought, *now he thinks I have a thing for him.*

Once he was far enough out of sight, I straightened and stopped pretending like I was dying. I quickly looked at my watch—6:45 exactly. I needed to be back on this spot by 6:55. I didn't have much time. Looking around and noticing the street still completely empty, I floated off the ground. Flying was the only way I'd get there and back in time.

I stayed near the ground as I sped down the street. The sidewalk skimmed by below me as I whizzed past the hotel and out into the open courtyard in front of Turin Cathedral. I felt Ethan on the far side, near the tower. I flew across the white bricks and landed in front of the structure.

Ethan was nearby but I couldn't see him. I checked my surroundings and noticed no one that could have seen my flight in. I reached out, able now to concentrate all my power on locating Ethan and felt him behind a sign hanging on the iron fence to my left. I found a gate, and walked rather than floated to it.

As soon as I stepped through the gate a pair of arms seized me and dragged me behind it. Before I could mount even a little resistance I was spun around and found my lips locked against a very familiar pair. I closed my eyes and savored the feel and taste of my boyfriend's mouth. Too soon we broke apart and I opened my eyes.

"Why can't you greet me like that every time we see each other?" My voice fluttered, and I cleared my throat so I didn't sound like such a lovesick girl. "What's up?"

Ethan gave me that lopsided smile of his and all I wanted to do was kiss him again. However, I glanced at my watch and saw we only had eight more minutes before I had to be back, so I practiced my self-control.

"How was your trip?" he asked.

"Uneventful," I said. I had no reason to tell him about Klaus' abuse on the plane.

Ethan stepped away and leaned his elbows on a metal rail overlooking some old ruins. There were several different levels, each going deeper into the ground than the last, creating a quarter circle around what appeared to be a raised platform.

"Was this a theater?" I asked.

Ethan nodded, as if the answer should have been obvious to anyone with half a brain. "A really old theater."

For some reason, I couldn't take my eyes off it. All it appeared to be was piles of old bricks very large steps down into a pit. I probably wouldn't have been at all interested in this place if I'd been reading about it in a book. However, being there at its edge, staring directly at the ancient structure, made it the center of my attention. I really wished I hadn't left my camera in the room. I took my cell out and snapped a picture with it instead.

"I wish I was on a real vacation. Then I'd actually be able to enjoy this," I told Ethan.

He nodded. "I know what you mean."

I looked at my watch—six more minutes.

It was all the motivation I needed to stop marveling at the antiquated theater. I turned away from it, so as not to be tempted to keep looking. "Ethan, I don't have much time. I have to get back before I'm missed. What did you have to meet me for?"

"I just missed you."

It was sweet of him to say and I did blush a bit at the sentiment, but I knew my boyfriend enough to know when he wasn't being honest with me.

"What does Abby want?"

He knew he'd been caught and sighed in defeat. "That guy Smith met us last night and filled us in. By the way, you're right, the man is a huge ass—"

"Not the time," I interrupted.

"Right," he agreed. "So, anyway, we need to know when you're going to move on the shroud, so we can be there to… steal it from you, I guess. Abby and Smith weren't too clear on that. So, we need you to wear a listening device."

"A wire?" I said. "You think Quinn's not going to notice that?"

He held up his hands like he was surrendering. "First, I'm only the messenger, don't take it out on me." Then he reached into his pocket and pulled out a small box that looked like it could hold an engagement ring. "Second, I doubt he'd going to detect this one."

He opened the box and to my relief there wasn't a ring inside. Not that I thought Ethan was going to propose. I didn't want to explain why I suddenly had a ring on my finger.

Inside was a pendant shaped like a skull and crossbones. It was incredibly small, but it was the sort of thing most people would picture me wearing. I hadn't brought any jewelry with me for this trip, mainly because I didn't want to deal with it. I grabbed the item and unlatched the chain it was attached to and put it around my neck. It fit me nicely.

"The listening device is in the skull," informed Ethan, not that he needed to. "We'll be able to hear everything you hear."

"So, you'll know when the heist is going down and exactly what the plan is," I surmised.

"Right."

Checking my watch again I saw I had only three minutes.

"I have to get back," I said. "I'll text you later."

"Actually, that was the other thing I needed to tell you," said Ethan with a hint of sadness in his voice. This was something he didn't want to say and I already knew why. "Abby said you shouldn't contact us. We'll know if you're in trouble because of the pendant. It's too risky, because anyone can take a look at your phone and check your messages."

I didn't want to get into the fact I could always delete the messages as soon as I sent them, but I didn't. As much as I hated to admit it, Abby was right. And this time I would follow orders. "I'll send *you* a text only if there's an emergency."

He looked relieved. The whole non-communication thing didn't sit well with him either. "Okay."

"I've really got to go though." I only had two minutes before Klaus was expected back. "I love you." I gave Ethan a hug and a kiss, and then jumped into the air and flew back toward Mordillo. The whoosh of air behind me told me Ethan too had sped back to wherever my friends were staying.

I raced as fast as I could and made it back with only thirty seconds to spare. I landed and leaned back against the wall, pretending I'd been there the whole time. I was only back in position for a couple of seconds before Klaus raced around a corner a block and a half away and ran toward me.

The way he ran made him look like a world class athlete. Every motion he made was precise and meant to have the maximum result with minimal effort. He was standing in front of me at 6:55 on the dot. The boy must have had an internal clock or something.

He leaned and stretched on the wall next to me, never stopping his movement. He was sweating from his brief workout, but he wasn't breathing heavily. "Are you ready to finish?"

Pushing myself off the wall, I pretended like I was still a little tired. "Race you back?"

"Vee jog today," he said, eyeing my falsely shaking legs. "Race tomorrow."

And with that, we jogged slowly the almost half mile back to the hotel.

CHAPTER 14
EYES AND EARS

Breakfast was at 8a.m., and I had an Egg McMuffin at Mordillo's. It was the strangest thing ordering McDonald's food at a place which was clearly not a McDonald's. For one, the seats weren't those plastic benches like most McDonald's had. They were actually cushioned chairs around elegant looking tables.

Just a fun fact: Egg McMuffin is the same word in Italian as it is in English—go figure.

It was crowded in the place too, which is why I think Quinn picked it instead of something a little more upscale. During our meal, he explained exactly what we were going to do today. He made sure to keep his voice low enough in case someone in the crowd were listening, they would have an incredibly difficult time doing so.

I positioned myself next to him, so the pendant would pick up every word he said and send it back to Abby and my friends.

"Surveillance is the key. It is going to take an awful lot of data to pull this off. I've been inside before and I can tell you it is a rather large place. They keep the shroud in the main room, and there are literally a dozen access points and each of them will have to be watched. Jayson, I am putting you in charge of that.

"They also have a very sophisticated security system. Cameras are spread all around the cathedral, and we need to find the location of each and every one of them. Johnny and Gina, I am going to leave that for you. You'll need to make a map of the inside and pinpoint where these cameras are so we can come up with a plan to get around them.

"The crypt where the shroud is kept is heavily guarded, both day and night. We need to monitor the guards and document when they change shifts. Priests are constantly moving through the cathedral as well, and we'll need to see if they have any patterns. We're also going to need actual photographs of the inside. Christine, I thought that would be best suited for you as you're the only one of us who thought to bring a camera with you.

"Then finally, the outside. We don't want anyone coming in unexpectedly. And since this is the busy tourist season, we'll need a way to get people out of the building and keep them there. That means, finding and watching every access point. Klaus, that would be you."

We all nodded, understanding what we needed to do. Everyone, that is, except Johnny.

"All this for a crusty piece of cloth. I don't understand why I don't send a hundred copies of myself inside and ransack the place."

"Because then your face will be on every most wanted list from the Vatican to Interpol. Believe me, I know."

The way he said the last sentence left a big unanswered question in my mind. "Quinn, have you tried this before?"

He nodded.

"And obviously you failed," I continued.

Again, a nod.

"And that's why you need us. Because you can't get anywhere near that place without every alarm going off."

"That is quite correct, Ms. Carpenter."

Everyone at the table was silent. The little confidence we had this mission was at all doable, was crushed in that moment. If Quinn, with all his power and experience, couldn't get near the shroud, a group of teenagers didn't stand a chance.

"Is this why you've been off the grid for two months?" I asked.

A third nod. "My mistake was going it alone. I had no one to watch my back and I was caught before I even started. Some mental finessing and I was able to escape, but not before my image was plastered on every government website around the world. I was careless."

Which is also why he'd shaved off his goatee, I guessed. I'd been wondering why he'd done that since he appeared on my doorstep two weeks ago.

We finished our breakfast with Quinn going over a few more details. The weight of what we were now doing rested on all our shoulders. Most of us had finally come to the realization this wasn't going to be a game. We were really going to steal the shroud or suffer the horrific consequences.

We were a rather subdued group as we trekked from the café to Turin Cathedral. All of us walked in contemplative silence. When we reached the cathedral, the tension in all of us, even Quinn, rose to heights I didn't think possible. And we weren't even planning on going in there and stealing the thing today. I couldn't imagine how we were going to feel when the time came.

Not surprisingly, the calmest of us were Johnny and Gina, who were used to performing heists all the time. I hated to admit it, but the pair of them were going to have to take the lead on this one.

More people filled the courtyard now. Apparently many of the tourists had woken early to get to the cathedral and see the shroud before the crowds came. I didn't blame them. I myself was going to have to get most of my surveillance done before it got too crowded inside. There'd be no way I'd survive if I was pressed in with hundreds of people.

"Remember," Quinn said before sending us inside, "you're a group of American highschoolers on a history field trip."

Then we had no more choice. It was time for us to go inside. Pressing through the people scuttling about the white brick courtyard outside the cathedral, we climbed the steps and entered the center doorway of the cathedral. Klaus broke from our group right before we entered, off to perform his own task. I felt a brief stab of loss as he wandered away.

Why? I asked myself.

My family wasn't really what you'd call the religious type. I could probably count the number of times I'd been inside a church in the past five years on my fingers. But the one thing I could say was, I'd never, in all my life been in a church like this one.

As soon as we walked in I was amazed at the high stone arches and the great detailed architecture of the ceilings. I've stood in the center of Manhattan, gazed up at the Empire State Building and been blown away by its sheer size. However, the ceiling I was looking at might as well have been twice as large for the dumfounded feeling I had.

Inside the entrance was a small cauldron made out of the same white stone the rest of the building was created from. Inside was a small pool of water which people dipped their fingers into as they entered.

Holy water.

Ahead of us, were rows and rows of pews that seemed to go on forever. In front of all this was an altar, all primed to have a priest stand there and speak to his flock. A huge gold cross stood on a stand, rising above the altar and drawing the eye of everyone who entered directly toward it. A mural covered the back wall featuring another altar on which a glowing golden cross was held.

Honestly, I couldn't help but gasp in awe of the place.

To our left was the most dense portion of the crowd, and where I figured the shroud must have been held.

"Okay, I'm going to check out the shroud," I said to the others. "You know what to do."

We all went in separate directions. I was pretty sure no one would mess anything up today, I hoped everything we were supposed to do was covered.

There were probably about twenty people hovering around a section of wall. As I stepped over, I pulled my camera from my pocket, intending to snap as many photos as I could to analyze later. I waited patiently until I was able to get to the front, only to find that all I was looking at was a mock up of the shroud. Standing at the red velvet ropes I examined the object on the wall in front of me. As Johnny described, all it looked like was a crusty piece of cloth with only the faintest trace of an image on it. It could have been Christ for all I knew, but it could just as easily been King Arthur as well. If this was really was the shroud looked like, I wondered how anyone could be so sure it was actually Christ's shroud.

Below the image of the shroud were what appeared to be two giant photo-negatives resting upright on the floor. They more clearly showed what was on the shroud. Again, it certainly looked like every image of Jesus I'd ever seen, but I'm sure there were a hundred people who looked like him. As a matter of fact, take off the beard and the man on the shroud might have passed for my dad.

I snapped several photos at several different angles. There didn't appear to be much security in this area other than the red velvet ropes and a camera resting in the corner, which I also managed to get a shot of. It was like this section wasn't important.

Well, why should it be? The voice in the back of my head asked. *Why protect something that isn't real and is easily replaced?*

That's true, I responded.

I didn't dwell any longer on that spot, and instead moved to the right along the wall to where another crowd had gathered. Again, I had to wait patiently to move to the front of the gathered people. There couldn't have been more than thirty there, yet I still had to take deep calming breaths to make sure I didn't freak out. From past experience I knew if I freaked out, I could potentially hurt a lot of people around me with my powers.

While I waited I took more photos of the surrounding area, taking note of several cameras placed around where I stood. It might have been Johnny and Gina's job to locate the cameras, but an extra set of eyes couldn't hurt.

There were two guards in this area as well, not dressed like a typical security guard. Actually, at first I thought they were in costume, but the serious nature the pair displayed and the way they eyed anyone who wandered too close to the object I couldn't yet see told me they were definitely in charge of security. They wore blue and yellow striped outfits, with poofy arm sleeves and pant legs. Each wore a crooked black hat and had a sword in a sheath on their left hip. It was as if they were doing everything in their power to be seen, and maybe that was the point. No one would mess with something if they knew it was being guarded.

People were taking their own pictures of the two men, so I didn't feel at all out of place doing the same. These were the men I had to watch. It was going to be easy if they stood in one spot all day.

It took several minutes for the crowd in front of me to view the shroud. Even though I knew why people were taking so long, I couldn't help getting impatient. I knew it was a miraculous thing being so close to an artifact such as this, but I had actual research to do.

Finally, I was able to get up front and see the object for myself. There was a short altar for people to kneel and pray before the artifact. I was a little surprised that people were making such a big deal about it, now that I could see it. Actually, the fact was, I couldn't see it. The shroud was in a sarcophagus and covered by a white and red sheet. On the sheet was a golden cross and scattered about the top of it was a dried vine of thorns.

The worst part of it was the sarcophagus was behind thick looking, and quite possibly bullet-proof, glass. Looking at the wall behind the sarcophagus, I tried to find another access point, but couldn't see anything.

Without meaning to, I felt the people behind me growing agitated I was taking so long. So, I took a couple of photos and moved away.

Even though the people were getting frustrated at having to wait, there was an underlying feeling that won out. Most of them didn't just desire to see the shroud, it was more of a need. From what I could feel from them, it was like seeing the old relic would affirm their faith.

I shook my head. Thinking about it would only make me back out of stealing it. And this was something that needed to be done.

I wasn't sure how we could possibly get to the shroud. I doubted we could break the glass, but even if we could, it would make so much noise everyone within the building would be on us in a second. That was, unless we could get everyone out of the building, but that didn't seem to be an option either.

I walked back into the main area and sat in one of the many rows. I stayed as far away from everyone else as I could. It was bad enough the chapel was getting crowded and my people-claustrophobia was beginning to kick in, but the high volume of minds in my vicinity were also threatening to break through my brains mental barriers. I doubled my efforts to keep the voices out.

Setting about my next task, I looked for anyone in the chapel that could hinder our mission. On first glance, there didn't seem to be anyone other than the two guards I'd already marked. I knew there were priests, bishops or other clergymen about, but none were in sight.

On the other side of the church, Johnny and Gina sat in another pew. Being practically on top of each other, the pair looked like they could be a couple. I knew it was them being protective of the other, but knowing they were brother and sister made the scene look a little… disturbing. I swear, I kept expecting Johnny to lean over and kiss her. Thank God he didn't.

Gina drew in a sketch pad as Johnny pointed out the cameras to her. Where she got it, I don't know—probably stole it. Not exactly subtle, but the twins could easily have been admiring and sketching the architecture.

Jayson was walking the perimeter of the building, making note of every possible entry point.

Opening my cell phone, I decided to take on the Grand Master of my chess game again. Even as I played—and lost—several games, I made sure to keep an eye on the rest of the cathedral. Eventually, I would have to mark someone else. After an hour of sitting, not much had changed, though the crowd had grown quite a bit thicker. Thankfully, they were more interested in seeing the shroud than they were taking a seat.

I was about to lose my tenth game in a row when my attention was torn away from my cell phone screen.

"Holy crap! It IS her!"

My head shot up and stared at these two pimply faced boys gawking at me while continuously glancing at a cell. The two couldn't have been more than thirteen, wearing Star Wars t-shirts and jean shorts. One had a Yankees' baseball cap on and the other had thick rimmed glasses.

"I told you," the boy with the glasses said. "You owe me ten bucks."

"I never bet you," the other argued. "Besides, you still owe me ten because I beat you to the top of the leaning tower."

I looked around to see if the two of them were talking about someone else, but there wasn't anyone around me. I'd never seen these two before and was getting nervous that they recognized me. Where could they have possibly seen my face before?

"But you cheated!" the first boy insisted.

"I did not!"

"Umm… hi," I managed to squeeze out of my lips.

They stopped arguing and looked at each other, a spark igniting in their faces. It was like it was the first time a girl had ever talked to them before, and by the looks of them, I probably was.

"Hey," Ballcap said, jerking his chin upward. "You're the girl right? The one in the video?"

The blank look on my face was apparently not enough to tell them I didn't understand, so I asked, "What are you talking about?"

"The YouTube video," he responded. "You know, the one where you fly around outside The Plaza Hotel."

"Oh, right." It was my little bout with Abby some idiot recorded on their cell phone and uploaded on the internet. The last check, nearly a month ago, it had almost ten million hits. This was the first time anyone had recognized me in it though. I had to give these two boys some credit, because the image in the clip wasn't exactly the sharpest. "That was all done with wires."

"Oh, I know that," Glasses said. "I mean, it's not like you really can fly."

The two boys laughed, and I laughed nervously with them.

"It's the coolest video we've ever seen. We've always wanted to make something like this," Ballcap explained.

"You're our hero," Glasses added. His cheeks turned red and he looked to the ground.

At that moment, two priests entered the chapel from a door behind the altar. Both were older men, maybe in their fifties and wore black robes. They crossed the altar and strode to the side of the cathedral opposite the shroud toward these small booths lining the walls. I needed to get a picture of them before they went in.

"Umm, sure... hero... got it. Thanks guys, but I gotta go."

As I ran off, the sound of someone getting smacked. Then Ballcap's voice followed me along the row of pews. "You blew it! She was totally into us and you had to go saying something stupid!"

I caught the pair before they went into the small curtained rooms, and snapped two pictures, one of each. Then, knowing I'd drawn a bit of attention to myself in my quick flight, I decided to go lurk in a corner until people went back to their business again.

So, two guards and two priests, I mentally checked off in my head. I checked my watch and subtracted two minutes, making the latter pair's appearance in the cathedral at exactly 10:15a.m.

I made a note of the time, and waited a few more minutes before taking a seat once again. And there I sat, playing cell phone chess and watching the room for the next few hours.

And let me tell you, sitting around doing nothing is so incredibly boring. People ask what could possibly make someone want to kill themselves. The answer is, sitting for four hours silently in a church, people watching. And to make matters worse, with each passing hour, the room only got more and more crowded.

The two priests went back into the rear of the cathedral at about 12p.m. and two more priests came back out an hour later.

While the priests were in the booths, a line of people formed and they were go into the booths one at a time.

Confession, I gathered.

The guards were less lucky, having to stand at their post until the church bell chimed 1p.m.

That was something to watch, the two guards stood on either side of the glass protected shroud as two other guards marched out of a back room, parting the amassed crowd. They traded positions, and the ones who'd been standing their all morning, formally tromped away. No words. No ceremony. And yet, as the guards changed, hundreds of camera flashes lit the room. It was enough to blind someone.

I would have joined in the controlled chaos of camera clicks, but if I left my seat and waded into the throng, I would have lost all control. So, I remained where I was and watched from afar. If these two brightly colored guards were there for as long as the first two, I'd have plenty of time to snap a photograph of them.

The busiest time at the cathedral was right around 1p.m. too. The tourists didn't seem to care about being packed into the cathedral like sardines. It was a holy relic and the whole lot of them were like fanatics needing to see it.

The brief moments when my concentration broke and allowed thoughts through, all I could hear on their minds was how they were going to pray to the shroud to heal someone, or to grant a deceased loved one passage to heaven. It was like this old artifact gave people hope and something to believe in.

And we were going to steal it.

I sighed. Once again, I couldn't believe I would be able to go through with this when the time came. Every molecule that made me up screamed what we were doing was wrong. I wasn't even sure I could steal the shroud to protect it. Looking at all the people who'd come here to see it. Where would their faith go if the shroud suddenly disappeared? Could their God allow such a heinous thing to happen?

And yet, there was the possibility that if I didn't take the shroud everyone in this room would suffer because of it.

Neither option was good. The question was, which one was the lesser of evils?

And while the question would astound the more philosophical of scholars, I knew, for me, it was really a simple choice of who I trusted more: Quinn or the M.H.D.A.?

CHAPTER 15
THE TRUTH ABOUT JOHNNY

For the next five days we went to Turin Cathedral, watching and making notes. Like clockwork, everyday at exactly 10:15, the same two priests would come out, and at exactly 12 o'clock, they would go back. At 1 o'clock, the guards would change and the new priests would enter the confession booths. It was the same routine every time.

The busiest time was always between 1 and 2 o'clock and the crowd got so bad on the fifth day—a Friday—I had no choice but to remove myself from the tightly packed room and step out into the open air of the courtyard.

I didn't understand why we kept coming back each day. There wasn't anything to be gained by returning and doing the same thing over and over again. Jayson already mapped three back entry points and one front entrance to the main hall of the cathedral. Johnny and Gina had already determined there were exactly thirty cameras scattered about the room and their locations. Klaus had a detailed description of each of the outside entryways into the cathedral as well as an escape route for us. There was nothing else to be gained.

I breathed in the warm Italian summer air and let myself relax. As much as I would love to argue the point, no one would listen to me. Over the last week, I'd found they were pretty much all in Quinn's pocket and would do anything he said. The only hope I might have had was Jayson, who was about as conflicted as I was about stealing such an important artifact, but even he was motivated by Quinn's promise of reward.

It made me realize I was truly alone.

That night, over dinner in the Bar Conte Verde di Stinelli Giuseppe (please don't ask me what it means), which was only a half mile away from the hotel, Quinn informed us the heist would be the following Monday.

"That's a bit soon, don't you think?" I asked. "That only gives us two more days to survey the site. What if something changes?"

Quinn shook his head and scrutinized me. "Is there honestly anything you can't tell me about the cathedral after spending a week inside of it?"

"Probably not," I admitted. "But, we can't be too careful. Isn't that what got you caught in the first place?"

His eyebrow arched. He knew I was trying to stall the heist. Frankly, I wasn't trying that hard to hide it. The longer we had until we tried to steal the shroud, the longer I had to figure out a way to prevent it.

Which is probably why Quinn is being so hasty to begin with.

"Stop being such a loser," Johnny said.

Quinn gave the boy a nod of satisfaction. "We're lifting the item on Monday."

Looking at the rest of our group, I saw none of them were going to support me. Even Jayson averted his gaze when I looked at him. So, defeated, I gave up any further argument.

I leaned over, making sure the skull pendant would pick up every word Quinn said. It seemed my friends would have to save me. I hoped they were listening.

"We will enter Turin Cathedral at exactly 11a.m. and get into position. Johnny will be in charge of disabling one of the guards so Jayson can replace him—use a double so you can be seen by the cameras in the main cathedral in case something goes wrong. If this step is not executed perfectly, we abort."

Both Jayson and Johnny nodded.

"We wait until 1p.m. as the guards are changing and the cathedral is the most crowded. Christine will enter the minds of everyone in the cathedral and create some crisis that will cause everyone to stampede out of the building as quickly as possible, causing the most chaos.

"While this is occurring, Klaus will disable all the cameras. The guards will likely not leave their post, so Jayson and Johnny will once again be in charge of disabling any of the remaining guards."

"How do I disable da cameras?" Klaus asked.

"I have a few ideas," responded Quinn.

"So, we've cleared the building, disabled the guards and made security blind," I said. "You're forgetting the shroud is being held behind a couple of inches of bulletproof glass. How do we get around that?"

"I find the simplest measures are usually the most effective." Quinn explained it in such a way that said he'd known I would raise such an argument. "Explosives."

What have I gotten myself into? I put my head on the table and groaned.

****

The more Quinn went over the plan, the less enthused I was about the whole thing—which is saying an awful lot since I wasn't at all enthused to begin with.

Even though I was confident the conversation had been heard by my friends, I still texted the number Smith had given me telling him to meet me that evening. I needed a face to face with someone to tell me what exactly I should do, because for the first time, I was out of ideas.

I received a text a few minutes later simply reading: 10 o'clock.

It was only around 8p.m. As I sat, staring out the window at the darkening sky, I realized I only had two hours to figure out how I was going to get away from these idiots. Chances were, they wouldn't be asleep by then, so I'd have to sneak out another way without raising suspicion.

The rest of the team seemed to be in higher spirits—Johnny and Gina especially. It was as if they all felt their numbers had come up in the lottery. The thing was, I kept hearing Quinn promise each of them money as compensation, but I never heard a price. Would he actually pay them once he had his hands on the artifact?

Probably not.

"Yo, Carpenter!" Johnny shouted, snapping me from daze. I looked up as he sat on the bed next to me.

"Johnny, I'm in no mood to fight right now."

"Actually, if you ask me, you're in the perfect mood to fight," he said.

"And we wouldn't want to disappoint you," came his voice from behind me as well.

I didn't rise to the bait and simply turned to gaze back out the window, leaving my mind open to sense any kind of attack he might mount against me, just in case.

"I don't get you," Johnny pressed on. I felt him pull his double back into himself. "Ya act all self-righteous, pretending to be a hero, a leader an' a hundred other things, but when it comes down to it, you're still here wit' us other freaks, tryin' to steal some crusty piece of cloth."

I didn't respond.

Despite my silence, Johnny continued. "Face it. You're just like the rest of us."

"I'm nothing like you!" I snarled. "You're a thief and a degenerate! You care about no one but yourself! You want the truth? You want to know why I'm here? Because Quinn manipulated my parents into sending me to this stupid place! I got no offers for money or riches—only threats. Satisfied?"

The outburst had drawn the attention of Klaus, Jayson and Gina. All three were now staring at me and Johnny. One quick mental nudge and all of them went back to their own activities.

Johnny looked away, finding something interesting to stare at in the corner of the room. "That's where we have somethin' in common." His tone had changed, no anger in his voice which I was used to, only sadness. "He caught us on a train, like you did. But he wasn't satisfied with getting his bag back. He nearly killed me an' Gina, but at the last second, let us go. I thought we'd gotten off clean, but a coupl'a days later, he showed up and told us we could either help him and get more money we'd ever dreamed of, or he would finish the job."

He was telling the truth. Maybe Quinn had threatened all of us in some way or another. Maybe I had more allies on this mission than I thought.

If I could sway Johnny, I would get Gina too. So, I continued on, trying to understand a little more about the man in front of me. "You can be a good guy you know. You don't have to resort to stealing. With your gifts, you can help a lot of people."

"These aren't gifts, Carpenter," he told me. "When we were little, me and Gina didn't have many friends. So, it was us. But when I was five or six—I don't remember exactly—we were playing out in our yard when another me showed up. It was great. We had a bunch of fun. I didn't realize it at the time but it was my own need for a friend that made me split myself."

I was going to mention he had probably always had that power, but I didn't want to lose him now, so I remained quiet while he continued.

"We did that for years. And I got better and better at it, until I was able to make two, three, then four copies of myself. At the same time, Gina was discovering she could make herself invisible. At first she was only able to do it with her body, but as she practiced, she could make her clothes, and then eventually me disappear too.

"We kept the secret from our parents for years, until we were like ten years old. That's when it happened." His mind retreated as he was seeing a very traumatic memory from his past. "I... I can't..."

I would have told him it was all right, and he didn't have to tell me, but it was something I needed to know. So, instead, I concentrated on his thoughts and grabbed onto the memory until I could see exactly what he was seeing.

I was in a backyard, it was nice and big, with a swingset and a treehouse. The treehouse was at least fifteen feet off the ground, with an old wooden ladder reaching up to it. A high fence surrounded the yard and on the other side all I could see were trees. Wherever they'd grown up, Johnny and Gina didn't have any neighbors.

The house they'd apparently lived in was old, but well maintained. As a matter of fact, the house appeared to have recently gotten a fresh coat of paint. All in all, looking at this, I would have said the twins grew up in a typical household.

A scream from the treehouse caught my attention and I spun to face it. From out of the tiny door game a little girl, wearing a light colored sun-dress and her dark hair in pigtails. She had the same facial features as Gina, but this girl was much younger and her hair was only one color—brown. She carried a tiny clear plastic gun in her hand as she ran out onto the treehouse's platform.

The scream was followed by wild laughter as the girl spun and fired several spurts of water at the young boy chasing her out. There was no doubt in my mind this was Johnny. He looked almost exactly the same, though the current version had a few more pounds and facial hair. He wore a pair of shorts and a Ninja Turtle t-shirt. He too carried a clear plastic gun.

"I got you!" Little Gina shouted. "You're dead."

Little Johnny paused his pursuit long enough to look down at the wet spot on his shirt where Gina had "shot" him. "Did not!" he shouted and then fired water at her.

"Stop cheating!" Little Gina yelled.

"Would you two stop fighting," a calm and loving voice said.

I spun to where the voice was coming from. I hadn't noticed her before, a young looking woman, even younger than my mom, stood near the house pulling clothes out of a basket and hanging them on a clothesline. The woman had light hair like Johnny flowing down her back, stopping about six inches past her shoulders. She was a lovely looking woman.

"But ma," Little Gina whined from the railing of the treehouse. "I got him and he's supposed to be dead."

"I don't want you two playing like that anyway. Now both of you get down here and wash up for lunch." Even as she chided the two children, she still wore a pleasant expression on her face.

"Aww, ma," Little Johnny said. "Just five more minutes!"

"Pleeeeeease," Little Gina added.

The woman shook her head. "All right, five more minutes."

The two kids cheered then went back to their play-battle.

Johnny fired the first shot and got Gina right in the chest, a wet spot formed right where her heart was.

"I got you!"

"I'm wearing a bullet-proof vest." Gina said as she fired a retaliatory shot.

"No fair!" Johnny insisted.

He charged at her screaming, but playfully, not angrily. Gina stepped back, but her foot caught on an uneven board of the treehouse and she stumbled backward falling over the rail toward the ground.

Both Johnny and his mother screamed, "No!" at the same time as Little Gina tumbled toward the Earth.

On instinct, I tried to get a mental hold on her and prevent her from falling, but it was a memory, and I could do nothing to change it.

As it turns out, I didn't have to. Underneath the falling girl, a copy of Johnny appeared, his arms already outstretched to catch her. It was only a split second, but the girl fell into his arms, and was safely placed on the ground.

I breathed a sigh of relief.

Their mother, however, did no such thing. She stood by the clothesline, completely shocked by first seeing her daughter fall headfirst toward the ground and then having a copy of her son suddenly appear and catch her.

Looking at her, I could tell she was replaying the last few seconds over and over again in her mind.

Johnny's copy disappeared and the real boy quickly descended the ladder to stand next to his sister.

Across the yard, mother and children looked at each other, not knowing what to do or say. Johnny was the first to make any kind of movement. He took a step toward his mother. "Ma, it's okay."

But as Johnny took a step, his mother retreated. Without reading her mind, it was apparent she was suddenly terrified of her son.

"Mommy," Gina tried, also advancing on her mother, "I'm fine. And look, I can do something too."

Gina disappeared for a second, and as soon as she did their mother tried both to scream and to take in a breath of air at the same time. Then she started breathing very quickly— hyperventilating really—until her cheeks turned a deep crimson.

Gina reappeared. "Mommy?" she asked.

"Ma?" Little Johnny looked like he was about to cry.

Suddenly, their mother's eyes rolled up into the back of her head and she collapsed on the ground.

"NO!" Johnny yelled as he ran toward her. He never got there. The memory faded away and was quickly replaced by another.

They were inside a hospital. Little Gina and Johnny were both sitting on a plastic bench in the waiting room. They were both alone. Neither talked, and neither cried, but they looked on the verge of doing both.

A large man, who had dark hair like Gina, barged into the room like a madman. His wide eyes and slack jaw told the whole story. All he was concerned about right now was his wife and kids.

A doctor, ran into the room following the man. "Mr. Jackson?"

The man didn't respond to the doctor at first, he wildly scanned the room until he found his children. Once he saw them, and saw they were okay, he let out a long breath, then still wild-eyed, turned toward the doctor.

"I'm Dr. Steinberg," he said. "I'm supervising your wife's treatment."

"What happened?" His voice came out like a croak. "She was fine when I left for work this morning."

"You're wife suffered from a severe aneurysm," the doctor informed him. "It was probably due to some kind of shock or extreme emotional distress. It has led to some hemorrhaging in the brain. We're doing our best to stop the bleeding, but..." The doctor's voice trailed off. He wasn't at all eager to deliver the bad news.

"Tell me, doc," he said. "Please."

The doctor sighed. "It doesn't look good. At best, your wife will come out of this with mild brain damage, at worst..."

"She'll die," Mr. Jackson finished.

"I'm sorry," Dr. Steinberg said. "We're doing all we can. If you'd like to wait here with your children, I'll keep you informed with our progress."

"Can I see her?" he asked, already knowing the answer.

He shook his head. "She's in surgery now. We need to stop the hemorrhage as soon as possible."

The doctor left. Mr. Jackson's knee began to buckle and for a moment, I thought he would faint as well. But he put his hand on the wall and braced himself long enough to prevent it. Once he was calm, he looked at his children.

"What happened?" he asked them.

Little Gina was the first to look up. "It was an accident," she said.

"I know, honey," he said, sitting with them. His voice was barely above a whisper. "I know."

"I fell out of the treehouse, and Johnny used his power to catch me."

Her father looked at her, wondering what she was talking about.

"I'm sorry, Dad," Johnny said. "I didn't know what to do. Gina was falling and I didn't want her to get hurt, so, I made a copy and caught her before she landed."

"Then mom fainted," Gina added.

Their father was as shocked as their mother was. I was waiting for his response, but I never got to see it as the scene shifted again.

They were at their mother's funeral, watching the casket sink into the ground. Then back at home, where Johnny's father sat on the couch, crying into his hands. The well maintained yard and house deteriorated, the lawn overgrown, the paint on the siding peeling, the treehouse and swingset rotting.

Johnny and Gina's father never smiled in any of the memories I saw. He grew more and more angry with each one. Until I watched as he beat an unsuspecting twelve-year-old version of Johnny to a pulp.

"Oh my God," I said. And both Johnny and I were snapped back into the present.

I looked directly into Johnny's eyes. A flash of anger passed through them, but it quickly faded only to be replaced by despair. "You saw that?"

"Yeah," I said. "I'm so sorry. I didn't know."

"Well, once my father started hitting me, he never stopped," Johnny said. "I could handle it. In a way, I felt like I almost deserved it. But when he started on Gina…" His voice trailed off.

"You didn't kill him, did you?" I asked.

His head snapped up, and he stared straight at me. Again, I saw the heat of anger burn in his eyes, but the fire quickly died. "No. Of course not. He's my father after all. We ran away, and never looked back."

And you thought you have problems, the voice in my head said.

Shut up, I told the voice.

The story explained a great deal about Johnny, especially why he was so angry all the time. But it still didn't tell one thing. "Why don't you use your powers to help people though?"

Any sadness he'd been feeling, at least on the exterior, vanished in that instant. "Not that it's any of ya business, but saving people isn't exactly profitable. We did what we needed to survive. The world isn't exactly fair to a coupl'a teenagers on their own."

Even though that's what he kept telling himself, I felt the real reason lurking in the depths of his mind. He had tried to save someone once, and it ended in disaster. He wasn't about to go do it again.

He got up then, deciding I'd learned enough about him. "Tell anyone about that, and I'll kill you." He started for the door.

Before he made it two steps I said loud enough for him to hear, "Johnny."

He looked back over his shoulder.

"I know I'm not your favorite person, but if you ever need to talk…" I let the end of the statement in the air. He knew what I was saying.

He gave an almost imperceptible nod, then continued for the door. Walking out of the room, he slammed the door shut behind him.

CHAPTER 16
FOLLOWING A LEAD

Before I knew it, it was time for me to sneak out. Johnny hadn't come back yet and Gina was worried about him. Apparently it wasn't like him to wander off somewhere without telling her where he was going. So, I suggested we go out to look for him.

"Okay," she agreed.

"We'll be back in a few," we told Klaus and Jayson, who were too busy playing some stupid card game I didn't care to understand.

We went down to the street, and once again I waved goodbye to the man behind the desk, who happily waved us off without so much as a word. Once we were outside, I suggested we split up.

"I'll go up this way," I said, pointing in the direction I needed to go to meet Smith.

"Then I'll go this way," she said, pointing in the opposite direction.

"Meet back in a half an hour?" I asked.

She nodded, then walked off.

I thought for a second, it was nighttime and we were in an unfamiliar city. It might not be such a good idea to go wandering. Despite the things she'd put me through, I really didn't want her to get hurt. "Hey, Gina."

"Yeah?"

"I think you should do this invisible," I said. "You never know what might be lurking in the shadows."

She nodded, and then vanished.

Surprisingly, I felt better about myself after suggesting that. Not thinking about the girl any further, I ran up the street to the small grove of trees I'd met Smith in earlier in the week.

The place had an entirely different feeling than it had during the daytime. In the shadow of the building, and on a narrow street without any lights, the area was nearly pitch black. Only a small amount of light from the stars and moon trickled down through the trees onto the ground. I could tell I wasn't alone in the small yard, because there was a void, hiding among the trees.

"Smith?" My voice squeaked.

"I'm here, Agent Carpenter."

"Can you come out where I can see you?"

"Not this time," he said.

That was odd. He agreed to meet with me, then wouldn't even face me? Why even bother then?

"I have some information and I need to know what you want me to do."

"The mission stands, Agent Carpenter," he responded. "You are to follow the orders of Quinn and steal the shroud. Once it is in your possession, your team will move in and extract it."

"What about me? Once I give up the artifact, Quinn is going to know something's up."

"You will not be taken out of play until we are sure Quinn is out of commission."

"Gee, thanks."

"You will follow orders, Agent Carpenter."

"But there has to be another way," I argued. "I don't think I'll be able to go through with this."

"You will because you have to. There are more important things than your own moral values. The entire world is at stake."

I don't know why I even bothered. Smith wasn't the one to give me any advice. He was all about doing things by the book and didn't care one way or the other about the people he hurt. All he cared about was the mission at hand.

"Fine!" I nearly shouted. "Whatever you say."

"If we're done here," he said. "I have more pressing matters to attend to."

Even though I couldn't truly feel him, I could feel the void retreating further into the shadows. I don't know why, but I had an urge to follow him. Call it my morbid curiosity, or call it intuition, but instead of going back to the hotel, I flew up, landing on the rooftop. I saw him emerge from the trees and head down a tunnel. I followed him from above, and saw him emerge on the other side into another large stone courtyard, not unlike the one in front of the cathedral.

Once he stepped out into the well lit courtyard, I could see he was wearing a long black trenchcoat and dark hat. I shook my head at his complete obviousness. He might as well as screamed he was a spy.

I stayed at the edge of the roof I was on until he completely crossed the courtyard and wandered down a street—Via Roma. I followed him for nearly twenty minutes, staying out of sight high above him as he seemingly wandered the streets aimlessly. He would walk up the street and then cross over to the other side, and then go back in the other direction, only to turn and head back the way he'd originally been going.

He was checking to see if he had a tail. He did, but I was pretty sure he didn't know I was there.

Eventually, he turned down another narrow road, and then entered a bar. I waited a minute to make sure he wasn't about to exit and then floated down to the sidewalk.

A small, unlit sign read, "Bar di Valencia". Unlike many bars in the United States that try to hide what goes on inside, this bar had a wide open window letting everyone see in, or out, of the place. I stayed out of sight of the window, only venturing to peek around the corner. There were few people inside, maybe ten or twelve.

It looked like what I'd picture a bar to look like—not that I'd ever been inside one before—tables scattered about the room, with a main "bar" counter in the rear. Several televisions played various sporting events around the room. No one was really watching any of the televisions. They were more concerned with their own conversations. Three people were at the bar, four if you included the bartender.

As I surveyed the area, I saw one of the people sitting there was Johnny. His back was to me, but his tangled dirty blonde hair and grungy looking clothes was all I needed to see to know it was him. He took a shot or something and slammed the glass on the bar, pointing to it. The bartender quickly filled the glass again.

As Johnny was intent on drinking away his memories, a fourth person approached the bar. He'd shed the trenchcoat and hat and was now only wearing the black suit I was used to seeing him in. He approached a man sitting three stools to Johnny's left and began talking.

I needed to hear what he was saying, but with the thought inhibitor, I couldn't get into his head. The man he was talking to, however, wore no such device. It didn't take much for me to get inside his head. Once the connection was made, I could hear everything the two of them were saying.

"…interesting city. Once the sun goes down it seems like only the unsavory element sticks to the streets."

The man seemed to consider what Smith was saying, then took a swig from a bottle labeled "Birra Messina", which I assumed to be a beer. "What do you want?"

"Just to talk," Smith said. "I understand you have a passion for antiques."

Being inside his head, I could tell the comment had made the man incredibly nervous. However, he made no show of it, sipping from the bottle again. "Really? And I wonder who told you that."

"It's not important," Smith said. "I'm here to warn you, stay away from Turin Cathedral. It can only end badly for you."

"What are you? Some kind of cop?"

"Yeah, something like that," Smith said.

The man looked up as Smith smiled. It was the kind of evil grin Quinn had whenever a particularly sinister thought crossed his mind.

"Listen," he said. "I can go wherever I want, whenever I want. And some cop isn't going to stop me."

"What is your interest in the Shroud of Turin anyway?" Smith said without so much as a second's hesitation.

"Like you said, I have a passion for antiques."

My danger sense flared. I wanted to warn this man away, but I needed to know what was going on.

"No, there is something more than that. You know what the shroud can do. You know how it works. But I am here to tell you, the only way you will lay a finger on the shroud is if you work for us."

The man emptied the bottle and slid it across the bar. The bartender, quick as he was, caught the bottle before it shattered on the ground. "Another please," the man said. Then he turned on Smith. "I don't take well to threats. But I'll let this one go. Whoever you are, and whoever you work for, you can rest easy. I have no intention of stealing the shroud. I plan on analyzing it. And I've gone through all the proper channels, only to be denied time and time again."

"Yeah, the Vatican can be like that sometimes," Smith said. He chuckled. "But I really don't care if you plan on stealing it or not. You're not to go near it. Understand?"

The man got his beer and took a swig from the fresh bottle. "No," he said simply.

"No?"

"I don't understand. I've done nothing wrong, I plan on doing nothing wrong, and here you are harassing me and sending me empty threats. Go away before I hurt you." The anger in this man was beginning to rise, but I could tell he wasn't really going to do anything to hurt Smith. The same couldn't be said for the Agent however.

"No." Smith said and he pulled out his gun. "If you're not going to comply with my wishes, then you have to be taken out of the equation."

The man, didn't even react to the gun being pointed at him. It was like he believed Smith wouldn't do anything to hurt him.

But, the man was wrong. Smith fired the gun. BANG!

The bullet bounced off the man's cheek and ricocheted into a couple of bottles behind the bar.

The man sighed, but then turned angrily toward Smith. "You shot me in the face! Are you crazy?"

"You're a meta," Smith said, as if bullets bounced off people he shot everyday. "That explains a lot."

"Can we get back to the part where you shot me in the face?"

Something was wrong. I pulled back out of the man's head and reentered my own.

A gun was fired in a seemingly quiet bar, and the only person who reacted to it was Johnny, who had jumped off his stool and stumbled drunkly into the wall.

I reached out, trying to sense anyone else in the bar, and though there were nearly a dozen people, I only sensed two. Johnny and the man whose brain I'd been in. The rest were Agents.

Oh crap! This wasn't good, quite the opposite. This was very very bad. Johnny was in there with a bunch of Agents. If even one recognized him he'd be arrested in a second.

I had to get him out of there.

As my mind was forming some sort of a plan that didn't get Johnny captured or killed in the process, a hand slapped down hard on my shoulder.

Instinctively, I pushed the hand away and threw a full force mental jab at my assailant. If this was an Agent, trying to keep me in line, I would make them pay dearly before I went quietly.

Quickly I spun to face the attacker only to find a stunned Klaus holding his hands up in surrender. "I didn't mean to frighten you."

"What the hell are you doing here?" I whispered.

"Vent for jog."

I rolled my eyes. The boy had probably been following me. I wondered how much he knew. I had to think up something quickly before he suspected anything was going on.

"Look, Johnny's in there and there are a few Agents in the bar. We have to get him out of there." It wasn't a lie, which made it easier to tell.

Klaus peered through the window as I had, and seemed to survey the situation. His eyes momentarily went wide with shock. I supposed he saw just how tough a time we'd have extracting our teammate from the place.

"You should take control of him, and walk him outside."

It was a logical idea. One I could have come up with given a few more seconds' thought. I hated the boy for coming up with it first. "Okay, but watch my back. When I'm in his head, I can't see what's going on around me." Not the kind of thing I wanted to admit to a potential enemy, but it was better than letting an Agent sneak up on me.

Concentrating, I entered Johnny's mind. Once inside, I was greeted by a strange sensation. I was seeing through Johnny's eyes, but I couldn't see straight. When I tried to move his legs forward, they were sluggish and almost unresponsive. It was taking most of my focus to keep the boy upright. The blurred and out of focus images coming through the connection from Johnny's mind to mine, was also causing the contents of my stomach to start bubbling. I could feel my own cheeks turning green as I willed Johnny to step forward. I moved Johnny like a puppet, step by step through the bar, avoiding the particularly large blurs I took to be tables… or Agents. I couldn't tell which. *Why would anyone willingly do this to themselves?* I mused.

It looked like I was going to get Johnny out of there successfully, but then I lost control. The room began to spin and the bile in my stomach started to boil again. When I thought I would lose control and spew the contents of my stomach on the ground, Johnny emptied his.

My link with him instantly broke and through the dizzy haze left in my head, I gazed through the window to watch Johnny finish throwing up on an Agent, and then pass out at her feet.

Revulsion filled the woman's eyes as she looked at the mess left on her suit. She lifted her arm as if she wanted to reach for her gun but didn't wish to touch the chunks of vomit dripping down her front. As if was, shooting him probably wouldn't have done much anyway, the boy was already down and out—no longer a threat.

Unfortunately, the incident had also drawn much of the attention of the other Agents in the bar. Most of the others converged on Johnny's prone form. I'd made the situation worse.

Luckily, while I was coming up with another plan, Klaus was already taking steps to get our comrade out of there.

He grabbed a handful of pebbles and then swung the door open. Then, standing inside the doorway he flicked each pebble in quick succession at each of the Agents in the bar. Each tiny stone hit its mark on the side of the neck, below the jaw-line, exactly where Klaus had intended. One by one, the Agents fell to the floor, unconscious. It happened so fast, I barely had the time to process it.

The only one who didn't fall was the man whose mind I'd been inside. He simply stood for a moment, dazed, before running through the rear of the bar. *Who was he, anyway?*

"Get him before they vake up."

"But how?"

"Pressure point," he said pointing to the same spot on his own neck. "Hit vith enough force, and dhey fall asleep. I show you zometime."

"Okay." I was still not sure exactly how he'd done it.

"Now go, dhey vill vake in a few minutes."

I did, entering the bar and stepping over the knocked out Agents. I reached Johnny, and got nauseous when I saw him covered with much of the same colored substance as the Agent he'd thrown up on. I was definitely not touching him.

Mentally grabbing him, I intended to float him out the door. I could easily carry him like that all the way back to the hotel. However, another thought crossed my mind first and I lowered him back, much to Klaus' dismay. The boy was really afraid of me getting caught. It was sweet.

Smith's body still laid by the bar, right where he'd been standing a minute before. This was probably going to be my only chance to see how much I could trust the M.H.D.A..

Finding the near-microscopic thought-inhibitor, I crushed it with a mental push. Then, reaching out to his unconscious mind, I sifted through all of his thoughts, bringing the ones for his current assignment to the forefront.

I didn't like what I saw.

I heard a groan from behind the bar. The fake bartender was waking up. As quickly as I could, I mentally lifted Johnny off the floor and floated him through the door, running behind him. By the time any of them fully awoke, we would be gone.

Klaus ran beside me, hardly showing any effort to keep up, while I was using all the strength I had. Johnny hovered, following only a couple of behind.

"Vhat vere you doing?" he asked, not breaking a single stride. "You could have been caught."

Again, my heart fluttered, knowing how much concern he had for my safety. "I had to," I told him. It wasn't a lie. "The Agent in there knows all about what we're doing. He's planning on taking the shroud from us."

I didn't add the last part—the part even I had to admit Quinn was right about. I saw an army, thousands of soldiers bred from the DNA in the shroud. All of them, taught from birth to follow orders. An army that was unstoppable.

I couldn't believe it. Just when I'd hoped I could trust them, I learn their ultimate purpose. They didn't care about stopping Quinn—or at least, not ONLY about stopping him. They wanted the artifact, probably to replace the one I inadvertently stole from them a few months ago. Imagine what they could do if they had the shroud, the spear and Quinn's chalice. They'd only need one more piece and...

It was unfathomable the destruction that army would cause. I couldn't allow it to happen. It appeared I didn't have a choice. I had to steal it. Not for Quinn, or the M.H.D.A., or even myself. Like Quinn had lied to us about: I had to steal the shroud to save the world.

CHAPTER 17
TWO WORLDS COLLIDE

After getting Johnny settled into bed and calming Gina down, I stepped out into the hall under the guise of using the bathroom and sent a text message to my boyfriend. It was probably the longest text I've ever sent.

Dont let anyone c this... must talk to u... only u... meet me @ the spot tomorrow... 7am... dont tell anyone... important!!!

If those words didn't get the point across, nothing would.

I went back in the room, to find Gina sitting at Johnny's bedside. She held his hand like a wife might hold her dying husband's. Gina's greatest fear was losing her brother. The twins had been side by side since birth. Neither knew what it was like to be alone. I really felt for her—for both of them. I didn't know what I would do if someone important to me was suddenly ripped from my life. I couldn't imagine what it would be like if the only person I loved and trusted in the world was taken.

I walked past them to get ready for bed. Since I was getting up early again, I wanted to be rested.

"Thank you, Christine," Gina said in a soft, almost imperceptible voice. "I know you don't like us very much, but..." She choked off the rest of the statement.

"Don't mention it," I said. "What I did, I would have done for anyone."

I had only meant the statement to be a humble remark, but as I said the words, every one of them rang true in my head. The more I thought about it, the more I realized, even if Quinn had been in danger, I would do anything in my power to save him. The thought both filled me with pride and disgusted me at the same time.

"He's done this before," Gina continued, turning away to face her brother. "I don't understand. Why does he have to torture himself?"

I knew the answer. He blamed himself for what happened to their mother and drinking took that pain away for a little while. But I didn't think it was something Gina needed to hear at that moment. "I don't know. But he's fine now. Let him rest."

Despite my words, Gina didn't move from his side. She was still there, watching over him as I drifted off to a restless sleep.

I dreamed that night. The world was consumed in fire, and people were dying left and right. I was in the middle of a great battle, fighting against an army of super-soldiers, plowing through legions of men and women, trying to defend their homes. I fought my hardest, but every one of the soldiers I wounded, ten more would take their place. Despite all the death they were causing, I still wouldn't kill them.

Quinn appeared behind me, waving a flag above his head like a man rallying troops. The flag had a swastika on it. "Sometimes it is necessary to take a life," he said, his voice echoing through the chaos. "You need to know your limits."

An American flag appeared over the ranks of super-soldiers, only it was different somehow. Looking at it, I knew it represented my own country, but it was like I didn't recognize it anymore, like it was tainted. The tromping sounds of boots sounded like thunder, threatening to deafen me, but there was nothing I could do to stop it.

Then my grandfather appeared, looking much younger, like he did in the photo from his journal. He wore his old army uniform, and even carried a rifle like a soldier in his time would. "Make them think you're losing, only then can you win."

And then, the world exploded, claiming everything, every life.

I woke the next morning to the noise of creaking bedsprings. Opening my eyes, I saw a shirtless Klaus sitting up in bed, getting ready for his morning jog. Next to him, still sleeping, was Johnny. Gina sat in the chair, her head slumped.

"Hey," I croaked. "Let me get dressed. I'll run with you again."

Klaus didn't say anything, but nodded and pulled on a tank top.

Trying to shake the disturbing dream from my head, I groggily sat up and rubbed the sleep from my eyes. I felt like living death. I was in no condition for a run. Luckily for me, I really had no intention of running.

I changed into a pair of shorts, not even caring if Klaus saw me or not, and pulled a t-shirt over my head. I felt the skull pendant knock around when I put the shirt on, and I unlatched the chord and took it off, setting it on top of the small table next to the bed. I didn't want anyone hearing what I was going to say to Ethan.

Then I dragged my feet to the bathroom. Going down the stairs, I met Klaus outside. He was already warming up and doing some stretches.

"You look like you are still sleeping," he said.

"I am a little, but I needed to get out of there."

He nodded and slapped me on my shoulder again. I have to admit, the jolt did wake me up a little—not enough though for my retaliating strike to connect. "I thought you were going to stop hitting me."

"Dhat vas not a hit." He slapped me on the shoulder again, this time harder. "Dhat vas."

"Ow!" I was fully awake now and rubbing what would probably be a bruise later. "Stop that!"

He smiled and did a few lunges to stretch out his legs. He was so infuriating. If he hadn't saved the day last night, I probably would have sent him flying into the side of the building.

"Let's gets started," I said.

"All right." He started running down the street in the direction of the cathedral.

"Wait!" I called. "I thought we were going to go that way."

He spun around and started running backwards. "Vee already saw dhat portion of the city. Vee see this part now."

Great. How was I going to get out of it this time?

I jogged after him. Klaus continued his backwards trot until I caught up, then he turned again and ran normally. Our sneakers smacking on the cement was the only sound to be heard in the early morning. I did a better job of keeping up with him this time. We'd past the cathedral before I felt any cramping in my legs.

When we ran past the old ruin, I looked through the fence. Ethan wasn't there yet, so I still had time to lose Klaus.

We ran another block, passing a monument that could have been for Julius Caesar. Who knew if it was or not? Pigeons covered the statue, making the Roman Emperor look like a dirty sanctuary for birds. After we went by, I decided how I would get rid of Klaus. As usual, the simplest solution was easiest.

I had the power. So, why not use it?

Keeping pace with Klaus, I reached a mental tendril out and attached it to his mind. Once inside, I gave him the impression I was keeping up with him. As long as I kept the connection with his brain, he would believe I was right there next to him.

Having the connection to his brain, I also received some residual feedback. I saw some things I hadn't intended and probably had no business knowing. However, the knowledge was essential. If I wanted to keep jogging at that moment, I wouldn't have been able to. My muscles had to physically stop moving for my brain to process what I'd seen.

I slowed my run, and let Klaus with my mental phantom continue on the path. "There's another one?" I asked to the empty street. Of course, I didn't get an answer.

He hadn't been following me last night. He'd been going to the bar for another reason, and I was sure it centered around the man Smith was questioning.

Looking at my watch, I saw it was already a couple of minutes after seven. I jogged back the way I came, passing the pigeon covered Caesar statue on the way to the old amphitheater ruins. All the while, all I could think about was, *What am I going to do about Klaus?*

I entered the gates this time, and saw Ethan standing in the same spot I last saw him in. He looked as tired as I felt, like he hadn't slept a wink last night. I approached, looking around to make sure we were alone.

When I leaned in to give him a kiss, he pushed me away. "I don't have any time. As far as Abby and the others know, I'm taking a toilet break. What's the emergency?"

Though a little put off by the lack of affection, I simply went into why I'd told him to meet me. "No one can know I met you. Not Peter, not Savanah and especially not Abby."

He nodded. "Okay."

"We need to get away from the M.H.D.A.. The Agents want to use the shroud to create an army. I saw it in Smith's mind. After we take the shroud from the cathedral, he's going to take it from us. Then, he's going to start the process all over again. A brand new Project: Hercules, only with thousands of soldiers."

If Ethan was shocked by it, it didn't show on his face or in his thoughts. "So, what do you want to do? Hop the next plane back to Pennsylvania?" The words were angry and frustrated.

"What's the problem?" I asked.

"You do this all the time. We can't trust Abby, then we can, then we can't again. Which is it, Chris?"

"Right now? I guess we can't. I don't know. At least, not right now. If she knows about what Smith is planning on doing, then we can't trust her. But if she's as in the dark as the rest of us…"

"Chris, you know I love you. You know I'll follow you to the ends of the Earth on any insane mission to save the world. But you have to make up your mind. We're either with the M.H.D.A., or we're not."

"We're on our own team, Ethan. We have to do the right thing, and helping the M.H.D.A. create a super-powered army definitely qualifies as the *wrong* thing."

"What about Quinn? Are we still not trusting him either?"

"Definitely not. I still can't read his mind, but I can tell he's lying."

He sighed and shook his head. "I've got your back, Chris. So, whatever you need me to do, say it."

"On Monday, we're stealing the shroud. Smith has already told me he plans on moving in and taking it once we have it in our possession. I think he plans on waiting until we bring it back to Quinn so he can kill two birds with one stone. We have to figure out how to get rid of the shroud after we steal it and before Smith comes to claim it."

"And how are we going to do that?" Ethan asked.

"Yes, how do vee do dhat?" came the heavy German accent from behind me.

Klaus came through the gate, to face the two of us. It was exactly what I'd hoped to prevent. No one from Quinn's team could know I had my friends here to help me.

Ethan must have known who the boy was, because he looked about ready to attack. I jumped in front of him at the same time sending thoughts of reassurance to him.

"Don't worry, Ethan," I said. "We can trust him… I think."

"He better prove it, and quick," said Ethan. "Quinn can't find out about us."

"Well, why don't we let Klaus explain?" I gave Klaus a challenging look. "What were you doing at the bar last night?"

For a moment, Klaus looked as if he were going to come up with an excuse, but then decided he had probably already been caught. He crossed his arms over his chest and smiled. "I vould say I cannot tell you, but it seems I am not the only one playing double-agent."

"What is he talking about, Chris?" Ethan asked.

I shushed my boyfriend and motioned for Klaus to continue. "Who are you working for?"

"The German Government," he answered. "You?"

"Would you believe me if I said I didn't know?" Looking at his face, I could tell he wouldn't. "I'm supposed to be working with the M.H.D.A., but after what I found out last night, I'm not entirely sure who I should be working for."

Klaus looked over my shoulder, as if what I'd said didn't matter. He was staring at Ethan, who returned the stare with a none-too-cordial gesture.

"Who is your friend?" Klaus asked.

"Oh, right." I introduced Klaus to Ethan and vice-versa. Neither moved toward each other to shake hands, but at least Ethan gave a flippant nod. "Ethan's on my team—my real team."

"So, vhy vere you really at the bar last night?" Klaus asked, changing subjects on me again.

"I was tailing Agent Smith," I explained. "I had a quick meeting with him and something didn't seem right. When I got to the bar, I saw Johnny inside, and another person. Smith shot him and the bullet bounced right off."

"Yes, dhat vould be Kommandeur Dresner. He is my superior. I vas zupposed to meet him last evening."

"But you never got the chance," I finished.

"Nein."

"So, your little trick with the pebbles was as much to save him as it was to save Johnny?"

He nodded.

"This keeps getting better and better," Ethan muttered. "As if we don't have enough problems, now we have to deal with some rogue German spy too."

"It might not be as bad as you think," I said, trying my best to keep Ethan calm. "We don't know where he stands yet." I turned back to Klaus, who hadn't moved so much as a millimeter since he'd snuck up on us. "In other words, Klaus, what do you intend to do with the shroud once we get it?"

"My mission vas to prevent Codename: Quintus from obtaining the artifact. If I cannot prevent the theft, dhan I am to bring it to my government."

I attached my mind to Klaus' once again as I asked the next question. It wasn't his response but what he thought which would tell me if I could trust him or not. "What is your plan for the shroud once you have it?"

His response was almost immediate. "I don't know." The synapses flared to life and they showed me his words were absolutely true.

"And can I trust you to keep my secret if I keep yours?" I asked.

Again, no pause before he responded. "Yah." Again, his mind said the words were true. I could trust him at least that much.

Ethan grabbed my shoulder. "How can you believe him? You've known him what… a week?"

"I seem to remember telling you my secret the second time we talked."

"All I'm saying is you can't believe him because he says you can. I'm trying to protect you."

"I know. But I read his mind," I whispered, so Klaus wouldn't hear about the mental invasion. "Plus, he saved my butt last night with Smith and the Agents. He's okay. I promise."

"And how did he do that?" Ethan insisted.

"His power is," I paused, not knowing exactly how to explain what Klaus' power was, "super-accuracy?"

"Like he could split an arrow in half by shooting it with another arrow?"

"Yeah, I guess."

Ethan laughed, looking over my shoulder at Klaus, who still hadn't moved. "That's not even a real super-power!"

"Ethan, he took out an entire group of Agents with a handful of pebbles."

"It's still a stupid thing to say is your power. Why would Quinn even be interested in—"

Ethan's words were cut off as something smacked into his forehead. In the last second, he'd tried to move, but he wasn't fast enough. Let me repeat that—my boyfriend, Ethan Everett, the fastest boy in the world, couldn't move out of the way of the pebble Klaus shot at him.

"OW!" he shouted, rubbing his forehead. "What did you do that for?"

"To teach you," Klaus responded. "Keep your mouth shut."

"Okay," I said, getting between them again before there was a real fight. "Ethan, we need to go. All three of us are going to be missed if we don't get back soon. We can't raise suspicion."

"Right," Ethan agreed. He never took his eyes off Klaus.

Then, Ethan did something completely unexpected. He kissed me. But it wasn't like any kiss we'd ever had before. This one was long, passionate, and angry. He was almost violent in the way he assaulted my mouth, but I will admit it wasn't unpleasant. It was like my boyfriend was taking charge and...

He was marking his territory—making sure Klaus got the message I was his and pretty much off limits. Once the realization came to mind, I pushed Ethan away, not at all thrilled with his behavior.

"Go, Ethan! I'll text you later. We need to come up with a plan."

"I love you." He said, then was gone before I could tell him I loved him too.

I turned to Klaus. The boy still didn't look like he'd moved a muscle. His arms remained folded across his chest.

How had he thrown that pebble so quickly Ethan couldn't move out of the way?

I knew I could trust Klaus, but I wasn't sure how much I could trust his team. For all I knew, Commander Dresner wanted the same exact thing Smith wanted. If that was the case, then Klaus was as untrustworthy as the rest of them.

It would have been really nice to have another ally. So, I needed to find out exactly where Dresner stood. And there was only one way to find out.

"Next time you go to meet your commander," I said. "I want in."

"I meet vith him tonight."

CHAPTER 18
THE GERMAN KOMMANDEUR

Now that I knew what Klaus was, I couldn't help but be worried. Klaus didn't have a thought inhibitor like the Agents had, and from the ease at which I was able to read his mind, I knew it would be no trouble for Quinn to do the same. What if he found out what Klaus was?

What if he already knew?

I dismissed the idea. If Quinn knew Klaus was really working against him, he would probably get rid of him as quickly as possible. Unfortunately, "as quickly as possible," probably meant death.

Johnny slept most of the day, after waking up briefly about noon with what I expected was a major hangover.

The day passed quickly, with all of us pretty much hanging around. I spent most of my day talking with Klaus, deciding it was nice to finally be able to trust someone on the team. We took a couple of walks away from everyone, in which we talked about how we got roped into this whole mess.

I found out Klaus was actually eighteen and had just graduated high school, but had been an operative since he was only fourteen. The German Government Agency he was a part of was known as The Vril Society, or V.S. for short. Essentially, they were like the M.H.D.A., but with a more, shall we say, unethical past.

"Zome of the original members of the V.S. included Adolph Hitler, Alfred Rosenberg and Heinrich Himmler. Dhey believed dhey were descendents of an alien race of beings far superior to man. Dhey believed the Gods of Old…"

"Gods of Old?" I asked.

"Zeus, Jupiter, Odin, even the Christian God. The V.S. believed dhey vere actually aliens and had passed dheir genetic code down to a select group of people who vere meant to rule over all the rest."

"Let me guess, the Aryans."

"Yah."

"And I thought Hitler was psychotic before I knew he believed in aliens."

"You mean you don't?"

"No."

"Zo, vhat you're saying is that people can have super-abilities, but dhere can't be aliens? Very interesting."

Okay, he had me there—I can admit at least that much. But that didn't change the fact the whole belief of alien ancestors was completely ludicrous.

"Fine, maybe I'm wrong," I conceded. "But let's get back to this whole V.S. business. You don't seem to want to dominate the world, so why on Earth would you join the Vril in the first place?"

"Christine," he said, shaking his head. "You don't understand. Vee call ourselves the Vril because vee are the Vril. You and I, Johnny and Gina, Jayson and Quintus, even your boyfriend. Vee are vhat the V.S. is all about."

"So, we're aliens?" I asked. If my eyes could have rolled all the way into the back of my head, they would have. This conversation just jumped out of the pool of ludicrous and into the pool of "holy-hell-insane".

He shook his head again. "Vee are the superior race."

I raised my eyebrows. I certainly didn't feel superior.

"Okay, I think I understand now. The Vril were started by a group of people who believed they were greater than everyone but weren't, and was continued by a group of people who really are greater than everyone."

"That is right."

Now, it would have been at that point I would have walked away from him. Anyone having delusions of grandeur was a person to stay away from. I'd learned that the hard way—Tommy, Eddie, and even I had fallen victim to the power trip our powers could cause. But even as he talked of his superiority over the rest of humanity, he didn't give the sense he actually felt that way. I had the feeling that while the Vril had started as a force of evil, it had morphed over the years to be a force of good.

We talked for a while longer before finally going back to the room to join the others for dinner.

Quinn once again went over our plan for storming the cathedral come Monday, and everyone listened intently. When I voiced an objection to the plan again, Johnny remained quiet. He never actually said anything, but I knew it was his way of thanking me for saving his butt last night.

When dinner was finished, we went back to the hotel. Klaus was going to get a text on his phone when it was time to meet. So, he and I sat in the room and waited. He was acting completely normal. I on the other hand, couldn't help but fidget all evening. It was nerve racking knowing we could be caught at any moment. It was bad enough I had to protect my secret. Now, I had to protect his as well.

It was about 9:30 when his phone beeped. He didn't even pull it out of his pocket, but nodded in my direction. The meaning was clear—*It's time.*

We exited the room, telling the others we were going on another walk. None of them even cared.

We closed the door and started down the hallway to the stairs, but were stopped after two steps. "And where do you two think you're going? It's late."

Turning, we both faced Quinn. My stress level spiked. If I had a full bladder at that moment, it would have emptied itself. He'd caught us. He knew. We were in deep trouble. Who knew what he would do to us?

"Ve're out for a valk," Klaus explained as calm as could be.

Quinn took a step toward us, his eyes narrowed. "You two have been spending an awful lot of time in each other's company. This is the third time you've wandered off today."

Oh crap! He definitely knew. He'd been watching, maybe even following, us. Now, he was going to eliminate us for trying to foil his plan.

I felt him try and reach out tiny mental fingers to pluck thoughts from Klaus' mind. He didn't get the chance thankfully, because my mental hand swatted them away. He winced but then turned to me and smiled.

"Fine, keep your secrets, Ms. Carpenter." He strode toward us, covering the space in a few steps. When he leaned in, and whispered in my ear, I expected to hear some kind of threat. Instead, his words were soft, but firm. "Let me remind you, before you do something you will regret—you do have a boyfriend, Ms. Carpenter, and guilt can be a terrible thing."

As he stood straight and walked passed us, climbing down the stairs, I thought about arguing. After all, who was he to think he could meddle in my love life. Not that anything was really going on between me and Klaus—I didn't like how he was so presumptuous.

However, if Quinn thought we were an item, it did give us the perfect cover story for sneaking off every now and then—like tonight, for instance. So, instead, I said nothing until he was well out of earshot.

"Can you imagine? Me and you? What was he thinking?"

"Yah," Klaus said, nervously rubbing the back of his neck. "Vhat vas he thinking?"

****

It took us nearly thirty minutes to walk to the where we were to meet Commander Dresner. We walked along this long road through a park called Giardini Reali (Real Garden?). I really wished my powers would translate the stupid signs too and not only speech. There were many trees here, but it didn't feel enclosed like the courtyard where I'd met with Smith. Flowering bushes and other plants dotted the landscape, making the place feel like paradise—even in the dark.

We trekked hand-in-hand through the park, wanting to look like a couple taking a quiet walk rather than two government agents on their way to a rendezvous with an officer.

Anyway, we finally reached a bridge that passed over either a river or a canal—I wasn't entirely sure. It was called the Dora Riparia—my previous complaint still stands.

We walked over the bridge, the only noise I heard was the water calmly flowing beneath our feet. Thinking about what Quinn thought about us, I couldn't help but think of how romantic this stroll would be if I was actually doing it with someone I cared for. Looking over at Klaus, and seeing how he avoided my gaze, I could tell his thoughts mirrored mine.

When he finally did turn to look at me, he smiled. Maybe it was the light, maybe it was the fact we were still holding hands, maybe it was quiet meandering of the river—hell, maybe it was all of the above—but my heart fluttered.

Okay, so I'll admit, he was good looking, and despite his incessant need to hit me, he was a really nice guy. He was definitely a guy I could go for if the circumstances were at all different. But, I was in love with Ethan, and no matter what, I wasn't about to fall for this buff, dreamy, foreign guy.

He squeezed my hand a little tighter, and when he did, I pulled it from his grasp. We were almost at our destination anyway, so we really didn't need to keep up the romantic-couple pretense any longer.

When we reached the opposite end of the bridge, we made a left and stopped in a small clearing next to the Dora Riparia. Cars lined both sides of the road, and a few lights were still lit in the apartments across the street. Where we stood, however, looked like a place to park more cars. It was probably a place where people stopped to take a stroll along the riverbank, but at night, all the spots were vacant.

We were only standing for a few minutes, leaning against an iron fence and watching the water, when a car pulled up. The headlights washed over us, temporarily blinding us with their brightness. I couldn't begin to tell you what kind of car it was, but it was silver and didn't have a straight line on its entire frame. There was a small blue shield on the front of the car that read Lancia. The engine stopped and the light cut off, leaving us in the dark for a second. As I blinked the blue and red spots out of my eyes, a man stepped out of the vehicle.

I recognized him immediately as the man from last night. Tonight he wore a black leather jacket, with tight black jeans. His hair was slicked back and he wore a pair of sunglasses that probably cost more than my house.

He jerked his head down the tree lined path along the river. "Let's take a walk."

He began down the path at a quicker pace than we'd been moving, but not so quick I'd have trouble keeping up. We walked, Klaus in the middle, me on the left and Commander Dresner on the right.

"I would ask what she is doing here, but after last night, I'm pretty sure you've told her everything. When are you going to learn never to fall for a pretty face?" He did have a German accent, but his English was a hundred times more clear than Klaus'. Dresner could probably pass himself off as an American with very little trouble—which was probably why I didn't think of him as a German when I was in his head last night.

"Hey, I'm in the same situation here as you," I argued. "I'm trying to prevent Quinn from getting his hands on the shroud too!"

"Really? And what do you plan on doing with the Shroud of Turin once you have it in your grasp, young lady?"

"The name's Christine, thank you very much. And I was going to ask you the same question." I didn't think it best to include the fact I was here working with the M.H.D.A., especially considering Smith shooting him last night and all.

As it turns out, it didn't matter anyway. "She is vorking for the American Agents."

"And you brought her here?" Dresner reprimanded. "They are just as dangerous as Quintus. None of them can be trusted! You're a fool, Klaus—a damned fool!"

"Look, I know you don't have to trust me," I didn't allow my voice to raise above a normal speaking level, even though I felt like shouting, "but I think we're on the same side here. I don't want the M.H.D.A. to take possession of the shroud either. I've seen what Smith plans on doing with it, and I can't allow it. So, the question is: what about you? What do you want the Shroud of Turin for?"

He stopped walking and leaned against the backside of a bench. He folded his arms and looked at me. I concentrated on his thoughts, breaking through into his head for the second time in as many days. I monitored his thoughts as he formulated his answer.

Dresner gazed at Klaus. "I can see why you like her, boy. She's got spunk."

Klaus looked like he was going to argue, but instead shrugged and turned away.

Then Dresner faced me. "I on the other hand, don't get taken in as easily. I suppose the M.H.D.A. wants you to spy on us now."

"The only person they want me to spy on is Quinn. From what I know, they don't even realize Klaus is one of your operatives."

"Oh, they know all right. At least, if Agent Smith is at all competent he does," he said. "But I still don't trust you."

"So, don't trust me. I don't care. To be honest, I'm having trouble believing you too. I know what I want to do with the shroud. I've asked you once already. Tell me what you're going to do with it."

Again, I made sure my mind was locked on his.

He didn't answer at first. He thought about what might happen if he told me. He kept himself absolutely alert to his surroundings, believing I had led an entire team of Agents here to capture him.

"There's no one here but us. I promise. No one will be hauling you away tonight."

"Okay," he said. "So, I guess we've discovered your power. So, why don't you rip it out of my head? I can't stop you."

"I'm not like that. I only use my powers when I need to. All I plan on using my power to do is check what you tell me is the truth."

"Noble," he said. He moved toward me. If I hadn't been locked into his head, I would have believed he was going to attack me. However, his thoughts were nothing but peaceful. "If I had your power, I doubt I'd be able to show the same restraint."

"I'm sure Quinn would agree with you."

He nodded. "To be sure. Quintus would have probably ripped my mind apart and lobotomized me before even asking a question." It took him a while to think about anything. It was as if he was trying to clear his mind before answering. If that was true, he was doing a pretty poor job of it. "I'm sure you know what the shroud can be used for. I too have no intention of allowing anyone to possess it. I have orders to destroy the cloth by any means possible."

What he said was true. Those were his orders and he planned on carrying them out.

"Then I think we're on the same page here."

"Kommandeur Dresner," Klaus said, "this is vhy I brought her to you. I know vhat she has gone through with Quintus. She vill never let him have the artifact. She can help."

"Okay," he said. "I leave her in your charge. But if she betrays us, she won't be the only one we mark for death. Do you understand?"

Klaus and I both nodded. And with those words, I went from being a double-agent to a triple one. Playing for three teams now, my nerves were going to be at their breaking point. At least I finally had a side I could honestly put my faith in.

My phone rang and I pulled it out of my pocket. I figured it would be Ethan, wondering why I hadn't texted him, or Quinn trying to find out where we were. But it was neither. The screen on my cell read, "Home". My parents were calling.

"Excuse me," I said and then walked away. Once I'd taken a few steps, I could hear Dresner giving Klaus some orders, hoping I wasn't eaves dropping. I wasn't.

I, on the other hand, walked about twenty yards away before answering my ringing phone. I didn't even get the chance to say hello before a voice came blaring through the earpiece. "It's after ten-thirty there, young lady. Why haven't you called us yet?"

"Hi, Mom," I said. Then, I settled down on a bench for a long lecture about responsibility. I sighed. If only she knew how responsible I was actually being.

CHAPTER 19
HERO HEIST

12:45

"I can't do this," I said for the fifth time Monday afternoon. This time, I words were uttered as we climbed the steps of Turin Cathedral. I rubbed the skull pendant, knowing at least if I got into trouble, my friends were nearby—even if they would have Abby and the rest of the M.H.D.A. with them.

"Shut up," Johnny said. It hadn't taken him long to forget the events of the other night.

The warm Italian air cooled instantly as we stepped through the large cathedral doors. Even with the lower temperature, my skin still felt hot. My heart was definitely pumping twice as fast as normal as the time drew closer. Looking at my watch, I saw my time lessen by one minute.

12:46

I took my designated spot in the pews nearest the shroud. It was the easiest part of the mission. After this, we'd be moving, to quote Ethan, "at light speed."

Klaus stood in the exact center of the cathedral, chewing gum. If someone was watching him, they would think he was studying the architecture. He was really looking and locating each of the cameras. In a few minutes, he was going to disable them all.

Gina stood off to one side, carrying a giant purse way too big for her small frame. She was a remarkable actress though, because she made it look perfectly natural over her shoulder.

12:47

Johnny and Jayson disappeared into the back of the cathedral. The next time they emerged, Jayson should be dressed in the blue and yellow colors of the Vatican guards.

12:48

Gina took a spot in the lengthy line of people waiting to see the shroud. She tried to keep the "package" in her purse from being seen by any prying eyes. This was such a bad idea.

12:49

I sat and waited.

12:50

I waited some more.

12:51

More waiting.

12:52

My nerves were getting the better of me. My hands trembled and my breathing grew rapid. My heart felt like it was ready to explode.

12:53

I connected to Klaus. His thoughts were so calm. It was like he did something like this every day.

Klaus?

12:54

Vhat do you need? Even his thoughts had an accent. How strange is that?

Are we doing the right thing? I mean, look at all these people. What are they doing to do when they find out we stole it?

It is not our place to question, he responded. *Vee are soldiers, vee follow orders.*

You can't always follow orders, you know. Sometimes you have to think for yourself.

12:55

Vee have job to do, Klaus explained. *Let us do it.*

I cut the connection. With only a few minutes remaining, I had to connect my mind to everyone in the room—no easy task, even for me. So, one by one, I reached out mental tendrils, and formed a vast network of minds, with me at the center.

12:56

The priests came out of the back and made their way over to the confession booths, like they'd done every day the previous week.

12:57

The priests entered the booths, disappearing from site—for a few minutes, at least. I made sure both of their minds were linked into the network.

12:58

I had a strong connection to everyone in the cathedral. Once the pair of guards stepped out, in less than two minutes, things were going to get ugly.

12:59

Half-closing my eyes, I did deep breathing. The clean air went in and the bad air went out. Unfortunately, I couldn't exhale all of my doubts along with it. This was really going to happen. I was really going to steal the Shroud of Turin.

1:00

The bells in the cathedral chimed, ringing in the new hour.

Here we go.

Right on time, the two guards stepped through the doors from the rear of the cathedral and marched toward the shroud. The second guard, was Jayson in disguise. He'd morphed himself into the man, whom Johnny was supposed to have detained in the back.

I had to admit, Jayson did have a cool ability. Who wouldn't want to be able to turn themselves into someone else? Jayson could literally be anyone he wanted and all he had to do was think about it. What I wouldn't give to be able to change into someone else for one day.

1:01

Jayson and the other guard reached the shroud and relieved the two guards from the morning. As the four brightly colored men switched positions, I knew it was time to act.

1:02

I'd been holding tight to the minds of everyone in the room for nearly five minutes. Now, I pushed, giving everyone a single, simple suggestion.

Screams broke out and people started for the exits.

"Fire!" someone shouted as he dove over the rows of pews to get ahead of the crowds.

It took less than ten seconds for a scrum to form at every exit. The panicked people couldn't get out of the room fast enough. Someone was going to get hurt, and it would be all my fault.

Klaus acted quickly, pulling the big wad of gum from his mouth and tearing tiny pieces from it. He flicked the wet, sticky wads of gum at each and every camera in the room, hitting each lens dead center. Within only a few seconds, all the cameras were effectively blind.

1:03

The priests tried in vain to calmly direct everyone out of the cathedral, but their voices could barely be heard among the yells and screams of the terrified tourists.

With all the commotion, all three guards and Jayson had taken positions around the shroud. They actually drew their swords and stood before the glass, as if to protect it. Jayson stood behind one of the blue and yellow clad men. When the time was right, Jayson bashed the man on the back of the head with the hilt of his sword.

The other two Vatican Guards took notice of this and advanced on Jayson. I was about to give them the suggestion the imposter was actually the man Jayson had taken down, but as it turned out, I didn't have to.

Three copies of Johnny suddenly appeared in front of the guards, blocking their path. They attacked, swinging their swords at the fake Johnnys, but every time they hit one of them, he disappeared and another popped up in his place.

One of the Johnny copies pulled the sword from one of the guards hands and hit him with the hilt as well. The man fell, sprawled on the ground. Then the other two Johnnys grabbed hold of the last guard's arms and disarmed him, while the Johnny holding the sword approached the man, the weapon held high as if he were going to stab him.

I couldn't let that happen. So, I lifted one of the pews and sent it flying in their direction. It struck all three Johnny copies, causing them to disappear and the sword to clatter on the marble floor. The guard was confused long enough for Gina to thwack him on the head with her very heavy purse—which was a bad idea in and of itself.

1:04

The last of the frightened people scrambled through the doors to escape the fire I'd created in their minds. Taking one last look around, I saw that my team of six and the three guards, unconscious on the floor, were the only ones left in the building.

1:05

Klaus clapped me on the arm as he ran passed me on his way to the glass enclosed sarcophagus. "Come on," he said in a heavier German accent than usual.

I followed him and we were joined by Johnny, the real one this time, as he stepped out of the back room, dragging the fourth guard behind him.

"Why'd you stop me from hurting that guy? He'd have done the same to us," he shouted.

"Because the man was only doing his job. No matter how you look at it, we're the bad guys right now. I'm not going to let you skewer some guard because it was his turn to protect the shroud."

Jayson's skin rippled and his clothes changed color. In a few seconds he was back to his original appearance. "What now?" he asked.

"Gina, do jou have the bomb?"

And this is why I think Gina was insane to whack the guy on the head with her purse. From inside, she pulled out a good half-pound gray brick of C-4, rigged with a very simple detonator. It looked like a piece of Play-Doh, only a great deal more dangerous.

Gina handed the explosive over to Klaus, who attached it to the plate glass.

"Step back," he instructed us all.

1:06

Klaus hit a button on it and the digital readout on the front of the bomb started counting down from fifteen seconds.

We ran away from the bomb and hid among the pews for protection. I hoped we were far enough away, otherwise this would end badly for all of us.

I couldn't see the timer from where I crouched, and the anticipation of the inevitable explosion was worse than any anxiety I felt leading up to this moment. My hands were actually shaking with the thrill of the impending bang. At the last second, I threw my arms over my head and ducked even lower behind the wooden bench.

BOOM!

A brief flash of light, and a concussive wave that felt like someone had punched me in my chest, and the glass was broken. Shards flew in all directions. One of these pieces cut Jayson's cheek and another Gina's hand. Both of them were extremely lucky, because an inch in either direction would have meant disfigurement or death for them.

I waited a count of ten before lifting my head. Smoke filled the area where the glass had been, and strangely, I didn't smell any smoke or fire. I figured I would at least have the smell of gunpowder—you know that same smell you get on Fourth of July after all the fireworks have been shot off—but there was almost no odor at all.

This part was all me, not because Quinn had assigned it to me, but because I was the only one I trusted to retrieve the shroud. Klaus had everyone else hang back as I crept over the pool of shiny broken glass. Each piece crackled beneath my feet as I crushed them under my weight.

1:07

As I neared the sarcophagus, the wailing of sirens filled the air outside. It had only taken five minutes for the authorities to arrive. We only had a couple of minutes before they burst in. Hopefully they'd send in the firemen first, so we wouldn't all be arrested immediately.

I pushed the dried bramble of thorns off the coffin with my mind, not wanting to touch them. Then I pulled the red, cross embroidered sheet off the top and flung it aside. Every fiber in every muscle of my body begged me to stop. It felt like I was desecrating a tomb, even though I knew there wasn't really a body inside. I grabbed the white sheet now, and pulled it off as well, revealing the stone sarcophagus for us all to gaze upon.

It was pure marble, and had a lid that looked like it weighed at least a half-ton.

Looking over my shoulder, I stared directly into Klaus' eyes. Without having to connect to his mind, I sent a very clear message. *There has to be another way.*

He simply motioned with his hand for me to continue. He was so much better at this spy thing than I was.

More sirens joined the others outside, and now shouting bellowed through the open door. It was a fireman wondering why there was no smoke coming from the building if there was such a large fire inside. Thankfully, the anomaly made him cautious and he didn't step through the door.

1:08

I turned back to the marble coffin and grabbed hold of the lid. With my mind, I nudged it. The grating sound of stone on stone filled the room and the unmistakable scent of old dust filled my nostrils. I opened it just enough to be able to stick a hand inside.

The sarcophagus was deep, much deeper than I expected. I was almost shoulder deep before my hand hit the cold bottom. I reached around, feeling for the shroud. It took a few seconds, but finally I gripped what felt like an old, brittle, dried out piece of cloth. It was folded neatly into a square.

The worst part was, as soon as my hand met with the cloth, I knew something was wrong.

1:09

I glanced over at the rest of my team, waiting at the edge of the broken glass pool as if stepping on it would set off some unseen booby trap. They looked at me expectantly, waiting for me to pull out the prize. The problem was, it wasn't the prize.

I lifted the skull pendant to my lips and whispered as softly as I possibly could. "Do not move in. I repeat, do not move in. The shroud is a fake. I'll explain later."

Then I pulled the cloth out and without any ceremony, floated over the field of glass, back to my team. They wanted to be happy. They wanted to cheer. But the look on my face told the whole story.

I landed next to Gina. "Give me the bag," I ordered.

"But I'm—"

I grabbed the bag off her shoulder and yanked it away. "Give it to me!"

I thrust the cloth into the bag and then pulled the strap over my arm and head so it rested across my chest. That way Gina couldn't take it away from me.

"What's the matter?" Jayson asked.

"Later," I said. Then I turned toward the door. Long shadows spread across the marble floor. Several men were ascending the stairs and about to come in. "Right now, we need to get out of here."

1:10

Joining hands, our group formed a long chain with Klaus at the front. When Gina locked hands with her brother, all five of us instantly became invisible.

We crept along the wall as the firemen came inside, and slipped through the doorway, unseen, after they had all entered. I allowed myself a sigh of relief as our group made our way across the courtyard to the gathered crowd of tourists, being kept in check by a few Italian policemen.

We wound our way through the crowd, keeping a good grip on each other's hands. If even one of us broke off, we'd become visible. None of us wanted to explain how we'd suddenly appeared in the middle of a gawking mass of people.

A few times I felt my grip slip from Klaus', but every time I thought I was going to lose him, he tightened his fist around my hand. He held hard enough to make my knuckles grind together, but at least this time I knew he was hurting me for the right reason.

Getting through the crowd proved to be easier than I thought it would be. We were soon a block away from the onlookers. Only then did we break our grips and reappear to the world.

1:13

"Okay, Christine," Johnny said. He tapped the bag which concealed the old cloth. "Tell us what's up wit' this thing."

"It's a fake."

Several emotions filled my team at that moment. Gina was surprised. Johnny was angry. Jayson was upset. And Klaus was amused.

"The question is," I said, "what do we tell Quinn?"

CHAPTER 20
HEADING TO ROME

It went against my wishes, but the group decided we should tell Quinn the truth. Johnny and Gina were the most vocal of my opposition, insisting they would never get paid, handing over a fake artifact.

The only reason why I ended up going along with it was that once Quinn held the crusty cloth he would probably figure out it wasn't authentic anyway.

Before I could tell Quinn, however, I needed to inform my team—my real team. My phone was in my hand in an instant and I rushed through a text to Ethan.

Meet… NOW!!! U-Peter-Savanah. No Abby. Café Mordillo.

I tucked the phone back in my pocket and turned back to the others. "We can't go directly back to the room. We need to split up for a while. Meet back at the hotel in two hours."

I received no objection from Jayson, Johnny or Gina. We said our goodbyes and they walked off. Klaus on the other hand, stayed behind.

"I vill speak with Kommandeur Dresner," he said. "How do you know it is fake?"

"It's kind of hard to explain," I said. "Let's just say, I've come across objects like the shroud before, and I've been able to feel them—especially after I've come into contact with them. And this," I patted the outside of the bag, "is just a piece of cloth."

He nodded, but I could tell he was still confused.

"The objects speak to me. This one doesn't. So it can't be real."

"I understand," he said even though we both knew he didn't. "I vill zee you in two hours."

"Yup. See you then."

Klaus strode off in one direction, and I tromped off in the other. If my friends really were in a position to help me, they would be close by. So, it wouldn't take them long to come and find me.

Passing the Hotel Chelsea, I walked to the fake McDonald's. Once inside, I simply sat at a table, not ordering anything to eat. I wasn't very hungry anyway. There was too much on my mind.

First and foremost, I'd made myself a criminal, even though I hadn't even stolen anything of any real value.

I also had to think as to why the artifact in the bag slung across my chest was a fake. It didn't make any sense. Why go through all the trouble of displaying and protecting a supposed holy relic, if it wasn't even real to begin with?

One unlikely response came to mind. It was possible the church actually didn't know it was a fraud. That couldn't be true, because the shroud had been kept under lock and key for hundreds of years. If someone had taken and replaced it, they would have had to have done so centuries ago. Plus, if the shroud was as powerful as people claimed, then someone would have used it by now.

No. The church knew what I possessed wasn't the real shroud. But then the question still remained—why the charade? Why let people believe it was the authentic artifact?

Another question popped into my head then. Where was the real Shroud of Turin? It didn't disappear, and with all the people still looking for it, no one had managed to steal it.

I really had to think about it. I had to clear my head and let the answer come to me. I concentrated, trying to empty all the extra baggage I had in my mind. I threw each and every thought out until I could only focus on one thing.

"Hey, Chris," came a voice I hadn't heard in a couple of weeks. He sat in the chair across from me, looking at me from under his woolen hat.

"Pete," I said, a little startled. I'd been trying so hard to think I didn't notice anyone come up. "Where's everyone…?"

I cut myself off as Ethan and Savanah sat at the table with me. I stifled both a gasp and a groan as a fourth person pulled a chair up to our table.

I didn't even look up at the unwanted guest, and instead turned to Ethan and said through clenched teeth. "I thought I said no Abby in my text."

"Relax, Chris," Ethan said, backing off in case I tried to hit him—like he needed the extra space to evade one of my swings. "She knows everything."

And that statement stunned me into silence. My lips moved to form words in what I'm sure could have been a really good protest, but my vocal chords refused to work. He'd gone behind my back and told Abby everything, even after everything I told him—even after I asked him not to.

"Christine, believe it or not, I'm not your enemy. Please stop treating me like one." She stopped me from saying anything with a simple a glance. "I don't know what Smith is up to. I can tell you his actions the other night you witnessed, were in no way sanctioned by our agency. He was working on this alone."

"How can I believe you? You could be telling me what I want to hear."

"Oh, Chris," Ethan said, rubbing his forehead.

"You don't," Abby responded, over Ethan's words. "What you need to do, however, Christine, is get over these trust issues of yours and put faith in someone other than yourself. Your friends all trust me. And I think I've proven time and again I am on your side. So, I think it's time you—"

"Okay, fine, I believe you" I said. "Please don't try and give me anymore speeches. You sound like my mother."

Peter and Ethan chuckled at that. Abby didn't look at all amused.

"So, tell me how you know it's a fake," Abby prodded.

I pulled the bag over my head and plopped it on the table. I opened it and revealed the relic to them. I didn't think it was best to actually take it out of the bag. By now the police had to know the "shroud" had been stolen and would be looking for it.

"The Spear of Destiny was at Camp Hero," I explained. "When I grabbed it, I felt... something. It was almost like the spear itself was alive and I could hear its thoughts like I can hear anyone's. When I touched the Holy Grail in Quinn's classroom a month ago, it was the same thing. The objects have a mental presence. I touch this," I put my hand on the cloth and patted it several times, "and nothing."

"But then... where is the shroud now?" Ethan asked.

"I don't know," I neglected to mention I'd been wondering that myself.

"I think I might know," Peter said. We all waited in anticipation for Peter to complete his sentence, but it appeared that was where he planned to stop.

Savanah prompted him to continue by saying, "Are we supposed to guess, or something?"

"I figured Chris would read my mind."

"And what about the rest of us, huh?"

"Savanah, drop it," I interrupted. "Pete, where is it?"

He seemed to shrink back in his seat. He never did feel comfortable talking to us all. So, I wasn't surprised when he spoke, his voice was very hoarse. "Well... ummm... you know how you said those Vatican Guards were watching over the shroud?"

"Yeah, that's their job."

Peter shook his head. "Not exactly. When my parents took me and my brother to Rome two years ago, we did a tour of Vatican City. On the tour they said—"

"Wait a sec! You've been here before?" asked Ethan. "Don't you think that might be something useful to tell us?"

"Ethan, back off!" I shouted. If I let him continue, Peter might shut down totally. And I really didn't feel like violating his brain for the info. "What did they tell you on the tour?"

Peter turned his body so he was only facing me, making it as if he and I were the only two sitting at the table. "They said the Vatican Guard only has jurist diction within the walls of Vatican City. They aren't supposed to be here in Turin."

"So, why were they here then?" I asked.

"It's a decoy," Abby said, more to herself than the rest of us. Her head was bowed for another ten seconds, as if she were going through massive amounts of data in her head. Then she leaned in and began talking in a conspiratorial tone. "Don't you see? Our friend, Quinn, was caught in an attempt to steal the shroud several weeks ago. The Vatican probably feared another theft, so without telling anyone, they replaced the artifact—probably in the middle of the night—and set up the guards so anyone watching would think the shroud was still here in Turin. But it was moved to the only place they'd trust to keep it safe."

"Vatican City," Ethan, Savanah and I said at the same time.

Savanah then smiled, and almost jumped from her seat. Her voice squeaked as she asked, "So, we're going to Rome?"

****

"Rome," said Quinn when I told him what we figured out. As usual the disappointment he felt at the failure didn't resonate on his face. He simply stood, back totally straight, watching the five of us as if we were little children. "Vatican City is one of the most protected places in all of Europe. Thousands of tourists visit Turin Cathedral everyday, but tens of thousands visit Vatican City everyday. They also have their own private police and army force, along with a group that is something akin to the Secret Service in the United States. There are literally miles of tunnels running beneath it and it could be kept in any one of them, though I suspect the shroud is in the secret vaults. If the shroud has been taken there, I'm afraid we can never get our hands on it."

It was a total reversal. I figured he was so obsessed he would stop at nothing until he took possession of the shroud. As it turned out, there was one thing that could stop him: fear.

Quinn was too afraid to go after the shroud. If the idea of going up against the Vatican frightened him, then the shroud had to be safe. Mission accomplished. I could go home early and enjoy the rest of my summer vacation like a normal teenager.

Except...

"Vee still get paid?"

"Yeah, whatabout our money?" Johnny agreed. "We got your stupid crust cloth."

If possible, Quinn got taller, looming over the five of us like an angry giant. A dark shadow spread across his face. I realized then Quinn had never truly showed his dark side to me, but there it was leering at us. A chill ran through me. I was glad I could keep my dark-side from showing itself.

"Do not presume to make demands of me. You failed to retrieve what we came for and now the item is out of reach. You will get nothing. You should be thankful I'm even going to pay for your plane ticket home."

Of all people to continue arguing for money, Klaus was the last one I expected. He should have been as happy as I was this whole foolish crusade was over. But instead, he seemed to get angry. I say "seemed" because I didn't feel an ounce of negative emotion from the boy. And if I felt it, Quinn felt it too.

"I vant my payment. You owe it to us."

"You want your money? Fine." Quinn began rummaging through a bag he'd left on the bed. He pulled out a wad of hundred dollar bills. He counted them out and then handed us each five hundred dollars. "Just enough for each of you to get home. Now get out of my sight. I don't want to see your faces ever again!"

He shoved the remaining money back into the bag and turned to the window. It was like he was daring one of us to reach into the bag and take the rest of the money. None of us moved.

"This is not what you promised me," Jayson said softly. I'm not even sure Quinn heard him. But with every word he spoke, he grew bolder and his voice got louder. "I'm not leaving until I have enough to take home to my mom. I'm going to take care of her for a change, and you're going to make that happen."

The strangest thing happened then as well. Jayson's arm began to ripple—just his arm. First it turned a blue-green color and then his skin became hard, like a shell. Then his arm grew fat and wide, until it resembled something more like a crab-claw. I jumped back, and so did Johnny, Gina and Klaus. None of us realized he could do that. I, at least, was sure he could only perform human transformations.

Quinn didn't turn around. I wasn't sure if it was because he didn't notice Jayson's morphing or if it he didn't perceive the boy as a threat. I was willing to bet on the second option.

"Reach back into your bag and give me what you promised." Jayson's voice was firm, but there was no hint of a threat in it. It seemed now that it was time to act, Jayson no longer had the will to do anything.

Johnny and Gina, now following Jayson's lead, both appeared ready to attack if the situation presented itself. Klaus and I both glanced at each other, both of us knowing this was going south and in a hurry.

As I reached into the three minds and attempted to calm them all down, Klaus tried a different tactic. "Vhat must vee do? You still vant the shroud. Vee can get it."

Quinn looked over his shoulder and smiled. It was what he'd been hoping one of us would volunteer to do from the beginning.

I simply rubbed my head. This German guy was going to be the death of me—if, of course, I didn't kill him first. He must have had a reason for continuing this idiotic quest. So, instead of arguing, I figured I'd go with it.

"The train for Rome leaves in two hours," Quinn said. "Pack your things. We need to be on it."

CHAPTER 21
VATICAN CITY

Wow!

Yeah, that about covers it.

The ride overnight on the train was uneventful—thank God. Though I did have to prevent Johnny and Gina from going on a little hunt and grab mission of their own—if you know what I mean.

But, I will say, nothing compared to the astonishment I felt when the train pulled into Rome as the sun was rising. As impressive as Turin was, with its old architecture and beautifully paved roads, it was nothing compared to the glory of Rome. The glass windows gleamed in the sun, making the city sparkle with a magnificence I had never seen before. Buildings older than I had ever seen mixed company with newer ones, and yet, they all seemed to match, like they had all been designed by the same builder.

I checked my watch, it was about 6a.m., and already there were people in the streets. Unlike the people of Turin, the ones in Rome didn't seem able to wait and start their day. Even as we left the train station there were a hundred cab drivers waiting to take us where wherever we wanted to go. Men shouted at us as we passed, offering to sell us maps of the city. This place was definitely more of a tourist spot than Turin was, and the locals treated it that way.

Quinn led us to a van. It said taxi on the top, but it wasn't like any cab I'd ever seen. For one, it was green, and who ever heard of a green taxi-cab? It was also vaguely shaped like a Volkswagon Beetle, but larger, more like the size of a mini-van. Also, and maybe I was being dense, but I couldn't figure out where the engine went on the thing. It had a rather flat front and rear, and with three rows of seats, it didn't seem like there was a logical place for the motor.

We jumped in and Quinn immediately said to the driver, "Vatican City."

The driver nodded and we immediately pulled away from the station. He took us north and after about a mile he turned to head west. As we drove, Quinn turned from the front seat to face the rest of us.

"It's 6:17a.m. We should arrive at the Vatican by 6:30. The museums won't open until 9a.m. and by then the crowd at the gates will be enormous. We need someone to go into the museum and do some digging, there are sub-basements upon sub-basements underneath. Those basements are the most logical place to find the artifact. Any volunteers?"

"Not me," I said almost immediately. Everyone, except the driver of course, who hadn't given any indication he'd heard anything Quinn said, turned toward me. "What? I'm not exactly compatible with crowds, okay?"

"I'll do it," Jayson volunteered. "Besides, if I can change into a guard or someone who works there, I can get into places the rest of you can't."

Quinn nodded at Jayson and then continued. "The Sistine Chapel will also open at 9."

"Whoa!" Jayson interrupted. He was staring out the windshield at the structure growing ever closer before us.

On his exclamation, we all turned to follow his gaze, even Quinn, though he did turn back almost immediately, suppressing the need to roll his eyes. "Pay attention," he ordered. "We have plenty to do before…"

None of us were listening. The site before us was… amazing. I've been to New York and seen the Statue of Liberty and stood at the top of the Empire State Building, looking down at the world. Neither of those sites compared with the Roman Coliseum.

The cab turned and rode around the outside of the building as five teenaged faces pressed against the left side windows of the cab. The Coliseum showed its age. The gray crumbling stone arches, one on top of the other, turned an orange-brown in the early morning sunlight. The long shadows stretched through the open spaces, making the resolute building seem even larger than it was.

Through the spaces, I could barely catch glimpses of the stadium inside. So much had happened within those walls. And though gladiators weren't exactly my thing—though from the amount of times Ethan made me sit through *Spartacus* and *Gladiator*, he would disagree—I had to sit in awe of the history this building represented.

I snapped a picture.

"Can we stop?" Jayson asked, sounding like a boy half his age.

And even though I wanted to act like I didn't care, I sounded exactly the same way, "Yeah, please stop for a minute."

"No!" Quinn said. "We have a mission."

"Vee can zee it later," Klaus whispered in my ear. "I promise, before you go."

We turned down another street, still heading east, and left the Coliseum behind us.

Only then could Quinn regain our attention, "As I was saying, the Sistine Chapel also opens at 9. There are several vaults in the rear of the church, which would also be a logical place to hide the shroud."

"We'll do that," Johnny volunteered himself and his sister.

"St. Peter's Basilica is always open because of the cathedral inside. There are vaults there as well, but more important are the catacombs below. It is a maze of tombs, holding the remains of each and every important Catholic figure in the last two-thousand years."

"I guess that's us," I said, looking to Klaus. He nodded his approval.

Of course, hanging around with dead guys wasn't the ideal choice, but it beat having to deal with a being pressed into a stampede of people. I only hoped Klaus and I found the shroud.

In another ten minutes, we'd arrived at Vatican City. The place was already swarming with people, though it was only hundreds compared to the thousands which would be here by the end of the day. I'd seen pictures, I knew how crowded things could get. By noon, it would look like an ocean of bodies, rather than the river it was now.

The cab pulled up to a large square. When we stopped, Quinn ushered us out, demanding we move quickly. I didn't know why, especially since it was still over two hours before the museum and chapel opened.

"What about our bags?" Gina asked, as she jumped out of the taxi.

"They'll be safe," Quinn assured her.

"We can't leave them in the cab," I insisted. I had all my stuff in the bag, including my passport. I couldn't leave it.

"The driver is going to drive around the city all day," Quinn explained. "I planted a suggestion in his head to pick up no passengers all day and to return this evening to pick us up. Your luggage is perfectly safe."

I was going to continue arguing, but by the time the protest made it to my lips, the door shut and the taxi was already pulling away.

"Saint Peter's Square," Quinn announced, opening his arms as if to take it all in, "the gateway to the Vatican."

He started walking, and we followed, giving the appearance we were some kind of tour group. If I wasn't so worried about my bag, I might have had the sense to be embarrassed. As it was, we were hardly in the square before Quinn and Jayson both walked off together, apparently to the museum entrance.

"I don't like 'dis," Johnny said, as soon as Quinn had disappeared around a corner. "I know when I'm bein' played. And 'dis guy's playin' us."

"What do you mean?" I asked, playing ignorant. If I told Johnny he'd been "played" from the beginning, he wouldn't be too happy about it.

"This whole thing stinks. He just happened to have train tickets to Rome waitin' for us? Then he knows exactly where we need'ta look for 'dis shroud? Come on!"

"It is a little convenient," I responded. Actually, it was a little too convenient, and I mentally kicked myself for not realizing it before. Quinn had intended for us to come here all along. At least, he had the plan in mind in case we failed at Turin Cathedral. "Whatever the reason," I continued, "the quicker we find the shroud, the quicker we get paid and can get away from him. Got it?"

"Yeah," he agreed. "But I ain't handin' the thing over 'til he forks out the money."

"Okay."

Gina remained quiet. I didn't have to read her thoughts to know she wanted out of there as soon as possible and didn't care one way or the other about the money anymore. She was coming to the realization Quinn was probably never going to pay them.

She was probably right.

The four of us walked together into the square, which wasn't really square at all, it was more of a large oval. We were

surrounded on all sides by large white marble columns. On the
tops of these were hundreds of statues, all of them seeming to
look down into the square like stone sentries protecting the
Vatican. In the center was a large obelisk, kind of like the
Washington Monument in Washington D.C. This was one much
smaller, of course, and it had a cross stuck in the top.

In front of us stood what I assumed was Saint Paul's Basilica.
It was the largest building I was able to see. The dome on top
reminded me a little like the Capital Building in Washington D.C.
too. I was willing to bet the people who first built D.C. were
inspired by Roman architecture.

Ahead and to our right, people were congregating. They were
waiting for a small kiosk to open, one I assumed sold tickets to
some of the sites in Vatican City.

I pointed to the line and said to Johnny and Gina, "I think
you guys better get in line."

"You mean I gotta pay to get in?" Johnny complained.

"Looks that way," I responded.

"To hell wit' that," Johnny said. He pulled Gina's arm and
dragged her away from us. "You'll hafta make us invisible and
sneak us in."

"Johnny, I don't think you should say Hell," Gina said as they
walked off. "I mean, look where we are."

I shook my head as they went off. They were certainly a
unique pair, and sadly, they were beginning to grow on me.

"Are you ready?" I said, looping my arm through his and
strolling toward the basilica like we were a couple.

"Yah." He tried to do it discreetly, but I still noticed as he
looked down at our joined arms and smiled.

"Don't get any ideas," I told him. "We're doing this for
cover." Of course, we could have simply walked in like a couple of
teens on a school trip and no one would be any the wiser. So why
had I grabbed his arm like that?

I didn't think about it anymore as we ascended the staircase
and entered the front of the building unhindered.

As easily as we were able to enter the front doors, we were
stopped as soon as we crossed through. Now, I would like to say
there was security, and they stopped us, made us empty our
pockets and whatnot, but it would be a blatant lie.

We were stopped by ourselves, upon seeing the site that greeted us as we entered. It was a huge gallery, with large columns reaching at least thirty feet in the air. Every one of them was decorated with paintings adorned with gold. Statues rested at the bottom of almost every column, depicting several... Saints? Popes? I really couldn't say, because the writing around each one, also in gold, was in Latin. I only knew it was Latin because I recognized a few of the root words we'd talked about in English class—I guess that proves I do pay attention, sometimes.

We walked into the room slowly, not only marveling at the amazing artwork, but also the looking for anyplace that might hide the shroud.

"You never told me why you decided to continue this mission," I whispered.

"Orders," Klaus replied. "Dresner said we had to get the shroud at any cost."

"So, he doesn't believe the shroud is safe here in the Vatican?"

"Oh, it is," Klaus said. "But what happens when they decide to move it back. You know it will happen eventually."

There were only a few people scattered around the hall, and even though they tried to be quiet, every sound reverberated off every wall, causing a magnified echo heard across the large room. So, every time someone spoke, including us, someone would look in their direction. Attention was one thing we didn't want right now.

I continued whispering. "Okay, you have any idea where these catacombs are?"

Klaus shook his head.

"Great," I muttered. The entrance to the lower levels could be anywhere. Behind any door, or up any passage, and from the size of the room, I would say that only left us about a thousand places to check. It wasn't like there was a staircase in the middle of the floor leading down to the tombs below.

"Look, over here," Klaus said. A little bit of excitement could be heard in his voice.

He dragged me along through the gallery, keeping a tight grip on my arm with his own. I followed his gaze until we reached the thing he was looking at.

"Well, what do ya know?" I had to shake my head at the sheer irony of it all. "A staircase."

The stairs only went down and from the looks of them, they went down pretty far. The only obstacle in our way was a red velvet rope hanging across the entrance. It was easily overcome and Klaus and I quickly darted down the stairs before anyone could see us—or so we thought.

"Hold it!" someone shouted.

We both froze, only three stairs down as a man raced after us, stopping at the velvet rope. He was dressed in a gray suit, with a white shirt and a black tie. He had an earpiece in his ear, not unlike what you'd see a government agent wear.

He flashed some kind of I.D. in our faces and said, "Swiss Guard. Would you please step back up here?"

I did as he said, giving Klaus a mental nudge to stay put. I ascended the stairs until I was on the same level as the man. His arm reached out, as if to grab me and yank me back over to his side of the rope, but before he could, I attacked his mind.

We're supposed to be here. We have special clearance. I sifted through his thoughts and lifted a name who would be high enough in rank to give us permission to enter the catacombs. *Camerlengo Viggiano said we could look for a research project we are working on.*

I have no idea who or what a Camerlengo was, but he was apparently one of the highest ranking people in Vatican City. I pushed into his mind, implanting the suggestion into his brain so he would believe it to be absolutely true.

The Swiss Guard's arm stopped in midair inches before reaching me. A blank expression crossed his face for a moment, but he made no other move. He simply stood, staring blankly into my eyes. As I was getting frightened the suggestion wasn't sticking in the man's head, he lowered his arm and nodded.

"If Camerlengo Viggiano gave you clearance, I guess that's good enough for me."

He turned and went back the way he'd come. As he stepped away, I had another idea. We had no idea where we were going, and this guy probably knew the layout of the catacombs, or at least had a better idea of where to go than we did.

Camerlengo Viggiano also said you should escort us. I planted the suggestion firmly into his head. *He would like you to show us where they've hidden The Shroud of Turin.*

The man turned around again. "He's right, you shouldn't be without an escort. Let me show you around down there. But I don't know what he's talking about. The Shroud of Turin was stolen yesterday afternoon from Saint John's Cathedral. So, I'm afraid I can't show you that."

He stepped over the velvet rope and joined us, taking the lead. "I am Major Gianni. It would be my pleasure to show you a part of the Vatican few have ever seen."

Klaus eyed me with a sort of "What the hell are you doing?" look. I wasn't about to explain, and I wanted to keep a firm mental grip on the now kidnapped Major, so I shook my head and said, "Not now."

There was one thing I knew though. Major Gianni wasn't a high enough rank to know the truth about the Shroud of Turin. If it wasn't down in the catacombs, I would have to find someone who was.

CHAPTER 22
THE CATACOMBS

Dark dungeons where people have buried their dead for a thousand years is definitely a place to add to my "Never Want to Visit Again" list.

I used the think the only thing that could really scare me was being in a crowd. But as it turns out I have cryptophobia. I know, cryptophobia isn't a real fear, but the closest thing I could find to describe it was placophobia: the fear of tombstones, or taphophobia: the fear of graves. Since neither of those sound even remotely interesting, I'm going with cryptophobia and you're going to have to deal with it.

Anyway, I think I'm justified in saying being in the catacombs really freaked me out. It took nearly all my energy to keep myself focused on Major Gianni and not have a massive panic attack.

It wasn't so bad at first actually. We walked down a brightly lit and wide open corridor, with a regular hardwood floor and saw each of the tombs, also brightly lit with statues hanging over each of the sarcophagi, representing angels protecting the bodies of the dead.

After the first level was when I began to lose control. Have you ever seen one of those old horror movies, where the heroine goes down into some dark dank cave with only a flashlight to light the way and the darkness seems to close in around her like it was some living entity? Okay, well now add to that, open chasms in the walls, each about two feet tall and six feet wide, holding an incredibly decayed and rotting skeleton sitting out where anyone can see, and I think you'll get an idea as to why I was freaked out.

Also, I neglected to mention, the stench of rotting flesh, mixed with the aroma of mold and dust filled every breath I took. Breathing through my mouth was no better, because not only could I smell it then, but I could taste it too. The odor actually made my stomach churn.

While all my concentration was essentially on Major Gianni, I still managed to feel inside all of the chasms we passed in search of any hint the shroud was about. But the further we went down, the harder I found it to concentrate. By the third level, I couldn't focus at all.

Thankfully, Klaus stood close beside me, holding me in his arms as we walked. Strangely, the big German boy's arms did lend some comfort. It was almost like having a substitute Ethan for a few hours.

Which reminded me, I'd have to check in with them soon. This far below the surface, I doubted my skull pendant was still transmitting. They'd be worried about me—at least Ethan would.

Major Gianni, for his part, acted as the perfect tour guide, pointing out interesting specimens and showing us important tombs. I had to admit, the man did know his stuff. It was a shame I was using him as a human marionette.

On the fourth level, and what I hoped was the final level, we reached the oldest tombs, the ones that were built when the Roman Empire still held much of the known world in its grip. Once we reached that far, I knew the shroud wasn't down here. I had no sense of it at all. If it was here, I would have felt it by now.

Deciding it was pointless to continue the charade any longer than we had to, and wanting to get out of the dark depths of the crypt as soon as possible, I had Major Gianni, leading with the only flashlight, take us back up.

I did my best not to touch any of the walls, though as narrow as the corridor was at times, it was unavoidable. All I knew was, after being down there, I needed to take a really *really* long shower when we got to whatever hotel we were staying in that evening. I felt like I needed to wash the feeling of death from my body. The thought of it made me shudder.

When we reached the third level again, I stopped. There was something there, ahead and on the right. It wasn't there before, or if it had been, I'd been so engrossed in keeping focused I'd missed it. We walked up several feet, and there was an alcove in the wall, like any of the other hundred or so I'd seen on the trek down—two feet high and six feet wide, and there was a skeleton in it. There didn't seem to be anything out of the ordinary, but there was definitely something there, and it had a familiar presence, not unlike the spear.

I made Major Gianni stop a good six or seven feet ahead of us. Then I reached into my pocket and opened my phone. The little bit of light shining from it was enough to light the dark alcove. Yes, there was a skeleton in there, perfectly preserved, with cobwebs spanning between the bones and the sides of the chasm.

Shuddering, I closed my eyes and took several deep breaths, forcing myself to calm down.

"Are jou all right?" Klaus asked. A wave of concern splashed upon me, and instantly I felt better—at least, well enough to continue.

"I'm fine," I said, though my voice shook slightly. "There's something back here. I don't think it's the shroud, but it's… something."

I opened my eyes then and used my cell to light the inside of the tomb. I noticed, laying on top of the body, underneath a blanket of dust, was a sword. The skeleton had it clutched in its hands, but I had to check it out.

My hand shook violently as I reached into the alcove and put my hand on the sword. As soon as I touched it, I knew I'd been right. As with the spear and the Grail, once my hand came into contact with it, it was like a psychic burst of information hit me. Only it was information I couldn't understand, like in a language I couldn't comprehend. It felt the same, and yet different from the other two artifacts. I couldn't explain it.

Without realizing it, I'd pulled the sword free of the skeleton's hands and they crumbled to dust, leaving the rest of the skeleton intact. I guess it wasn't like the movies after all. In the movies, if I'd pulled this free, it would have taken one of the hands with it.

I studied the blade, seeing if there were any markings on it which could help me identify it. There was nothing. The blade was covered in a blue/green substance, not unlike what covered the Statue of Liberty, it was hard, but felt strange to touch. Could the blade be made of copper? The hilt was nothing special either. As I ran my cell phone over it, all I could see was a straight hilt with no markings whatsoever. It appeared to be just an old sword—much like the Spear of Destiny looked like nothing more than a rusty spearhead and the Holy Grail nothing more than an old goblet. Yet, like the others, there was something special about this object.

I turned to ask Major Gianni if he could tell me anything about the ancient blade, but when I looked up, he was gone.

Damn. I'd broken my concentration and he'd woken up from the trance I'd had him in. He'd probably figured out I'd done something to him and run off while I was distracted.

Panic was setting in again. Not only was I lost in some old crypt, but now I was lost with only a phone to light the way.

Klaus hadn't noticed a thing, and his own fear was now apparent. His heart had begun racing faster, and his breathing had become shallower. I had to admit, he was still taking it better than me.

"What are we going to do?" I said quickly, and louder than I'd intended. My voice echoed down the corridor. When the echo came back toward us, it sounded like someone completely different—like a ghost.

I'm smart enough to know it was the sound of my own voice, but it still send a chill down my spine and caused goose bumps to appear all up and down my arm.

"Relax. Vee find our own vay out." He held me tight, knowing I was scared out of my mind.

I hated looking so weak and vulnerable in front of Klaus. For some reason, I felt the need to have him see me as a strong leader, as someone he could depend on. But I was acting like a frightened little girl who was afraid of the dark.

Putting on as brave a face as I could—not that he could see it with only my cell lighting the corridor—I nodded. Then I put the sword back on top of the skeleton. I couldn't really take it out with me. It was way too big to hide, and carrying it would draw too much attention to us. I knew it was here, and the thing had been laying here for at least a thousand years, so no one would bother it. If it turned out to be important, I'd know where to find it.

I let Klaus lead the way, handing over my cell phone. We moved nearly silently, only crunching some gravel under our feet as we walked. Every sound made my heart skip a beat. I didn't know why, but I did know all too well someone could actually be scared to death—I'd almost done it to Peter.

Eventually, Klaus stopped and I nearly crashed into him. I wondered if he saw something and found myself hiding behind his larger frame.

Why am I being such a coward? I asked myself. It wasn't like some zombie was going to spring up from one of the open graves and eat our brains. The worst that could happen would be getting caught by one of the Swiss Guard, and we could probably get away from them, but I didn't want to hurt any of them to do it.

"Why did you stop?" I half-whispered.

"I heard zomething," he said.

I listened, but didn't hear anything but our own breathing. Maybe his hearing was better than mine—it was possible. So, I reached out with my mind, trying to sense if there was anyone, or anything, in the corridor with us. I sensed nothing on our level, or the   level   above. I was about to say there was no one there when a noise did travel down the corridor. It was a voice, a deep male voice. I couldn't hear what he said, as it was more echo than anything else, but I knew it meant only one thing.

"They're coming," I said.

They had to still be on the first level, but the narrow corridors made the voices carry much further than they should have.

"Vee have to hide," Klaus said, pulling me along behind him. He shone my cell phone left and right as we stepped up the corridor. Finally, he stopped tugging my arm and crouched next to one of the open graves in the wall. He stuck his hand into the alcove, and my cell lit it up in an eerie blue light. He turned and nodded at me. "In here."

I backed away, shaking my head. "Are you crazy?"

"It's empty," he assured me. "No body in there."

He held out his hand, but I still hesitated. Dead body or no, the place was still a tomb, and I couldn't lay down in a tomb like it was no big deal.

"Christine, dhere is no time to wait. Dhey are coming."

I heard the voice again, and this time I was able to sense the presence that accompanied it. There were five—no, six—of them. They were rushing down the corridor, eager to catch the intruders who'd entered their holy place. As much as I believed Klaus and I could take them, I wasn't eager to find out.

I stepped toward Klaus, whose hand was still waiting to meet with mine again, and allowed him to pull me down until I could see inside the chasm. The only thing in the space was dust and cobwebs. At least he'd been honest about there being no corpse in there.

I crouched and then rolled into the opening, sliding in until my back hit the rock wall. There was plenty of room, and Klaus slid in beside me. He positioned himself so his back was to the corridor beyond and his face was only inches from mine. It wasn't the most comfortable position, but it would be manageable for a couple of minutes. I hoped the guards wouldn't think to look here.

The voices were now joined by echoing footfalls as the guards quickly marched down the corridor above us. The deep male voice I'd heard earlier was now recognizable. It was Major Gianni. He'd been quite fast in getting reinforcements.

"They must have drugged me. There's no other explanation." He sounded angry, like he'd never forgive himself for being tricked. "But, I left them in the dark, there's no way they could have found their way out. We have them."

"With all the extra security, because of yesterday's theft," another, much higher toned voice said, "there's no way they'll get by us."

Great, I thought. They probably had someone watching the entrance, which meant we wouldn't be able to leave now even if we wanted.

"Just make sure we grab them before the museums open," Gianni said. "We don't want to cause a scene."

The footfalls were really close now. They were in the corridor with us. My body tensed as they passed, and I tried not to breath, fearing even the smallest noise would give us away. Klaus must have had the same thoughts, because his chest stopped moving.

The six men went straight passed though, not even bothering to look in any of the open tombs, and soon the stomps faded to echoes again. When they were gone, I could breathe again.

"Okay," I said, pushing against Klaus' chest. "Let's get out of here."

"No," he replied. "Vee vait."

"Vee vait?" I asked, mocking his accent for the first time. He didn't even notice. "We have to get out of here before they come back and try to bust through the guards they have at the entrance."

"No," he repeated. "Vee vait."

I pushed against him again, this time using the back wall as the leverage I needed. But his body didn't budge. "Let me go!" Even though I wanted to shout, I made sure to keep my voice low so the guards wouldn't hear. "I can't stay here. This is too much.

We're laying in a tomb! We need to find the shroud! I'm leaving with or without you. I'm…"

I was cut off by a warm, soft pair of lips meeting mine. At first, I continued pushing against Klaus. I had a boyfriend. He shouldn't be doing this. And we had a mission to complete. We didn't have time to lay around, making out.

But the longer he kissed me, the more I couldn't think of why I was protesting, and eventually gave in. I closed my eyes, wrapped my arms around him and kissed him back.

CHAPTER 23
TOTAL CHAOS

I don't know how long our lips were locked, but it felt like half-an-eternity. The guards, at least some of them, returned, passing us by again, but we remained connected. Then, as suddenly as it began, the kiss ended.

"You talk too much," Klaus whispered.

My mind clicked back to before the kiss began, and I remembered my rant Klaus had cut short. But then I forgot it again as my mind was racked with guilt.

I didn't fight him when he kissed me. Worse—I'd kissed him back. I'd cheated on Ethan and I'd never be able to forgive myself for it. I'd never be able to face him again. All at once, I wanted to be as dead as the corpses all around me.

While warring with myself for several minutes about what I should do, I decided two things. 1) I could never, would never tell Ethan a thing about what happened between me and Klaus, and 2) If Klaus ever tried to kiss me again, I had to punch him in the jaw and knock out some teeth.

Thinking about Ethan made me think of a way to escape. What Klaus and I really needed was a distraction.

When I knew it was safe, I opened up my phone again to see if I could get a signal. If I could call Savanah, or even Abby, one of them could help get us out of here. Unfortunately, we were too far underground and there was no signal to be had. I was sure my skull pendant was in the same state of uselessness.

The Swiss Guards charged passed our hiding place at least a dozen times. Each time they did, I tensed and held my breath until they were gone.

Klaus, even though I could feel his apprehension, remained cool-headed, as if he knew exactly what to do if we were caught. How much training must he have gone through to keep such a level head in a crisis? The only answer I could come up with was, More than I'm willing to go through.

An hour past, then two, and we were still stuck in our hiding spot. Major Gianni and his men didn't quit. Any hopes of waiting the search out, as Klaus planned on doing, were dashed to bits when we heard Gianni giving orders from up the corridor.

"They have to be down here," his voice echoed loudly through the catacombs, actually disturbing dirt and dust that had clung to the walls for the last century. "I want three more squads down here. Start a systematic search of every tomb."

"But, Major—" the guard protested.

"No buts, Lieutenant," Gianni growled. "Pull them off museum detail if you must, and disturb every grave in these walls, but I want the two intruders found."

I sure picked the wrong guy's mind to control. He was completely obsessed. Any normal person would have figured we'd escaped by now. But no, I had to pick the guy who was even more stubborn than me.

"Yes, sir." The guard's echoing footsteps faded as he ran back up to get a radio signal.

I checked my cell again. Still nothing. Closing it, I shoved it into my pocket.

"They're bringing down more people to find us," I informed Klaus, who was about to ask me what they said. I guess the major was speaking Italian. This personal translator thing my brain did actually was kind of useful after all, I guess.

He didn't say anything, but he nodded—at least I think he did. The darkness made it impossible to tell.

"We have to go," I whispered only loud enough for him to hear. "There's no way we'll get out once more guards come down."

"Vee not get out now either."

"We have to try."

More footsteps approached, and as usual, my lungs stopped sucking in oxygen. This time, Klaus had no such emotional failing.

"Vait here. I have a plan."

He rolled out of the alcove before I could question him. He left me alone. I felt the void he left like it was a physical thing. Suddenly, I couldn't survive without him laying next to me.

I couldn't see a thing, not even a shadow, but I listened closely as Klaus scooped a pile of pebbles from the ground.

The guards were getting closer, and their flashlights caused a dim glow to fill the corridor outside the crevice. The glow brightened as the guards must have turned a corner, and suddenly their footsteps were deafening.

A "whoosh" followed by another "whoosh" and the sounds of objects hitting the floor replaced the footfalls. Then, for a second, there truly was silence.

The light was still shining and I heard no shouts. So, the real question was, "Who got who?" Had Klaus taken them by surprise and subdued them, or had it been the other way around? I couldn't bring myself to look.

Moments past, with only the sounds of scuffling in the corridor. Every second that ticked by made me more and more apprehensive, until I couldn't take it any longer.

I was about to stick my head out to see what was going on, but shrunk back as a thick silhouetted leg stomped down in front of me.

I readied myself for an attack, putting a defensive shield around me. They weren't going to get me without a fight.

"Come out," came the thick German accent from Klaus' mouth. "It zafe now."

The sound of his voice seemed to warm my frightened body. I slipped out of the open tomb and stood on legs that didn't seem capable of supporting me. Laying there for all that time, my legs had fallen asleep. I had to lean against Klaus for a minute before blood circulated through my lower half again.

When he was sure I could stand on my own, he stepped away toward the fallen guards. "Come here. Take his clothes off."

My first reaction, as I lumbered over to the downed men was to ask, "Why?" But my mind was already way ahead of me and formulated its own answer.

We were going to dress as guards and slip out without anyone even noticing us.

I stripped off one guard's blue and yellow uniform with haste, as Klaus did the same with the other. Then we both slipped the incredibly loud colored garments on, and buckled the belts around our waists so the swords could dangle from them.

I was so short, or the sword was so long, the blade scraped against the ground. I had to keep my left hand on the hilt to keep it from contacting the floor and making any noise.

"Grab his arms," Klaus ordered me.

Without hesitation, I took the underwear clad man by the hands and dragged him along the floor. The guard was heavy, and

I couldn't move him with physical strength, so I used my telekinesis to bring him along.

Klaus and I must have finally been on the same wavelength. Not only were his orders easy to follow, but it seemed I knew exactly what he had in mind—even without my powers. We shoved the two unconscious and near-nude guards into the alcove we'd been hiding in a few minutes earlier.

"Are you ready?" he asked. He shined the guard's light in my eyes to see my face, but it caused me to be momentarily blinded by the bright light.

I held a hand over my eyes to block the beam of the flashlight. "Yeah."

"You make mental projection, so no vill one look at our faces?"

I wasn't sure if he was ordering me, or asking me if I was capable of doing it. It didn't matter, distracting anyone we came in contact with from gazing upon our faces would be a simple enough task, even if I was still fighting the uneasy feeling about being down in the catacombs.

I nodded, and then created an aura around both me and Klaus which would prevent anyone from staring directly at our faces. "Done."

"Let's go," he ordered.

He shone the light up the corridor and began a brisk walk. I followed, not two feet behind him, keeping my hand on the hilt of the sword and preventing it from touching the floor.

We made it up to the second level without running into anyone, and for a moment I thought we were home free. But we turned one corner and found Major Gianni shining his flashlight into one of the other recesses in the wall—looking for us, no doubt.

When he saw us, he immediately turned away from the open tomb and stared directly at Klaus. I pumped more mental energy into the aura around us, and watched in satisfaction as Major Gianni approached, but kept his focus on the walls of the corridor. "Captain, did you find anything?"

Klaus didn't respond. He stood, back straight, like a proper soldier would do when standing before a superior officer.

When it was apparent Klaus wasn't going to answer Gianni, he took another step, turning his head to gaze directly into Klaus' eyes. As soon as he did, his eyes averted again. "Is there a problem with your hearing, Captain?"

I knew at once Klaus didn't understand what the man was saying. Neither he nor I had considered he would actually be asked any questions.

Thinking quickly, I immediately connected my brain to both Klaus' and Gianni's. My hope was, if I connected their minds to mine, I would act automatically as their translator without either one noticing.

"What did you find?" the major asked again.

After only one more second's hesitation, as Klaus' mind came to the conclusion I had something to do with Gianni's sudden shift in language, he responded, "Nothing, Major. They seem to have escaped."

"They couldn't have escaped, Captain," Gianni said, still shifting his neck to look in any direction but Klaus' face. "No one could get passed us. They're hiding. Continue your search."

"Yes, sir," said Klaus in almost perfect military style. The only thing missing was a salute.

We were about to slip by the major, and make our way further up in the underground corridors, when another of the Swiss Guard ran up. He was out of breath and his eyes her wide. He looked like he was going to trip himself up several times before he clumsily stopped in front of Gianni.

"Major, we've been… trying to reach you by comm. We have… a situation."

Even here on the second level, it appeared we were too deep for any signals to get in or out.

Gianni turned from Klaus and I, and looked the disheveled guard directly in the eye. "Yes, Lieutenant?" He sounded impatient, but hopeful they had at least located the two of us.

"We have a break-in at the museum. Someone has slipped past security and entered the archive rooms."

"Do we have a description?"

"No, sir."

"It could be the two intruders. Maybe they did escape the catacombs after all." Gianni took a moment to consider a plan of action. Still being connected to his mind, I saw him weigh the options of abandoning the search in the catacombs, or letting someone else deal with the situation at the museum. He reached a decision quickly. "I want double the guards posted at the entrance to the catacombs. No one goes in or out until I give the all clear." He then started running up the corridor toward the exit. "You three are with me. We'll deal with this intruder."

Great, I thought as we followed the major up and out. *We've made our escape, but we're still trapped.*

I contacted Klaus via our mental connection. *We need to get away from Major Gianni so we can continue looking for the shroud.*

Or vee can help Jayson out at the museum, Klaus responded.

That was true. It was probably Jayson who'd broken in. Did we go and prevent Gianni from finding him and continue risking ourselves being caught, or did we trust Jayson to get himself out of this mess?

It was another decision I thankfully didn't have to make. When we reached the velvet ropes where Gianni had first laid eyes on us, another yellow and blue clad guard charged over to us.

"Major, someone has—"

"I know," Gianni cut him off, "we have an intruder in the archive room."

"Well, yes, that too, sir. But we also—"

"Something else?"

"Yes, sir. There's a disturbance at the chapel. Two guards have been assaulted by a pair of men."

Johnny, my mind automatically concluded. A few hours trapped in a hole and the whole world had gone to hell. He and Gina had obviously run into trouble during their search, and instead of simply turning invisible, Johnny had to go and attack someone.

"Why did the world have to go crazy on my shift?" Gianni muttered as he pinched the crown of his nose. "After today, I'm officially on vacation."

The two guards, plus Klaus and myself, stood as the major racked his brain. Then he tapped his hand to the comm unit in his ear and spoke loudly. "I want twelve men to the Sistine Chapel, and I want twelve more to meet me in the museum. Cancel all tours for today and evacuate every building. Call in every guard on staff—I don't care if they're sick or if every bone in their body is broken. I need a hundred men standing around the perimeter of Saint Peter's Square. We're shutting down the Vatican until we can get this straightened out."

"But, sir—"

"I'll deal with the colonel later," Gianni said. "Until then, I have full authority."

"Yes, sir."

"You two, with me," he said, pointing to the two guards. Then he turned to me and Klaus, averting his gaze when he tried to look us in the eye. "You two, stay here. No one is to leave or enter the tombs without direct authorization from me."

"Yes, sir," I said.

Without another moment's hesitation, Gianni and the two guards ran off. "Code: Orange. Everyone, out of the building. NOW!"

The floor of the basilica was full of people. All the tourists looked up in confusion as ten guards swept in and began ushering them through the door. A couple of people argued, but offered no resistance as they were taken outside. More people were taken out of the cathedral and escorted from the building, all of them unhappy, most of them because their vacation plans had been spoiled.

In only a few minutes, Klaus and I were the only two people left in the basilica—talk about efficiency. I'd never seen a building evacuated so quickly. Hell, it took twice as long to get everyone out of my high school when we had a fire drill.

The lightning-fast response to the possible threats was probably why Quinn hadn't wanted to come here in the first place. This city-sized tourist spot might as well have been a fortress. Even those of us with super-powers didn't stand a chance against the Vatican.

When everyone was gone, including the guards, I turned to Klaus. He played his part well. He stood at attention like a guard should, relaxed, but ready in case someone actually came. As a matter of fact, if I didn't know any better, I would swear he was a Swiss Guard.

"We should get out of here."

"Agreed."

"This mission is a bust, we need to gather everyone and leave before anything bad happens."

Anything else, you mean, the voice said.

Don't remind me.

"Agreed," Klaus said again.

We walked through the lobby toward the front doors. Before we reached the door, Klaus stopped and looked around.

"Take off your clothes," Klaus said.

I raised an eyebrow at him. It appeared the broken jaw I had promised earlier was about to come about. How dare he suggest I strip, and in a moment such as this?

But then, I calmed down as I noticed Klaus taking the blue and yellow uniform off. "Vee need to look like regular people," he continued.

I would have to smack myself later. Of course, he wanted me to take off the uniform. I did, so quickly and was once again in my regular clothes. I threw the garment on the floor, thankful I'd shed the ugly uniform from my body and sprinted for the door.

Klaus, with his long strides and being in better shape than I would ever be, made it to the exit first. He swung the large door open and the hot summer air washed over us like a hot bath. It was quite a contrast to the coolness of the catacombs. The sun, now high in the bright blue sky, spilled its light through the open door into the basilica. Its rays also shone brightly on the mass of people being corralled in the square.

And there were a lot of them—more people than I'd ever seen in one place in my life. The blue and yellow colored guards were herding them into a giant, angry, frightened and frustrated throng of people.

I ducked back into the building, hiding in the safety of the shadows. My heart was racing and I already felt dizzy thinking about approaching the crowd.

Klaus rushed back in after me. "Vhat's the matter?"

"I… I can't go out there," I admitted.

Twice now—worse, twice in one morning—I'd acted like a terrified child in front of Klaus. What did he think of me? He probably thought I was weak and couldn't take care of myself, which was totally untrue. Of course, I could have delved into his brain to find out, but like the rest of my friends, I didn't want to invade his privacy.

I could tell, however, from both the frown on his face and the dark aura radiating from his body, he was frustrated.

"Vee cannot vait here. Vhat is the problem?"

"I told you in the cab. I don't do crowds," I explained. He didn't seem to understand and opened him mouth to ask a question, but I cut him off. "It's like claustrophobia, only with people. I get horrible anxiety when in a crowd. I lose control of my powers and... bad things happen."

A brief flash of the comic convention Ethan and his dad had taken me to raced through my head. I'd nearly scared half the people on the show floor to death when it got to crowded, and there were at least ten times as many people outside.

Klaus leaned against the stone pillar next to the door and banged the back of his head against it. It was probably his way of thinking.

I peered through the open door again. The situation outside was getting worse. More people were being forced into the square, and though it appeared they had the option of leaving—since I saw no one blocking the street leading out into the city—no one was. Instead, many, especially at the front of the crowd, argued angrily with the guards. Some of them even raised their hands as if to attack the men if they didn't let them passed soon.

It apparently hadn't occurred to anyone there was an actual danger at the Vatican and the guards were only trying to protect them. No, all they cared about was the inconvenience this was causing them. They would rather sacrifice their own personal safety than come back another day when they'd be free to roam around. I would have been angry, but the site of the soon to be uncontrollable mob didn't leave room in my brain for fury.

I pulled my head back inside before I unintentionally projected some of my own fears on the men and women outside. If I panicked a mass of people that large someone would definitely be hurt—or killed.

Leaning against the wall again, I closed my eyes, trying desperately to calm down. It seemed we were officially trapped.

I reopened my eyes when Klaus muttered something in German that must not have had an English translation—probably swearing. His eyes were closed and his face was tilted upward as if he was praying for some divine intervention.

Then his eyes shot open and he pushed himself off the pillar. "You could fly over the crowd. I could meet you on the other side."

"Are you crazy?" I stepped further away from the door, irrationally fearing he would throw me out through it. "There are thousands of people out there. They'd see me!"

He grabbed me by the shoulders and gently pushed me into a corner. "You Americans are so... vhat is vord... uptight. Relax. Calm down. You vill zee this is the only option."

"Nope. I can always wait here and let them capture me. Or find another way out."

He leaned in again, and I thought he was going to kiss me like he'd done in the tomb. But the punch I'd promised never came. As it turned out, he only wanted to whisper in my ear. "Vhat vould your grandfather do? Vould he cower here like a baby, or vould he march outside and take off to escape?"

Wonderful. I tell him about me and my grandfather, and what does he do? He uses it against me to win an argument. But he neglected one tiny detail.

"You're right. My grandfather wouldn't just sit here. He would act. He'd have his next twelve steps planned out to have his enemy right where he wanted them. But he wouldn't, under any circumstances, reveal himself to thousands of onlookers. He's fought hard to keep his powers secret for years—decades. He'd think of something else before revealing his powers or identity to the world."

Klaus didn't say anything for a moment, but his face hovered only inches from mine. Again, I thought he might actually kiss me and again, though I didn't want him to, I did nothing to prevent it. But again, I was wrong. He gave me a cock-eyed grin and said, "You are pretty when your angry."

He was very lucky I wasn't Savanah. She would have literally punched him through a wall.

Klaus took a step back, holding his hands up in surrender when he saw the scowl on my face. "If I give you a vay to hide your identity, vould you listen?"

It sounded an awful lot like a challenge. But I had to admit, if he could hide who I was, then I'd really have no more reason to argue. "Okay."

He backed up a few more steps, arms still raised, before turning and picking up the uniforms we'd thrown to the ground. He picked up one and brought it back to me.

"You can still see my face in that."

He shook his head , but smiled. "Vait." Then he reached into his pocket and pulled out a little red rectangle. He carefully flipped up a small one inch blade.

"Seriously? You've been carrying a knife around this whole time? Why bother throwing pebbles?"

He held up the poofy hat and examined it. He turned it around several times, trying to find the front. Then, deciding which way was best, he plunged the knife into the fabric.

"Sviss Army Knife," he mentioned as he tore the cloth with the tiny blade. "Very handy tool. I never go vithout it."

He looked me dead in the eyes and cocked his head. Then he squinted at the hat before sticking the knife into the fabric again.

"What are you doing anyway?

"I am making jou a mask."

Why is it every guy I like wants me to put on a mask?

He tore a bit of the fabric, making the holes bigger, then held the hat up in front of him and scrutinized his work. Then, deciding it was good enough, he tucked the knife back in his pocked and handed me the hat. "Put it on."

Another order. I was getting tired of him telling me what to do, but without complaint—other than a drawn out sigh—I slipped the blue and yellow hat over my head. I pulled it down until my eyes met with the holes he'd cut. Luckily, the hat was poofy, because it had enough fabric so I could pull the garment down over my nose, obscuring all of my face except for my mouth.

I had to hand it to Klaus, he was a quick thinker. No one would be able to indentify me like this. The only hang-up I still had was I'd still be revealing my powers, and even if they couldn't identify me, that could still be a bad thing. After all, it wasn't everyday someone flew away from the Vatican.

"Put the uniform back on," Klaus ordered.

"Yes, sir," I said with as much sarcasm as I could muster. I did as instructed and redressed in the obnoxiously loud colors of the Swiss Guard. Why couldn't they wear black like any normal guard? At the very least, they could have made the colors darker.

I looked out the open door. I still wasn't sure I could do this. They couldn't recognize me with the hideous outfit I'm sure made me look like a clown. Even so, I didn't want to go out there. But I had to. We had to get out of here so we could do something to help the others.

What? I didn't know, but we couldn't sit here.

"Okay, I'll meet you on the other side of the square where the taxi dropped us off this morning," I told Klaus. Then I turned to step outside and pretty much let the world know super-powered beings existed.

I made it one step before a heavy hand clamped down on my shoulder and spun me back around. Before I could even let out my gasp of shock, his lips covered mine once again.

Dammit, I thought as I closed my eyes and enjoyed the feeling of the kiss for a second time. *Fight him, Christine. Tell him no. Tell him you have a boyfriend.*

Even though my mind protested, the words never made it to my lips which were passionately kissing the older boy back. I was a bad person and a horrible girlfriend. Not once, but twice, I'd given in to Klaus and allowed him to do this to me.

When Klaus pulled away, I was left there, eyes still closed, wallowing in the sheer bliss of his kiss. I hated myself.

I opened my eyes to find him standing there, looking into them through the holes he'd cut in the hat. That lopsided grin returned. "For luck," he said.

"I hate you," I said, turning away from him. "I want you to know that."

I didn't let him say anything word. I walked out, stepping into the light like someone reaching the ultimate goal of their enlightenment. The only thing was, I would be the one enlightening the thousands in the crowd.

The people toward the front of the crowd were really getting violent now. One man placed his hands on one of the guards and pushed him. "Tell me what's going on?" he demanded.

Two other guards rushed over to help out their comrade. They grabbed the violent man by the arms, but as they attempted to restrain him, the mob jumped on them.

I was torn between trying to help them and making my escape. If I didn't help the Swiss Guard, this was going to quickly turn ugly, but if I did, I might not ever get away. I stood on the top step for a moment, unsure which the right course of action would be.

And then the voice in my head spoke up again. *Just fly.*

It wanted me to escape and abandon the guards to the rage of the crowd. It seemed so wrong, but the more I thought about it, the more I knew it was the right thing to do.

So, I floated, first only a foot off the ground, then higher, and higher, until I was halfway to the roof of Saint Peter's Basilica. I went slow, because if something didn't change with the attacking crowd, I wouldn't have any choice but to go back and set things right.

It looked like that was exactly what I'd need to do, as more guards rushed into the outskirts of the square to try and keep order. Now, it seemed if I didn't do something, someone was really going to get seriously hurt.

Just then, there was a loud shout from somewhere in the corralled people. "Look!"

The next thing I knew, a chorus of Oh's and Ah's filled the air. First only a few people noticed me, then more, until much of the mob, including the guards struggling with the attacking people, were staring up at me.

Then, the crowd went silent. I didn't know it was possible to make that many people stop talking all at once. It was so quiet in the square as the people stared at the seemingly impossible floating Swiss Guard, if someone had dropped a pin at the back of the crowd, I'd probably have heard it.

Now that I'd prevented the crowd from rioting, I wasn't sure what to do. *Should I say something like the hero would in a comic book?* I didn't know what to say—probably something about treating your neighbor how you wanted to be treated or some other inspirational quote.

I didn't say a word. I simply hovered, drawing the crowd's complete attention. Then, I figured, if I lingered, someone would figure out a way to bring me down and that was not something I wanted or needed. So, deciding I'd done enough, I shot like a bullet off into the sky, leaving the awe-struck crowd, flabbergasted in my wake.

CHAPTER 24
GETTING THROUGH SECURITY

I found an alley about a quarter mile away. I landed, stripped off the ugly uniform for a second time and left it on the ground.

I stepped out of the alley and got my bearings so I could make my way back to Saint Peter's Square. While walking the distance back the way I'd come, the sky darkened. Looking up, I noticed clouds covering the sun. Further inspection showed darker clouds in the distance, moving in. The beautiful, warm morning was apparently going to turn into a pretty dismal afternoon.

It took me about ten minutes to jog back to the square—I made two wrong turns. When I got there, I found the crowd, apparently still in the eerie calm they'd experienced when I'd floated over them. Not only that, but (and I know this is going to sound completely insane) they were singing.

Yes, that's right, thousands of people all singing the same song.

"Ye watchers and ye holy ones, bright seraphs, cherubim, and thrones…"

Apprehensively, I approached the rear of the crowd. All backs were turned to me and not a single one of them noticed my approach.

"Raise the glad strain, Alleluia!"

It was like they were all mind controlled. How did they all know the words?

"Cry out, dominions, princedoms, powers, virtues, archangels, angels' choirs…"

There was a middle-aged woman, wearing white and with short brown hair, who appeared to be in some kind of trance. Her eyes were half-closed and her head was tilted toward the clouded sky. A quick scan of her head told me she was of perfectly sound mind. I also discovered this sudden hive mind of the crowd had everything to do with my appearance.

"Alleluia! Alleluia! Alleluia! Alleluia! Alleluia!"

I tugged on the woman's sleeve to get her attention. She stopped singing and turned in my direction. Her mind was in a state of absolute peace which considering all that had gone on, was the complete opposite of what should have been.

"Excuse me," I asked the woman. "What's going on?"

"A miracle," she said. She let out a contented sigh and with it, the feeling of sheer joy washed over me. "He sent us a sign. Proof from above that He does exist."

The crowd continued their singing. "O higher than the cherubim, more glorious than the seraphim…"

"One of His angels appeared before us," she explained. "It stopped the men in front fighting."

"Are you sure it was an angel?" I asked.

"Lead their praises, Alleluia!"

"Oh yes, definitely." She pulled a pink camera from her bag and brought up a photo she'd taken. "See? It's right there, watching us."

There I was on the tiny camera screen, floating above the mob. She'd zoomed in as far as she possibly could, but the quality of the picture still wasn't that good. But she was at the back of the crowd. Who knew what kinds of pictures they had of me in the front?

"Thou bearer of th'eternal word, most gracious, magnify the Lord…"

Why, of all things, would they think I was an angel? It's not like I had wings or a golden halo over my head.

They are standing on holy ground, my mind informed me. *You showed them something they've never seen before. Something they've never imagined. Of course they'd think it was some sign from God.*

I shuddered to think how many "Cults of the Angel" I had inspired to form.

"Alleluia! Alleluia! Alleluia! Alleluia! Alleluia!"

"Thank you," I told the lady.

"You're very welcome, dear. Praise His Holiness."

I rolled my eyes as she turned and rejoined the singing crowd, who'd begun the song again. These people were insane. No other explanation made any sense.

The icing on the crazy-cake was, and I could barely make them out, but at the top of the stairs in front of the basilica stood several bishops who were apparently leading the crowd in song. If only they knew it was me and not some divine spirit.

Klaus hadn't shown up yet, but I was really getting uncomfortable and wanted to leave. The thought I was the one who confirmed many of these people's faith made me physically ill. I couldn't be in their vicinity any longer. I wasn't going to abandon the boy though. So, instead, I waited across the street where I'd be able to see him when he emerged from the crowd.

Minutes ticked by and the mass of people repeated the song another two times. I shook my head. *The next time Klaus suggests something, I'm going to hit him.*

Thinking of Klaus automatically made me think of Ethan. I wondered where my boyfriend was. They had to be in Rome by now. I hadn't heard from them since the meeting yesterday, and I was worried. I know we weren't supposed to be in contact, but the game-plan had changed once Quinn decided to storm Vatican City like a rebel army fighting to regain a lost treasure.

I pulled the pendant up to my lips. "I don't know if you're still listening. But if you are, things have not gone well so far in Vatican City. I need you guys. Contact me."

I was about to send a text to Ethan too, when someone emerged from the crowd, walking briskly away from the square. He didn't look back and wasn't at all concerned with what was happening behind him.

I'd expected Klaus, but the boy had either not made it through the crowd yet or he'd been distracted by something else, because he was nowhere in sight. Instead, who stepped to the curb behind the bursting-at-the-seams square, was none other than our fearless leader: Quinn.

I hid myself as best I could, so he wouldn't see me, and observed him.

He whistled, carrying a bundle under his arm. It shone in what little light there still was coming through the ever-thickening clouds. It looked like a metallic cross with pictures on it. He gripped it by a small handle and cradled it close to his side. The way he was holding the cross, told the whole story. What he had was very important to him and he'd fight tooth and nail to keep it. I had a sinking feeling in the pit of my stomach about what the case contained inside.

He stood on the curb for about a minute when the cab that had dropped us off that morning pulled up. He opened the back door and stepped inside without so much as a glance over his shoulder.

The worm was going to leave us here. I knew he was going to betray us, but not like this. He was going to leave us, alone in a foreign country, with no money or passports (at least mine was in my bag) to fend for ourselves. I could have killed him. I should have killed him. But, I stayed in the shadows, out of sight until the taxi pulled away.

Okay, what do I do? I asked myself. Did I stay and wait for Klaus or another member of my team and let them know what happened, or did I go after Quinn? Both options felt wrong. On the one hand, if I waited, Quinn would probably get away. On the other hand, if I left, I'd be no better than Quinn, abandoning my team when I could help them.

Like I said, neither option was a good one.

I looked back into the throng of devout angel worshippers one last time. I could see no one from my team. The way Gianni had been set on capturing us, it was a good bet Johnny, Gina and Jayson were all under arrest at that very moment. And I had no idea where Klaus was, he should have been there by now.

Quinn's cab was a block away, and would soon be out of sight. My time to make a decision was running short.

The decision I made was for the good of the world, rather than the good of my group. I lifted the skull pendant to my mouth again. "If you can hear me, Quinn took off with something under his arm. I'm going to follow him. Home in on my position and bring backup as soon as possible."

And with that, and not worrying about being seen this time— I doubt I would since everyone's focus was pretty much on the basilica, hoping the "angel" would make another appearance—I jumped into the air and flew a hundred feet above all the buildings.

I was a dark black streak with dark gray clouds in the background. Anyone peering up would have a difficult time seeing me—I hoped, anyway. There was no time to worry about that. Quinn had the artifact, and I needed to get it back.

A clap of thunder filled the air as followed the green vehicle in the traffic below. Though the loud bang had scared me, I never took my eyes off the cab. I was determined not to lose this time.

The cab twisted through the streets of Rome as if it were trying to lose a tail. If Quinn was looking over his shoulder for someone following him though, I doubted he'd be looking a few hundred feet above him.

The rain began. It was very light, but the winds were starting to make it difficult to fly. I hoped wherever Quinn was going, it wasn't going to take him long to get there.

Eventually, the cab turned south and headed away from the city. It rode down the highway a few miles before turning and heading west. From where I was, I could already see the unmistakable glint of the ocean—or was it the sea—in front of us. That wasn't the only thing. Long cement runways crisscrossed the landscape just before the water.

Quinn was headed straight for the airport.

Of course, I thought, *he has what he wanted. Now he's making his escape.*

How do I stop him? I asked.

I don't know, the voice responded.

You are so helpful.

Lightning arced in the sky over the sea. The storm was approaching, and fast. Luckily, Quinn's taxi was only a few miles away from the airport, so I'd be able to land soon.

I shouted Quinn's destination into the pendant and then made my descent. I had to think of something, and quickly. There had to be some way to prevent Quinn from getting on a plane. I had to come up with something that didn't reveal myself. Alone, I didn't stand a chance of beating Quinn.

The cab pulled up to the airport and Quinn got out. I landed on the opposite side of the cab, as Quinn entered the doors to the airport. I hadn't been seen, thankfully.

The taxi driver was about to pull away, when I sent him the suggestion waiting around for a few minutes would earn him a really big fare. I almost felt bad for the man. He'd been manipulated by two mind-controllers in one day. While I had him in the trance, I opened the back and removed my bag and Gina's.

I told the driver to drive around, but to come back about every twenty minutes. I hope my suggestion was strong enough, because I didn't want everyone else to lose their possessions. I memorized the number on the back of the car just in case.

The cab drove off, and I ran inside, hoping I hadn't lost track of Quinn in the process. When I stepped through the doors, I saw him, waiting in line at the Air Italia ticket windows. He was still cradling the silvery cross under his arm, and I doubted he was going to let the object out of his site.

I would have loved to rip the case out from under his arm and taken off, but I knew I wouldn't get very far. Not only would Quinn be after me. But I was pretty sure airport security would try and stop me as well.

I stayed well enough away from Quinn, hiding amongst the others in the terminal. With enough minds around me, it might very well mask my presence. Hopefully, it would mask me long enough to come up with a proper plan—or for the cavalry to arrive.

"Where are you guys?" I muttered.

It took several minutes for Quinn to reach the front of the line. In the meantime, the skies outside had pretty much opened up, and a deluge of rain fell onto the pavement. Lightning struck every few seconds, always followed by a loud rumble of thunder. Quinn purchased a ticket and then casually walked to the security checkpoint. He stopped in the middle of the floor and looked over his shoulder. A strange look crossed his face. I would have said it was worry, but it was more like suspicion. His eyes narrows and his brow creased as his jaw went slack.

Thinking he might sense me, I pulled back even further, hiding amongst the customers at a magazine stand.

He shrugged his shoulders and then continued on his way. I didn't have much time. Unless I had a ticket, I'd have to bust through security to get to Quinn, which...

Which might be exactly what I need to do.

A plan quickly formulated in my head. If I shot past security right after Quinn, they'd have to chase me. And then I could have them do the work for me. I'd bump into Quinn and knock the case out of his hand, and when they saw what was inside, they would have to stop him. At least, they would in theory.

There was one thing I needed to do first. If I burst passed the checkpoint as I was, they would surely get my face on camera, so the first thing I needed to do was hide it. So, instead of following Quinn, I ran into the ladies' bathroom.

As with most women's rooms, there was a line to use the toilettes. So, impatiently, I waited, hoping Quinn didn't get too far ahead of me. Once it was my turn and a stall opened, I jumped inside and ripped the zipper open on my luggage.

I dug to the bottom to grab what I hoped I wouldn't need on this stupid mission: my mask and the bio-suit Abby had given me. I'd dyed the white fabric black—there was no way I was running around in a pure white outfit. I quickly stripped off my clothes and shoved them into the suitcase, then pulled the uniform on, adjusting the mask over my eyes to cover my face.

Both items would be a necessity. First, the mask to hide my features so no security cameras could pick me up—I eventually did want to go home, after all, and having my face on the "no fly" list definitely wouldn't allow that. Second, the bio-suit, because for all I knew, there was some trigger happy airport policeman who wouldn't hesitate to take me down at the first sign of trouble.

I couldn't get over how undignified this was. When have you ever seen a superhero changing in a bathroom—never! But I've learned things never worked like they did in comic books.

Gina's bag, with the fake-shroud in it, was slung across my chest.

I extracted my passport, my cell phone and my wallet and tucked them into pockets in the bio-suit. Once they were concealed inside, I could hardly tell they were there. I left the luggage with the rest of my clothes behind. For the moment, I wouldn't need them, and carrying all that with me would only slow me down.

The women in line to use the bathroom all fixed me with confused stares. All of them wondered what I was doing and why I was dressed like that. I did my best to ignore them and ran from the room, using very little effort as the bio-suit took most of the strain off my muscles.

I immediately caught the attention of airport security. Two guards standing by a kiosk selling sunglasses picked up their radios and made a call as I sprinted by. I wasn't too concerned. Even if Quinn had made it through the security checkpoint, at the speed I was now moving, I would still catch him quickly.

Something stopped me before I could make it down to the checkpoint, allowing Quinn to get a few extra seconds ahead of me. Like all airports, this one in Rome had televisions playing the news all throughout the airport. On the bottom of the screen in white letters over a red background said, "Angelo Visite Vaticano". Now, I couldn't really be sure, since the text didn't translate in my brain the way words did, but I'm pretty sure the headline read, "Angel Visits Vatican".

Above the words, was a short video, showing me hovering over the crowd in the Swiss Guard uniform and then taking off into the sky. The scene replayed, this time at a different angle. Then a third time, at yet another angle.

Oh crap. This was only going to get worse. Hopefully, like the YouTube video from a couple of months ago, people would eventually see this as some form of camera trickery. I doubted it.

"There she is!" came a shout from behind me.

I spun away from the television to see three men in brown and gray uniforms running toward me. The one in the lead was pointing in my direction, making it perfectly clear I was the target.

"Time to go!" I shouted, then I bolted down the corridor toward the security checkpoint.

With the enhanced speed the suit gave me—though it was nowhere near as fast as Ethan could run—the men didn't stand a chance catching me.

"Excuse me," I yelled as I darted between an old lady and a man in a business suit. "Sorry," I said after nearly knocking down a couple of kids.

Then in front of me was the checkpoint, with a rather large line in front of it. I didn't have time to wait. Not only could Quinn get away any second, but if I stopped, there was a good chance security would catch me.

I picked up my speed, running as fast as my legs and the suit would allow. Moving at such a high speed, it seemed like the checkpoint sped up on me. The police running the checkpoint had already stopped anyone else from passing through, as they obviously got the bulletin about me. I could see two of them moving forward in the crowd, hands already on their guns.

Taking a few more steps, bringing me dangerously close the end of the line, I leapt high and used my powers and momentum to soar quickly over the travelers, through the metal detector, through the x-ray machine and out before even one of the officers could react.

I landed on the other side, tucking and rolling and using the forward motion to spring back up on my feet and continue my sprint. I paused in front of the outgoing flights board just long enough to find the flights to the United States, since I was almost positive that was where Quinn was headed. There were two, both leaving within the next thirty minutes.

I looked at the signs—thankfully numbers were the same in every language. One was going to Atlanta and leaving in fifteen minutes from gate twenty-three. The other was headed to New York and left in thirty from gate four.

"Opposite directions," I muttered. "That so figures."

I decided to try the New York plane, since it was closer to Pittsburgh and the more obvious choice. If I was wrong, I hoped I had enough time to double back and get to the other gate without being caught.

Following the sign pointing toward gate four, I ran as fast as my legs would carry me. At this point, I had almost every officer in the airport coming after me. I would have to be quick. Dodging through people, faster than security could react, I bounced from wall to wall on my way toward the gate I prayed Quinn was waiting at.

I used my telekinetic powers for an extra burst of speed. At this point, I had to be moving along at the rate of a slow car on the highway.

"Freeze!" one officer shouted as he burst through a door I'd run passed. He had his gun drawn, but I was confident he wasn't going to fire it while the corridor I sprinted down was so crowded.

Three men tried to block my path, all of them with guns in hand. I didn't stop. I jumped, flipping over the trio, and blew a kiss to the middle one as I landed and continued on my way.

Yeah, I don't know why I blew the kiss either. I guess it was one of those "caught up in the moment" things.

I was getting close, passing gate ten, and seeing gate four ahead of me. Even as I ran, dodging both security and innocent bystanders, I scanned the area in front of the gate for Quinn.

My eyes shot from face to face, and my mind reached out to sense the man. Both were dangerous, Quinn could see or sense me at any time and prepare some kind of defense against me. But let's face it, if he didn't know something was up with the officers running around and the constant shouting, then he was even dumber than I thought and it would be all too easy to take him.

I spotted him. He was there, in front of the large plate glass window, a lovely view of the airport and the sea behind him. Well, it would have been lovely, anyway, if it weren't still pouring down rain. I wasn't going to stop. He saw me coming, but hadn't made any more yet, which meant he wasn't entirely sure I was going to attack him yet.

But that was what I intended to do.

If I jumped into him, like I'd jumped through the security checkpoint, I might catch him by surprise and knock the wind out of him long enough to wrestle the cross-shaped case from him— which by the way, I'm kind of shocked he was able to get through security. My only theory is he did a little mind-manipulation to make the officers believe it was a box of candy, or something. But that's besides the point.

I didn't break stride as I reached the gate. I'd slam him into the window and then grab the box from him. Then I'd run off before anyone could stop me. If I did get stopped, I'd quickly hand over the item to security and surrender. They'd have no choice but to search it, especially after I explain I thought it was a bomb. Then they'd know what Quinn was up to and he'd be in as much trouble as me.

Quinn watched me coming, but still made no motion as if to stop me. He probably still expected me to stop in front of him and want to talk. But there would be no more talking today. There would be no more manipulations. There would only be pain—his.

I was about fifteen feet away when I bounded into the air, straightening my body like an arrow and using my powers to make sure my aim was precise. Fists outstretched, I would hit him square in the chest, knocking him into the bullet-proof glass and watch him slink slowly to the ground.

I flew through the air, feeling like I was moving in slow motion. Quinn must have finally realized I wasn't there for any negotiations, because his eyes widened in panic. He tried to move himself out of the way, but it was far too late for that. I was shooting at him at sixty miles-an-hour, and at that short distance, he wouldn't be able to move in time.

Sucks to be him.

My fists made contact with his chest, and as predicted, he fell backward into the plate glass window. Only, I'd miscalculated. Instead of him hitting the window, which should have been sturdy enough to take the blow, the glass shattered and both of us fell, tumbling through the opening to the wet tarmac below.

CHAPTER 25
SHOWDOWN

I'd love to tell you I fell gracefully, but it's kind of like when you're running upstairs, and you think there's one more step, but there isn't, you really have no choice but to fall flat on your face. That's kind of the way Quinn and I fell.

The good news was, I'd figured out what it took to break bullet-proof glass. Apparently, all you needed was about three hundred pounds moving at sixty miles-an-hour. I know it seems like useless information, but think of what I could have done with that knowledge back in Turin when I was trying to steal the fake shroud. You never know when useless info might come in handy.

Anyway, Quinn and I fell smack down on the wet pavement, amid shards of broken glass. I'd managed to throw a mental barrier around my body out of sheer reflex and Quinn had done the same, but I'd still gotten a few cuts from crashing through the window.

The metal cross clattered across the ground, landing about ten yards away. Now aching, I managed to get myself to my feet first and ran over to it before Quinn got up. Once I touched the uneven etchings on the metal case, I knew what was inside was special. I could feel the contents, like I could feel the spear and Quinn's cup. This was what we'd been after.

I opened the case, but made sure to cover it with my body to prevent the rain from pouring onto the contents. A 2,000-year-old piece of cloth probably wasn't the best thing to get wet. Once it was open, I brownish shroud came into view. It was folded tightly within the cross, but that wasn't all. Laying atop the cloth were four long splinters of wood, each no bigger than my finger.

I reached out and touched one and had to recoil from the mental blast I'd received. They had to be small pieces of the True Cross, what was left of the artifact anyway after thousands of years of decay.

By now, there was a crowd forming at the windows, looking at the two crazy people who'd crashed through outside. I could feel the amazement of a few of them we both weren't dead. I rolled my eyes. As usual, a crisis erupts, and all people can do is watch. *Does no one have any sense of danger anymore?*

Resealing the contents within the metal cross, I stood once again.

The officers chasing me were bound to come out at any moment. So, I had to get out of there with the case.

I jumped into the air, intending to fly off with the cross and its contents, but I didn't make it five feet into the air before a force slammed be back into the ground.

"Give it back to me and I may not kill you," Quinn groaned.

Dazed as I was, I managed to tighten my grip on the case. As I propped myself up on my other hand, I saw Quinn, still about three yards away, standing over me.

"I can't do that," I told him.

"I train you. I keep you safe. And this is how you repay me? You ungrateful little bitch!" He reached out with a greedy hand, taking another step toward me. As he lifted his leg, I grabbed the opposite foot with my mind and pulled it out from under him. Quinn fell onto his back with a loud "Oof!"

I stood up, and keeping an eye on Quinn's fallen form, I backed away slowly. He was going to get back up, and when he did he was going to be furious. I needed to put as much distance between him and I as I could.

KRACK-KABOOM! A bolt of lightning sizzled through the clouds, causing me to go temporarily blind for half a second in the flash.

When I was able to see again, Quinn had disappeared. "What?" I said in confusion. Quinn couldn't have possibly moved that fast.

Suddenly, I was pushed hard from behind and was sent sprawling to the ground. I almost fumbled the metal cross.

For the third time, I rose to my feet. It was amazing how much more of a beating I could take in the suit. It was as if the material absorbed the blows being wailed upon me. Don't get me wrong, I still felt them, but I should have been a lot more hurt than I was.

The airport police officers forced their way to the broken window. "Hold it right there!" one shouted at me. He had his gun aimed in my direction. His hands shook, which told me he'd never actually fired at another person before.

The other officers disappeared into the gathered spectators, probably to find a way out onto the tarmac. I wasn't at all worried about the officer's gun aimed at me, when and if he fired, the bio-suit was more than capable of handling the bullet. I'd learned that first-hand when Samantha jumped in front of a bullet to save my life.

I was even less worried as the gun was seemingly yanked from the hands of the now confused officer by some invisible force.

My neck craned as the gun spun through the air, over my head, into the waiting hand of Quinn, who stood five feet behind me.

He aimed the gun directly at my head, and for a half-second I was sure Quinn was going to shoot. I took a breath—maybe my last.

"Drop the gun," the nervous-looking officer shouted from the window.

Without hesitation and barely looking, Quinn raised the gun and pulled the trigger.

My eyes closed as the gun flashed. It took a split-second to raise a mental shield around myself. I waited for it to be struck by the bullet, but after another second, I realized it wasn't going to come.

Opening my eyes, I saw the gun had been pointed over my head. I spun to see the officer, clutching his chest where he'd been hit. Blood stained his brown shirt and hands. He looked into my eyes, completely shocked, before he fell out the window.

I should have saved him. I should have dove under the window and caught him, or grabbed him with my powers and floated him gently. But I did none of that. Instead, like my body was firmly rooted to the ground and I had no control over my movement, I stood and watched the man plummet to the pavement, and smack head-first into it. He was dead.

I turned back to Quinn, my eyes wide and my jaw hanging open in disbelief. He'd killed the man for absolutely no reason. I tried to utter a curse, a sound, anything, but my vocal chords refused to work.

Quinn casually tossed the gun to me. On instinct, I caught it, almost dropping the box in the attempt. I stared down at the weapon, still warm in my hands, the faint smell of gunpowder reaching my nostrils. It was heavier than it looked, but I still found myself thinking, *How can something so small, kill so easily?*

Then, hands shaking and a deathly glare crossing my features, the real question formed in my mind. *How can Quinn kill so easily?*

"His blood is on your hands, Christine," Quinn shouted above the gale. "None of this would have happened if you hadn't come after me. Now, give me the box and no one else needs to get hurt."

I could feel his manipulative tendrils of mental energy attempting to break through the barrier around my mind. In response, I pushed more of my concentration to keep the barrier intact. This was the easy part. I could repel his controlling thoughts all day. When he tried to get physical, and my concentration was torn, was when I'd run into trouble.

Which was why I had to stall until help arrived—if help arrived.

They had plenty of time to get here by already. The tracking systems implanted in me still should have worked. Not to mention my dash through the airport had to be all over the news by now. So, where were they?

"And what are you going to do with it if I give it to you?" I asked.

The winds and rain carried my voice away, and I wasn't sure Quinn heard me, until he responded. "We've been through this. I'm trying to save the world."

"Save it?" I yelled. "Or change it?"

A loud clap of thunder shook the air when Quinn responded. I couldn't be sure, but it sounded like he said, "What's the difference?"

For a moment, I wondered if there really was a difference. After all, saving the world would require some amount of change, wouldn't it?

I shook my head. I couldn't think like that. I couldn't think like HIM. The only way to save everyone would be for the item inside the cross to be destroyed. And that was exactly what I intended to do.

I tossed the gun aside, thinking once again about the innocent man who'd wielded it. The sickness I felt at the thought of what Quinn did to him quickly turned to anger—anger at the man before me who was intent on committing who knew how many more atrocities against humanity. He needed to be stopped.

I didn't stand a chance at fighting Quinn one on one, and if I lingered too much longer his limited patience would fail. So, I had one option—run!

A door behind me burst open and several officers poured out into the rainy afternoon weather. Their guns were already drawn, and I'm surprised they didn't open fire immediately upon seeing us.

Even without any gunfire, it was the distraction I needed, and without waiting another second, I leapt over Quinn, landing in a deep puddle and sprinted off along the runway. The metal cross was tucked safely under my arm, as I ran headlong through the torrents of water dumping down on top of me.

I never looked back, even as I heard the unmistakable sounds of gunfire behind me. While I hoped the airport officers would be able to take Quinn down, I knew realistically, the men didn't stand a chance. All I needed was for them to keep my former teacher busy long enough for me to get away.

I pelted down the runway, splashing through puddles in my haste to escape. As I ran, I shoved the metal cross inside Gina's bag with the faux-shroud. Another crash of thunder startled me, and caused me to break my stride for an instant. I quickly righted myself, and continued on my way to what appeared to be an empty hangar.

The long half-cylindrical building was huge. I guess it had to be if they were able to park a full-sized jet in there. There was no one in there and no planes in sight, but even before I made it inside I suspected there would be hundreds of places where I'd be able to hide the box. As long as it remained hidden, it wouldn't have to worry about it, and could more easily confront Quinn.

Only when I made it under the cover of the high round ceiling did I slow down and allow myself to look back. There was no sign of pursuit, but I wasn't stupid enough to think Quinn wouldn't follow me. He'd be coming, and soon.

The hangar had to be twice as big as the football field back at school, and looked like it could fit several planes at once. Glancing around, I noticed there were fewer places I could hide the box than I'd originally thought. The hangar had, as one would expect, way too much open space. They could literally hold a concert for a few thousand people in this place, and still have room to spare. However, it seemed while I thought there'd be tool chests, and equipment laying around where I could stash the box, there wasn't much.

There were a few cabinets on the left side of the hangar, where they must have stored some equipment to fix planes, and I figured it would have to do. I rushed over and flung the door of one cabinet open. Inside were a bunch of blue work uniforms, hanging neatly in a row. On the bottom were black work-boots.

Well, it's better than nothing I guess.

I shoved the case inside, and slammed the door shut, running the length of the humongous building in a few seconds. On the wall was a glass case, and inside emergency equipment, including a fire hose, fire extinguisher and a med-kit—nothing I could really use against Quinn, but that wasn't the point. I removed the fake shroud and stuffed it inside with the hose.

I stood there, with my hands inside and waited. He would be along any minute in search of me and the case.

"If anyone's hearing this," I said into the pendant, "I'm in a hangar, about a mile from the main terminal. Come quickly, I don't know how much longer I can hold Quinn off."

As if on cue, the man descended from the sky, into the hangar. I made sure he saw me, and when he did I pretended to struggle and then nervously slammed the glass emergency case shut. I backed away, and came to the center of the room.

Quinn landed easily on the ground, and dripping wet from the storm, he spoke, "Foolish, Christine. Clever, but foolish none-the-less. You will not stop me from taking my prize, and you along with it."

"Me?" I asked. "What do you want me for?"

He ran his hand through his hair, trying to shake loose the water clinging to it. "I think that should be obvious. Although, you never did learn how to fully use your brain, did you?"

"What are you talking about?" I'd play the stalling game as long as possible. The longer I did, the more of a chance help would arrive. So, I'd let Quinn talk until he was blue in the face. Let him, as Ethan would say, monologue his entire plan. Maybe he'd reveal something I could use against him.

"It's always been about you, Christine. Haven't you come to realize that yet? I've tested you, right down to the genetic level, and you are the one it must be."

He stepped toward me, arms raised, but this time almost as if he were going to embrace me rather than attack. I stepped away just as quickly. No matter his motive, I didn't want the murderer anywhere near me. I had plenty of room to back up, and at the rate we were going it would take several minutes before I was up against the wall.

"I must be what?" I asked.

"You are the only one who will be able to take the full genetic code."

I didn't quite comprehend, and even though I was keeping my distance from the man, who could very well lash out at me at any given moment, the look on my face was unquestionable.

Quinn shook his head, and kept advancing in my direction. "You can be so completely clueless sometimes, I begin to wonder myself if I haven't been mistaken. Let me spell it out for you plainly. I have the Grail, you have the Spear. In the box you were so obviously hiding as I came in, are the final two pieces of the puzzle. Inside are the real Shroud of Turin and the last few splinters of what remains of the True Cross. Each one of them has touched the blood of Christ. Each one of them has one piece of his genetic code. Put all four of them together and..."

"And you make the ultimate human being," I finished for him.

"No, you make a god. And you bring about the change this world needs to survive."

Okay, I realized I had never actually been scared before in my entire life. The look of seriousness on Quinn's face, and his talk about turning a person into a deity, was... scary. The worst part was, somehow, he thought I was the key to all of it, which meant he wanted to involve me in some crazy way.

I know I shouldn't have. I should have remained quiet and not said another word. Or maybe I should have struck and let him end me right then and there. But I couldn't help myself. I had to know. "Why did you say it's always been about me?"

"You're the only vessel that can hold the genetic code. My research has shown, given to just anyone, even one who is gifted with our talents, the genes would burn that person up from the inside out. Oh, they would have great power for the last few days of their meaningless lives, but in the end, their bodies wouldn't be able to handle it. You are different. It's like you were built specifically for the purpose of holding the genetic material."

I closed my eyes and imagined myself having limitless power. I could do almost anything I wanted. I would have the power to do anything, to save anyone. I could even put down evil in the world once and for all.

My eyes sprung open as Quinn spoke again. "Why do you think I have so much patience with you? Anyone else, and I'd have destroyed them eons ago."

I had to think about that for a second. Once I thought about it, I realized it was true, though he occasionally lost his temper with me, he'd shown more patience and understanding with my arguments than he had with anyone else. When Johnny had thought to question Quinn's authority, the man almost lost it, but when I had done the same, it had been more of a discussion.

It was too much to take in at once. I needed to change the subject.

"Can I ask you something?"

He nodded.

"Did you know the shroud in Turin Cathedral was a fake?"

He nodded again. "They moved it days after my first attempt."

"Then why go through all the trouble of having us steal it? Why didn't we go straight to the Vatican in the first place?"

"The alarm had to be raised at the Vatican. Once they realized the artifact was in danger, they moved it to the vaults underneath the city—the most secured area where the most important documents and artifacts are kept."

"And using us as a distraction, you slipped in unnoticed and took them," I said. My anger was boiling again and threatened to burst out. "You used us?"

"To use a term I'm sure you'll be familiar with, sometimes you have to sacrifice a few pawns to claim victory."

Was this what you were really trying to teach me, Grandpa? Had the whole stupid chess teaching been a warning about how Quinn would try to use me? No. That couldn't have been it.

"And what if I'd been captured, or killed? You said you needed me. What would you have done then?"

"Well, recently—quite recently, in fact—I have determined that your genetic code wasn't as unique as I'd originally thought. If you had perished in my attempt to steal the shroud, I would have been upset, but I would have gone with an alternative. Your brother shares your ability to handle the full genetic code. I'll admit, it wasn't easy obtaining a blood sample from him, seeing as your house is watched almost around the clock, but—"

"Shut up!" I shouted. "You go near Conner again and so help me…"

"You'll what? Kill me?" The way he said it caused every muscle in my body to tense. He was mocking me. His eyes narrowed and a wave of his anger crashed down upon me. "You don't do that, remember? You said it yourself. You couldn't sacrifice even one life to help the greater good. So, don't try acting all tough and threaten me. It won't do you any good."

I thought seriously about rushing him and attacking then and there, and the hell with the backup that was probably never coming. This man had broken into my home and hurt my brother, all for some sick science experiment. He deserved to die. He needed to be tortured, nice and slow until he begged to be killed. *But are you willing to do it, Christine?*

A loud boom broke the tension I thought might have been thunder, but it didn't sound quite right. I looked away from Quinn then, and walking in, gun with smoking barrel held over his head, was Agent Smith.

Quinn too turned to look at the intruder. His lip curled with disgust at the sight of the man.

Smith, not in the least afraid, even knowing the things Quinn could do, charged forward in sort of a walk/run until he had the barrel of his gun pressed directly against Quinn's lips. "Just give me a reason," he said.

CHAPTER 26
STANDOFF

When I'd asked for backup, Smith was definitely not the person I had in mind.

He looked over his shoulder at me and said, "Nice work, Agent Carpenter, but I'll take it from here."

Like hell you are, I thought. I was about as likely as stand by and let him get his hands on the artifacts as I was to let Quinn run off with them.

I didn't move, but remained ready. Once I made my intentions known to Smith, I'd be in danger of both him and Quinn.

Smith stepped up behind Quinn and forced his gun into the back of Quinn's neck. With his free hand he placed a small round device, about the size of a quarter, on Quinn's neck behind his ear. Instantly, Quinn's mental presence disappeared.

"Don't even bother trying anything now. You couldn't even lift a paperclip with that thing on. Now give me your hands!"

Quinn didn't immediately comply, but didn't say anything either. When it was clear, he wasn't going to move, Smith pressed the gun further into Quinn's neck. "Do it, or I'll blow your head off right here!"

Quinn half-closed his eyes and turned his head slightly as if to see Smith over his shoulder. Then, he moved both of his arms back behind him, sighing like an impatient boy waiting in line for lunch.

Smith worked quickly, and with one hand cuffed Quinn's wrists behind him. With his hands bound and the large inhibitor on his head, it pretty much rendered any resistance from the man absolutely useless.

"So, let's begin," Smith said. Moving beside Quinn now, and stepping back a pace so the gun wasn't directly against his head anymore. "Where's the shroud?"

Quinn looked at me, then over at the barrel of Smith's gun as if bored. Then he looked down at the ground, saying nothing.

"Where is the shroud?" Smith repeated—this time shouting. His eyes were wide and maniacally looking at Quinn. He'd gone off the deep end. Obsession had taken over his mind now, and he was beyond reasoning with. He was also desperately close to pulling the trigger and spraying Quinn's brains all over the floor.

The worst part was, I actually considered letting him. With Quinn out of the picture, I'd have so much less to worry about. There'd be one less idiot out there trying to reshape the world.

Right, like you're going to let that happen.

I tried sending soothing, calming thoughts to Smith, but he had one of the inhibitors on too, so I wasn't able to break through. I didn't dare break the device like I knew I could. If Smith felt it, in his irrational state of mind, he'd probably pull the trigger out of agitation.

A loud click echoed through the silent room. Smith had cocked the handgun. "I'm only going to ask once more."

Quinn gazed directly in my eyes. It was an intense stare, one that said I'd better do something.

Why doesn't he do something? the voice asked.

I sighed. Again, I could have let Smith shoot him. But I couldn't even allow Quinn, a man who'd admitted to harming my brother and using me for some foolish attempt to change the world, to be murdered.

Hating myself, and promising a self-inflicted mental beating when this was all over, I pointed and said, "It's in the emergency case on the wall."

Quinn closed his eyes as if relieved I'd revealed the artifact's location.

Smith merely glanced over at the case where I'd stashed the fake shroud, but he didn't take his eyes off Quinn. Keeping his gun aimed at my former science teacher, he backed away toward the wall.

"Excellent diversion," Quinn whispered. "You almost had me convinced. Now, where is the real shroud?"

"Like I'm going to tell you," I whispered back.

Without averting his gaze, Smith reached behind himself and opened the emergency cabinet. Then he felt around until his hand grasped the rough fabric of the shroud. His eyes lit up with delight, when he extracted the item and saw it.

There didn't seem to be any doubt in his mind he was holding the genuine article. "Good work, Agent Carpenter. I can see now how useful you can be."

"Yeah," I agreed. "I guess I'm just full of surprises."

He walked back toward us, fake shroud in one hand, gun pointed at Quinn in the other. As he drew closer, I could see the look in his eye. It was the look of a power-crazed man—one that saw his competition as a threat he had to eliminate at any cost.

"And now that I have what I want, I see no more reason to keep you around." He pressed the gun barrel against the side of Quinn's head.

The man, my former teacher and mentor, totally helpless and knowing he was out of options, looked to me once more for help. It was kind of pathetic actually for someone so old to plead for his life—albeit silently. It was the first time I'd seen genuine fear in Quinn's expression. And if he hadn't been such an evil dirtbag, I might have felt sympathy for him, but I couldn't.

On the other hand, I also couldn't let Smith kill him. Fortunately, as I prepared to jerk the gun from his hand, and totally ruin any notion I was on Smith's side, I was saved the need to do so.

"Drop it, Smith," Abby's voice was even as if she were greeting a coworker coming into the office. Of course, her tone didn't need to be forceful. The long-barrelled rifle she had pointed at Smith, and the fact her eyes was against the sniper-scope mounted on the top, pretty much said one false move from the man would mean the end of his life.

Behind her ran in Ethan, stopping cold beside her. Then Peter and Savanah joined them. All three wore costumes similar to what I wore, masks and all. For the first time, my chest swelled with pride seeing my three friends in uniform, and knowing I matched them.

Ethan attempted to meet my gaze. I had to look away, as glad as I was to see him, I still couldn't face him. Somehow, I knew if I looked directly at him, he would figure out what I'd done not two hours ago. It had been a stupid mistake, but Ethan wouldn't understand.

"Okay, so who's the bad guy here?" Ethan asked the others.

"They both are, Loser," Savanah responded. "Don't you pay attention?"

"ADHD," Ethan responded. "Side-effect of my powers."

"You really have issues."

"Agent Davidson, shut those damned kids up!" Smith howled. He dug the gun deeper into the side of Quinn's head, causing the man to wince in pain. He finger tightened ever so slightly on the trigger as well, and I feared the gun might go off. Yet, I still did nothing.

"Actually, I'm done taking orders from you," Abby said. She didn't falter at all, keeping Smith directly in the sight of the scope. To prove she was serious, she lit up the laser sight, placing a bright red dot on Smith's forehead. "Christine, would you be so kind as to retrieve Mr. Smith's weapon?"

"With pleasure."

I reached out to grab the gun with my mind. I had a grip on it, and was about to yank it from his clenched fingers when…

"I am your superior officer," Smith ranted, though I wasn't sure if it was directed toward me or Abby. "You would be nothing without me, Davidson!" Okay, guess that answered the question. "I deserve your respect and loyalty!"

"You deserve nothing!" Abby spat back. She took a few steps closer to the man, making her chance of missing him even slimmer. "I trusted you, and I was loyal to you until Christine told me about your outing the other night. So, I did a little digging of my own." She was angry, she felt betrayed, and yet, as she spoke, it sounded more like she was reading from a police report rather than pointing an accusatory finger at her own former mentor. "When did it become M.H.D.A. policy to hire mercenaries to pose as Agents on an intel mission? Or should I call it an ambush? Because the last I checked, you didn't need over a dozen men to question a potential informant."

Well, that certainly explained a lot. I thought they'd been Agents, but they were nothing but hired guns, which might have explained why Klaus was able to take them out so easily.

Smith looked at me, eyes red with anger. He thought I'd been the one to cause his plan to go awry.

Only one question formed in my mind. It was a simple one, but I knew the answer would be complicated. I cast a narrowed eye at Smith and simply asked, "Why?"

Though the question had been meant for the aged Agent, Abby was the one who'd answered. "He's been double-dipping for months, as far as I can tell. I've gone through all our records for the last six months. Three trips to Jerusalem at $250,000 each? A work order to refurbish a facility in the Rockie Mountains we don't even own for $20million? Recon on four German and six

American geneticists, who have all mysteriously turned up missing in the last two months? Two leaves of absence for two weeks at a time? Does anyone else find this suspicious?"

Ethan raised his hand and pronounced, "I do."

I seriously had to have a talk with that boy about rhetorical questions.

"What are you building Smith? And why is that thing in your hand so important?"

I closed my eyes, and once again saw the images I'd seen in his head the other night. The army he planned to create, more powerful than any other—a force no one on Earth could dare oppose.

As the spark of Smith's plan ignited inside my head, Quinn's lips turned upward in a vicious looking smile. "I think Ms. Carpenter knows the answer."

All eyes were on me. Even Smith, who seemed less interested in the laser sight burning a hole in his skin than what I was about to say. He looked at me fearfully, as if I might very well out his whole stupid scheme.

"He's building a cloning facility. With the shroud's genetic code, he's going to create an army of super-powered men." I paused and gazed into Quinn's eyes as I prepared to let out the next part. "Exactly like the Nazi's did when they created Quinn."

"So," Ethan asked, dragging out the vowel a little too long, "are we talking like the clone army from Star Wars?"

"Actually, yes," I wanted to beat my head into a wall for the fact I knew exactly what he was talking about. "Thousands of soldiers, exactly the same—except for their super-powers."

Quinn's grin of satisfaction, despite the gun still held against his head, made me shudder. He had a look that said, "I was right all along."

Smith, who'd been surprisingly quiet, finally spoke up. I think it would've been perfect if he'd said, "And I would have gotten away with it too, if it hadn't been for you meddling kids and your dog." But, alas, those particular words did not spout from his lips. Instead he said, "You're all fools! All of you! Can't you see this is the next necessary step for the survival of the United States? We have enemies at every corner of the globe, all trying to tear us down! What I'm proposing is insurance. Insurance for our very existence. And I'm not about to let you, any of you, thwart me!"

And at that point, I burst out laughing, causing everyone to look at me once again. Of course, laughing at a person with a gun to someone's head was never the right thing to do, but I couldn't help myself. "Thwart? Are you trying to sound like a 60's comic book villain?"

Abby and Smith were the only two who didn't join in my giggling. Even Quinn let out a small chuckle, until Smith pushed the gun into his skull again.

"Smith, don't you see what you're doing?" Abby said, trying to be the voice of reason, even though she still had her own rifle poised to put a hole in her former boss' head. "You're going to create an army more powerful than you. How can you ever hope to control them?"

"Oh, that's quite simple, Agent Davidson," Smith said, with a psychotic-looking grin that made him look ever-more like an old comic book villain. "I already have prototypes. I will implant tiny devices inside my soldiers. They will be completely undetectable. And if my men get out of line—BOOM! I assure you, the other soldiers, seeing the remains of their comrade, will keep them firmly under my thumb."

"And you expect your men to let them put these things inside them?" I asked.

"You did," he responded, with another devious grin.

I'm pretty sure my heart stopped then. I thought about that day Smith first showed up in my house. The tracking devices he'd implanted in me, were they really explosives? Could I, at any moment, spontaneously combust? Was it as simple as the push of a button? Could Smith set them off at any given moment?

I turned to the only person I could—Ethan. I gazed directly into his eyes from across the room, and I got what I was looking for: sympathy. Of everyone in the room, Ethan would feel the most pain if I were to suddenly become a fireball of flying body parts.

Knowing my life could end at any given second, I sent my boyfriend the most important message I could think of at that moment. *I'm sorry.*

"Am I your simple villain anymore, little girl? Or have I finally gotten the respect I deserve from a little whelp like you?"

I was going to answer, but was interrupted by yet another person entering the hangar seeking the prize of the shroud. "Everyone hold it!"

I had to turn and search for the source of the voice. Another group strode forward. The leader, a man in a black leather jacket with slick backed hair, and still wearing sunglasses despite the cloudy sky outside, held a pair of silver handguns out in front of him. His arms were straight as arrows, and the guns were aimed at Smith and Abby.

Commander Dresner stopped three feet behind me. And flanking him, all appearing quite displeased, were Klaus, Jayson, Johnny and Gina.

In response to the new gun pointed at him, Smith threw the shroud to the ground, and drew another black handgun from inside his jacket. He pointed it over my shoulder at Dresner.

"You know that won't do any good," Dresner said. "Bullet-proof, remember?"

Abby sidestepped to her right, keeping Smith in her sights at all times, but moving to be in a position to shoot at Dresner, or any of his accomplices if she had to.

Dresner ignored the pair of Agents, even as he continued aiming at both of them, and turned his head to face Quinn. "Long time no see, eh Quintus? Sorry about commandeering your team, but they were more than willing to switch sides when they learned you'd left them to rot in a Vatican jail cell."

"Are you all right, Christine?" Klaus asked.

I simply nodded, not sure if I should say anything about the bombs I was apparently carrying inside my body.

Dresner glanced my way this time and said, "By the way, girly, nice work. You've got the entire continent believing in angels. I didn't think it was possible, but there have been more trips booked to come to Rome in the last hour than in the last year."

I wasn't sure if he was complimenting me, or making fun of me. Not wanting yet another psycho to worry about, I really hoped it was a compliment.

"Dedrick," Smith said plainly. "Drop the guns. I have you outnumbered, and I have Quintus. He's my prisoner, and I don't intend to give him up.

"From the looks of things, Agent Smith, I'd say you're the one who's outnumbered. Or am I mistaken in thinking you're team here has all but deserted you. So, I believe it will be you who will drop your weapons and hand Quintus, and the shroud, over to me."

"Over my dead body," Smith said.

"That's the general idea."

This was it. This was going to come to the point of no return in a couple of seconds unless I did something. Once that first shot was fired, I doubted anything would be able to stop the three gun-toting adults until everyone was wounded or dead.

Quinn simply smiled.

I wasn't about to let them all kill each other for the stupid rag laying on the ground at Smith's feet. *Ethan, you need to grab the guns from everyone.*

From the corner of my eye, I saw Ethan nod and get ready to run. Before he even took one step, all hell broke loose.

CHAPTER 27
DEMONS OF THE PAST

I'm not sure who fired first. One second I'm giving Ethan instructions and the next, bullets were flying.

Abby had switched targets, firing several bullets from her laser guided rifle at Dresner. Unfortunately, as Dresner had predicted, the bullets merely bounced off his hard skin. Smith had fired both guns at once, one aimed at Dresner, which was as ineffective as Abby's rifle, and the other at Quinn.

What Smith didn't realize though, was Quinn's head was no longer against the barrel of his gun. Instead, the bullet whizzed passed the end of Quinn's nose, doing no damage to anything except the wall it embedded itself into.

I was practically in the crossfire between the three gun-toting idiots, so I ducked and covered, putting a protective shell around my body once again to stop any strays from reaching me. The next thing I knew, I was on the other side of the room, in Ethan's arms.

"Thought you could use a pick-me-up," he said. Laughing internally at his own non-existent wit. Oh, how I loved that non-existent wit!

I planted a big, wet kiss on his lips, and then jumped from his grip to land on the floor.

The three adults, pretty much oblivious to the rest of us in the room, ran around firing blindly at one another, twisting and turning, ducking and rolling. Abby would fire at Smith, then spin and take another shot at Dresner, while dodging the bullet coming her way from Smith. Several shots found there mark, hitting a combatant in the shoulder, the chest, or some other body part. But none of the bullets did an ounce of damage.

I mean, Dresner was bullet-proof. Abby's bio-suit, which matched mine was pretty much bullet proof, and I wouldn't be surprised if Smith was wearing the same thing under his suit. So, each futile attempt to kill each other ended as one might expect—with no one dying.

Klaus, and the others had pretty much scattered when the shooting had begun and were trying, as I was, to figure out how to get this all to stop. There was a very simple solution, we had powers, they didn't. We could force them to stop.

While I was discussing what to do about the situation with my friends, and among the battle of the whizzing bullets, Quinn had laid himself down and pulled his legs through his cuffed wrists, so his hands were in front of him.

He quickly yanked the inhibitor from behind his ear and crushed it between his fingers. Then using telekinesis, he unlocked the cuffs and threw them aside.

I should have been paying attention to him, but I was so focused on Smith, Abby and Dresner I let his actions slip buy. I could have stopped Quinn if I'd realized what he was planning. Now that he had the use of his powers again, it was going to make this much more difficult.

Only when Quinn stood, did I truly take notice, because the instant he was on his feet the guns were ripped from each of their owners' hands. The weapons were tossed aside casually, scattering about the floor.

He stepped forward and the three formally armed operatives floated gently into the air.

This is going to be bad.

On the other side of the scene, Klaus looked on, wondering if there was something he could do. Johnny and Gina looked practically terrified at the sudden shift in power to Quinn's favor.

I got no reading from Jayson at all, which was strange, because the boy was usually as easy to read as a text message.

Quinn examined his now helpless victims, moving them so they floated in a perfect line a foot or so off the ground. For his captives, that foot might as well have been a mile for all the movement Quinn allowed them. He paced before them, as if he were a drill sergeant on inspection.

"Okay, we have to do something," I whispered to my friends while Quinn was distracted.

Quinn stopped in front of Smith first. "There's an old adage, Mr. Smith, I'm sure you're familiar with. It goes something like, 'Those who do not learn from the past are doomed to repeat it.' You are a fool to think you could control an army of supreme beings. Hitler thought the same thing, until I forced him to shove a gun down his throat. And I assure you, if someone ever succeeds in creating your dreaded clone army, the same will happen to them as well. All it will take is for only one of your creations to start thinking for himself. The chain reaction will be an unstoppable force that will end with the demise of millions."

I continued whispering through Quinn's speech. "Clear your minds as best you can, and don't move until I tell you what to do. He can't even have a second to read your thoughts. If he does, we're dead."

Abby was the next in line for Quinn's scrutinizing gaze. "You're no better than these kids half the time. Oh, you have maturity on your side, but no wisdom. After all, you're what—nineteen, twenty? You're barely an adult yourself. You can't possibly understand how the outcome of today will effect every single life on this planet. How could you?"

He looked as if he was going to continue on to Dresner, but after only a step he narrowed his eyes and backpeddled to her. "You know, I'm curious. Mr. Smith wants his army and Mr. Dresner wants to halt the human races natural genetic evolution. But what do you want Ms. Davidson?"

Abby spit in his face. "I want you to die."

Quinn didn't even flinch. He simply raised a hand and wiped the spittle from his eye and cheek. "Lesson learned. I take back what I said about the maturity."

While this was going on, I kept giving instructions to my friends. "We have to wait for the perfect moment, when he's the most distracted. As soon as I give the orders, move. Don't let him get a read on you."

Quinn had to sense an attack was imminent. Even I could feel the anticipation from my friends. My only hope was, he wouldn't know when or from where the attack would come. If we could at least surprise him, we'd be in good shape.

From what I could make out, Klaus was trying to rally the others on the other side of the hangar. First, he'd slipped over to where one of Smith's handguns had landed, then he picked it up, seemingly unnoticed, and then slid back over to where Johnny and the others were. He went over his plan with them.

I hoped he didn't plan on killing Quinn. If Klaus had the inclination, he could very well end the man with one bullet. After all, he never missed his target. Severely wounding him would be enough. I would have sent these sentiments to Klaus, but it would have been too dangerous. Quinn could potentially pick up any thought I projected.

Quinn stepped in front of his last victim. "Fifteen years it's been, hasn't it Dedrick? Longer than half of these kids could walk. How are the Vrill these days anyway?" He waited for a response, but Dresner didn't say any a word. "I see you've gotten some new members since you removed me."

His gaze fell upon Klaus. No words were exchanged, but it was like Quinn knew the gun was in his hand. His eyes lingered on Klaus for a few moments before they returned to Dresner.

"I guess the Society must be desperate, taking on kids so young. In our day you had to prove yourself before we'd even consider you. What happened? All the old members dying off?"

"That boy over there is a better operative than you ever were," said Dresner. "He isn't driven by the need for power. And for the record, you left us."

"And you've been hunting me ever since."

"Only because I know what you're trying to do."

"I'm simply ushering a new era for humanity."

"By destroying this one!"

"And thus, saving us all!" Quinn backed up and now spoke in a loud voice to make sure we all would hear. "None of you have the experience I have. I've been around for longer than all of you and will be around long after you're dead. This world is not going to survive for long if something drastic isn't done. The weak have ruled the Earth for too long now. They have led us into countless wars and endless violence. Terrorist attacks, mass suicides, attempted genocide. The Doomsday Clock is only seconds away from midnight. Yet all of you, the ones who could actually have done something about it, have sat back and let the world go about its business. My solution will put an end to all of that, and all I've been met with is resistance."

"Because you're solution will kill us all," Smith shouted.

Quinn shook his head. "How limited your little minds are. You can't see outside of your own little world. Yes, there will be loss of life, but what war doesn't. At least my way, those who are taken from this world will go peacefully, without any pain."

Was I missing something here? Or did it seem everyone knew what was going on except those of us under the age of eighteen? Seriously, adults don't tell kids anything!

"And it all rests with this girl," Quinn said, spinning to point directly at me.

And it was then, when Quinn had turned to show everyone how his plan was coming together, a single shot rang out with a loud BANG!

It surprised us all, and I know I wasn't the only one in my group who jumped at the sound.

Quinn, on the other hand, seemed ready for the attack and waved a hand, deflecting the small projectile, sending it on a new course which embedded it in the hangar's ceiling.

This was the chance I'd been waiting for. Quinn was distracted and we wouldn't get a better shot at him. "Ethan tackle him. Peter hit him with some lightning."

They'd been waiting for the order and immediately sprang into action. Ethan disappeared with a burst of speed. At the same time, Peter unleashed a torrent of crackling blue energy from his clenched fists, aimed directly at Quinn.

They were quick. Quinn was quicker. He created some kind of force bubble around him which diverted Ethan's course and dissipated Peter's lightning. Ethan skidded to a stop on the far side of the room, and turned, confused, as he wondered how he could have missed.

Quinn turned on me and darkness covered his features in shadow. "Did you really think that was going to work?" He lifted off the ground and floated ten feet in the air. He looked positively terrifying, and my whole body shuddered at the sight of the man, slowly coming my way. "You think your little friends have a chance at destroying me? Your grandfather's tried many times, and they were fully trained soldiers. But I'm still here, young and strong, while your grandfathers are decaying or dead. What chance do you have?"

I didn't know what to say. I didn't know what to do. The only thing I was sure of was, no matter what, I was going to stand my ground. Together, my friends and I would come up with some solution. We always did.

A cold sensation crawled up my spine when Peter stood in front of me. Pete had been the most loyal and best friend a person could ask for this last year. Though he was quiet, we'd grown to rely on him. Now, he was taking a stand between me and Quinn, lightning arcing up and down his arms, telling the man, if he wanted to hurt me, he'd have to kill Peter first.

The cold sensation didn't come from Peter's action though, it was from Quinn. Once Peter had taken his position and Quinn took notice of him, the dark shadow fell upon my friend. "I wonder if you would take the same stance if you knew what a good friend Christine really was."

I knew exactly what he was going to do. "Quinn, don't!"

"Maybe this will teach you a lesson."

I tried to put a mental shield around Peter's mind to stop Quinn from doing what he intended, but I was too late.

At first, Peter's shoulders relaxed and the lightning causing his arms to glow dimmed. He turned, his mask covered eyes staring accusatorily at me. "It's true?" he asked. "I thought it was a dream."

"Yes, Pete," I said, a tear escaping the corner of my eye, "but I didn't know what I was doing."

"You tried to kill me," Peter said, as if not able to believe the words. "You tortured me!"

"I'm sorry, Pete. I'm so—"

The blue energy in his arms crackled to life again, and this time it rose up to his neck until his eyes glowed with the blue light. And before I knew what was happening, a burst of energy shot from his fingertips and knocked me to the ground. My skin sizzled with the electric current.

Stunned, I managed to lift my neck as Peter stood above me, hand lit up with pure blue energy. The look in his eyes reminded me of the time he'd trapped Tommy in the supply closet at school, intent on snuffing out the boy. Those same eyes fell upon me now. Anger had completely taken over his rational thought. It was like the Peter we had come to know since that day in November had been swallowed up by this monstrous Peter who now towered over me.

He pointed a fist in my direction and it lit up as it charged with energy.

Instinctively, I pushed out mentally, sending him staggering back. He fell right into Savanah's waiting arms. She squeezed him tightly, pinning his arms to his sides. Lightning shot out straight down at the ground as Pete struggled to break free.

"Calm down," Savanah ordered. She struggled to keep her grip as some of the potent energy coursed through her body. "We're still you're friends."

"Let go of me!" Peter squirmed in her tight embrace, using his power to shock her to break free. In response, Savanah only held tighter. Several loud snaps filled the air over the unending thrum of the electric bolts hitting the ground. She'd inadvertently cracked a few of Peter's ribs. He howled in pain.

"Don't hurt him!" I shouted, getting back to my feet.

"I'm… trying," she said, as she continued to fight against the electric jolts and Peter's thrashing.

With us, occupied, Quinn had the opportunity to turn on the others. I barely noticed as Klaus fired several more bullets at Quinn, which were apparently as ineffective as the first. And it wasn't until there were two dozen of them surrounding Quinn on all sides, did I see the constantly replicating Johnny copies fill the room.

I had more pressing matters to deal with though. With Quinn dealing with the others, I had a chance to undo what he'd done to Peter. At the very least I could calm him down long enough to actually talk to him.

I reached out to Peter, allowing my mental fingers to touch his mind. At once, I was met with resistance. Not only was Peter fighting me, but Quinn had left some mental blocks on my friend to prevent me from doing exactly what I was trying to do.

"Get out of my head, Carpenter!" Peter screamed.

"Pete, I'm sorry, but this is for your own good."

I pushed passed the first defense, after eroding away Quinn's mental wall. It took a lot of concentration, and it was even harder with Peter pushing back against my mind as well. I got brief flashes of Peter's memory, while going deeper into his mind.

I saw Peter playing as a kid in his backyard. Then a brief flash of him having dinner with his family—his whole family, like twenty different people—filled my vision. A third scene came to mind, this one of an old man I assumed to be his grandfather, holding a lightbulb in his hand and turning it on and off. All in all, he had a very happy life it seemed.

But those were the memories on the surface. The memory of that dreadful day when I'd hurt Peter—the day Tommy Fulton died—was buried far below. I pushed through, encountering more mental blocks. Each one I pushed through got harder and harder. And the further I went in, the worse the memory flashes got.

Tommy beating him up on the playground, Peter accidentally exploding his X-Box when he first discovered his powers, his grandfather dying—murdered—were among the memories I saw.

Why didn't Pete ever tell us about that?

Three boys grabbing him in the bathroom, another large guy shoving him inside a locker—there were so many instances of Peter being beaten up or bullied.

Apparently, Peter had been picked on quite a bit until he'd fallen in with our group. It was no wonder he had such a chip on his shoulder when it came to bullies. I couldn't believe it. I never knew any of this about the boy I called a friend. I just thought it was Tommy, but apparently there was a long line of people who'd hurt Peter.

And I was one of them.

Savanah was struggling terribly to keep a grip on the boy. Peter was shooting more lightning in every direction he could, which was still limited by Savanah pinning his arms. I didn't have much time.

At last I found the memory I was looking for. I saw that morning when I'd made Peter believe he was being buried alive. I needed to erect a wall around that memory and make Peter forget it again, like Quinn had done months ago. The only problem was I didn't know how. I'd never done something like this before. I understood the concept, but it didn't mean I could perform the action.

I trapped the memory deep within his brain, and raised a cage around it. But even as I set about keeping the memory contained, it fought to break free. The harder I pushed, the more it fought. Peter didn't want to forget. His rage had gotten the better of him.

"I... said... get out!" One burst of electric energy shot from him in all directions, forcing Savanah to let go. She shot back, hitting the nearest wall, denting the solid structure with her body.

With a deep breath, Peter stood tall, focusing all of his attention on me. He advanced, his hand alight with glowing blue electricity once again.

I gave up trying to contain the memory, and instead focused more on calming him down. I sent soothing, happy thoughts to him, trying to change his emotions. He slowed his advance, and looked as if he was going to turn back into the Peter I knew. I pushed harder, keeping the gentle thoughts caressing his mind.

His eyes lit up, and a snarl crossed his face. "You think you can change me again? Make me into your puppet?"

"Pete, it's not like that at all. I'm trying to help you."

"I don't need any help. I can see you for what you are now. You can't change that with the flick of a switch."

As he pointed his fists at me once more, I knew I'd failed. Unless Quinn helped me, and I knew he wouldn't, there would be no more Peter in our group. Another tear rolled down my cheek as I threw up a force shield to dissipate the torrent of energy soon to be unleashed on me.

The lightning discharged toward me and I prepared myself for the shock, but for the second time, one of my friends got in between Peter and me. This time, Ethan took the strike right in the chest, but still managed to wrap his hands around Peter's wrists. First he threw, the boy's arms aside, sending the arcing lightning shooting harmlessly into the air. Then he pushed Peter down so quick and hard, Peter slid along the floor on his butt for at   least   twenty   feet.
Then he spun and grabbed me. "Are you okay?"

Of course I wasn't. Quinn had turned one of our friends against us and forced us to attack him. Still, I found myself nodding. "We have to get Quinn."

The man was still floating, fighting off the horde of Johnnys that were climbing on top of each other in vain attempts to pull the man down. Slight flicks of the wrists and tiny nods of his head sent dozens of the boy flying in all directions. Each one of the copies vanished in mid-air, only to be replaced by another on the ground who would then make another attack.

I was actually awestruck by the sight. There had to be over a hundred copies of Johnny, all of them with a single purpose—destroy Quinn.

Jayson and Gina were both standing next to each other, both unsure what to do. They could only watch as Johnny continued his unending onslaught. Jayson's skin rippled several times like he wanted to transform and jump into the fray and help, but he didn't move. Klaus too, had given up trying to shoot Quinn, and instead he was going after the immobilized prisoners.

"What do you want me to do?" Ethan asked.

I shook my head. "I don't know. Give me a second to think."

I had to think. How could we get to Quinn without him knowing it? I was the only one who could mask my intentions from him, but I still wasn't going to be nearly fast enough—unless Ethan gave me a hand.

"Okay," I said, "here's what we're gonna—"

My idea was cut off by the loud heart piercing scream of Ethan, as he was hit from behind by a large electric discharge. Peter was back on his feet and angrier than ever. His skin crackled with energy now, as he unloaded a stream of lightning into my boyfriend.

"Peter, stop!" I screamed.

My words were ignored, as he continued unleashing his unbridled fury into Ethan. I had no choice. I had to stop him.

"Tell me, Pete, what do…" My voice caught in my throat as the reality of what I was about to do hit me. The words "you fear" never did escape my larynx, but my power worked on him just the same.

The last time I'd tried to do this to Peter, my own mind wouldn't allow me. It was because of the guilt I'd felt for almost killing him in the first place. Now, my brain must have known I had no choice, either that, or protecting Ethan far outweighed my need to keep from hurting Peter. Either way, the lightning stopped and for the second time since I've known him, I forced Peter to thrash on the ground, believing he'd been buried alive.

Tears rolled down my cheeks, wetting the fabric of the mask as I continued the assault on Peter's mind. I saw everything he did. I felt the terror he felt. His heart was racing and his breathing was quick and uneven. But I couldn't let up. I had to make sure he was completely incapacitated before lifted the illusion, otherwise he'd come back at us again.

"I'm sorry," I kept repeating. The words came out of my mouth, but I also projected them to Peter. I hoped at least the message would get through to him I didn't want to do this.

Every one of Peter's yells for help stabbed me like a sword through my heart. But I forced myself to keep pushing. He had to be stopped before he put us all in jeopardy.

Only when I felt a hand shake my shoulders did I pull back out of him mind. The illusion from inside the coffin faded away to be replaced by the face of my boyfriend. "I think he's had enough, Chris."

I looked over to Peter, laying motionless on the ground. Fear still radiated off him like heat from a fire, but he was unconscious—for now.

"Oh, Ethan!" I collapsed into his arms and let him hold me as I sobbed into his shoulder. Only Ethan could understand why, even if he'd never understand the pain I went through to do it. "He's our friend. I shouldn't have."

"You did what you had to, Chris." He rubbed my back consolingly.

"Hey, Losers," Savanah called from where she'd struck the wall a couple minutes before. "Don't you think we should—oh, I don't know—kill the bad guy?"

"She's right," I said between the last of my sniffles. I wiped the remaining tears from my eyes and composed myself. There'd be time for me to feel sorry for myself later. No matter what, I resolved to make my friendship with Peter right again. Only this time, I'd do it without lobotomizing him.

"Savanah, be ready!" I called over her. Then I turned to Ethan, who though a little singed around the edges, still looked eager to get back into the fight. "Right. So, here's what I was thinking."

CHAPTER 28
CHECKMATE

First, let me say what a horrible idea this was. I didn't even like going on the teacup ride at Disneyworld because the spinning made me sick. So, asking Ethan to spin me around at mach one and hurl me at the floating Quinn didn't go quite as I'd hoped.

Ethan held my right arm and leg and spun in a clockwise motion. He started off slow, but quickly reached speeds that threatened to dislocate my shoulder and hip. It was only a few seconds into the spin when I began to feel that drunken-queasy feeling. My vision blurred, and by the time he released me, I literally couldn't see straight.

This was a problem, because I was supposed to use my powers to guide me so I could grab Quinn around his neck and not only bring him to the ground, but touch his head and invade his mind. My brain was so muddled, I was lucky to be flying at all.

I did manage to keep a mental shield around myself, but it wouldn't matter at all if I missed my target.

The flight from Ethan to Quinn took just under a second. I was pretty much moving, and I hate myself for using the phrase, faster than a speeding bullet."

Not being able to see straight, did cause my course to shift a bit, but I still hit my target—sort of.

With my shield around me, and my astounding speed, I punched through Quinn's shield with little difficulty. Then I slammed into the man at full speed and wrapped my arms around him. The only problem was, instead of being near his head, like I'd hoped, I'd grabbed him more around the thigh area.

Using my momentum, and holding with a vice-like grip, I dragged Quinn down into the horde of Johnnys still trying to attack him from below. He hit the ground before me, which was good because his mass served to cushion my fall. And let me tell you, the impact still hurt.

The shock of my airborne tackle caused Quinn to lose his concentration, and his shield not only dropped, but I felt him release his hold on Abby, Smith and Dresner.

Though my head was ringing and every limb felt like it had been ripped loose, I scrambled amidst the surrounding Johnny copies to get to Quinn's head. I'd found over the last ten or so months I'd had my powers, the closer in proximity I was to someone, the easier it was to get into their head. Once I placed my hands on Quinn's head, it was my hope I'd finally get access to his mind.

Thankfully, he was still a little stunned from hitting the ground so hard. When I reached his head, I smacked both my hands on either side of it. At once, what felt like a warm rush of water ran over me and my vision was filled with hundreds of thousands of images all at once.

It was too much to make sense of. It was like someone had their finger on the remote control and hitting the channel up button as super-sonic speed. If I didn't do something soon, my brain would shut itself down due to information overload.

While my mind was among the vast array of images, I pushed into Quinn's head looking for one specific item. For the second time in only the last couple minutes I found myself asking, *What do you fear?*

Instantly, the images vanished, washed away from the imaginary world around me, plunging me into darkness.

What do you fear? I repeated, then concentrated on the deepest, darkest fears he had trapped in his head. Nothing. All I saw was darkness.

Everyone was afraid of something, weren't they? Was it possible there was really nothing Quinn was afraid of?

Okay, let's see what Quinn plans on doing with me when he gets his hands on the shroud and the cross.

Again, nothing.

He was preventing every attempt I made at gaining access to anything important in his mind. I had to get creative. I needed access, and I needed it now. But what could I do?

Somehow, I needed to make Quinn drop his guard, but that was unlikely to happen while I was making attempts at entering the dark recesses of his mind where he kept all the good secrets.

"What did you think you would accomplish here, Christine?" A mental projection of Quinn appeared from the darkness as if emerging from a shadow. Though it was still total blackness around us, as Quinn approached, I could see him as clearly as if we'd been standing in a field on a sunny day.

"You can't keep me out forever," I told the projection. "I will find a way in eventually."

"Of that I have no doubt," the Quinn image responded. "But while I have you trapped in here, the real me will simply decimate your friends out there."

"I'm not trapped."

"Are you sure?" I hated even the projection Quinn had sent in here to talk to me. He was as cocky and condescending as the real man.

I closed my eyes and tried to pull my consciousness back into my own head. But when I opened them again I was still in the darkness, alone with Quinn.

"It was rather foolish of you to come in here by yourself. I dare say, I'd actually call your actions rather rash." Fake Quinn strode around me, like the real one did when giving me a lecture. "Did you really think you'd get me to reveal my deepest fear to you? Did you think even if you did find out what I was afraid of, you'd actually be able to project that fear into my brain? I'm not one of your adolescent friends, Christine. I have all the mental power you do, and I have about a thousand times the experience using it. That means, no matter what you try, I've already set up a defense for it."

"I made it this far into your mind," I said defiantly.

"And I applaud you for it." He actually stopped his circular pacing, looked me in the eye, and clapped his hands. I was amazed when the claps echoed.

I rolled my eyes, the applause was meant to mock me. But I wasn't going to give him the satisfaction of letting it bother me. "I will beat you."

"But why do you have to?" The Quinn projection resumed his strides. "Wouldn't it be so much easier if the two of us worked together?"

"No. You're insane!"

"The distance between insanity and genius is measured only by success—or so it's said."

"I suppose you're going to quote me scripture next?" I asked.

"If you insist. Now let me see, which would be the most appropriate?" He stepped around me, making two more full circles with a hand on his chin as he thought about it. "Ah, yes. John, chapter ten, verse twenty. 'Many of them said, "He has a demon, and is insane; why listen to him?"'"

"Right. Why should I listen to someone who's insane?"

"Because I'm far from insane. I would say, of all people, I have seen what must be done most clearly. Others understand the human race cannot and will not survive if it is allowed to continue on the track it is on. I am the only one who is willing to throw the switch and change our course."

"And does that include killing millions of people?"

"Some will die. I don't deny this. But it's for the greater good."

I rolled my eyes. The more he spoke, the more insane he sounded. But, instead of arguing, like I knew I could, I played along. "Can you explain how it's for the better when we'll have to kill innocent people?"

He stopped in front of me, and turned in my direction. He shook his head. "No, no, no. You misunderstand, Christine. Those who will die will be the unworthy, and I promise you they will be far from innocent."

"Listen, Quinn," I said, feigning actual interest in what he had to say, "if you want me to cooperate with you, and I mean really cooperate, you're going to have to explain exactly what you're trying to do."

"All in good time, Christine. All in good time." He paced around me again.

I could feel fissures in the darkness opening. I wouldn't be able to siphon any of the information I needed without him knowing it and trapping me in here again, but I would be able to jump back into my own head, and the real word, soon. I had to keep him thinking he was turning me to his side.

Just like, Grandpa Carpenter told me: make my enemy think he's winning, keep him confident until I make my final move.

"Okay, let's suppose I do decide to help you. How do I know someone in my family wouldn't be considered one of the 'unworthy'?"

"Fortunately, that's up to you to decide," he explained. "You see, you would be the one to choose who was worth saving and who would be cast out."

"And you'd take the chance I wouldn't cast you out if I had the power?"

He smiled. For the first time in a long time, I believed the smile was genuine. "I would like to think once you see things my way, you'd realize I've had our race's best interest at heart all along. That fact alone would make me worth saving."

I played it cool, even though I was fuming. I needed to keep him thinking I might help him, but there were too many questions I wanted answered.

"You're still not telling me anything. If I'm the only one who can help you, then why all the secrets? If you'd be open with me, maybe I'd be more willing to help you."

"I know you, Christine," Quinn retorted. "You're just like your grandfather—always trying to get as much information as possible before you make a decision. While the trait is commendable, sometimes you need to go with your gut reaction."

"You're avoiding the question."

"Am I?" he looked at me with an expression I would describe as "fake-shock". "I don't seem to recall you asking one."

"It was implied!" I shouted before I could stop myself. I was sick and tired of these mind games. Why couldn't he give me a straight answer?

When I yelled, I felt the holes I intended to make my escape through contract. So I quickly calmed myself down and said, "I'm sorry. It's frustrating. Why can't you tell me what you intend for me?"

The holes reopened.

"I cannot risk you opposing me. Its best you learn a little bit at a time. That way you get used to your destiny."

So, now I was destined to help destroy the human race? This man really was insane. It was time to get out of there.

I didn't move at first. Instead, I asked, "So are you going to keep me trapped in here until I agree with you?"

"No."

"Then why hold me here for so long? It has to have been like fifteen minutes since I entered your head."

I pinpointed one of the larger holes, one that would take me out of Quinn's mind. I still couldn't see it, but I sensed where it was.

"Actually, the mind works much faster than the outside world, it feels like fifteen minutes, but it's really been about two seconds."

"Good to know," I said. Then I decided to add a little sugar to the statement by adding, "I could learn so much from you. I want to help you Quinn, but I don't know."

His defenses were relaxing even more. It wouldn't be long.

"You have no idea how much I could teach you. You have only just begun to tap into your powers. Wait until you open up your mind to the impossible."

"When you give me that extra DNA?"

"Yes," he nodded.

"Okay."

Then I launched myself—at least the projection of myself—up through the blackness to the hole I sensed. I'd taken Quinn completely by surprise.

It didn't take him long to react. Even as I sped toward it, I could feel the hole closing again as Quinn tried to trap me.

It worked. I couldn't believe it. Letting Quinn think he'd beaten me, even if only half-heartedly, caused him to lower his guard. I hoped I was quick enough to escape before he completely sealed me in.

Faster, I pushed myself. The opening was closing at a rapid rate. So quickly, in fact, I was afraid I wouldn't make it. I willed my imagined body forward, determined to make it to the hole.

Closer, closer and...

I shot up to my feet and found myself surrounded by the many Johnny copies, all trying to get a piece of Quinn. Or at least, that's what I assumed.

The Johnnys definitely had me surrounded, making me incredibly nervous being in a crowd like that, but they weren't attacking anyone. I looked down at my feet where I'd slammed Quinn down before I'd entered his brain. He wasn't there.

"You know, Christine," Quinn's voice echoed from above, "you forget I am always ten steps ahead of you. Did you really think your ruse would fool me?"

"Actually, it did," I responded with complete confidence. The fact he didn't answer right away told me I was right.

Being right, however, didn't change my situation. My breathing was already getting more rapid and my heart was racing. Quinn, still above me, watched in amusement as, caught in the center of a sea of Johnnys, my body betrayed me. This was a point my former mentor was quick to point out.

"Having a panic-attack are we?" he let the question hang in the air for a moment while I continued to slip into an uncontrollable state. "You know, the only thing preventing you from being pummeled to death at this moment is my patience, which is about at its end. I've tried reasoning with you. Now it's time for threats. I can easily pull your brother into this, in which case, I no longer require you. So, you can join me, and no one else need be hurt, or I can unleash my fury on all of you and watch as you destroy each other."

This was the part where someone was supposed to rescue me—not that I was trying to be the damsel-in-distress or anything. But sometimes a powerful girl could use a knight-in-shining-armor to whisk her away from danger too.

I sought out Ethan or Savanah, desperately attempting to locate their thought patterns—I even reached out for Klaus, but either because Quinn was blocking me, or they were no longer there, I sensed no one who could help me. No one except Johnny, but the boy was completely under mental control as his thought signature was a reflection of Quinn's.

Glaring at the aged clone, and resolved to my fate, even though deep down I really hoped he was bluffing, I defiantly said, "I guess you're going to have to kill me."

He shook his head, closing his eyes and tightening his lips. "Such a waste, but if that's your wish then…"

There was a pause then, as if Quinn were hoping I would rethink my response. He was wrong. There wasn't even the most infinitesimal chance I would ever agree to help him exterminate a portion of the "unworthy" human population. No matter what he threatened me with, I would stand by my morals.

If what Quinn said was true, and I did indeed have some preordained path set in front of me, then that path saw me stopping Quinn—not helping him.

The pause was brief. He looked down on me with disgust. Then, with a wave of the hand, the battle for my life began.

I was grabbed from one of the zombified Johnnys from behind, his thick arms wrapping around my torso, while another one punched me in the face. I spat blood in his eye and kicked hard between his legs. He made a cross-eyed face of pain, then disappeared. Another Johnny took his place.

I fought off several Johnnys while trying to pinpoint the real one in the crowd. I was having a hard time of it, not only because of all the punching and kicking I was doing, but because the crowd was definitely causing me to lose all control. I tried to hold it back as much as I could, but it wouldn't be long before I projected something horrible that scared the crap out of everyone in the room.

When I took another hit, my vision blurred. I couldn't help but wonder why I was fighting back what came naturally. If I let loose my fears and scared everyone in the room, it might save me.

So, I stopped fighting, both physically and mentally. I took several more punches and kicks from the Johnnys, the ones that didn't land on my face were mostly absorbed by the bio suit, so they weren't too bad. As I kept taking the hits, my mind slipped into oblivion.

I'm not sure when I blacked out, and I'm really not sure how long I was out for. But I was awoken by the sounds of my own scream along with the echoed screams of hundreds of others. My eyes were still closed, but I could feel the cold, hard cement floor against my cheek.

Opening my eyes, I watched the sea of Johnnys vanish a few at a time, all of them crying out in terror as they disappeared into nothingness. Eventually, they all winked out, leaving only the original Johnny behind.

Who knew my fear of crowds would actually save my life one day?

Beyond Johnny stood Jayson, Gina, Klaus, Savanah and Ethan. Smith, Abby and Dresner were nowhere to be seen.

Quinn still hovered high above me. "Impressive," he said. "Too bad you can't repeat it."

I didn't respond to his jibe, but lifted myself from the floor and stood once again. Reaching out, I felt for the minds of the others, wanting to relay orders to them, but I received nothing. Their minds had been cut off from me. And there was only one person who could do that.

I glared up at the man, determined not to show him anything but pure hatred. He had my friends under his control, and I was going to get them back.

But then, I felt something. There was one mind in the group not being effected by Quinn. Jayson was still there, for some reason. He had all of his thought patterns intact. Quinn didn't have a hold on him. So, I reached out to the boy.

Jayson, can you hear me?

There wasn't even a second's hesitation. *Yes.*

You need to help me. Come here.

Jayson didn't respond mentally, but walked over to my position. As he got closer, and my muddled brain was able to see him more clearly, I noticed the grim expression on his face. He didn't seem like the nervous little boy he usually was. There was something different about him. But I didn't have time to dwell on it.

Can you turn into anything?

Yes.

Glancing up at Quinn, I wondered why he hadn't done anything to attack me. He simply floated above, watching the exchange between Jayson and myself with interest.

I quickly turned back to Jayson. *I need you to turn into something that can fly and help me out up there. I need to take down Quinn.*

No.

The statement was simple, yet it spoke volumes. I hadn't expected the negative response, and so I was completely unprepared when a long, coiled, leathery tail wrapped around my neck and tightened.

The next thing I knew, Jayson was no longer standing in front of me, and instead there was a large, green boa constrictor, swaying from side to side, wrapping more and more of its tail around me.

"Very good, Jayson," Quinn finally spoke again. "I knew you would be able to get near enough to her."

The coiled length of the tail tightened its grip around me, as the snake looked up at Quinn and nodded. It had been all been another of Quinn's elaborate tricks. He'd had Jayson all along. The boy didn't seem to be under his control. Instead, Jayson was serving Quinn under his own free will, which meant he was really no better. The boy had been a spy for Quinn since this whole thing started, probably feeding him all the information he could get from us. It's why he'd stayed so quiet and off to the side all the time. He didn't want to draw attention to himself. If I survived this, I would really have to beat myself up for not noticing earlier.

With the ever tightening lengths of Jayson's newly formed scales winding around and around my body, I wasn't really sure if I'd live through this. Quinn and his new sidekick were really determined to annihilate me. Without the help of my friends, they could very well succeed.

A loud snap and pain surged up my arm from my wrist where the pressure had crushed it. My left arm was all but useless now. I would have cried out in pain, but the tail around my neck choked off my oxygen supply. My cheeks were tingling and I knew I was close to blacking out again. I needed to do something to get this stupid snake off me.

I tried flying, to pull myself free of the slippery scales, but Jayson's grip was much too tight. I tried getting into Jayson's mind, but I felt Quinn blocking me. Maybe that's how he'd hidden Jayson's true feelings for so long.

I was seconds away from unconsciousness when I tried one final act of desperation. I created a skin tight shield around myself, and then I expanded it. It loosened the coils around my body and I sucked in a good deal of life-giving air. My cheeks, which had been blue only seconds before, returned to their normal pale color.

After taking a few breaths, I was ready to tie the snake into a knot. I flew out of Jayson's grip and watched as the snake expressed his anger by hissing at me, baring his fangs.

I did the only thing I could think of, I kicked with my right leg as hard as I could and knocked the boy's lower jaw into the top one. The snake didn't seem to like that very much, and after shaking off the blow I'd inflicted, it lunged. Its teeth extended as if to rip my flesh from my bones.

This time, I was ready. I moved to the left and the head shot passed me. I grabbed Jayson with my good arm around his neck— did snakes have necks—and then flew down to the ground as quickly as I could. I slammed the snake's head into the ground as hard as I possibly could, and then, seeing it wasn't completely knocked out yet, I did it again. Three times I wailed Jayson into the cement floor before his body stopped moving.

I reached out with my mind to sense him. Yes, he was definitely out, but not dead. He would have a horrible headache when he woke though.

My arm hanging limply at my side, I spun. I was going to tell Quinn what he could shove up an orifice I shouldn't mention in polite company, but when I turned to face him, I found Savanah standing in front of me.

"Hey, Loser," she said, a blank expression on her face.

The next thing I knew, her fist connected with my jaw and I was flying toward the ceiling. Luckily, I'd managed to throw up my mental shield in the last second or she would have caved in my skull. The last thing I remembered before passing out for the second time was seeing the roof of the hangar careening toward me and then smacking headlong into it.

CHAPTER 29
ENDING QUINN

You ever have a dream where you're falling and then you realize it's a dream and suddenly you're able to fly? Well, it's nothing compared to waking up and finding yourself actually flying.

Okay, so flying probably isn't the most accurate way to describe what was happening. I was in an uncontrolled freefall speeding down to the Earth at terminal velocity.

After shaking the latest blow from my head, I managed to slow my descent to a hover. I was high above the clouds, the storm now below me. Savanah must have hit me incredibly hard, because I had to be at least a mile in the air. I'd venture a guess to say it was even more than that.

The bright sunlight warmed my damp and aching skin. I went to raise my arms to bask in its glory but the pain in my wrist and forearm kept my left arm planted firmly at my side.

I reached out and located the hangar. Quinn and the others were still there. All of them were back under their own brainpower. I guess with me out of the way, Quinn saw no reason to keep his mental leash on them.

I was miles away though, how was I able to sense them? I usually could only feel people in my immediate vicinity—at the most across a building. I hadn't ever been able to read thoughts over such a long distance before.

Then I realized I wasn't actually hearing any thoughts. My head was as empty as it had been before I could read minds.

Ha! Ha! Yes, I have an empty head. Good one.

It was strange not needing to block out everyone's thoughts. It was peaceful, relaxing—a relief. I'd have to fly up here more often—whenever I needed to clear my head.

But that wasn't the priority now. As much as I would love to float above the clouds all day, I had more pressing matters to attend to. Namely: Quinn.

One way or the other, my friends were in trouble and Quinn was the cause. Hell, not only my friends, my brother and family too. Even worse, the whole world's fate hung by a thread, determined only by the outcome of what happened here. One way or the other, this would end today.

But I couldn't kill Quinn in cold blood.

He threatened Conner, the voice reminded me.

I can't.

He's going to kill your friends!

I CAN'T!

Then how are you going to stop him?

Take away his powers.

I didn't know how. It wasn't like I could force him to imagine his abilities away like I'd done to Eddie. But somehow, it seemed like the right answer.

With or without a definite plan, I had to go back, and in a hurry before Quinn had the chance to do anything to my friends. Or worse, escape with the metal cross which, at this moment (I hoped), was still hidden inside the tool chest.

I flew in the direction I knew the hangar to be, not yet with any urgency, only because when I returned, I really needed to have some kind of game plan. If I didn't, I'd probably get flattened again like I had a few minutes ago.

The one thing I did have on my side this time was surprise.

Behind me, I heard the roar of twin engines quickly approaching me through the vast blue sky. I turned, flying backwards, so I could view it, and more importantly, make sure it wasn't going to hit me.

It was a smallish plane. Don't get me wrong, it was still about forty feet long with a wingspan longer than my driveway. Each blade of the rapidly spinning propellers was at least as tall as I was. And those propellers were coming right at me!

Straight up I shot, getting out of the way before the blades chopped me to bits. Seconds later, the metal shell passed harmlessly beneath me, engines whirring as it disappeared into the thick gray clouds below.

Then and idea stuck me, and I shot like a missile into the cloud-wake the plane had created.

Grandpa Carpenter was wrong—sometimes you couldn't lull your opponent into think he'd won. Sometimes you had to go for an all-out assault and remove as many pieces from the game as possible and go straight for the king.

And that's where the plane came in.

Through the thick cloud-cover I made out the tail of the plane. I sped forward, until I was about even with it. Then I brought myself along the top until I was above the cockpit and grabbed on with my one good arm. I mentally glued myself to the metallic exterior and stood. The winds buffeted me and nearly knocked me backward, but I used my power to keep myself upright. I felt two men inside the cockpit, who were oblivious to my arrival. I sent an image of the plane in an uncontrolled dive to both their heads.

They grabbed the controls and tried to correct, which really did start the plane tumbling. So, doing my best to keep rooted to my spot, I sent another image to them telling them the controls were dead.

Needless to say, the two pilots panicked and rushed out of the cockpit without any further hesitation. I heard a loud bang a few seconds later, as the hatch burst open and the pair jumped from the plane, disappearing into the thick gray nothingness.

I did a mental scan of the rest of the plane and found nothing. At least I didn't have to worry about harming any innocent people.

Actually, there were a few innocents I still had to account for, but I'd have to wait until I was closer. I couldn't worry about that yet. Right now, I had a plane to control.

This is really going to hurt.

I'd never moved anything this large before, and I prayed I had the power to do it. I reached out until the entire plane was wrapped in an invisible aura. I used that aura to fly the plane in the direction I needed.

Fly is probably the wrong word for it—it was more like guiding a dead ten-ton bird in for a crash landing. And what a spectacular crash it would be if I did this right.

My head pounded and my limbs ached as I controlled the heavy vehicle's descent. It tottered and wobbled, but using Quinn as a homing beacon I kept the craft on course. The further along I went, the faster and harder to control the plane became. It was almost as if the vessel was attracted to the ground. I did nothing to slow it down, the faster I moved, the greater the chance I would catch Quinn by surprise.

By now, every air traffic controller had to know something was wrong. I had the plane in a rather steep dive, and they would have no luck contacting the pilots, since they were most likely floating calmly to the ground somewhere behind me.

Suddenly, the clouds cleared—or rather I broke through the bottom layer—and I could see my target. Rain pelted my damp skin as it had before, this time stinging my face. I had maybe twenty seconds before the plane crashed into the hangar.

Hey, I said no innocents would be hurt. I made no claims about destruction of private property. Besides, I'd already accumulated two felonies on this trip. What was another one tacked on at this point?

While keeping the plane on as steady a course I could make, I attempted to contact Ethan. Between guiding the plane, holding myself in place and reaching out, it was too much for my brain and it felt like someone had stabbed deep into my skull with an ice pick. The copper taste of blood filled my mouth as it flowed freely from my nose. I was on the verge of blacking out again, but I pushed myself harder until I knew I'd made a connection with my boyfriend.

I could only concentrate long enough to send a simple message. *Everyone out. Find Abby. Ten seconds.*

Feeling, rather than hearing, his acknowledgement, I shut the connection down so I could better concentrate. I was homed in on Quinn, letting his brain pattern guide me right to him. The plan fell almost straight down, aimed at the roof of the hangar, directly above where Quinn was still floating.

Through the rain and wind stinging my eyes, I could barely make out the tiny people appearing outside the building. Ethan was doing his job perfectly. I would join them in a moment, but I had to make absolutely sure the plane found its target.

I had no doubt Quinn would survive. There was no way I'd get enough of a jump on him he wouldn't be able to throw up some kind of shield. Chances were he already had a shield up. The purpose of this wasn't to kill him. It was to hurt him, distract him, and give me time to get Abby.

More and more the hangar filled my vision, seeming to get larger every second that ticked by. Still, I stood firm, attached to the roof of the falling vehicle.

The nose had almost contacted the top of the hangar when I finally jumped off, confident it would topple down on top of Quinn. At that speed, the man would barely have time to react. Crunching and scraping metal exploded behind me, as the speeding aircraft punched through the hangar's roof. My own flight ended in much the same way, only much quieter. I unsteadily brought myself to the ground, crashing hard and skidding along the wet pavement until I reached the feet of my friends.

My motion hadn't stopped for less than a second when two rough hands lifted my battered body from the ground.

"Are you okay?" Savanah asked.

I winced at the additional pain in my left arm. If the limb wasn't broken before, it definitely was now. Despite the pain, I still nodded.

"You look like hell," she added.

"Gee, thanks," I responded.

Another loud crash drew my attention and I spun. The tail end of the plane fell through the hole, broken off from the rest of the plane which crashed to the ground and exploded. The outside walls of the hangar billowed outward from the pressure wave, and a half second later, I felt a thud in my chest, as if I'd been punched when the shock wave reached us.

"Cool," Savanah said.

The tail fell down and crashed among the fiery remains of the former aircraft. Another loud crash filled the air.

And among it all, I could still feel Quinn.

Quickly, I looked through those gathered here. Savanah stood right next to me, then Klaus, Johnny, Gina and Jayson. All five stared in awe of the humongous explosion within the hangar.

"Where's Ethan?" I asked. Then, looking closer at the gathered group, I also asked, "Where's Peter?"

The only two to turn and look at me were Savanah and Klaus. The others didn't even hear me. Johnny was too busy restraining Jayson, while Gina watched.

Savanah shrugged and Klaus shook his head gravely.

"No, no, no!" I turned again toward the hangar, the fire seeming to grow larger as whatever fuel in the plane burned. Hot plumes of black smoke billowed into the air. Were my friends in there? I couldn't tell. No matter how hard I concentrated, I couldn't feel anything but Quinn.

I started to run, no longer sure I would be able to fly, toward the hangar. I'd pretty much spent all my mental energies bringing the doomed flight in for a landing. I'd made it exactly four steps when another pair of hands wrapped around my shoulders.

The hands twisted me around so I could see their owner. Ethan was standing in front of me.

I threw one arm around him, then pulled back and punched him. "Don't you ever worry me like that again!"

Standing with the group now was Abby. She looked perfectly fine, like absolutely nothing had happened to her. I should have smacked her.

"Christine," she said with a nod of acknowledgement.

"Where the hell did you run off to? Ever think we might need your help?"

"Once you broke Quinn's hold on us, Agent Smith took off. Commander Dresner and I chased him down. We thought you had Quinn handled. It appears we were right."

"It's not over yet," I told her. "I need your help."

She smiled. It was that sort of smug smile someone got when they were expecting an apology. Abby was going to get no such apology from me. "I'm all ears, Christine. Let's hear what you've got."

I quickly went over what I thought was a good plan. Abby and the others still looked skeptical.

"I don't have time to argue," I finally said when they looked as if they were going to protest. "Quinn isn't going to stay down for long, so I have to act now. Just give me what I need, and back me up in there."

"Well, look who's giving orders now," said Abby.

"Hey, you've always said I was a leader. So, what's it gonna be?"

She loaded and then handed me the device I'd asked for. "You better hope this works."

It fit in the palm of my hand. It looked exactly like the device Smith had used to plant the tiny trackers/explosives inside my body. I shuddered to think I could potentially blow up at any moment if Smith decided it was my time to go.

Shaking the thought from my head, I prepared to reenter the burning hangar.

"You don't have to do dhis," Klaus said, grabbing me by the arm. "Let me. I am better shot."

Ethan flashed a jealous look at Klaus, but thankfully didn't rush over to punch the boy in the face—though I could tell he wanted to.

I pulled free from his grip before he got the idea in his head to kiss me again. "I'm the only one who'll get close enough. And I can't have him using you against me."

I stepped backwards, wondering if I was seeing these people for the last time.

"If I'm not back in ten minutes, come charging in," I said, looking at each of my friends in turn.

I turned and ran for the wide open hangar, limping only slightly. I didn't trust myself to fly any longer, I really didn't think I had the power. I clutched the device in my good hand and used my forearm to cover my nose and mouth as I entered the hot, smoky building.

For the second time in my life, I really understood how dangerous smoke inhalation could be. I was immediately coughing as I climbed through the wreckage which only moments before had been a cargo plane. Now it was only recognizable as burning, twisted metal.

Black smoke filled the large room, and the smell of that, mixed with petrol gas overloaded my senses. And the worst part was, I had to go deeper into the hellish place if I was going to find Quinn.

BOOM!

A mini-explosion from off to the side startled me, and instinctively I turned to see what it was. As I turned, there were two more. Whatever the cargo was in the plane was something under pressure, and the added heat was causing all the items to burst.

I turned back to continue my search for Quinn, only to find him standing right in front of me, completely unharmed.

"Hello, Christine."

My arm shot up, to jab him in the neck with the device, but he was too quick. He slapped my arm away and shoved me back. I stumbled, and tripped over what I think used to be part of the pilot's chair, but surprisingly didn't fall.

"I no longer have any use for you." He sent a mental blast in my direction which did sent me tumbling backwards and landing on my butt. He continued advancing on me, "You have become too uncooperative to deal with any longer. You simply cannot follow orders."

I scrambled backward as he stepped toward me, trying to buy more time.

"You need to be taught a lesson," he said. "One you will never forget."

Before I could do anything, I was lifted off my feet and found myself floating, as helpless as Abby, Smith and Dresner had been. Then, through the wafting smoke, floated another body—Peter. He looked as if he was struggling to break free, but was equally immobilized. When he caught sight of me, however, his attempts stopped and he glared at me, as if this whole thing was my fault.

"I'm sorry," I tried to tell him once again, even though in his state of mind, he wasn't going to listen.

"Go to hell!" His anger still overpowered his reasoning.

My own anger got the better of me too. I could feel the rage boiling in every blood vessel. All of that fury was directed at Quinn, where it belonged. He knew the best way to hurt me was through my friends, and he'd taken Peter away from me. If I could break free of his mental grip, Quinn would feel my pain.

"I really hope you have nothing more to say to each other. Because I'm afraid you're never going to speak again."

"Wait," I began, looking confusedly at Quinn. "What are you—" My question was cut off.

"I hate you!" Peter spat at me.

Then he was gone. Quinn flicked his wrist and Peter's head turned to the right sharply. The outline of his spine jutted out at an awkward angle beneath his skin. His mouth hung open limply, and his eyes stared ahead blankly.

"NO!" I screamed.

Desperately, I tried to get a read on him. It couldn't be true. It had to be an illusion, playing on one of my worst fears. But no matter how hard I pushed, there was no longer any trace of Peter's mind. He was dead.

Still hanging in the air, I dropped my gaze to the ground. I couldn't look at Peter any longer. I wanted to cry, but no tears came from my eyes. If I allowed myself to cry, my tears would make it true. And it couldn't be true. Pete couldn't be dead. I couldn't—wouldn't—accept it.

The rational part of my mind had already accepted what happened though. One second Peter was there, yelling at me, and the next, he was gone. What bothered me the most were his last words. He was my friend, and he died hating me. That was the part even my rational mind couldn't accept.

Peter's body fell to the floor. Quinn tossed him aside like a worthless piece of trash that had outlived its usefulness. I stared directly into Quinn's eyes. Instantly, my grief flashed to vengefulness, like water flashing to steam after being poured on a red hot piece of metal. The man had gone too far.

I flexed my arms, using my rage to refuel my body. I pushed against Quinn's mental hold and found I could move. I pushed further and completely broke his hold on me. As I hit the floor a shadow filled the edges of my vision. I thought it might have been from the slight jolt my body had taken as if fell to the ground again, but when I stood up, the shadow lingered.

Now it was Quinn's turn to look frightened. I could sense no one had ever broken free of his mental snare before. He backed away as I advanced upon him. He heaved large chunks of burning metal in my direction, but I batted them away as easily as I would a mosquito.

I sent a blast of mental force at him this time and sent him sprawling on the floor. He scrambled backwards as I had only minutes ago, looking up at me with nothing but terror filling every pore of his being. He was forced to stop by the still intact wall of the hangar. With nowhere else to go, he looked up at me, defeated.

I stepped up to him, no longer feeling any pain in any part of my body. The anger flowing through me was enough to keep any agony I may have felt at bay.

"You killed him." I was surprised to hear how deep my voice sounded. It was like I wasn't the one speaking. "You hurt my brother. You threatened my family. What else have you done, Quinn? Did you kill Savanah's grandparents too?"

He shook his head, holding up a hand as if he could defend himself. "No. No, I had nothing to do with that." His voice shook, and had a plea in it. If this were any other day, under any other circumstances, I might have felt some sympathy for him. But after what he'd done...

I also was inclined to disbelieve anything the man told me, but I had a deep connection to his mind now. His sheer terror was making it impossible to block me out. He was telling the truth. He wasn't responsible for what happened to Savanah's grandparents.

That simple fact didn't change his fate though. I turned my head for a moment and saw the shining silver object laying on the floor ten yards away. I pulled it toward me, sending it flying through the air into my outstretched, left hand.

Then, just as quickly, I spun and pointed Dresner's gun right at Quinn's forehead. "I hope you don't have anything left to say," I repeated his fateful words to him. "Because I'm afraid you're never going to speak again."

The shadow almost filled my entire vision now, leaving only one image in my sight: Quinn.

"Chris! No!" It was Ethan, he'd come in, ahead of schedule. He tried to reach for me, but I sent a mental blast in his direction and sent him sliding across the hangar floor.

"He killed Peter," I simply said. "He is going to pay."

No one was going to stop me from what I had to do. I took another step closer to Quinn, to ensure I wouldn't miss.

A pair of strong arms wrapped around me, and tried to pull me back. I didn't budge. I hit Savanah with an equally potent blast that sent her crashing through what remained of the plane's hull.

They didn't understand. It was time to end Quinn.

"Goodbye." I pulled the trigger.

Click.

I took a deep breath and shook the gun as if that would help matters.

Click.

I pulled the trigger several more times.

Click. Click. Click.

It was empty, yet I continued my attempts to shoot him. With each squeeze of the trigger, the shadow dissipated, until it was gone and all that filled my vision were tears.

I collapsed onto my knees and let the water works flow, all the while continuing to shoot Quinn with an empty gun.

I don't know how long it was, but eventually Abby came and took the weapon from my hand. Then she hugged me. She'd never done that before, but it felt natural coming from her, almost like being embraced by a sister.

I stopped my blubbering long enough to notice I still held the small device in my hand. If I couldn't kill Quinn, I'd at least end his reign of terror. I leaned over and pressed the device against the base of his skull, behind his ear and pulled the trigger.

He winced in pain as the device injected the thought inhibitor under his skin. I'd effectively taken away his powers, and he wouldn't be able to remove the inhibitor this time.

He made no move to attack me, but he did say one thing. "Now, you're ready."

I punched him with the hand that still held the miniature injector, knocking him unconscious.

CHAPTER 30
AFTERMATH

You know how in the movies, right after all the action takes place, that is the exact moment when the authorities and reporters show up? I used to think that was all part of the Hollywood charm, but as it turns out, it's completely true. I barely had three minutes to rest before the sirens started wailing and a slew of Italian police and firemen charged up the runway for the hangar.

They were followed by no less than seven vans from various news channels.

They formed a perimeter, as we stepped out from the dilapidated hangar. The police raised their weapons, but made no show of force, nor any demands.

Abby flashed her badge, holding it high over her head for everyone to see. "I am a United States Federal Agent, responding to a terrorist threat. The situation is under control."

"What did she say?" Ethan whispered in my ear.

I never would have guessed Abby could speak Italian. I repeated what she'd said and continued to translate.

"Please lower your weapons," she continued. "We are no danger to you. My team has eliminated the man responsible for this travesty."

"Ma'am," one of the reporters interrupted, trying to push passed a policeman, "can you please tell us what happened?"

"I'm afraid that's classified," Abby responded.

Three other reporters, all jockeying for position now asked questions.

As Abby, held off the torrent of queries, I looked around. Myself, Savanah, Ethan and Klaus were the only ones left. Johnny, Gina and Jayson had disappeared. Seeing how Johnny was treating Jayson when I last saw him, I almost felt sorry for the boy—almost.

There was also no sign of Smith or Dresner either, I couldn't help but wonder what happened to the two of them.

After fielding a few questions, but not really answering any of them, Abby decided to stop acknowledging the reporters altogether. Instead, she turned back toward us and spoke. "You've all been seen and by now your pasted on every news channel from here to London. I'm going to come up with a cover story. Whatever you do, don't remove your masks."

A minute later, a black SUV pulled up and two men dressed in suits sprang from the car. Abby simply pointed to where we'd left Quinn inside the hangar and said, "He's in there. No need to be gentle."

Quinn was dragged out of the hangar by the M.H.D.A. Agents a moment later in cuffs. He was awake once again, but looked like he had a nasty bruise on his jaw where I'd slugged him. As they loaded him into the car, he turned back to me and said, "If you're really eager to find the Stephenson's killer, I suggest looking a little closer to home."

The door slammed on him, and even though the windows were tinted, his satisfied smile could still be seen as the SUV pulled away.

"What did he mean by that?" asked Savanah. "Was he talking about my grandparents?"

"I don't know," I responded to the first question. "And yes," I said to the other.

"Go back to the safehouse," Abby ordered.

Having never been there before, I asked the logical question, "Where is it?"

"Just follow me," Ethan said.

"You better run slow." My angry fit had served to recharge my powers, but I wasn't nearly at full strength anymore, and the shooting pain running up and down my whole body also would lead to a pretty slow flight.

Abby turned to Klaus, who hadn't said much since our romp with Quinn had ended. "You better find your commander. He's going to need some help if he's going to track down Agent Smith."

Klaus nodded, then turned to me. "I guess this is goodbye."

As much as I'd miss the annoying boy, I desperately wanted him to leave. The longer he lingered, the higher the chance was of Ethan discovering what had happened between us—twice. I loved Ethan and he loved me, and I didn't want anything to change that.

"Yeah. Goodbye." I acted as nonchalant about it as I could.

He grabbed my hand, lifted it to his mouth and gave it a little peck. Then he let go and ran off.

"Get going," instructed Abby.

Ethan grabbed Savanah, but I thought of one other thing. "Wait!"

Limping, I went back inside the wrecked hangar. A few smoldering fires still remained, but for the most part everything had pretty much burnt out.

I saw the cabinet I put the metal cross inside and went right to it. I'd taken down Quinn, now I had to make sure no one else got their grubby little hands on the artifacts.

I threw open the door and was delighted to see the metal case still laying inside. I placed it on the floor. Then, undoing the latch, I opened the cross-shaped box. It was empty.

"No!" I cried, lifting the box to check every corner, in case I missed something. I hadn't. The only thing inside the metal cross was... well, the inside of the metal cross.

Where did the shroud and pieces of cross go? I'd felt them inside when I threw the box in there. They couldn't have vanished—could they?

I didn't want to think about it anymore—not at that moment anyway. I had too much to think about already. All I wanted was to go someplace safe and rest.

Depressed at yet another failure, I limped back out of the hangar. "Let's go," I said to Ethan and Savanah. Then I once again took to the skies, floating high off the ground without even thinking.

There was a collective gasp from the crowd of both officers and reports alike, as they caught sight of what I was doing. We needed to get out of there before there was any time for questions. I didn't feel like answering questions.

Ethan sensed it too and, holding tightly to Savanah, disappeared into the wind. I likewise sped off as fast as my battered mind and body could handle, following my boyfriend to the safehouse.

****

The problem with taking time to rest: you also allow your mind to wander. And unfortunately, laying on the hotel bed, I had a lot on my mind to wander through.

I still hadn't totally accepted Peter had been lost. I kept replaying the scene over and over again in my head, searching for something proving he was still alive. Each time I came to the same conclusion: he couldn't have survived.

What bothered me the most—he died hating me. His final words replayed over and over too.

I would never be able to make amends. I would feel guilty about that for the rest of my life.

Another thought infiltrated my mind too. I almost killed Quinn, and it wasn't by accident. I willfully pulled the trigger with the intent of murdering the man. If the gun hadn't been empty, I would have succeeded.

I'd let my anger take control of me again, and almost let it consume me. I couldn't let it happen again. The effects were too dangerous to predict.

The only thought that offered me any solace was the slightest possibility that, at least subconsciously, I knew there were no bullets in the gun. It was the only thing that gave me any peace-of-mind. The alternative was knowing how easily I could be led to kill someone.

And I wasn't a murderer.

The other thing bothering me about the incident with Quinn was his comment before I knocked him out. "Now, you're ready."

Ready for what?

I tried distracting myself by turning the hotel TV on, but it seemed no matter what channel I switched to, the only things on were coverage of me flying away from the Vatican or escaping from the airport.

I couldn't understand a word they were saying, but if they hadn't made the connection between the two mysterious flying beings yet, they soon would. Abby was going to have a hell of a time covering this one up.

Hitting the power button, I threw the remote on the floor. The back came off and the batteries sprang out and scattered across the room. Even the TV couldn't provide any comfort.

So, I decided to try closing my eyes and falling asleep.

Unfortunately, even my dreams had turned against me. I was jolted awake several times by images of Peter's broken body. Sometimes it looked as it had been in real life, and other times his snapped neck was grossly exaggerated, like being turned completely around, or tied in a knot.

Once, when I woke from one of these mini-nightmares, I saw Ethan sitting next to me in the room's only armchair. He had a wrapped sandwich in his lap.

His voice was calm, soft and soothing. "I thought you might like to eat."

He thought wrong. I was in no mood to eat, and the way my stomach felt, I doubted my ability to hold down food anyway.

I took the sandwich, giving Ethan a peck on the cheek, and promised I'd eat it later. He seemed to accept that, and leaned back in the chair. He stared up at the ceiling, looking bored.

He wanted to ask me about me and Klaus, the question was at the forefront of his mind. He was worried I'd been taken away from him by the older boy. He sat awkwardly in the seat next to me for nearly a minute as he debated broaching the subject. Instead, when he finally spoke, he simply asked, "How're you doing?"

"I don't think you're going to like the answer."

"Probably not, but I still want to hear it." He had a stupid lopsided grin on. I wanted to smack it off.

Instead of answering, I asked, "Why aren't you upset? Don't you feel anything?"

His mouth opened and his eyes went wide with shock. "How can you even think I'm not upset?"

I didn't know what to say. I stammered for several seconds before I finally got words out. "You just seem, all right with it. Like it didn't even happen. You're acting... normal."

"You really must have turned your powers way down," he said. He leaned toward me and showed every single worry line on his face. There was no longer a hint of a smile. "I put on the brave face for your sake, Chris. I know how guilty you feel and I know of all of us, you need to be cheered up the most. Believe me, I'm as torn up about it as you."

"It." Neither of us could bring ourselves to say Peter, or murder. So we referred to "it." It was so degrading, and not worthy of Pete's memory.

I didn't mention any of these thoughts to Ethan. I didn't want him to know how much what had happened effected me. In a way, I was trying to put on a brave face, like he was. Instead, I simply said, "Thank you." Then, a second later, I thought to add, "For being strong for both of us."

He nodded, then slumped back in the armchair. He looked as worn out as I did. "Abby called. They recovered your bags. And a medic is coming over to look at your arm."

"Great," I said, meaning it, but showing no real enthusiasm. I didn't have any room in my life for enthusiasm anymore.

We sat in silence and I eventually drifted back to sleep, only to be awoken by yet another dream, this time of Quinn. He'd killed Peter, and now he was coming after everyone else I cared for.

This time when I sprang back from my dream it was to a terrible pain in my arm. The medic Abby had sent over had set the swollen, black and blue mess my arm had become by quickly jamming the bone back into place. It hurt, but I'd been beaten so much today, I hardly noticed.

He started scanning my arm and other parts of my body with what looked like a long metal wand, like they use at security stations in the airport. I didn't know what he was looking for, but he apparently didn't find it.

I fell asleep again as he wrapped my arm.

My eyes shot open after an angry Peter, head flopping down off his neck, though still attached to his body, shot hot, blue lightning at me. The echoes of "I HATE YOU" still filled my ears as I blinked the dream out of my vision.

The room had grown darker, and I strained to see the window. The light outside was dimmer too. The sun must have been setting, if it hadn't already set. Either way, I'd been laying there for a few hours. I looked to the armchair. Ethan was no longer there.

I was still very tired, almost like in a daze, and finding it hard to focus, but I could tell someone had changed my clothes. There were also voices outside the doorway in the suite area of the room. I could hear Ethan, Savanah and Abby talking.

"What are we going to tell her?" Savanah asked.

"For now?" Abby responded. "Nothing. There's no reason to worry her. She's been though enough."

Ethan came to my defense. "If we can handle it, she can handle it."

"I think we should let her rest, I had the medic give her a tranquilizer, she should be out until morning. We'll see how she is then," Abby said.

What were they talking about? I needed to know.

"Ethan, you know how Christine gets. She says she doesn't want to go running off to save the world, but she's always the first one on the battlefield," Savanah argued. "She can't help it. If we tell her now, she's going to want to do something about it."

Ethan sighed. "Maybe you're right."

Now I had to know what they were talking about. Whatever it was, couldn't have been good.

I sat up and suddenly felt light-headed. Whatever tranquilizer they'd used on me was still apparently doing a number on my system. On shaking legs, and feeling more groggy with each step, I stumbled over to the door. I stepped sideways, and knocked into a lamp with my bad arm. I stifled my cry of pain, but they had heard me anyway.

The door swung open and Ethan was by my side, holding me. "Chris, are you okay?"

"I'm fine." My voice sounded so far away.

"Get her back into bed," Abby ordered. "She shouldn't even be awake, let alone standing."

Ethan forced me back into bed. I protested, but was too weak for it to do any good.

"I'm fine," I repeated. "I heard you talking. Tell me what's happened."

"No," Abby said forcefully. "You get some rest, and we'll talk about it in the morning."

"Tell me," I insisted.

"Loser, lay there and go back to sleep."

I shook my head. "I want to know. Please."

Abby looked at the other two, then down at me. "The fact your even awake is amazing in and of itself. Where you find your strength, I doubt I'll ever know."

"Stop stalling and tell me. I'm not sleeping until you do."

She rolled her eyes and sat on the bed by my feet. "Fine. But this isn't news you want to hear."

Ethan sat next to me and grabbed my good hand, squeezing it gently. Savanah stood next to the bed like a sentry—I guess in case I decided to bolt as soon as I heard what Abby said.

"Dresner , Klaus and three other V.S. operatives took Smith into custody a few hours ago," Abby explained.

It sounded like good news. I couldn't understand why they wouldn't want to tell me.

I quickly found out, as Abby continued. "They were working with us, and he was to be extradited back to the United States, for the M.H.D.A. to deal with. I was going to see him put away for the rest of his life. We had him in holding, awaiting orders to ship him back when..." She trailed off, her face turned red and she looked away from me.

I tried sitting up, but between the sedative they'd given me and Ethan's arm on my shoulder lightly pressing me down, I didn't budge more than half-an-inch. "What? Did he kill himself?"

Abby shook her head. "No. I got orders to release him. My superiors say he's committed no crime."

"But... how... I don't understand? Didn't you say he was spending all that money and going against orders?"

"Yes, he was. At least, I thought he was. How could I have been so stupid?" In a move so unlike her, she punched the mattress in anger. "The whole thing was setup so if things went downhill, one person would take the blame, so the whole agency wouldn't be implicated. Smith was their fall guy, but apparently, they weren't ready for him to fall just yet."

"So, he's going to get off scot-free?" I couldn't believe it. After all he'd done, they were going to let him go.

"Yes."

I lay there, in shock. It was like we hadn't accomplished anything on this whole mission other than capturing Quinn.

"Tell her the rest," Savanah said. "Let's see what she thinks of that."

I had a sinking, aching feeling reaching from the pit of my stomach all the way up my spine. "What?"

"He's taken Quinn," Abby said. "And we think he may have the shroud too. We think he's going to use them both to complete his army."

Okay, I have to admit, Abby was right. They should have waited until morning to tell me.

CHAPTER 31
HOMECOMING

I wasn't able to stay awake after hearing the news about Smith and Quinn. Again, the drug they'd sedated me with, had to be something powerful. Despite the grogginess, I was still able to ask one more question before totally checking out.

"What did you do with Peter's body?"

"It's already on its way back to the States," Abby said. "I'm going to tell his parents when we get back tomorrow night."

Then as hard as I tried to fight it, I fell back into a deep and thankfully dreamless sleep.

I don't know how they got me through security, but the next thing I knew I was sitting on a plane, in coach, in between Ethan and Savanah. My boyfriend stared out the window like a five year old watching the white fluffy clouds pass by. Savanah listened to her mp3 player with her eyes closed.

But when they felt me move, their attentions were instantly focused on me.

"Hey, you're awake!" Ethan said—his powers of observation never ceased to amaze me.

"Where are we?" I asked.

Savanah pulled the earbuds from her ears and rolled the wire around the mp3 player. "Somewhere over the Atlantic."

Ethan handed me a bottle of water. "Bought this in the airport for you. Abby said you'd need something to drink when you woke up."

Seeing the water made me realize how thirsty I was. My tongue felt like sand, and that sand was running down my throat. I opened the bottle and drank greedily, finishing off half the liquid before coming up for air.

"Thanks."

"Don't mention it."

I leaned back and closed my eyes again. Even though I must have slept for hours, I was still tired. " I don't suppose I was dreaming last night when you guys said Smith had gotten away."

"Nope," Savanah said. "He's long gone."

"The good news is you don't have to worry about those explosive-thingys he put in you. When P... when you got shocked, they all shorted out." Ethan sqeezed my hand as he said this, obviously as a way of comforting me.

I pulled my hand away. "Would you say his name? Say it! Say Peter!" I said. "We can't keep avoiding his name. Say it so you don't forget."

"Okay," Ethan responded. "Peter."

There, we said it. Now the healing could begin.

"Where's Abby?"

"The witch got herself a first class ticket." Savanah sounded none-too-happy about this turn of events. "Stuck us back here to ride with the rest of the cattle."

I didn't mind being stuck in coach. All I cared about at this point was getting home.

"I half-expected Abby to come and check on us at some point during the flight, but we didn't see any sign of her until we arrived at J.F.K. Airport in New York.

She was waiting for us inside the terminal as we exited the plane. "Come on, we have to get moving. Our connecting flight leaves in twenty-minutes."

"Couldn't spring for a direct flight, huh?" Savanah asked.

Abby ignored the question and started walking.

"Wait, can I call my parents first and let them know I'm coming home?" I asked.

"Already taken care of," Abby told me as we walked to the new gate. "I called them last night and explained everything."

Apparently "everything" meant the cover story. We had been doing a dig with Quinn when there was an accident. Several beams holding up the roof gave way and the tunnel collapsed on top of us. Apparently I was lucky to come out with only a broken wrist and a couple of bruises.

There was more to the story, but I got distracted as we passed a newsstand. I stopped and the others continued for a few steps before realizing I was no longer following.

There it sat, plain as day, the *New York Times*. Normally, a simple newspaper wouldn't have distracted me, but I was on the cover. Yes, that's right, me, on the cover of the *New York Times*. Two pictures—one of them in the Swiss Guard outfit, the other in my black mask—sat under the headline that read, "Black Angel—Savior or Menace".

I couldn't bring myself to pick it up and read further. When Abby came to stand beside me, all I could ask was, "This isn't good, is it?"

"Nothing we can't handle," she answered. Then putting a hand on my shoulder, she guided me away from the newsstand. "We have to catch our plane."

Thankfully, the ride from New York to Pittsburgh was short, and when we disembarked and found baggage claim, my parents were there waiting for me. Ethan and Savanah, thankfully had separated themselves from me and Abby.

I have no idea how much time had actually passed since the battle with Quinn, but I do have to say, when my mother pulled me into that worried/relieved, incredibly tight embrace, it felt like every one of my injuries was brand new. I winced, but my mother either didn't notice or refused to let go.

"You are never leaving my sight again," she squealed. "Every time you go anywhere, you get hurt."

I wasn't going to argue with that. I couldn't even if I tried.

When my mother finally let me go, it was my father's turn. At least he was more gentle, and didn't make every nerve in my body feel like it was on fire.

"You had us so worried," he said. "I'm so glad you weren't in Rome."

"There was a terrorist attack there yesterday," my mother added. "They crashed a plane and everything."

I let out a nervous laugh, but made no comment.

"Yes, we were far from the action, I'm glad to say," Abby mentioned. "Mr. Quinn is sorry he couldn't bring her back personally, but he has a lot to deal with, with the accident and all. But he sends his regrets."

My dad shook her hand. "We're glad our daughter's home safe. Thank you for everything, Ms. Davidson."

We got my bag and my parents took me to the car. My dad turned on the radio after we pulled out of our parking spot.

"And have you heard this story coming out of Rome?" the radio announcer said. "There are reports this supposed Black Angel may very well have foiled the terrorist plot. Instead of crashing into the airport terminal, as is officials initial theory of the intended target, it seems the angel guided the plane into a vacant hangar, where no one was injured."

I shrank back into the back seat, my cheeks reddening in embarrassment as the announcer continued.

"We have the video up on our website, where you can clearly see someone jumping from the top of the plane, as it crashes into the hangar and explodes. This is truly an amazing thing to see."

The man gave the website where people could view the video and opened up phone lines to hear his audience's comments.

"Can you believe that?" my mother asked. "All these people thinking an angel saved them?"

"Sounds more like a superhero to me," I commented. A mental slap followed for saying anything at all.

"You've been hanging around with Ethan too long," my father said. "Superheroes. If only there were such a thing."

"I'm so happy she was in Turin yesterday and not Rome," my mother commented. "Can you imagine if Christine had been at that airport trying to come home?"

"Yeah... imagine."

I tried not to listen as my parents talked about the Black Angel and the terrorists in Rome. I didn't want to think about it. I would have been perfectly happy if no one ever mentioned this ill-fated trip again.

I would like to say this is where the story ends, however when I returned home, I realized it had only just begun.

When we walked in the door, we found my grandparents sitting and watching the news with Conner. Even they couldn't be torn away from the Black Angel story. As soon as I stepped through the door, my grandfather gave me a look as if to say, "What were you thinking?"

My grandmother looked away from the news report long enough to greet me. "Hi, Christine. How was your trip?"

"Fine," I lied. She wasn't listening anyway.

She hadn't even bothered to ask how my arm was, and if I was okay. It was strange, being ignored. But, at the same time, they were paying attention to me, only they didn't know it.

My parents sat on the couch with my grandparents, all of them transfixed. I couldn't understand why. It wasn't like it had happened here. It was half-a-world away—surely the incident didn't require this much media attention.

Not wanting to watch it, I grabbed my luggage and said, "I'm going upstairs to unpack."

As soon as I turned around and took one step, the sound on the television cut off. "Hold on a second, young lady."

Oh, this is bad. I could tell by hearing his tone. It was the kind of tone that said, "You're in deep, deep, deeeeeeep trouble, Christine."

I closed my eyes and turned around before opening them again. *Oh yeah, I'm in trouble.*

My mother and grandmother stared at me, jaws hung open with shock. My father scowled, his brow furrowed so much, his eyes were almost completely obscured by the shadow it formed. My grandfather continued with his, "What were you thinking?" look.

"Is there something you'd like to tell us?" My father pointed at the television, where he'd paused the live news report. *I am so sending a threatening letter to the guy who invented DVR after this is over.*

It was a close-up of my face, covered by my mask. Though the mask covered the top half of my face and would fool the average person, anyone who knew me would have no trouble recognizing me—not from that close anyway.

My first reaction was to act confused. Then, I thought about denying the whole thing. I could always claim the whole evil twin thing. My mother and grandmother enjoyed enough soap operas to actually believe it. But, I figured, what was the point? I'd been found out. It was time to come clean.

"Okay," I said. "But you've gotta promise not to freak out."

****

Well, my parents took it better than expected. Not that they took it all that well. As a matter of fact, I think when I mentioned I could fly and read minds, the words actually took ten years off my father's life. Then he turned a sickly shade of white when I proved it.

I told them everything: when I discovered my powers, what I could do, what really happened at the school the day of the fire, what really happened in New York, and what really happened on my latest adventure in Italy. I even told them about Ethan, Savanah, Peter, Abby and Quinn. The only piece I didn't mention was my grandfather. He'd asked me to keep his secret, and I would.

My grandfather remained silent through much of my talking, his arms crossed over his chest, as if disappointed in me. It wasn't until my parents asked the big question when he finally chimed in.

"Why didn't you tell us?" my mother asked.

"You know you can talk with us about anything, Christine," my father added, turning even paler by the second. "Even this."

"That would be my fault," my grandfather said before I could answer. I let out a sigh of relief. "I told Christine not to say anything to you. Neither of us knew how you would react?"

"She told you?" my father asked. He looked at his father with such raw anger, I thought he might actually get up and hit him. "Dad, how could you condone this? What if she'd gotten hurt?"

My grandfather held up his hands as if in surrender. "Oh, I've told her time and again she shouldn't be gallivanting off, looking for trouble." He looked my father dead in the eye. "Besides, what would you have said if I told you your little girl was flying around in spandex, acting like a vigilante?"

The words seemed to subdue my dad, who no longer appeared as if her were about to perform patricide.

"Christine and I share a bond," my grandfather continued. "She feels she can share things with me that she can't share with anyone else. Understand that she has been helped through these troubling times by someone who loves and cares for her a great deal. Take comfort in it."

"Why you, Frank?" my grandmother asked. She was less upset by what I'd been doing and more upset that I'd confided in my grandfather and not her.

He hesitated answering. It looked as if he was going to say something several times, but each time thought better of it. I couldn't blame him. This was a secret he'd kept for nearly seventy years, and once the words came out of his mouth, there would be no undoing them. "I think the only one who could answer that question is Christine."

Great, put all the pressure on me.

All eyes were on me at that point, even Conner seemed interested in what I had to say.

Did he want me to lie for him? Or did he want me to tell them? I looked him in the eye to see if he would give me the answer. No answer came. I didn't know what I should do.

"Well…"

There was a knock at the door, cutting off any further conversation. Inwardly, I breathed a sigh of relief—at least I had a few seconds to think up what I was going to say. Any break in the tension was very welcome.

Or so I thought.

"Don't move," my father grunted. He rose and went to the door.

He swung it open violently, his anger getting the better of him. The knob banged into the wall, putting a dent into the sheetrock.

"What do you... Oh, I'm sorry."

He backed away from the door and an officer stepped inside. He held a badge out for all to see, but dressed in a nice shirt and pants. For a second, I thought it might be an Agent, here to silence me for spilling secrets. It turned out, he was from the Pittsburgh Police Department. And he wasn't alone.

Two other men stepped through the door behind him, similarly dressed, but hands resting on their guns. There were three more squad cars sitting in front of the house. Several officers could be seen through the window, dressed in the typical black uniform of the Pittsburgh Police, approaching the house.

Again, I feared for myself. They had to be here because they ran my face through some database and found out I was involved in the Roman airport fiasco. They had to be here to take me in for questioning.

Wrong again.

"I'm sorry to bother you sir," the lead officer said politely, "but we're looking for Frank Carpenter."

My father, trying to look over the officer's shoulder to see the action taking place outside, asked, "What's this all about?"

All politeness left the officer, and he too glanced over my father's shoulder at our gathered family. "Is Frank Carpenter here?"

My father purposely blocked his line of sight. "I'm not answering any questions until you tell me what you're doing here. Why are there so many officers on my lawn?"

"Tell me where Frank Carpenter is, or I'll have you arrested for impeding a police investigation."

"It's fine, Larry," my grandfather said to my father, rising from the couch. "I'm Frank Carpenter. What's the problem?"

The officer pushed my father out of the way and walked straight to my grandfather. "I have a warrant for your arrest, Mr. Carpenter." He produced a pair of handcuffs.

If my grandfather was at all surprised by this statement, it didn't show.

"Frank, what's he talking about?" my grandmother wailed.

I grabbed Conner from her, fearing she would drop him, as she rushed over to my grandfather's side.

"It's okay, Sandra," he told her.

"My grandmother wasn't listening. She strategically placed herself between the officer and my grandfather. With her being half the officer's size, it made for a pretty pitiful display.

He moved passed her as easily as he had my father, and grabbed my grandfather. "Frank Carpenter, you are under arrest for the murder of Mr. and Mrs. Thomas Stephenson."

"What?" I exclaimed, almost dropping Conner myself. "He couldn't have!"

Then Quinn's words echoed through my head. *If you're really eager to find the Stephenson's killer, I suggest looking a little closer to home.*

My protests were echoed by the rest of my family.

"My father's not a murderer!"

"He never hurt anyone!"

"You have the wrong man!"

Everyone was yelling at the officer—everyone, that is, except my grandfather. He stood, head bowed and silent, his hands extended in front of him for the officer to cuff.

How could he do that? He was innocent. He had to prove it. He shouldn't walk away with this policeman to be locked in a cell. My grandfather couldn't kill anyone!

As the officer tried to put the metal cuffs on my grandfather's wrists, I nudged the man's arm so he'd miss. His arm swung down awkwardly since he'd expected to contact my grandfather's flesh.

Grandpa Carpenter looked at me, knowing what I'd done. He shook his head slightly and sent a simple message. *Don't. I've been expecting this.*

No! Don't let them!

The officer, a little confused for a second, quickly decided my grandfather had moved to make him look foolish. He slapped the cuff on one wrist this time, wrapping my grandfather's arms behind his back before binding the other wrist.

The three officers then lead him out of the house, followed by the rest of my family. By now, all of our neighbors were out in the street, watching the events and wondering what was going on.

"Christine, don't you leave this house. Watch Conner," my mother shouted as she went out the door to help my father and grandmother plead my grandfather's innocence.

But was he innocent? He said he'd been expecting this, and Quinn had said to search closer to home. Did that mean my grandfather really had killed Savanah's grandparents? If he had, then why? I had to find out, but now wasn't the time as my family fought to get passed the line of officers to stop my grandfather from being put in the back of a squad car.

I couldn't stand. I collapsed on the couch. What was I going to do? Every time I think things can't possibly get any worse, they do.

What happened Grandpa? a tiny voice filled my head.

Normally, the voice in my head didn't squeak so much, and it spoke in proper English. So, I knew the voice hadn't come from my own head. But there was no one else in the room with me except for...

Conner? I asked mentally.

The little boy giggled. His eyes focused on me. *Silly sissy.*

Oh, this is soooo not what I need right now.

He giggled again, then stuck his tongue out at me.

All I could think was, *I'm going to kill Quinn if I ever see him again.*

CHAPTER 32
JUNIOR YEAR

The rest of my summer was dreadfully boring. Thankfully, the whole situation with my grandfather distracted my parents enough that they didn't think questioning me about my powers was a priority any longer.

My grandmother had moved in with us in a more permanent way, while we waited for my grandfather to go to trial. They set his trial date for the beginning of October, which I hear is rather speedy in today's legal system. My grandmother went to the prison to see my grandfather three times a week. I went with her the first couple of times, but he seemed rather distant and cold toward me every time, so I stopped going.

I didn't know what to believe anymore. No matter what, I couldn't picture my grandfather as a killer, but the more I heard about his arrest, the less I could deny the possibility he had actually done it. They found his DNA underneath the Stephenson's fingernails, and traces of his blood were found nearby. What the police had first thought of as a wild bear attack, now pointed more and more toward my grandfather.

I was kind of surprised that Savanah still talked to me. She seemed to have more faith in my grandfather than I did at this point. "Someone's obviously framing him," she said. "It's probably Quinn."

I wanted to believe her, but she hadn't been there. She hadn't seen my grandfather leave with them, acting like a guilty man.

Conner's sudden ability to read minds and speak mentally also had me worried. I had Abby bring in a team to check him out. They couldn't detect anything abnormal about him, other than the same genetic markers that gave me my abilities. I couldn't help but believe his sudden use of powers had something to do with Quinn's blood test though.

But by far, the hardest thing I had to do that summer was attend Peter's funeral.

Only the first few rows of the church were filled. The casket was closed, which I thought was wrong. It was the thing Peter had feared the most, being inside a closed casket. I know the thoughts were irrational, but I wanted desperately to open it up so he wouldn't be frightened anymore.

His mother was a wreck. I'd only met her once, back in February. She'd seemed like such a nice, pleasant woman then. Now, she was nothing but a broken woman, completely empty of happiness.

Peter had a little brother who couldn't have been more than five or six years old. I never knew he had a brother. The little boy didn't understand what was going on, and kept asking his mother when Peter would wake up. Each time he did, his mother's sobs grew louder.

Only a few people showed up from our school. Me, Ethan and Savanah were the first to arrive, but Tiffany, Sam and Samantha soon followed us in. I could tell Samantha didn't really want to be there, but at least she was respectful enough not to throw any insults in my direction. The only other people I recognized there were Brian Falkner, from our chemistry class, and Wesley Holton, one of Peter's skateboarding friends. Mr. Philmore also attended, but sat in the back row, away from everyone else.

Ethan had been a little off lately, I think it had a lot to do with my spending so much time with Klaus in Rome. I never did tell him what had gone on between us, and with Klaus an ocean away, I didn't feel the need to. I would gain Ethan's trust again, and telling him about a simple kiss I shared with another guy I had no feelings for, would only ruin that.

A priest stood before us, in front of the casket and led us in a prayer. "We are gathered here to say farewell to Peter Michael Perkins and to commit him into the hands of God."

I couldn't pay attention. I wanted to, but at this point, I was nothing but a sack full of tears, and my eyes were two giant, leaking holes. It was all my fault Peter was dead. If only I'd been stronger. If only I'd not hurt him all those months ago. If only I hadn't trusted Quinn as much as I had. I couldn't take it.

If only I'd given into the madman.

"God, we thank you for the life that you give us. It is full of work and of responsibility, of sorrow and joy. Today we thank you for Peter, for what he has given and received."

He continued on for a while, talking about how we are all destined to leave the Earth eventually and ascend to heaven to be at God's side. And as much as I wanted to be comforted by these words, I couldn't find any peace within them. Every time I thought about it, all I could see was Quinn twisting his neck around and snuffing out that existence too early. How could that be destiny? How could anyone even think that a senseless murder could be part of some greater being's grand scheme?

When Peter's mother got up to give the eulogy, face covered with wet tears, I had to leave.

"Christine?" Ethan whispered as I walked down the aisle. I ignored him and left the building. I waited outside for the service to be over.

It should have been me lying there. Quinn should have killed me instead of him. Why did he let me live? He should have killed me as soon as he figured out I wasn't going to play his game, not toy with me and use the lives of others as pawns in his evil game of chess.

Fifteen minutes later, everyone filed out of the church. Mr. Philmore stopped next to me long enough to offer his condolences before getting into his convertible and driving off.

"Chris," Ethan said, placing a hand on my shoulder. "Are you okay?"

"No," I admitted.

"We can go home. We don't have to go to see him buried."

"Okay," I said.

"Savanah, can you get Chris' car? I'll drive us back."

"Wait," I said. "I still have to say goodbye."

I waited until everyone left the building, and then reentered.

The church was now empty, other than the priest who'd offered the prayer and a man in a dark suit.

"The hearse is running a few minutes behind," the man said. "We'll move the casket as soon as it arrives."

"Good," the priest said. "I'll tell the family we'll be a few more minutes until we leave for the cemetery."

Then, they both left the room, leaving me completely alone.

Slowly, I stepped up to the casket. I fidgeted a while, not knowing what to say, or if I should even say anything. After about a minute of standing there, feeling like a fool, my mouth spewed out words.

"I don't know what to say, Pete. I don't even know if you can hear me. I know when you died, you said you hated me, but somewhere deep inside you, I hope you know I was your friend. I've never been very good at making friends, and I know you were the same way. But who would have ever thought a skating punk and a goth chick could hit it off like we did?

"I blame myself for what happened between us, and I want you to know how sorry I am for it. Yes, I knew what Quinn had done to you, making you forget, and I always wanted to tell you, but I was afraid you'd react just like you did. I didn't want to lose you, Pete. But now, I can't help but think if I had opened my mouth months ago, this wouldn't have ever happened.

"I know you can't say anything, but I'm begging for your forgiveness. You need to understand I never meant for any of this to happen."

I stopped, looking at the closed casket and thinking again about how his greatest fear was becoming a reality again. True, Peter wasn't being buried alive, but he was still in a cold, dark casket about to be put under the Earth. But I couldn't bring myself to push aside the flowers laying atop the coffin and opening it up for him.

"I guess this is goodbye," I said. "But I promise you one thing. I will see Quinn brought to justice if it's the last thing I do. Goodbye, Pete. I hope wherever you are, it's a better place than this."

I kissed my hand and lay it atop the casket. Then I turned and walked out of the church.

Ethan, Savanah and I went back to my house and we hung out, telling stories about Peter and the good times we'd shared with him. They stayed until pretty late that night—thankfully my parents understood. When they finally left, well after midnight, I went up to my room.

I flopped down in bed, but couldn't sleep. I was angry—at myself mostly—and now I didn't even have my grandfather to confide in.

Opening up my closet, I slipped on my costume, threw on my mask and flew out my window. Alone that night, I nabbed four would-be criminals. Two young teens tried to break into a car on Grant Street in Pittsburgh and another pair, much older made an attempt to hold up the 7-11 in Bigelow Square. In both cases, I pounded on them with my powers until they gave up, then unceremonially dropped them on the stairs of the nearest precinct with a simple note:

Courtesy of the Black Angel.

And that's how the legend began. At first, it was a way to let out my frustrations. I would let loose my powers on those who deserved it and it would make me feel better—for a little while. But the pain would always return and I would need to find someone else to pound on.

The rest of the summer flew by, and before I knew it, September was here again and it was time to begin school. The newspapers reported in the month of August alone there were no less than fifty criminals brought to justice by the Black Angel.

I couldn't take all the credit though, after news got out of those first few night's adventures, Ethan and Savanah were more than eager to help. We were the super-team Ethan had always dreamed of. Using our powers for the good of mankind.

Until, of course, that first bell of the fall semester rang.

"Carpenter, Christine," Mrs. Steinbrenner, my new World History teacher called first period.

I waved my hand casually, not really paying attention to her. Who cared about school anyway, when there were bad guys out there that needed a walloping.

Ethan sat next to me, and whispered in my ear. "I heard she's like the hardest history teacher in the school. You better pay attention or you're gonna fail."

All I cared about that day was getting my schedule, seeing what my classes were, then going home, getting my costume on and going flying around.

At least things had gotten back to normal with me and Ethan. Over the last couple of weeks it was like our trip to Italy had never even happened. By the time we'd stepped back into our hallowed halls of education, we were as inseparable as we had been when we'd left.

I shared two classes with Ethan, my first period, history, and my last, gym. It seemed this year Ethan was going to see what a horrible athlete I really was. We also had lunch together, along with Tiffany, Sam and Savanah. It felt like old times.

We found our table immediately, and sat, leaving one seat empty for our missing friend.

"So, how was everyone's summer?" Tiffany asked. "I feel like I haven't seen you guys in, like, forever. I had a great summer. My family went to Vancouver. I've never been to Vancouver before, but it's a really cool city. They put gravy on their fries there instead of ketchup. And boy are they into hockey. We stopped in Seattle while we were there. Did you know Seattle is only like forty miles from Vancouver? It's weird, right?"

"Tiffany," I said, interrupting her. "Take a breath. Jeez, you saw us all last week."

"I know, but I'm so excited."

I didn't see anything to be excited about. With all the problems I was having, and everything I'd have to deal with in the coming months, like finding the shroud and cross, my grandfather's trial, figuring out what Quinn did to Conner, stopping Smith from creating an army. There couldn't be an upside to anything.

"Tiff," Ethan said, "we all heard about your trip to Canada. I think you need to get some new stories." He laughed, and everyone but me joined.

Without missing a beat, Tiffany continued. "Well, it's over between me and Ryan."

"Oh, he broke up with you?" I asked.

"No. I dumped him. He was just too boring, all he ever wanted to do was hang in his room and play video games." She looked around the table at each of us and laughed. "I'll tell you, I'm through with boys. They're nothing but a headache."

"Hey!" Sam said in mock-offense.

Everyone but me laughed again.

He squeezed my hand and turned on me. "Come on, Chris. Cheer up. Everything's going to work out. You'll see."

"Yeah," Sam agreed. "You've been in a funk all summer. We're back in school now. Time to take your mind off things a while."

"Yeah, Loser," Savanah added. "We've got your back. Just trust us and live a little."

"So, I've been thinking," Ethan said, turning away from me. "Superman and the Hulk. Who would win in a fight?"

"Which Hulk?" Sam asked.

"Green."

"Oh, Superman all the way," I said.

"No way," Savanah argued. "The more Superman pounded on him the angrier Hulk would get. And when Hulk get mad, Hulk get strong!" She pounded the table to emphasize her point and we all laughed. Maybe they were right. Maybe I really needed to take my mind off things.

And then, the last nail was put into the proverbial coffin.

The empty seat reserved for Peter was taken and all eyes turned to the newcomer. Tiffany's heart fluttered as she saw him, and she was already picturing this cute boy asking her out on a date.

Sam looked at him, wondering what the boy was doing there. "That seat's taken," he said to the newcomer.

Ethan stared at him with a contemptuous glare. Savanah's gaze was indifferent.

With his spiked hair and plain white t-shirt and jeans, the boy paid no attention to Sam and looked at me. "Vell, are you going to velcome the new exchange student to the school?"

He's lucky I didn't punch him.

ABOUT THE AUTHOR

James Mascia is the author of many great young adult books, including his wonderfully reviewed series, *High School Heroes*. When James isn't writing, he is teaching English and Literature in a high school in Maryland. When he isn't writing or teaching, he usually dons a black mask and hops around from rooftop to rooftop, making the world a better place for all.

His wife and son are very tolerant of him, especially when he drags them around to many sci-fi and comic conventions.

Other Stories by James Mascia
All Available on Kindle, Nook, iPad or any e-reading Device

Graphic Novels –
High School Heroes (Volume 1)
The Poe Murders

Short Stories –
The Collector
City of Darkness
High School Heroes: Cold Lies
High School Heroes: Rescue Mission
High School Heroes: The Guardian
High School Heroes: Imagination
High School Heroes: Secrets of the Past
Even Heroes Have the Right to Bleed

Novels –
High School Heroes
High School Heroes II: Camp Hero
High School Heroes III: Hero Heist
High School Heroes IV: Hero's Burden (Coming Fall 2013)
The Island of Dren
Urban Jungle

Made in the USA
Las Vegas, NV
16 December 2021

38192604R00164